SHADOW
OF
THE
ENDLESS

ENDLESS UNIVERSE

SHADOW
OF
THE ENDLESS

S T E P H E N G A S K E L L

TITAN BOOKS

SHADOW OF THE ENDLESS

Print edition ISBN: 9781835410448
E-book edition ISBN: 9781835410455

Published by Titan Books
A division of Titan Publishing Group Ltd
144 Southwark Street, London SE1 0UP
www.titanbooks.com

First edition: October 2024
10 9 8 7 6 5 4 3 2 1

© Amplitude Studios, 2024. All Rights Reserved.

Stephen Gaskell asserts the moral right to be identified as the
author of this work.

A CIP catalogue record for this title is available from the British Library.

Printed and bound by CPI Group (UK) Ltd, Croydon, CR0 4YY.

For Dad, who always believed

ONE

◁ ३ ६

Waking up, I'm all tangled up with Rina. Her braided dreads spill over my face, tickle my bone-dry lips. I turn my head, spluttering out a few strands. My little sister's asleep, her chest gently rising and falling, but her limbs feel hot and heavy, her embrace surprisingly tight. She must have had a nightmare and climbed up to my bunk.

Then I remember why.

Today is the Ceremony of Duties.

Carefully, I lift her arm off my chest, tilt my head up. A handful of votive candles send a dim, flickering light across our family chamber, and I spy Mother's sleeping form on the bottom of the other recessed bunk. The candles are an indulgence, but Mother insists we sleep by their light, that the illumination holds the wisdom of the Endless and wards off evil. Often her sleep is troubled, but this morning she looks relaxed, the deep lines of her forehead almost invisible.

Sometimes I can still recall the sound of her laughter.

I disentangle myself from Rina, softly kissing her cheek, before gracefully swinging off the top bunk, crouching as I land. Already, just from this little exertion, I can feel the beads of perspiration prickling my brow. The air is sweltering, thick and heavy; the *Reverent*'s cooling systems have cycled down to the bare minimum where life is just about tolerable. As a kid it'd always confused me that the ships' internal climates were hot and balmy, when deep space was as close to the coldest temperature imaginable.

Life in space is often like that.

Confusing.

Endless guide us, for we know nothing, Mother likes to say.

I can't remember a time when the air's been hotter though. Every breath is an effort, my lungs both rejoicing and recoiling as they draw in the blistering air. Energy rationing. It invades every facet of every Pilgrim's life on the ships that make up the Horizon of Light fleet.

That's what comes from being a hunted animal.

I slip into my flight suit, pull on my climbing boots, and tie up my braid in a swirl. As I clip on my caving belt, I feel a familiar tightening around my ankles as the joins between boots and suit become airtight.

Brushing my fingers over the tip of our chamber's condenser, I bring a few drops of warm water to my lips, just wetting them, despite my thirst. I should be able to chip off some ice chunks down in the cave system, save our own water rations. On the table, under a plastiware bowl to protect it from the scuttling bugs that infest near every one of the 147 vessels of the arcological fleet, sits a handful of blackberries.

I smile. A gift for me on the day I learn my duty.

Rina must've squirreled them away for me ages ago; we lost the hydroponics ship that was the sole supplier of such fruits weeks back when its core drive failed and couldn't be repaired.

I pop one in my mouth, savoring the sweet juices, and put the rest in our otherwise empty cold store. I grab my pack, and I'm on the verge of stepping out, when Mother croaks my name.

"Sewa," she whispers. "Even today?"

"Yes," I reply, trying to keep the frustration from my voice. "Even today."

I've spoken louder than I intended, and I glance back at my bunk, hoping I haven't woken my sister. Thankfully, in the half-light, I see that Rina still sleeps.

I step over to my mother's berth, crouch down.

"Tomorrow I'll answer to Cavemaster Kalad," I whisper, softly. "Today, I still have my freedom."

She props herself up on one elbow, so that we're face to face. Her tattoos are as prominent as the day they were inked, speaking the story of her life. Mother, entwined, acolyte.

Tonight, I will be inked too.

She nods, wearily. "I pray you get your wish."

Despite the incessant heat, a chill skates up my spine.

"You know something?"

She shakes her head. "Only that life doesn't always go the way you think."

Just Mother's usual foreboding, then.

"Anything but history," she adds.

History was Father's assigned duty, archeological trips his passion. Mother believes his vocation was instrumental in his desertion of the Horizon, his abandonment of us. I don't know. I was only nine at the time. All I remember is his warmth and love. And our caving sessions.

He loved nothing more than exploring digs and brought me along whenever a site was deemed safe, even if Mother protested. Beyond his family and his colleagues, it was the caving team who knew him best. Always seeking tips and techniques, we'd often scout underground sites together with the cavers, and when he disappeared it was Cavemaster Kalad who most understood the kind of father I'd lost. Among the rest, even today, I still catch the odd Pilgrim staring at me with a mixture of pity and disdain, Father's flight an indelible stain on our family name.

I kiss her forehead. "Let's not go there today."

It's funny. Deep down nobody's madder with Father than me for how he left us, but at the same time I won't hear a bad word said against him. Even from Mother, who has the most cause for her anger. Over the years we've had some terrible fights.

We still don't know what happened to him.

Before she can say more, I slip out of the chamber.

Usually, at this hour, the passageways of the *Reverent* would be crawling with Pilgrims heading out for their first shifts. Shattered bodies and minds hauling themselves out of their bunks once more to put their all into the ongoing evasion of the United Empire hunter fleet, their eyes red, their faces sunken. Mining crew, weapon techs, engineers of every persuasion, and, of course, the clerics. But today, the ashen, sweltering passages are quiet. Doorways to the chambers are closed. The Ceremony of Duties isn't until later in the day. May as well get some extra shuteye if you can.

Naturally, tradition would go out of the airlock if the Empire were in close attendance, but the Horizon seems to have caught a break in the last few days, with the immediate threat of the hunter fleet waning. In fact, Overseer Liandra ordered every Pilgrim with non-essential duties to observe the custom of rest on this sacred day. Smart. Even in flight, people need a break.

Not that the Empire is resting.

If the last two years has taught us anything…

I think back, remember when Oba and I were secretly exploring a derelict vessel near an abandoned Empire outpost, when one of their gargantuan mining ships showed up on the other side of the system. The evacuation order went out immediately. Although we scrambled, got back to the fleet double-quick, Overseer Liandra was waiting for us on the *Reverent*'s flight deck by the time we arrived. She didn't hold back, dressed us down in front of half the deck crew. We scrubbed floors and cleaned vats for a month afterwards. That's a smell you never forget.

I shake away the memory.

Threading my way along the hot, dark walkways, I imagine scenes playing out behind the closed doors. Some Pilgrims will be using the free time to sleep, still curled up in their bunks, while others indulge in a traditional daybreak meal. I picture a family elder laying out an impoverished feast for their kin from stockpiled scraps. Thin pickings based on the recent wares I've spied in the black markets.

Many will be prostrate in prayer or meditation.

Mother would be. Probably bent down in supplication at this very moment. She'd like me there, joining her in worship, no doubt beseeching higher powers to give me a worthy duty, but I don't have much belief in the Endless. "The *Reverent*. Where blind faith will get you everywhere," I mutter. I turn my head, check I haven't been overheard. Every vessel of the Horizon is united in worship of the Endless, but no ship is more devout to the creed than the *Reverent*. Disrespect of the faith can mean anything from creeping ostracism to outright exile.

Over the years I've learnt to hold my tongue. When I was little I used to scare my mother half to death, the things I'd spout about the Endless, about the Pilgrims' exodus from Raia, about our very own Scriptmaster. Eyebrows would get raised, small talk would get briefer, rations less generously cut. *What kind of Pilgrim are you raising?* Eventually, I understood nothing good could come from my words, and I kept them to myself. Keep your head down, do your studies, be a good role model for your sister.

Caving would be my out.

And I didn't need to pray for that.

Nobody among my cohort is a better caver. Even Oba. Tomorrow, I'm certain, I'll officially be under Cavemaster Kalad's mentorship. That'll be enough for me. More than enough.

Mother will be happy too. And Rina.

Caving's not the most glamorous duty, but for me it's everything. Escape from the suffocating existence of day-to-day life and the stress of constantly being hunted, feeling like prey. Contributing to the Horizon's survival by securing real, physical resources that you can touch, smell, sometimes even taste. Most of all, for the pure physical joy it brings me—rappelling down subterranean cliffs, hiking along vaulted fossil galleries, swimming through bone-cold flooded passages.

Nothing comes close to its majesty.

Even if the zealots will have us scouring the depths for Endless relics once we've escaped the Empire's reach. Given the last two years, they'll be champing at the bit.

For Mother, the appeal is different. Cavers don't get seen in the same light as the medics or engineers or acolytes, but few duties offer more lucrative sidelines. Whether combing derelict space wrecks or searching for underground Dust sumps, cavers have envious opportunities to grab something for personal trade.

Once I've been on a few expeditions, we'll be rich.

Mother's stock would rise.

For Rina, it's all about where I end up living. That's why she's having nightmares. Her greatest fear is that I end up relocating to another of the Horizon's vessels. The military barracks of the *Judgment* or the dorms of the *Dawn Skies* repair yards, maybe even a private chamber aboard the seminary vessel, the *Ecclesiastic*—

I give out a blurted laugh. Me? Proselytizing for the Endless. Wearing robes, quoting scripture, cementing faith. Absurd.

I'd be useless.

No, they won't have me.

If you get chosen for caving, you stay in your family chambers. Sure, expeditions can last days, even weeks sometimes, but most of the time when the arcology's traversing deep space, the nearest moon or world or space wreck is light years away, and there's no call for cavers.

Rina would see her big sister plenty.

So, me getting caving would see us all happy.

Still, confident as I am, I can't help but feel nervous. Until Overseer Liandra reads out my name, speaks my duty, those nerves aren't going to go away. And the only time I can really lose myself, forget my troubles, is when I'm deep in the darkness, fingertips grappling the rock.

Hence my little act of rebellion.

I'm just lucky we're taking refuge where we are—

I stop dead.

The *Reverent*'s concourse would usually be chaotic at this time, but today there's only a smattering of folks. Even the chai seller's little stand is all folded up, the sweet aroma of tea absent. Aside from the odd Pilgrim making a beeline, two distinct groups loiter.

The first is a mix of younger kids hanging out, some cross-legged on the floor playing games, others pulling stunts on the cubic sculpture that sits at the heart of the concourse. Cavemaster Kalad told me it was originally a symbol of the Pilgrims' belief in science and knowledge. Now it's more associated as an emblem of the Endless' infinite wisdom.

The second group, sitting at a couple of little tables near the chai stand, is a handful of my fellow year mates, killing time before the ceremony. They're acting nonchalant, arms draped over chair backs, cracking jokes, but I can see the tension in their movements, in their faces.

I know how they feel.

Even with the relentless heat, sapping everyone's energy, they're coiled tight, on edge.

Nobody's spied me yet.

I could skirt the periphery, get out the airlock onto the surface before anyone even knows I'm here. I start to do exactly that, before a cry of anguish stops me in my tracks. A few of the bigger kids have hoisted a smaller, scrawny kid aloft, and are carrying him towards the sculpture. The kid's struggling, pleading for them to put him down, but he's no match for their combined strength.

I want to step in, but I hesitate, knowing that if I do all eyes will be on me. Someone will notice I'm in my caving gear, and then I'll have hell to pay later.

Come on, put him down.

I hope it's just a lark between friends, hope to see signs of laughter on the boy's face, hope that any moment they'll drop him down again and they'll all joke about it, but all I see on the boy's face is his terror.

"Let me go! Let me go!"

One of the kids doing the carrying breaks away, springs up the oversized cubes, then crouches down on the flat top of one near the summit. He leans forward, extending his arm...

I know exactly where this is going.

The three kids still carrying the boy fake drop him, before thrusting him up higher into the clutches of the ringleader on the sculpture. Gripping his wrist tight, he hauls him upwards, not caring as the boy's side slams against the hard edge of the cube, making him scream in pain.

"Stop whingeing, maggot," his tormenter yells. "Up here you're the Overseer, see. Enjoy the view." He skittles back down to the ground, making short work of the tricky descent, joins his mates, laughing and pointing at their victim.

High above, the boy's all balled up, gripping the edge tight, fingers white. He stares over the lip, terrified. The other kids pack up their games and amusements, begin leaving the concourse, not wanting to be around for the fallout.

They're going to leave him up there.

I glance over at my year mates, hoping somebody's going to intervene, but they're all studiously ignoring the commotion even if they know full well what's happening.

Ah, hell.

I step out of the shadows, mentally throwing daggers at my useless cohorts, before confronting the bullies. Putting on a measured, authoritative tone, I address their backs.

"You think this is funny?"

All but the ringleader tense.

They turn in unison, worry on the three sidekicks' faces, defiance on the ringleader's. I recognize one of the sidekicks, the son of one of Mother's friends from daily worship.

"It's Agha, isn't it?"

He hangs his head, but before he can speak, the ringleader raises a hand, signaling that he shouldn't answer.

"Where are you heading, blindworm?"

Little tyrant has already clocked my gear. Blindworms, creepers, maggots. Pilgrims have many terms for cavers, most of them unfavorable.

"On this day of all days," he adds.

Knows who I am, too.

Around, I can feel all eyes on me. Some of the kids who were leaving have stayed back, watching to see how this plays out.

"You are going to help that boy get back down," I state, staring down the bully. "Then you're going to apologize to him. All of you."

"Oh yeah, says who?" The bully grins. "You?"

And they're going to obey you because…?

"Yes, me."

He laughs. "I don't think—"

"But not just me."

That gets his attention.

Who though? Where am I going with this?

"You know who else?" I ask, buying myself some time.

The concourse is deathly silent, even the victim's whimpering quieted.

I know what to say.

"Every single Pilgrim on the Horizon."

I turn full circle, meeting the eyes of as many of the assembled youths as I can. On the edges of the concourse, a few older Pilgrims linger in the shadows.

"Everyone on this concourse. Everyone from your closest blood, to strangers on the other side of the arcology that you've never set eyes upon. They too ask that you make this right. You know why?"

The bullies have shrunk into their shells, no answer.

"Because we're at war. Because we've been hunted, mercilessly, since the first day we left Raia's skies. Because a vast, powerful empire seeks to crush us, and our only chance of survival lies in our spirit of togetherness, our unity." I glance up at the boy marooned on the sculpture, smile, before returning my gaze to the chief bully. "If we sow discord and hatred among ourselves then we die. That's why."

The bully's gaze flickers across the onlookers, before he stares down at his feet.

"And I don't care if you snitch on me," I add. "As long as you make this right."

Slowly, methodically, the bully climbs up the sculpture, whispers a few words to the boy, then eases him down into the arms of the trio. I start to relax, glad this is over.

Then behind me, I sense somebody approach.

"Overseer!" I gasp.

"Alright, show's over," she says, addressing the entire concourse. "Everyone back to their chambers. Rest and reflect."

Guess, there'll be no caving session today, then.

She turns to the boys. "I hope you heed Sewa's words. Everything she said was true."

Everyone begins to disperse.

I start moving off too.

"Just a moment, Sewa."

"Overseer?"

I brace for a reprimand, awkwardly clutching my caving belt, but she stands stock still, attention consumed by the sculpture.

"You know," she says once the concourse has completely emptied, "this thing represents something to do with hyperspace entry, but no matter how many times the engineers explain it, I can't get my head round it." She turns, smiles. "Guess that's fitting on the *Reverent*."

"Hyper-geometry's never been my strong suit," I reply, for want of anything better to say, "so I can't help you there."

Come on, read me the riot act so I can get out of here.

"Caving's your passion, isn't it?"

I nod. "It is."

She grunts. "You handled that situation well."

"Somebody had to do something."

"And you did," she says. "Things like that. They're easy to overlook. But left unchecked they can do enormous damage in the long run."

Is the Overseer looking to offload?

"It can't be easy," I say. "Anyway, I should get back to my chambers."

"Weren't you heading somewhere else?"

No point in straight-up lying. "Yes, Overseer."

"Then I think you should carry on as planned."

"Overseer?"

I can't believe she's okaying my little caving jaunt.

"Let's say you earned it."

Before she can change her mind, I'm halfway to the airlock, grinning like a maniac.

TWO

ㅈㅅく

Stepping out onto the comet's surface, I raise my hand, momentarily blinded by the glare off the volatile ices. Between my contracting pupils and the darkening visor, the dazzling ground fades to a manageable off-white, while above the starfield dims.

A sense of peace washes over me.

Out here is where I can escape.

Most of the Horizon's vessels are camped on the comet, a ten-klick wide ball of ice and silicates hurtling out of the local system, but a couple dozen maintain low orbits, their shadows occluding the stars as they pass overhead.

Keeping watch.

I set off, aiming for the *Dawn Skies*, its upper decks still visible above the curvature of the comet. Gravity's weak, of course, and I skip along the glittering ground, careful not to push too hard. Even with propulsive jets in my boots, drifting off into space isn't much of a risk, but it would be fairly embarrassing if somebody spied me cartwheeling off into the void.

Glancing back, I see the local star through the comet's long tail, an unremarkable yellow disc growing smaller with every passing day. A bittersweet feeling. Pilgrims hide in the darkness, seeking sanctuary where we cannot be seen, yet, like moths, we're constantly drawn back to the flames despite the dangers.

Light, warmth, life.

Nothing can survive too long in the pitch-black.

A vision of the bullied kid, frightened out of his wits at the apex of the sculpture, comes to me. I can still hear his whimpering. A microcosm of Pilgrim life. Only a few weeks back the majority of the Horizon was up-in-arms against one of the small cargo vessels, who were accused of siphoning off grain supplies. They vehemently denied it, but were made to feel like pariahs.

Scapegoats for the sake of the pack.

The truth is, no single vessel of our 147-strong arcology could survive alone, yet relations between the ships aren't always harmonious. Fault lines are plentiful—working conditions, medical access, food supplies. Our faith in the Endless binds us, yet tensions still simmer. And with the threat of the United Empire looming large, nerves are especially frayed.

The paradox is that we *need* rivalry as well as unity.

Well, healthy rivalries, at least.

I'm still some ways from the *Dawn Skies,* so when my path winds through a smattering of rocky outcrops, I take the opportunity to plant myself down and enjoy the cooling feeling of the cold stone against my sweltering suit. I take a long draw of stale water from the helmet straw, the faint taste of my sweat lacing the fluid. Always a pleasure.

Resting, I gaze up at the heavens, attempt to identify some constellations, even an odd star. It's not easy with all our movements. Nothing's familiar. Somewhere out there, though, glides the Shining Faith, the Nightstar, the Luminous Truth, and the rest of the Pilgrim arcologies. Our siblings, all in this together, all fleeing into the dark night from the clutches of the Empire.

For now, we're on our own. Usually, we'd periodically gather—two, three, sometimes even four arcologies—coming together at a carefully choreographed time and place. A time of companionship, celebration, exchange. Light in the darkness. Right now, though, a rendezvous is impossible. Not with a hunter fleet so close on our tails.

Nobody blames the other arcologies for their absence.

They do what they can, but they won't risk their own survival. We'd do exactly the same, should our positions be reversed. According to the faith, so long as one Pilgrim arcology discovers Tor, the homeworld of the Endless, the sacrifice of the rest is a price worth paying. Needless to say, there's plenty of sibling rivalry among the arcologies. Some religion, huh?

I get up, march on, a gravitationally-assisted skip in my step as I get closer to the one person in this world who I can be myself with. Oba. I find him in the usual place we've been using as a meeting place over the last few days: a small, hidden ridge beyond the makeshift cargo yard. He's sitting on the scree, looking out over the desolate, yet beautiful valley, and seeing him there I feel myself physically relaxing.

"About time, Ess," he says, voice crackling in my helmet.

He hasn't turned round, but somehow, he always knows when I'm approaching, like he's got a sixth sense. That's Oba in a nutshell—always one step ahead of whatever's unfolding.

I remember one time we got caught exploring an empty UE transporter vessel before it had been signed-off 100 percent safe by security. Well, I got caught. Somehow, even though he'd been right next to me a moment earlier, he slipped out of sight of the search lights, leaving me blinking in the glare alone.

Naturally, I didn't snitch on him.

No point us both getting in trouble. And it's not like he hasn't taken the fall for me numerous times.

"You forget the day?" he adds, turning his head.

Through his visor I spy a mischievous smile.

He's teasing me. He knows I'm nailed on for caving duty, but he also knows I'm not sleeping well from the butterflies.

I play along.

"Is it your name day?"

"Actually it is." He levers himself up. "Where's my present?"

"Here." I punch him on the upper arm, his muscles firm against my knuckles even through glove and suit.

He rubs his bicep, feigning hurt. "How did you get so strong, Ess?"

"Shut up."

"Well, not much of a gift, but I guess it's the thought that counts." He veers into a firebrand delivery, gesticulating with his arms while mimicking Scriptmaster Artak, the head of the Pilgrim faith on the Horizon. "Pilgrims! The journey is hard, but the rewards are mighty!" He offers his hands out, palms to the sky. "Sacrifice today—"

I copy the gesture. "—enlightenment tomorrow!" I finish with a flourish, bringing up my hands, fingertips together. We laugh, but it's a bitter laugh.

Sacrifice? Like the church would know.

We make fun, because the alternative's too depressing.

"So, what really kept you?" Oba asks, as we hike off, heading downslope towards the rift on the far side of the valley. "I *know* you didn't oversleep."

"Fat chance with Rina crawling into my bunk at some ungodly hour." He shakes his head. "That kid."

"She's just terrified I'm going to get taken away."

"You'll get caving, I know it."

I watch him navigate down a steeper incline, perfectly balanced, the definition of his calves and thighs stark against his suit. Great ass, too, if anyone's asking. Sometimes, when we're together, the other girls give me jealous looks—a few of the boys too—not realizing we're not into each other like that.

We're just friends.

"And you'll get…" I trail off.

"Yeah, that's me," Oba says, laughing. "Jack of all trades, master of none."

"Hmm, jack of all trades is pushing it—I'd hate to see you plot a star-lane entry—"

"Smart-ass."

"But you are an all-rounder, sure. Strong, agile, able to count. I can see you in plenty of duties."

"High praise, indeed," Oba replies. "As long as I can get off-ship from time to time, I'll be happy."

I tell him about my run-in with the bullies, how the Overseer showed up at the end, gave her unspoken consent to this little illicit caving expedition.

"Are you kidding?" Oba asks, twisting round. "She okayed this?"

"Guess she does have a heart."

Near everywhere you go on the arcology, everyone rags on the Overseer, says she has a heart of stone. I just think she has to make hard choices and showing too much compassion gets you accused of weakness.

Maybe that's what being a leader means.

Oba shakes his head, hikes off.

We come to the rift, a dark slash in the landscape that leads to the comet's subterranean realm. Oba perches on a nearby outcrop, while I check over my gear. Finishing, I glance up to see him gazing at the starscape. I join him, peer up at the shining vault. The dense tapestry of stars that forms the galaxy's plane looks like a roiling storm front with ceaseless lightning crackling its edges. So many worlds out there. Most lifeless. Barren husks or toxic hellholes, no good for anything except maybe mining ore or siphoning fuel.

Yet the sheer numbers mean there's more living worlds than a single Pilgrim could hope to visit in their lifetime. Everything from mono-grass worlds to ocean wonderlands, each inhabited by creatures beyond imagination. And then there's the civilizations, ordering the chaos, raising up dizzying metropolises, building spectacular marvels, inventing philosophies, every mind of every soul a universe unto themselves. I would like to roam that galaxy, set eyes on its wonders—perhaps even discover Father's fate. But instead, come this afternoon, we must be standing in the Overseer's Gardens waiting for our assigned futures.

Oba picks up a loose piece of ice, throws it skywards like he was skimming stones. The projectile curves downwards, but the comet's gravity is no match for his launch, and it sails over the horizon, glittering away forever in the starlight.

"You think we'd make it?" Oba says softly.

"What?"

"If we left. You and me. Flee the Horizon, abandon the Pilgrim life." He tosses another rock into space, the missile easily reaching escape velocity. "I think we'd be alright."

I'm speechless. This is crazy talk.

"Roaming round, hustling, scavenging," he continues, warming to the idea, "no United Empire dogs on our tails. Going where we want, seeing what we want, doing what we want. We'd be free, Ess, really free."

"You're shitting me, right?"

A pause.

"Yeah, course," he says.

"Endless above, you're serious!"

He makes a fishing motion, pulling back on an imaginary rod. "Reeled in, good!"

I'm not buying it. He *was* serious. Now he's just trying to backtrack, make it all seem like a joke.

"We got people who need us, O."

Our siblings for starters. Rina. Oba's three younger brothers and lone sister. And you got to count our mothers too. Mine a shell of the woman she once was, Oba's exhausted from juggling parenthood and logistics duty. Even Oba's father needs help these days, an industrial accident a few years past severing his right forearm. One day he'll receive a replacement limb. One day. Until then, and until the kids grow up, it's on us to provide everything beyond the standard gruel and water rations. Scavenged things from our expeditions traded for real vegetables, medicine, repairs. Sometimes we even hunt when planet-side—if the local wildlife is edible and there aren't too many apex predators.

"Like I don't know that," he snaps.

"So why bring it up?"

"Is it wrong to daydream?"

Us? Running off together? Rina would be devastated. I certainly couldn't do that to the person I love most in the world. And Oba, for all his frustrations, is dedicated to his family. They'd be lost without him. We just can't leave. We can't. Even the idea of it is making me feel uncomfortable. Besides, I might not know much scripture, might not care about the Endless or their legacy, but I do believe in this Pilgrim society, believe it is something worth defending. If Pilgrims just upped and left when things got hard, the Horizon would fall apart.

Loyalty's important.

Oba doesn't want to hear a lecture, though.

Especially from me.

"No, it's not wrong," I reply. "Maybe… maybe when we've shaken off this hunter fleet we can get some leave, have an adventure in a nearby system. We'll be of age—"

"Can we drop it?"

I nod.

Maybe he's more tense about the ceremony than he's making out. Duty assignment cuts both ways. More privileges, more allocated essentials, but less time for side ventures. Sometimes much less time. Take ship maintenance crews. They work grueling shift schedules keeping all our vessels flightworthy. Oba gets assigned something like that, his scavenging missions will be over for the foreseeable.

"We should get on," I say. "Snag some swag."

"Music to my ears," he says, marching over to the jagged entrance to the comet's interior. "I was thinking we could comb one of the secondary cave systems we haven't explored yet. Easy pickings."

That'd be great. Land some iron or nickel, trade it for something nice to eat tonight. A celebratory meal in honor of our new duties, even in these dangerous times.

Assuming we want to celebrate.

The secondary system ends up being a washout, though.

"So much for easy pickings," I say, resting in a small, pitch-black chamber, my headlamp's light scattering off the dirty ice walls.

We've navigated through its twisted geography easily, the channels wide and smooth, the weak gravity forgiving, but of riches—even algal gunk—it possesses none. Even the ice looks extra dirty, not worth the effort of hacking off, hauling back to the *Reverent*, and cleansing of impurities.

Gruel tonight, then.

Maybe that's a sign.

"Let's do something fun," Oba says, chirpily. "Might be the last time we get to do this for a while."

"Fun?" I ask, trying not to sound too deflated.

"Hide-and-seek?"

Are we kids? We haven't played anything like that for years. Games are for children, not young Pilgrims about to be given their duties. Especially, when we're in such danger. All I can think of is Mother's admonishing look when I return empty-handed. *But we had fun, Mother!*

"Come on," Oba says. "What have we got to lose?"

I glance around the grey, rocky chamber. "Sure, why not?" I turn to Oba, dazzling him. "Gives me a chance to prove my number one credentials! I'm hiding first. Give me fifty!"

Before he can agree, I take off, navigate deep into the warren of tunnels, getting as far away from him as I can. Before I know it, he's almost finished his count.

"…thirty-seven, thirty-eight, thirty-nine…"

His words crackle in my headset, the interference already swallowing some of the numbers. His voice is deep and assured. I'm breathing hard, but the narrow fissure I've just squeezed through has opened out into an expansive cavity and I pause to plan my next move. My head-beam lances over the inky blackness, throwing a shaft of light onto a rippled surface of gleaming ice speared with strange geometric protrusions.

Peachy. For a geologist.

I'm likely the first soul in the history of the universe to lay eyes upon this chamber, but I don't have time to marvel.

"…forty-zzzz, zzzz-four, forty-five…".

I spy a crawlspace—and leap.

Caving in near zero-gravity has its advantages. Like not breaking bones when falling, for example. Getting lost, on the other hand, is an all too real problem. With up and down fuzzy, cave systems can become three-dimensional mazes where retracing your steps is harder than deciphering Endless runes. Normally, you'd unspool a line of microfiber, but if you're playing hide-and-seek where's the fun in that?

I stretch out my arms, ready for impact.

"…forty-eight, forty-zzzz…"

Fifty. Coming to get you.

I brace myself, bending my arms and colliding with the far wall with an inelegant, painful jolt. Thankfully, I manage not to make any giveaway noises, and I scramble into the crawlspace. Weird dark slashes mark the wall, no doubt formed from some ancient geological process. I don't stop to study them, eager to put distance between myself and Oba. It's a tight, jagged tunnel but not narrow enough to prevent my passage. A few meters in, it tapers further. I stick my arms out, corkscrew my body, and turn my head to get through the pinch point. Cold seeps through my suit.

Kalad tells me that even in the short timespan of a couple of generations of space-living, Pilgrim bones have elongated and Pilgrim muscles have softened, making caving expeditions easier. I guess I should be grateful for that, but I've never had a problem with the claustrophobia.

But the darkness?

Sometimes the darkness gets to me.

Ahead, the passage opens up into a small cavern. Dead end, though. No time to double-back. I kick back to the entrance, so I can watch for Oba. *Time for lights out.*

I take a deep breath, kill my head-beam. The darkness washes over me like a hungry wave, thick and unabating. My breaths come fast and shallow, and not just from my exertions. *Easy, easy.* I find a little sanctuary in the green light of the data streams edging my visor, but I know it's giving me away.

I switch it off.

The darkness becomes absolute. My breaths quicken, my heartbeat too. I taunt myself. *How can you ever be a real caver when you're afraid of the dark?*

The barb works, my pride stung.

I can and I will. Deep breaths.

Gradually, my breaths slow, and my heart no longer hammers against my chest. It's not pleasant, but it's tolerable. I wave my gloved hand in front of my visor. Nothing. Not even an inkling. I could be a ghost. Alone at the end of the universe.

Is that why I'm afraid of the darkness?

Static crackles, breaking my thoughts.

"You think I'm in with a shot at caving duty?" Oba says cockily. The interference is minimal; he must be close.

No chance.

Being a small team without much prestige, a lot of the years, *nobody* gets assigned to caving. So the odds that Cavemaster Kalad is going to swoop in and call up not one, but two, cavers is a long shot. And no way is Oba above me in the pecking order. Free climbing, navigating crawlspaces, rappelling—I'm better in every department.

"Sewa?"

He wants me to reply, but I won't take the bait. Given we're in a hard vac there's little danger I'll give away my location, but I want to unnerve him.

Alone in the darkness, I wait. Except—

Light.

It's faint, barely perceptible, but unmistakable. And it's not Oba. He's still out there, somewhere in the riddle of shafts and caves from where I've come, but this light emanates from behind me, within this tight cavern.

I turn, freshly fearful, ice running in my veins.

A comet is an unlikely place to harbor strange, deadly life, but the universe is full of surprises. Who knows what other passengers this icy rock might've picked up as it traveled the cosmos, thawing in the warmth of nearby stars, and freezing again in the depths of space?

The light's coming from the wall, suffusing the space in a dim green glow. Microbial life? Phosphorescent algae? *I can hope.* Reaching over my shoulder, I draw my climbing pick from the side of my pack, clasp it tight. I flick on my head-beam via the resurrected HUD and drift closer.

Squat shadows skate across the terrain.

What in the Endless?

The source of the light isn't microbes or algae or a weird, terrifying monstrosity. It's a device. I can feel the relief flooding my body, but beyond it I can already feel a grim foreboding.

"Gotcha!"

Somebody grips my shoulder, and I spin, brandishing my climbing pick.

"Easy, Ess!" Oba cries. "It's me."

I see his face through his visor, his eyes fighting to hide his fright. I'm sort of glad I've given him a taste of how I'm feeling. I lower my makeshift weapon.

"Why'd you turn on your head-beam?" he asks, before teasing me. "Did you get scared of the dark?"

"No!" I snap, too fast.

He holds up his hands in mock surrender.

Nobody knows about the unease I sometimes feel in the darkness. Not Cavemaster Kalad, not Mother, and not even Oba. And I wouldn't dream of mentioning it to Rina, afraid it might instill in her a similar fear.

"I found something," I say. "Look."

The device is a black polished disc, as wide as the span of my hand. An unfamiliar script scrolls around the edge, glowing with a faint green light. Crampons at the base of the machine embed it in the icy surface.

Neither of us says anything.

Ah, hell.

"If you're not going to say it, I will," I say. "We need to show this to someone."

"Are you crazy?" He shakes his head, his head-beam dancing over the walls. "Even if the Overseer turned a blind eye, Artak will demand we be given penance for weeks." He balls a fist and strikes at the gleaming ceiling, sending down a shower of fragments. "And on the Ceremony of Duties day!"

"I know, I know."

Admitting we'd caved deep into the cometary core would lead to punishment. *If we're lucky?* Cleaning the foul-smelling agal vats or working in the sweat-dripping heat of hydroponics. *And if we weren't?* Reciting scripture or singing hymns, most likely.

I could live with that.

What would be harder to bear would be losing our chosen duties. *They wouldn't, would they?*

I grit my teeth. *Doesn't change what we need to do.*

"This thing," I say, gesturing at the device, "might be a danger to the whole of the Horizon. It could be a beacon, an eavesdropper, maybe even a dark bomb."

"Or it could be nothing!" Oba cries. "Maybe it's been sitting here for thousands of years, or maybe it was set up yesterday by one of the science geeks."

"Maybe," I say. "But we don't know."

Oba shakes his head again, sighs. "Alright."

I flinch as he rips the device off the ice. The digital script scrolling around the perimeter fades to black.

"I guess it's not a dark bomb, then," I deadpan.

Not the brightest star in the cosmos, Oba.

"I'll take it to Kalad." He gives it the evil-eye, as if it could feel anything. "There's no point both of us getting into trouble."

But I can't fault his heart.

"No," I say. "I found it. I'll deal with the consequences."

Before he can argue, I take it off him, slip it into my pack. I pirouette away, launch myself into the adjoining passage.

I just hope Kalad is in a forgiving mood.

THREE

ᚩᛉᛉᛖᛖ

We exit the cave system, trek our separate ways across the barren, dirty ice to maintain the solo ruse. Above, the stars are bright and breathtaking, no sign they harbor a United Empire hunter fleet who would seize us without hesitation. Oba heads to the *Lexurus*, one of the main communal vessels, while I aim for Cavemaster Kalad's ship, the *Mestaphos*.

When I call him on the grainy, low-res monitor outside his vessel, he looks surprised to see me, but buzzes me inside. After decontamination and recompression in the airlock, I enter. Kalad prefers his artificial gravity a little heavier than most, and I clamber over the threshold with an energy-sapping step.

Cavers need muscles, he's always preaching.

Without a helmet supplying the chemically-tinged, carefully-calibrated air mix, I breathe in a rich mix of smells. The faint acridity of the decontamination spray clinging to my suit; the mossy, earthy smell of caving equipment that's spent too long in the field; an edge of something somewhere between lubricant and home-brew.

Caver smells. My smells.

"Come through, Sewa," Kalad calls, urgency in his voice.

I navigate through the cramped passage overstocked with equipment and consumables, no time to let my eye wander over the cornucopia of marvels, seemingly more crowded than usual.

Are you planning a descent, Cavemaster?

Even in the circumstances, a visit to Kalad's personal vessel still feels a rare treat, a chance to learn some arcane knowledge.

"Cavemaster," I say as I emerge onto the *Mestaphos'* compact bridge. "May the Endless guide you."

Kalad mutters something, but it's not the usual rejoinder.

Back to me, he sits in the cockpit's command seat, a bulky chair studded with controls, suspended from the rafters. A holographic occupies the space in front of him: a stellar chart with comet 27-B-2431 at its origin, colorful trajectories spiraling away from our icy refuge.

"I can't wait to get off this rock, too," I say.

The holographic disappears, and Kalad spins round.

Shaven-headed with a craggy, weather-beaten face that wears the scars of a hundred expeditions like a call-to-arms, today his lines are extra stark, his eyes extra sunken.

On edge.

"Like me, I know you're not one for traditions, Sewa," he says in his gravelly voice, "but I'm surprised you're not getting ready for the ceremony."

"But that's after midday repast."

"Not anymore. Overseer Liandra announced an emergency decree only an hour ago. Ceremony begins shortly. I'm surprised—" Kalad's jaw tightens. "You've been exploring the ice caves, haven't you?"

Busted.

"I can explain, Cavemaster—"

"But why have you come to me?" His eyes narrow, calculating. "You found something."

I nod. No point denying it.

That's why I'm here.

Kalad steps down from the command seat, wincing as his knee bends. His body is a wreck. He's spent a good part of his life underground, accumulating a litany of injuries and afflictions. Broken ribs, half-destroyed lungs, popped eardrums. He never hides the traumas, always lets us know the stories. Our medical knowledge is second-to-none, but without advanced facilities and specialized medicines, Pilgrims have to carry many of their pains. Especially in these times.

"This needn't become common knowledge," he says, reassuringly, no doubt clocking my anxiety. "I know it couldn't have been easy coming to me."

That's Cavemaster Kalad. The nearest thing I have to a paternal figure on the Horizon. I think he's pitied me since my real father left. Trouble is, I never know if I'm going to get the unforgiving or the sympathetic version on any given day.

Looks like I'm in luck, today.

"So, what did you find?" he asks.

I delve into my pack, carefully retrieve the device like I'm handling an Endless relic. He picks it up, cradling it between his hands, and examines it with complete attention.

"What is it?" I ask.

"Best guess?" he says, inspecting its underside. "A geological instrument collecting seismic data or some such. Pilgrim origin, clearly."

I close my eyes, relieved. "That's good to know."

Kalad drops it on a workbench, chuckles. "Worst case scenario, you've derailed some poor Pilgrim's geology research."

"I can't say I'm sorry." I smile. "Well, maybe a little. We were—" *Shit*. "I mean, I was terrified it might've been some kind of threat to the Horizon."

"We?" Kalad cocks an eyebrow. "You weren't down there alone, Sewa?"

My big mouth. *Sorry, Oba.*

I hang my head. "I was with Oba."

"Obafemi Naia, of course."

Kalad turns away, studies the rugged cometary landscape and the overarching vault of stars beyond.

"Are you going to punish us?"

"Do you think I should?"

I want to mention Overseer Liandra's blessing of our little expedition, but that tactic might well backfire. If she takes flack, *we* might well end up being the ones paying the price.

"Yes… No… I don't know."

Kalad remains silent.

"I mean, we were wrong to go down to the caves, but… we were right in bringing this thing to somebody's attention… so you could say everything balances out."

Faultless logic.

I stare at the device, thinking.

Kalad turns. "You should get to the ceremony," he says. "You still have time. And I'll think some more on an appropriate punishment for you both."

Ah, sheesh. I take a breath. "I was thinking, Cavemaster…"

"Yes?"

"Whoever planted this thing… they'll discover—sooner or later—that it's gone, right?"

"Makes sense." He narrows his eyes. "What's your point?"

"My point is… when they do, they'll wonder who tampered with it, and they'll alert security, or whoever. There'll be an investigation. Maybe we're better off coming clean now?"

"Or," Kalad says, "it'll all blow over, and you'll have stirred up an ants' nest of trouble for no good reason." He smiles. "It's a tricky one though. Your choice."

I step over to the workbench, pick up the device.

Fucking seismology. I wish I'd never found it.

No, that's not true. What if this isn't some innocent seismic instrument? What if it *is* a threat? What if our discovery of this thing is the difference between the Horizon's survival and its destruction? Catastrophizing, maybe, but we don't *know*. Not 100 percent.

"I want it checked out."

Kalad nods. "Maybe it's good to be prudent."

"Whatever they throw at me and Oba, it'll be worth the peace of mind." I give him the device.

"I know just the right person for this." He gives it another once-over, then places it back on the workbench. "Someone in Analytics on the *Dawn Skies*. He'll be rigorous, but discreet. I'll drop it off later today."

"Later today?" I say. "I can take it now."

"Better this comes from me." Kalad grabs the device again, stows it in his pack. "I'll come with you. Hell, I should attend the ceremony for once anyway—save myself an earful from Scriptmaster Artak," he says with a wink.

"You're coming?" I say, unable to hide the glee in my voice.

Even though all Masters are expected to be present, Cavemaster Kalad usually dodges the Ceremony of Duties, not wanting to undermine his cantankerous recluse image. But if he's coming? A good sign he's lining up somebody for caving duty.

Somebody like me.

"I know, I know," he says, holding up a hand. "I'll be breaking my run. And it is a colossal drag—no offense—but maybe I should go for old time's sake, eh?"

I smile. "I think so."

A vision comes to me. Rina and Mother in the crowd, beaming with pride—well, Rina, at least. My name is called. *Sewa Eze. Chosen for the duty of caving.* Cheers and laughter. Afterwards, feeling like I'm walking on air, joining Cavemaster Kalad who introduces me to my idols: Argo Vela, the Lawal twins, and the rest of the caving crew.

"Cavemaster," I say, suddenly worried. "They wouldn't punish us by changing our assigned duties, would they?"

"No, of course not." He frowns. "But Sewa," he says, dropping a bombshell that shatters me into a million pieces. "You're not going to be a caver."

FOUR

ᗅ◁◊Σ

I trek across the icy landscape in a daze.

Cavemaster Kalad leads and I follow, my gaze trained on the hard ground. Unless it's a cruel joke, he's telling the truth: I'm not going to be chosen as a caver.

And he would know.

The leadership consults all the masters before assigning Pilgrim youths to their lifelong duties. It's one of the most important tasks the masters perform. The long-term survival of the Horizon depends on it. We've all heard the cautionary tales of when it goes wrong.

What Overseer Liandra has lined up for me, Kalad can't say. "All she told me," he says, with a sympathetic pause, "was that you weren't available for caving duty."

All Pilgrims have the right to challenge their assigned duty, of course. Nobody's done so for years, maybe decades, but the right exists. Let's just say it doesn't exactly enamor you to your fellow Pilgrims—and especially your new master—should you challenge.

We walk in silence. *Dawn Skies* looms out of the regolith, a beautiful sweep of vaulting arches and glassy galleries. Mentor Catryn always tells me—with a sneer of distaste—that it's a little *too* inspired by Raia's gothic period for her to admire it unreservedly, but even she cannot dispute its majesty.

Usually, during terrestrial ventures, the *Dawn Skies* remains orbiting whatever world, moon, or ball of rock we've stopped at, but with the hunter fleet hot on our tails, this time it's slumming it land-side with the rest of us.

After decompression we're inside.

We hustle along dim channels, Kalad walking as fast as his

wrecked leg permits. Everywhere's quiet and deserted, no doubt the majority already at the Overseer's Gardens. The few Pilgrims we do run across wear tense expressions and avoid eye contact. The fact the ceremony has been brought forward can only mean the United Empire has picked up our scent.

Soon we'll be running again.

Where the *Dawn Skies'* outer facade conveys elegance and grace, the inside tells a different story. Everything's smaller, more degraded. A tangled labyrinth of passages and spaces, choked with cabling and conduits, like the crammed, cancer-ridden innards of some gigantic beast. Flaking paint, frayed wiring, flickering lights. The whole orbital could do with an overhaul, but aside from the patch-up maintenance of the core systems, the only thing that gets regular TLC are the frescoes.

Or *propaganda murals* as Oba and I call them.

The one outside Analytics depicts the original twelve convening under cover of darkness on Raia, plotting their breakaway from the Republic. *Was life really so bad under the United Empire that our forebears decided fleeing into the hostile wilds of deep space was the answer?*

Kalad interrupts my thoughts. "Let's see if Tyjani can shed some light on this thing," he says, waving the disc. He presses a hand against the security scanner, and we head into Analytics.

We weave through the hangar-like space, passing groups of Pilgrims in deep conversation around various artifacts and machines. The place feels like a cross between a research lab and an archeological dig. To be honest, I've never been sure exactly what Analytics *do*.

"What happens here?" I ask, as we head off the main floor.

"Analysis," Kalad deadpans.

"Profound."

"Think of it like this," Kalad says, as we head down a long, crowded passage. "The galaxy is a dark, tangled forest, alive with dangerous rivals and predators. We creep around, keeping our heads down, but sometimes we stumble upon a curious trinket. Analytics studies these curios, try to work out their purpose."

"Like the disc I found."

"Like the disc you found." He stops, glances into a side room arrayed with standing workstations, half occupied by Pilgrims. "Here we are."

Kalad leads us to a station in the corner, our presence noted by the Pilgrims, but nothing more. The atmosphere feels tense, everyone focused on their work.

"Tyjani," Kalad says, softly.

The man turns his head, breaks into a warm smile. Of similar age to Kalad, his silvery hair is tied into a thick, multi-stranded braid, while his tattoos have faded a little with time.

"Cavemaster Kalad," he says, his voice deep and rich. "And who is this? One of your caving protégés?"

"Unfortunately not," Kalad replies. "Much to young Sewa's disappointment. Overseer's orders."

Tyjani gives me a long, sympathetic look. "Try not to be disheartened." He glances at Kalad. "I might even be counting my lucky stars avoiding this tyrant."

I smile, my despondency lifting a little.

"Now," he says, "I know this isn't a social visit."

Kalad shuffles closer, retrieves the disc from his pack, and carefully passes it to Tyjani.

He turns it over in his hands. "Seismological device?"

"That was my first thought."

The Analyst raises his eyebrows.

"In the ice caves," Kalad replies. "*Deep* in the ice caves."

Tyjani frowns.

"Yep," says Kalad.

They obviously know each other well, half the conversation unspoken. I wonder how far back they go, where they first met. I get the sense this isn't the first time Kalad has brought something to Tyjani's attention.

"I'll get on it right away," Tyjani says, then looks at me. "So, you're good then?"

At caving, he means.

That makes me feel good.

"Best in my cohort."

"I found it," Kalad says, giving the official line.

"Of course."

We wheel away, thread our way out. Once we've exited Analytics we make tracks for the Overseer's Gardens.

"Thanks," I say, talking to Cavemaster Kalad's back as he strides on. "Some of the other masters might've had me in penance for years."

"I might yet," he says, his gaze locked straight ahead.

I can't tell if he's joking with me, so I let it slide.

Besides, something else is eating me, and I might not get the chance to ask again. "Cavemaster, I need to know. Did you argue my case?" I ask, as we approach a crossroads. "For caver duty, I mean."

"I know what you mean," he replies, orienting himself. We head right, into a notably wider, less scruffy passage. "And I know you're hurting right now. The truth is, Sewa, I argued, believe me. And nothing I said shifted Liandra's stance one jot. I haven't had a more gifted maggot come to me for years, but the Overseer has something else lined up for you."

My hurt mingles with feelings of sadness—and pride.

"Who else would want me?" I ask, genuinely puzzled.

"That, I don't know. Obviously, I wasn't the only one who petitioned for your service, Sewa," Kalad says over his shoulder. "Overseer Liandra had to make a difficult choice. Her first consideration is always the needs of the arcology."

"I just wanted to be a caver," I reply, frustrated. "I don't care about the Endless or their relics or their damn homeworld."

I stop cold.

I've said too much.

Technically, I'm not *of age* yet, but I will be tomorrow when I've been entrusted to my duty. Pilgrims *of age* can be punished, even exiled, for speaking such blasphemous words.

A Pilgrim passes, giving me a hard stare.

"I know," Kalad says quietly afterwards.

He doesn't say more, doesn't chide me.

Sometimes I get the feeling he shares my thoughts about the Endless. Even in private he could never voice such heresies given his position, but his eyes and the small movement of his jawline give me belief. I realize I'm sounding a little like a whining child who's still waiting for their first tattoo, though.

"I mean," I say, "I don't judge anyone who worships or seeks the Endless. And I don't intend any harm to come to the arcology. As a caver I'd be more than happy to pull my weight, follow orders, undertake descents whether they're for ice, weapon caches, or Archivist Veltaros's very own private codex. And—"

Kalad raises a hand.

"You don't need to convince me, Sewa," he says. "But Overseer Liandra has made her choice." He looks pensive, almost brooding, before giving me a small smile. "Try not to be disheartened. Life is complex, full of events that we cannot anticipate." He clutches my shoulder, gives a reassuring squeeze. "Who knows what the future holds?"

He spins, sets off again. "We've tarried enough. Time for you to discover your duty."

FIVE

ᛒᚾᛁᛖ

Emerging from the murkiness of the *Dawn Skies'* intestinal tracts, we're pitched into the bright greenery of the Overseer's Gardens. We stop a moment, letting our eyes adjust to the false, thin blue light that washes down from the geodesic dome, a facsimile of an early summer's day on a real world. I can smell the grass, yet it's edged with a hint of decay.

Maybe a fifth of the Horizon's ten-thousand strong populace are here, packed together on the sloping lawn that gently descends to Kyrv's Rest—the seat of the Overseer on the Horizon—and the raised terrace where the masters gather. Their legion numbers hide the state of the turf, but the signs of the water shortages are still visible in the parched yellow leaves of the trees and shrubs, and the dry earth of the plant beds where only the most tenacious flora has survived.

Many of the rest will be watching.

We weave through the masses, aiming towards my cohort near the front, off to one side. This is usually a time of celebration, but today smiles and laughter seem in short supply. Conversations seem tense, while many wear anxious expressions. I overhear the word Empire several times, and I get the sense most just want to get this over with.

No doubt everybody's on edge.

The questions are the same ones I keep asking.

Why did the Overseer move the ceremony?

Is the Empire close?

Do we need to flee?

Understandably, they want to get back to their own vessels, be ready for a swift evacuation. Our arrival provides a small distraction, though. I can feel their eyes on us, probably wondering why Cavemaster Kalad has arrived late with one of the coming-of-age.

We get a few hostile looks, muttered reprimands. Maybe they think we're holding up the start of the ceremony.

Maybe we are.

Ignoring the unwanted attention, I focus on trying to locate Mother and Rina. They must be here somewhere. I half hope Mother might be carrying Rina on her shoulders, but she hasn't done that for a while. Guess my little sister got too big.

That, or Mother got too weak.

No matter where I look, I can't find them.

We descend the slope, the ground beneath our feet hard and unyielding. Skirting the edge of the koi pond, I see the water is low, scummy, and weed strewn, the fish long since gone. Among the onlookers I see pockets of demonstrators, Pilgrims here to publicly confront the Overseer.

There's Old Yaba, who's banged the same drum for as long as I can remember: a lone voice for merging the Horizon of Light with one of the larger Pilgrim arcologies. Or the terrestrialists over there, who believe the arcology needs to create permanent settlements where the eldest and youngest Pilgrims can live more comfortable lives before they pass away or rejoin the Horizon.

I spy Oba's father.

Of course, he's here for his son, but he's also one of the weapon-hunter advocates—Pilgrims who believe that *all* the arcologies need to coordinate and concentrate on uncovering Endless weapons' tech to truly counter the United Empire.

"Endless' blessings, Sewa," he says as I pass.

I wonder what duty they would want for me?

Healer? *I'm too blunt.* Cartographer? *Too restless.* Ranger? *Maybe... That wouldn't be so bad...*

"Cavemaster!" an oily voice exclaims louder than necessary as we get closer to the terrace. I turn in the speaker's direction, only to be greeted by an overfamiliar smile. "Late, but at least you're here."

"Scriptmaster Artak," Kalad replies, "always a pleasure."

Artak's facial tattoo depicting the Burning of the Prophet—micro-etched and exquisitely detailed—beguiles and appalls in equal measure.

"Is this your farewell?" Artak asks earnestly. "Is that it?"

"Don't get your hopes up."

"Really? I understood you might be hanging up the—" Artak's brow furrows "—what is it exactly cavers hang up? Chaps? Harnesses? Urinal bottles?"

Kalad grins. "Come and cave with me sometime, Artak," he says.

"And I'll show you."

The animosity between these two goes back decades.

Of all the Pilgrims on the Horizon of Light, Scriptmaster Artak is perhaps the most pious, the most dedicated to the Endless and the mission to discover their homeworld, Tor. He knows I'm not the most devout. Maybe if we worshipped the Lost—the actual gods of the Endless—it'd be different, but praying to a dead civilization, long gone, just seems... I don't know... indulgent? Pointless? Desperate? Not that I'd tell Artak. With his size, his fervency, the whites of his eyes stark against that scene of tattooed carnage, he frightens me.

A terrifying thought occurs.

I can't have been chosen by him, can I?

Elect the most faithless Pilgrim from the coming-of-age crop, and then slowly indoctrinate them until they became a shining beacon of devotion.

A challenge to overcome.

An example to make.

Yes, Artak would revel in that.

We push on, the two masters falling in behind me, conversing softly, their words a ritual dance. Shortly, I join the rest of the coming-of-age Pilgrims, while Kalad and Artak climb the steps to the terrace. I've just found Oba, just started to whisper that we're likely in the clear, when, on the other side of the terrace, the entrance to Kyrv's Rest opens.

Overseer Liandra strides through, trailed by High Counsel Ito. Both wear traditional Pilgrim robes—soaring collars, sweeping lines, flared sleeves. Whereas the High Counsel's attire is shimmering purple fabric inlaid with Endless runes along the hems, the Overseer's is a deep, dark burgundy, the only decorative embellishment the insignia of rank on the collar. Rumor has it that things are strained between the pair, the biggest flashpoint being the strategy for the Empire fleet on our tails. The Overseer takes up her position at the simple lectern at the front of the terrace, while Ito joins the masters.

The crowd falls silent.

"Pilgrims, may the Endless guide you," she begins, invoking the traditional salutation. "We are gathered here today for the Ceremony of Duties—an important day, perhaps *the* most important day in our calendar—where the future security of the Horizon of Light is entrusted to another generation.

"Novices," she says, turning her head to us, "today you take the first step of a long journey as you move from being the *protected* to being the *protectors*. Today you come-of-age. Today you receive your sacred duty."

"You hear that, Ess?" Oba whispers. "Even caving's a sacred duty."

He intends the words as a tonic, but he doesn't know I'm not going to be a caver. I glance at him, trying to grin, but it feels more like a grimace. Oba's eyes narrow, but I turn back to the Overseer, not wanting to get into this now.

Liandra looks up at the sky of the dome, like she can maybe see the stars beyond. "First though, I want to offer an apology. Late this morning, we detected troubling movements of the UE hunter fleet currently scouring the Kuiper region on the far side of the system. A thorough review of these movements determined that the fleet was likely still sweeping that region, but as a precautionary measure, the inner council elected to move forward the Ceremony of Duties."

Foreboding whispers break out across the crowd.

I can feel their anxiety. I can feel it myself. Outrunning the UE isn't an option. Once they know where we are, the only choice we have is taking flight via the galaxy's slipways—the fragmented web of threads that link the galaxy's stars. With the slipways we can travel light years in a matter of days, but always at a cost of leaving a mark of our passage in the long-trembling filaments. Sooner or later, they work out where we exited. And then the mouse hunt begins anew.

Using the slipways doesn't come cheap either.

Even with the 147-strong arcology packed up like matryoshka dolls into a streamlined set of twenty vessels, the fuel costs are considerable. And when I say fuel, only one substance suffices. Dust. That's why we're always hunting for the stuff. And right now, reserves are getting low.

But that's not even our biggest problem.

Our biggest problem is reaching the nearest slipway. The slipways link the galaxy's stars, but taking refuge on this comet has taken us away from the web. And that was the point. We deliberately put distance between ourselves and the slipways, because the UE weren't supposed to believe we'd ever endanger our escape route like that.

And it was working.

Everyone was starting to think that we'd shaken them, that this comet was a perfect hiding place from where we'd go on our merry way. And now? Do they know where we are?

Were we fooling ourselves?

The Overseer raises a hand, appealing for calm.

"Please, don't be alarmed," she says. "We are monitoring the situation closely. Although the hunter fleet's movements brings it closer to our location, it is *not* on an intercept path. We believe that it is making plans to investigate the system's inner planets, not us."

Exchanges break out across the gardens again.

"So?" Oba asks, his words almost inaudible in the din. "Did Kalad lose it?"

Classic Oba, still worried about our foray beneath the ice, when we might have a hunter fleet closing in.

"Not really," I reply, leaning close. "He was more interested in what we found than our trespassing."

"You told him I was there?"

"Sorry, Oba. First thing he asked."

He glances up, seeking out the Cavemaster.

"Don't worry," I say. "He's keeping it to himself."

Before I can explain more, the crowd quietens. Looking back, I can see that several onlookers are leaving the gardens, no doubt keen to learn more or get back on their own vessels.

"I repeat: don't be alarmed," the Overseer says. "I have given strict instructions to be notified immediately should there be any change in the situation. Now, please join me in a short period of reflection before we begin."

She takes a moment, tilts her head down, and closes her eyes. I see the slow rise and fall of her chest as she meditates. I feel her aura of tranquility mirrored in my own relaxed breathing. A wave of calm spreads through the crowd.

She lifts her head, eyes blinking open.

"Brothers, sisters," she intones, her words slower than before, coming from a deeper place. "Today we are gathered to see our novices be given their sacred duty." She turns to the eighty or so of us at the side of the gardens. "Today each of you will speak a sacred oath that commits you to a single lifelong duty. Your given duty is a reflection of your talents, your enthusiasms, and your character, but it is first and foremost a reflection of the needs of this arcology.

"But what are those needs?"

The Overseer leaves the question dangling, and the old Pilgrim mantra echoes in my head. *Our purpose is found in the communal not the individual.*

Eventually, she answers, an edge creeping into her voice. "Spiritual invigoration? A deeper understanding of the relics? Reaching the homeworld of the Endless?"

Everyone is still, captivated. Cavemaster Kalad and the majority of the other masters look on with inscrutable expressions. Scriptmaster Artak is nodding his head, but he stops dead with the Overseer's next words.

"No!" she cries. "Not at this time at least."

Murmurs of disquiet trickle through the crowd.

"For near two years," the Overseer says, "we have been running from a dogged, tireless United Empire hunter fleet, hiding everywhere and anywhere we can. Dead moons, gas giants, interstellar voids. Despite all our tricks, that fleet is still on our trail, closer than ever.

"Today we can be proud that we still stand here as survivors, but the price has been heavy. Failing systems, lost vessels, dwindling resources—but worst of all has been the assault on our resolve. Every day we pray and hope and beg that the chase will end, but this chase will not end through mere pleas."

I glance at Oba, his expression one of nervous anticipation, mirroring my own feelings. I feel a brittle electricity skating through the assembled ranks of Pilgrims.

What is the Overseer about to declare?

Is this why I can't be a caver?

"We carry on, attempting to honor our sacred duty to the Endless while fleeing from our enemy, but that division of purpose has seen our culture enter a spiral of decay. A spiral of decay that will be terminal if we don't act. Today we make plans to counter the United Empire threat. Today we start to fight back!"

There are a few cheers of endorsement, but the majority of the crowd remain quiet. Among the masters, Artak doesn't look amused, while Ito remains steely-eyed. I look across the sea of faces, witness fear and uncertainty.

"Fight the Empire?" somebody shouts. "They'll crush us."

Pilgrims are nodding, the man's words resonating.

Oba whispers, "See the masters aren't exactly banging the drum here."

"Jawa, you are absolutely right," the Overseer says, gesturing in the heckler's direction, "*if* we fight them head-on. And that's why we will not fight them head-on. Our fight will be the guerrillas' fight." Overseer Liandra paces as her voice grows louder. "Patience, subterfuge, lightning-fast strikes. We will lure them, harry them, spin them in circles. And then we will hit them. Hard. Every encounter will be on *our* terms, not theirs."

Her words are turning the audience, isolated cheers becoming islands of hollered support. She reaches down to her right, lifts a heavy, dark object. Thrust high, she grips it as if she were an ancient swordsman holding aloft the head of a beheaded foe, and I see that is not so far from the truth. It is the helmet of a rank-and-file United

Empire soldier, the distinctive curved cap unmistakable.

"The United Empire are not unstoppable. They are flesh-and-blood. They bleed. And they die!" She drops the helmet which hits the ground with a crash, then rolls onto its side. "If we are united," she says, pressing her heel onto the helmet, "if we are deft, if we are prepared to not waver in our fight then we *will* be victorious. They will suffer, they will doubt, and we will break *their* resolve. Pilgrims, our time for running is over. Pilgrims, our time to strike back is now!"

As she says the words, she kicks out, sending the helmet tumbling off the terrace into the crowd. The nearest Pilgrims flinch backwards creating a clear zone around the helmet as it lands with a heavy *thunk*.

"Who is with me?"

The crowd falls silent before a Pilgrim woman pushes through the onlookers into the cleared space.

"I am!" she cries, half stamping, half kicking the helmet.

When it comes to rest, another Pilgrim raises his foot stomps on it, sending it spinning. "I am!"

"I am!"

"I am!"

"I am!'

The shout becomes a rallying cry across the gardens, Pilgrims far and wide joining in unison as the helmet gets kicked back and forth. As the cry swells, fed by hundreds, I feel the hairs on the back of my neck rising.

"I am!" I cry.

For the first time in a long time, we feel together—we feel alive. The seeds of our survival lie in that rekindled spirit.

I can feel it.

Nearby, the helmet clatters across the flagstones. One of the ceremonial guards stops it with the toe of his boot, then raises his spear. The helmet shatters with a bone-splitting crack, and the chant dissolves into a wall of sheer noise.

"Today—" the Overseer shouts, struggling to be heard over the tumult. She lifts her hands, appealing for quiet, and the crowd complies. "Today, we assign a new generation to their duties—and we begin this fight!"

More cheers.

"Hesta Odemi, Medu Dwani," she says. "Approach."

Hesta and Medu—two quiet souls who I don't know so well—shuffle out of our throng, climb up the short stone staircase, and walk past the masters.

"To you both," the Overseer says, "the duty of healing."

Not gonna be a healer then.

They each make the traditional Pilgrim embrace with the Overseer, before she gives them the healer insignia that will pin on their breast, forever identifying their duty. As they make their way to the other side of the raised terrace, the assembled Pilgrims erupt into rapturous applause.

I turn to Oba, and we both can't help but grin.

In this way, the ranks of the coming-of-age Pilgrims around us are thinned as they are called up. Hyper-engineering, bioscience, infiltration. Sometimes it's a lone Pilgrim, most of the time it's two or three together. Wrangling, reconnaissance, raiding. The biggest roar goes up when six Pilgrims are chosen to go under the wing of Battlemaster Nedi, soldiers who will one day take the fight to the Empire. Ito gets some of the best and brightest under his political wing, and I wonder if that's a peace offering from Liandra. That or she's trying to buy his support.

"Check out Artak," Oba says over the din.

I scan the standing masters, locate the Scriptmaster. He's a little off to one side, close to the Overseer, his hands tightly clasped in front of him. He's furious—eyes narrow, jaw tight.

Holy shit.

"He's livid."

Oba nods, laughing.

Not a single Pilgrim so far has been assigned to the Scriptmaster or his traditionalist allies of the Horizon's religious-minded wing. If it stays that way this will be unprecedented.

Shortly, Oba's name is called.

He gets the lone caving berth, and although I'm disappointed it's not me, I cheer with the rest. He'll make a good caver, play an important role in making sure the arcology's drum-ships never run dry.

The Overseer continues, the numbers swelling on the terrace, while around me we're whittled down to a handful of remaining Pilgrims. After assignments to cartography, strategy, and—in the only bone thrown to the traditionalists—scripture, I find myself last Pilgrim standing.

What is the Overseer lining up for me?

"Finally," she says, looking over at me with kind eyes, "we come to our last Pilgrim, Sewa Eze."

I feel countless gazes on me.

Camaraderie and relief—and an odd expression of envy—among my fellow coming-of-age; judgment and curiosity from the few masters whose expressions aren't inscrutable. I feel uncomfortable with the attention, but less so than I might've imagined.

"Approach."

As I climb the steps to the terrace, I glance out over the masses. I can feel their joy, their encouragement, but also their need, like they're investing all their hopes in this new generation.

In me.

Before I reach the Overseer, I pass Scriptmaster Artak who gives me a scathing look. Disgust because he'll be the one dealing with my heathen ways, or because I'm yet another Pilgrim who's fated to be beyond his grasp?

"To you," the Overseer says, "the duty of leading."

Leading?

I blink, uncomprehending.

"Embrace me," the Overseer whispers.

I feel winded—like the time my rope once broke during a rappel. I ended up landing hard on my back, breath snatched from my lungs. I turn my head. All these Pilgrims, one day under my care. I'm drowning in this sea of faces, imagining myself being pulled under by a thousand grappling hands, when I spy Mother.

And next to her, Rina.

My little sister's face is flushed with fear. She doesn't know what this means. Not for the arcology. For her.

I muster all my strength, give her a smile.

I'll still be here for you.

Her fear evaporates and she smiles back—and in that moment my paralysis eases. I only wish Father could've been with them to see this day.

I embrace the Overseer, take my insignia.

He would've been proud, I think.

I join the others. Applause breaks out. Oba grabs me, his eyes wide with excitement, and I can't help but grin. He screams. I'm happy for him. Before long the clapping is drowned by an avalanche of whoops and cheers, deafening.

Among the masters, I notice Cavemaster Kalad has already taken his leave, while Scriptmaster Artak has joined the Overseer, face like thunder, launching into an angry tirade. I smile.

Times are changing, Artak.

Overseer Liandra's not listening though. She has a finger to her ear, straining to hear over the noise. Then her mouth drops, and her face goes white. Artak enquires. I read the Overseer's lips clear as day when she replies.

They're coming.

SIX

ᐁᓛᓂ

The sirens begin, a long skin-crawling wail that reverberates through the geodesic dome. The crowd disperses—orderly yet purposefully—but I stay rooted to the spot, like I've been pitched into darkness.

We've had tight scrapes before, but this feels different.

Like the UE knew we're here.

I know what I should be doing. I should be heading for the *Dawn Skies'* main airlock to get to my home vessel—or should I?

As of a few minutes ago, I'm no longer a novice.

I'm a Pilgrim with a given duty. Just like the rest of the new crop who loiter, unsure what they should be doing. We all have masters now. Mine just happens to be the Overseer herself.

Her wish is my command.

I can't approach her though, even if she stands not ten paces away. A scrum of masters surround her like barking dogs, flanked only by High Counsel Ito who remains tight-lipped. The exchanges are heated, Defensemaster Zaerva in furious argument with Battlemaster Nedi and Shadowmaster Bawa.

They're making a hard choice.

"What should we do?" Oba asks, uncertain. "Sewa?"

"I don't know," I whisper, glancing at him. "I guess we won't be getting inked tonight."

The Overseer lets both sides say their peace, then raises a hand, silencing further discussion. Except for the masters and us, the gardens have emptied, and the sirens echo unchallenged across the dry grass and desiccated trees. The Overseer turns and whispers a word to the High Counsel, who nods and departs. Without any fanfare, she quietly addresses the masters.

Afterwards, Bawa shakes her head and Nedi drops his in defeat, while Zaerva, the Defensemaster, touches the Overseer's forearm in solidarity. Then they all leave.

The Overseer turns and approaches us.

"Pilgrims," she says, "I wish you every success in your new duties, but we find ourselves in exceptional circumstances, so for now, I ask that you return to your home vessels until this crisis passes."

I feel my unease deepening. I don't want to sit on the sidelines while this plays out. Among the others her words have elicited mixed emotions. In some, relief, in others, exasperation.

We start to leave.

"Not you, Sewa."

I stop dead, turn.

"Overseer?"

Oba and a couple of the others have stopped too, curious, but the Overseer gives them a steely look.

"Stay safe," Oba says to me, and they head off.

"With me," the Overseer says, giving me no time to figure out Oba's feelings.

Before I reach her side, an announcement starts blaring over the noise of the rolling sirens.

"EVACUATE IMMEDIATELY. EVACUATION PLAN AZURE… EVACUATE IMMEDIATELY. EVACUATION PLAN AZURE… EVACUATE IMMEDIATELY. EVACUATION PLAN AZURE…"

Azure. Isn't that—?

"We're going to have to move fast," the Overseer says, turning and striding off. "No time to waste."

I follow her into Kyrv's Rest. Across the whole arcology I've never seen quarters so lavishly appointed, so spacious. Two high-backed armchairs, upholstered in thick, button-pocked leather are the centerpiece of the room, next to a low oval-shaped table brimming with papers and trinkets. The Overseer grabs something from the table, then disappears into the baroque, gilded library, all the while engaging in terse exchanges over her earpiece. Orders, I surmise, not debate.

While she rummages, I marvel. An antique globe from the age of sail depicts Raia's continents and oceans in sepia tones, while fleshy-hued, portentous paintings illustrate the original exodus. The only clue this place might not be a private study in a large manse on some venerable world is the holographic star-chart that slowly gyrates above the grand desk.

"—Sewa?"

"Sorry, Overseer?"

"Come on, this way."

We leave the study, hasten through another part of her quarters, before we're back in the *Dawn Skies'* maze-like passages, gradually ascending through the hub orbital's structure as the siren's wail.

"I brought you with me," the Overseer shouts over her shoulder, "because the next few hours—the next few days—will give you great insight into the demands and challenges of leadership. Just by observing you will learn a great deal—provided we come out of this attack alive."

My stomach tightens; another stab of fear.

"You think they're aiming to destroy us?"

"I do. The Empire despises the fact we're an aspect of itself that sought escape." She glances back, gripping a lower rung of a ladder we're about to climb. "Erasing the Pilgrims from the galaxy isn't enough for Zelevas, though. He wants to erase us from history too. We can't let that happen."

No, we can't.

"Not everyone wants to fight though," I say, thinking of the tension between the Overseer and the High Counsel.

"Sometimes that's the only way." Liandra begins climbing.

"You think I can be a leader?" I ask a moment later, shouting up the ladder shaft. "I've never thought of myself as one."

"I wouldn't have chosen you otherwise," she replies, voice echoing down the shaft. "Listen, Sewa. Our culture is dying. The Horizon—all the Pilgrim arcologies—are slowly losing their hunger, their survival instinct. Despite what Artak says, the search for the Endless is not enough. Every civilization needs to have a purpose, otherwise it dies." She catches her breath, the steady rhythm of our foot- and hand-falls on the rungs creating a discordant chorus. "The United Empire give us a cause to fight, but they are only a distraction. We need a new generation with new ideas."

I wonder if she's got the right person. Most of my ideas focus on first keeping Rina and Mother safe and fed. And then caving, a distant second. The Horizon's enduring raison d'être doesn't even cross my mind.

"And that's me?"

"I've had my eye on you a while, Sewa," she says, as she reaches the top of the ladder. "You're not in awe of the Endless like many of the other novices. From your earliest years, even before your father left, you've been skeptical of their elevation, recoiled against many of the teachings. I've seen that."

She's right, but I don't say anything.

I clamber up the last rung, breathing hard.

"Eventually," she continues, "many Pilgrims get to the same place, but they're usually too old or too comfortable or too afraid to agitate for change. I'm one of them. And so the cycle carries on, the culture slowly asphyxiating itself. But you're young. You know these thoughts you harbor are deemed heretical by the orthodoxy, so you don't give them voice; you ignore them or bury them, and you seek a life free from confrontation."

She lifts my chin, locks eyes. "Isn't that the real reason you've always sought the solitary life of the caver? To avoid conflict—to avoid the judgment and the shame that would follow."

Is she right? I don't know.

A message comes in over her earpiece, and she turns away, presses a finger to her ear.

"Understood," she says, then turns back to me. "Mutiny brewing on the bridge. Let's step it up. And Sewa," she adds, before she's off again, "under my wing you don't need to be afraid. I can protect you."

When we reach the bridge, Commander Ldeko, Battlemaster Nedi, and High Counsel Ito stand around the tactical hologrid, while several lower-ranking crew occupy the consoles positioned around the oval periphery.

High in the uppermost reaches of the *Dawn Skies*, we're a good distance above the cometary surface now, and the curved screen gives a panoramic vantage over the decamping fleet. Most of the arcology is still on the ground, but several vessels have already escaped into holding patterns above the regolith, vaporized ice trails glittering in the starlight.

The room is tense.

A look of disgust crosses Nedi's face as he notices me hanging back. Guess I wasn't *his* first choice for the duty of leadership. *Well, screw you.* I stride out of the shadows and join the Overseer on one side of the hologrid.

Ldeko glances between myself and the Overseer. He leans forward, hands gripping the edge of the hologrid. "Overseer," he says, unable to hold his tongue any longer, "this plan is a mistake."

Usually, he makes pronouncements dispassionately, without any sign of emotion, but I can hear his anger. *Dawn Skies*, the beating heart of our arcology, is Commander Ldeko's vessel.

"I understand your concern, Commander," the Overseer replies. "But our hand is forced."

"But giving up the *Dawn Skies*?" He sweeps his arm out, emphasizing the extent of the orbital. "It's unthinkable. And there are other options. We could run for Ictaz V, lay low in its helium oceans, or we could seek the aid of one of our brethren—the *Lago* and *Jarvad* arcologies—"

"The matter is settled, Commander Ldeko," the Overseer interrupts calmly, but firmly. "Defensemaster Zaerva has run the sims. Sacrificing the *Dawn Skies* gives us the best chance of escape with minimal casualties."

"Provided the UE take the bait."

"They will," the Overseer says. "The temptation to capture a Pilgrim hub orbital will be too great."

Ldeko locks eyes with Ito, but the High Counsel keeps his lips sealed and his arms folded beneath his wide-sleeved robes.

No help there, Commander.

Ldeko's assigned commission of the *Dawn Skies* was a proud capstone for many years of dedicated military service. After this, the command of any other vessel will feel like a humiliation. I feel sorry for him.

"The *Dawn Skies*," he says softly, "is the spiritual heart of the Horizon. We congregate here, reflect here, worship here—and lead from here. Losing it will be a devastating blow to morale."

The Overseer nods, but doesn't answer.

The crew stationed at the consoles around the bridge don't turn to look, but they cock their heads and stiffen, keen not to miss anything. The Overseer stays quiet, weighing her words, no doubt anxious that her choice to sacrifice the *Dawn Skies* isn't seen as a political act. After her speech at the Ceremony of Duties, the traditionalists will be sharpening their knives.

"Overseer," Battlemaster Nedi says, "give me full military authority over the Horizon and I will see off the enemy—without the loss of the *Dawn Skies*."

"And how many lives will that cost?"

"Any true Pilgrim would gladly give their life—"

"Enough! My mind is made up."

The Overseer raises a hand warding off any further dissent. She manipulates a touchpad, and a view onto the *Fount*'s concourse appears on the bridge's main screen. The *Fount of Hope* is the arcology's largest vessel, home to roughly a tenth of the entire population. Despite the emergency, the atrium is still crowded with huddled Pilgrims. Few traders are plying their wares today, only the skeletal frames of the stalls present, but the chai stand and the stewed rice eatery are thronged.

"Brothers and sisters," the Overseer begins, addressing not only the *Fount*, but every single vessel of the Horizon. On the grainy feed, a sea change comes over the crowd as they stop and listen. "No doubt all of you will have heard the sirens, will have heard the evacuation order, and are right now readying yourselves swiftly—but calmly—for flight. We had hoped this comet would offer us sanctuary from the enemy, keep us hidden while it carried us into deeper space, but recent movements of our pursuers indicate this is not the case. They know where we are, know our capabilities, and know they possess the superior firepower."

The Overseer ignores the Battlemaster's grimace.

"Desperate situations call for desperate measures."

Forcefully, but calmly the Overseer outlines the plan to split the Horizon into three parts. The first group, numbering the most vulnerable vessels, will escape along a trajectory that uses the comet's profile to keep them out of sight of our UE pursuers. The second group, comprising the majority of the vessels but disguised to appear limited in size, will head on a course towards the nearby Coronis star system. Lastly, but most vitally, the hub orbital *Dawn Skies* together with a few of the most decrepit vessels *and* our fastest warships, will set course in the opposite direction, heading for the Sareco nebula.

Dawn Skies is the bait.

The Overseer's banking on the notion that snaring the shining jewel of a Pilgrim arcology—a hub orbital—will be a prize too great to pass up for the Empire. At a suitable time the accompanying warships will break off and flee, rendezvousing with the remainder of the Horizon at a later date.

"Brothers and sisters," the Overseer says as she finishes. "May the Endless protect you."

Before she kills the feed, I see the assembled Pilgrims staring in shocked silence. The *Fount* will be one of the vessels walking a tightrope away from the comet, a difficult balancing act as they attempt to keep out of sight of our pursuers. One slip and they'll be exposed.

The Overseer orders everyone off the bridge—off the ship—except Commander Ldeko and High Counsel Ito.

And me, of course.

Soon we'll join them though—right after the scuttling commands are initiated and the vessel's in the hands of the auto-pilot system. Then the *Dawn Skies* will be entirely empty, a ghost ship carving a lonely course across the stars. Already I can feel the hurt of its impending loss—even if this *is* the best strategy.

I just hope it's not a terminal blow.

"I'm sorry, Ketchi," the Overseer says, gripping Commander Ldeko's arm.

"Me too."

SEVEN

ϴᛄᛃᛄᛃ

War in space involves a lot of waiting.

Away from the slipways, information can spread no faster than the speed of light. As the Horizon leaves our icy refuge, sundering itself into three distinct flotillas, it will take the light that betrays our egress eleven minutes to span the void between ourselves and our UE pursuers.

A further eleven minutes will pass before we might gain any inkling of our pursuer's response.

Twenty-two minutes of dead time.

And that's only the absolute minimum.

From the underbelly of our new de-facto capital vessel—the mid-sized scientific research ship, *Truthseeker*—I watch the pitted and scarred surface of comet 27-B-2431 recede to a jagged silhouette in the darkness. Another sanctuary left behind. Strange to think that only this morning, Oba and I were drifting through its icy caves, oblivious to what was coming.

I shake away the useless thoughts, focus.

The *Truthseeker*'s a sensible choice for lead, where communication and observation are more important qualities than military prowess, but that can't disguise the political statement the Overseer is making once again. She could've thrown a bone to the traditionalists and chosen one of the clerics' vessels—the *Faith and Glory* or the *Enlightening Light* would've both satisfied the operational needs of a capital ship—but she chose not to walk that path.

Eleven minutes pass.

I imagine the light reaching our pursuers.

They will see two flotillas escaping the comet in opposite directions, like a perfectly choreographed explosion. The *Dawn Skies'* presence in one of these armadas will be obvious from its engines' emission spectra, but the remaining compositions will be uncertain. They will speculate that a third flotilla might be escaping on a trajectory occluded by the comet—or even that a handful of vessels remain on the comet itself.

Our divergent escape will pose them a dilemma.

Another eleven minutes pass.

No reaction.

Our pursuers remain on an intercept course with the comet, but that doesn't mean they aren't *acting*. Vast computing resources will be brought to bear on the incoming light, sophisticated algorithms slicing and dicing up the spectra to best ascertain not only the anatomy of each flotilla, but also its likely destination. Like supercomputers analyzing the mid-game distribution of pieces on a cavat board, the routines will prune the mighty tree of near-infinite possibilities, eliminating the unlikely lines and offering the optimal responses.

The rest will be down to gut feelings.

Whoever's in command of this hunter fleet has been chasing us for two years now. In that time they'll have developed a sense of our strategies, our feints and bluffs, our very survival instincts. Likely, they'll know we'll have carefully calibrated the three-dimensional formations of our flotillas to misdirect, and they'll take that into account when they make their move.

The question is: Will they take the bait?

Another ten minutes pass, time flowing like treacle, the heavens fixed except for the steadily diminishing light of our sibling flotillas. To distract myself from the crushing wait, I head up to *Truthseeker*'s comms station and radio the *Eustatia*, Oba's family vessel, a few klicks away across the vacuum.

"Ess! Is it true?" Oba asks, after I get his father to pass over the headset. "They haven't made their move yet?"

"It's true," I reply. "We're all still on tenterhooks."

"Damn." Oba lets out a long breath. "I can't stand the waiting. Are they going to go after the *Dawn Skies* or not?"

"I don't know, O."

"I mean, if they ignore the *Dawn Skies* and come after us, we're going to be soup, right? Hey, you think they've clocked that we've split into three flotillas yet? Is that why they're still heading straight for the comet? They somehow know about the third flotilla, and they're going after our most helpless first? We know a lot of people over there, Ess. I mean, a ship like the *Tagma* could be incapacitated in next to no time. You think they'd send us to Raia? I hear they've got gulags in the frozen north—"

"Oba!"

"What?"

One of the *Truthseeker*'s comms specialists is giving me a stern look, so I lower my voice to a fierce whisper. "I called you for some *respite*—not to get more stressed!"

"Oh… right. Sorry."

The line goes silent. Seconds pass.

"I—"

"I—"

"You go," Oba says.

"I was just going to say it's good to hear your voice."

"Yeah, it's good to hear yours too."

I picture him in some nook of the *Eustatia*, the cramped ship offering little privacy for a family of seven. "How's your family holding up?"

"No one's tried to kill anyone else yet, so I'd call that a win."

"Obafemi!" I hear his mother shout in the background. "I heard that!"

"Give me a sec," he whispers, and a scraping noise follows as he moves. "So, you check in on your sis?"

"Not yet," I say, feeling guilty. "It's been non-stop, O. This is my first breather since the ceremony."

"Liandra working you hard?"

"Just watching and listening mainly. But it's intense."

"Enjoying it, then?"

"I wouldn't go that far." I imagine our splintering arcology moving away from our cometary refuge, the Empire closing in. "Not with everything happening."

"I was worried you'd be devastated, after—"

"Me too," I say. "Leadership has its perks, though." I want to tell him about the opulence of Kyrv's Rest, but then I remember it'll soon be in the Empire's hands—if the plan succeeds. "Anyway, I want to be there for Rina, but Mother will only stress me out if I call. Then I'll probably make them both upset."

"Yeah, I can see that."

"Can you do me a favor?"

"Sure."

"Can you pay them a visit—when the lockdown's over?" Inter-vessel movement is strictly forbidden while we flee. "I don't know when I'll have some downtime, and I know they could do with seeing a friendly face."

"Of course," Oba replies. "Not like I'll be doing any caving missions anytime soon."

"I owe you."

"Nah, I'll be happy to escape the cabin fever."

We fall to silence, just like we do when we're caving together, happy to just be in each other's company.

"You still there, Ess?"

"I'm here."

He hesitates, then gets the words out in a rush. "What I said this morning—about taking off. I was just letting off steam, you know?"

"I know."

"I'm not going anywhere, Ess," he says. "Like you said, people need us."

"I know."

"Especially if you're going to lead us someday."

That might've freaked me out if I hadn't started thinking about our morning's little caving adventure.

"Say, O," I say, dropping my voice to a whisper, "you think that thing we found has anything to do with the UE finding us?"

"I don't know," he answers. "I doubt it."

I glance at the nearest comms specialist; he's focused on a complex blizzard of data but that doesn't mean he isn't eavesdropping.

"You're probably right. Listen, Oba. I should go—maybe the UE have made a move. Stay safe, okay."

"Yeah, you too."

Another two hours pass before the UE act.

I learn the news standing alongside the Overseer on *Truthseeker*'s bridge. A chime sounds from the hologrid, and we watch the predicted trajectory of the UE fleet change as our pursuer switches course from the comet—to the *Dawn Skies* flotilla.

"Thank the Endless!" somebody cries.

The sentiments are echoed among other members of the crew, but I also hear mutterings of discontent.

The UE have taken the bait, though.

Relief floods through me, a weight lifted.

We're going to live.

I see the Overseer's fist clench with satisfaction too, but she's careful not to let her contentment be too obvious. I understand. She might've already moved on from the forthcoming loss of the *Dawn*

Skies, but many haven't. They won't forgive her if she seems happy in its destruction. But that's not why she's happy. She's happy because she's ensured the Horizon's survival—for now.

Battlemaster Nedi speaks first, hiding well any bitterness he might have. "It appears your plan's working, Overseer."

"Let's not get ahead of ourselves." The Overseer's gaze remains on the UE's trajectory. "We have a long way to go."

Before the day is out, the Overseer's words of caution turn out to be prophetic. Six hours after the UE watched us flee the comet, and three hours after they altered course to intercept the *Dawn Skies* flotilla, they make another strategic move.

One hunter fleet becomes two. Half carry on pursuing the *Dawn Skies* flotilla, while the rest change course to intercept us. Still occluded by the comet, our vulnerable sub-fleet carries on into the darkness, undiscovered.

Why did they decide to splinter themselves?

A deeper analysis of the flotillas' emission spectra? Clues from the rapidly approaching cometary surface? The suspicion of a ruse in the mind of the UE commander?

Who knows?

The only clear truth is this: they're coming for us.

"Overseer, incoming message."

Overseer Liandra is deep in conference with Cavemaster Kalad and High Counsel Ito discussing viable worlds for replenishment runs. They don't stop talking.

"From our pursuers," the specialist adds.

The conversation stops dead.

As does the rest of the chatter on the bridge.

"Let's hear it," the Overseer commands.

"Overseer Liandra," begins a strangled, rasping voice. "This is Commander Zarva Rachkov, leader of the United Empire fleet Inquisitor."

I flinch.

Each choked word is an assault on the ears.

The audio must be suffering some chronic distortion—a distortion that the comms specialist will shortly rectify. Then I remember.

The hunter fleet is being led by an Empire outsider.

Rachkov is a Niris, a naturally-aquatic species, not unlike the cephalopods that exist on Raia, and this must be its normal, modulated voice. Special breathing apparatus and other bionics permit the species to live outside underwater environments, although it's known that they prefer zero-gravity vessels when off-world.

I've never heard one speak before.

It's not pretty.

I shiver. They must bring something very valuable to the hunt to have even been considered for command by Emperor Zelevas, supreme ruler of the United Empire.

Maybe he's right to have had such faith.

We've never had a hunter fleet on our tail for so long—or one that's got so close.

"I applaud you and your people's tenacity, Overseer," Rachkov says, its half-mechanical, half-gargled words echoing across the bridge. "I have tracked many fugitives in my lifetime, but few have shown your stamina, ingenuity, and courage. Truly, you are a credit to all Pilgrims."

Battlemaster Nedi sneers. "Words of a snake."

The message plays on, as if Rachkov were swatting away a fly. "And a credit to Raia too, of course. Do you still remember Raia, Overseer? Deep oceans, vast continents, cities as wondrous as shining baubles. As a world, it really is something to behold. Much richer sustenance than the thin gruel that a life in space entails."

Naturally, like most Pilgrims alive today, I've never ventured within a half-dozen systems of Raia, never mind walking its lands. Countless trawls of the arcology archives, however, have seared its landscape on my mind. I've never known any home except for the Horizon, and yet, I think, there is something deep-rooted in my blood that yearns for a homeworld.

Around me, all are silent.

"That world can be yours again," Rachkov says, as if he was right here, right now, reading the mood on the bridge. "Yes, it can. I give you my solemn word, Overseer Liandra. Surrender your fleet now, and every Pilgrim under your command will be given safe passage onto Raian soil. There will be trials, naturally... the Pilgrim leadership should expect severe judgment... but every Pilgrim, provided they renounce their faith, will be granted full citizenship.

"You'll be free. And you'll be home."

"Lies!" Nedi shouts, throwing up his arms.

The bridge is silent, but Rachkov isn't finished yet.

"Whether you surrender now or not, the United Empire will repatriate *all* Pilgrims. On that matter, Emperor Zelevas has given me his personal assurance. But be warned—should you elect to fight, punishments will be far more severe for all the Horizon's Pilgrims. Believe me, the United Empire mourns every one of its lost as much as the Pilgrims, and you will be despised."

Rachkov lets the words hang in the air.

The collar of my uniform chafes against my neck, suffocating.

I see I'm not the only one who's frightened.

"We have you in our sights, Overseer Liandra. And we will not lose sight of our prey, irrespective of what happens over the next few days. Don't make a foolish choice."

The message ends.

Silence.

Then the bridge erupts into a chorus of voices.

I hear arguments about Rachkov's origin, appeals to the Overseer to ignore the demand for surrender, a rapid-fire analysis of the strategic situation, but my own mind is focused on the Niris's last words.

We will not lose sight of our prey.

"Pilgrims!" The Overseer raises her arms, silences the bridge. "Don't make me regret letting you all be privy to that message." She turns to Nedi. "Battlemaster. Analysis."

Collecting himself, the old Battlemaster adjusts one of his pauldrons, before letting his fingers play over the Pilgrim insignia etched onto his suit's upper arm. Stern-faced, he takes the measure of the room, then speaks.

"They're fishing. Their ponderous response to our flight from the comet demonstrates they know little of our strategy, tactics, or even the composition of our sub-fleets. They don't even know where the Horizon's command resides. I guarantee an identical message would've been sent to the *Dawn Skies* flotilla, all in service of an easy victory."

Nedi clenches his fist. "But we can win this fight!"

He moves to the edge of the dormant hologrid, grips its side.

"Overseer, frankly, Rachkov is not to be trusted." He shakes his head, almost incredulous. "Surrendering now will not see the United Empire roll out the red carpet for the Pilgrims. It will see incarceration at best, annihilation at worst. And it will be a complete and utter betrayal of our faith."

The Overseer nods.

"Cavemaster, what are your thoughts?"

Kalad gives the Battlemaster a long, hard look, as if sizing up an adversary. "Battlemaster Nedi speaks much sense," he says. "If we misjudge our enemy's intentions, we risk catastrophe. Can we trust the Niris's words?" Kalad's gaze dances over the assembled Pilgrims, before locking eyes with me. "Before that though, more vitally, each of us must examine our own hearts and answer a simple question: Am I willing to sacrifice my life for my faith?"

"Heresy!" the Battlemaster cries. "We are Pilgrims!"

The Overseer waves her hand. "Cavemaster, carry on."

The Battlemaster glances around, attempting to get a fix on the mood. Everyone is silent, calculating.

I'm stunned.

Mutiny is in the air.

"Call me heretic if you will," Kalad begins, "but I, for one, have witnessed too much death among our number. Let us face the truth! We are a dying civilization, Pilgrims! Our arcologies grow more decrepit with every passing year, and our response? To become more pious, to become more committed to our faith."

He fixes eyes with the Battlemaster, unafraid.

"This isn't rational," Kalad says. "This is desperation. Pilgrims, unless something changes, we are doomed to gutter out like a dying flame. Maybe we can win this battle, but the Empire has us in their sights. Wounded and weakened, it will only be a matter of time before we find ourselves in the same situation. The next time they might not be so merciful."

Nedi shakes his head. "Empire propaganda."

"I trust the Niris," Kalad says. "I say we surrender. I say we secure our future back on Raia."

"Future?" Nedi roars back. "That world offers us only incarceration and death. Even if only one Pilgrim arcology escapes the yoke of Raia, the sacrifice of the rest will have been worthwhile! We must resist, whatever the cost!"

The commotion flares again, even more heated.

The Overseer quiets the din, her voice soaring over all. "What makes you think they'll find us again, Cavemaster?"

"Zelevas."

"Zelevas?"

"The Emperor won't rest until we are subdued. Even all these years later our flight from Raia still eats away at him, day and night. The resources he can bring to bear... There is no escape for us."

The bridge is silent, all eyes on the Overseer.

"Kalad's words are poison," Battlemaster Nedi says. "And tantamount to treason."

The threat is plain.

Surrender and you will no longer command.

"You are on thin ice, Battlemaster."

The tension is becoming unbearable.

"Sewa," the Overseer finally says. "What do you think?"

The words are so unexpected that at first I don't hear my name. Everyone is looking at me though—some surprised, some disdainful—that the truth finally dawns.

"Me?"

"Yes, Sewa. You."

Is the Overseer trying to buy some more time?

That's the only reason I can think she would ask.

I can hardly believe she is actually interested in my thoughts.

"Well," I say, taking a deep breath and trying to forget that most of the Horizon's leadership are waiting on my next words. And that the fate of all of us hangs in the balance. "The way I see it..."

How do I see it?

"The way I see it, Overseer, is that... is that... we risk everything if we take the United Empire at their word. Rachkov is a UE fleet commander. Unless we know otherwise, we can't trust the Niris."

Nedi slaps the battle hologrid.

"Sense! Somebody speaks sense!"

Others nod their heads, relaxing. The mood brightens as if somebody undimmed the lights.

I feel myself flood with relief.

Only Kalad looks aggrieved.

After a long moment of quiet consideration, the Overseer lifts her chin. "Battlemaster," she says, "prepare us for conflict."

I am no authority on the intricacies of deep-space encounters, but I understand the broad strokes. Millennia past, when ancient armies clashed on grassy plains, victory or defeat was often determined before a single soldier fell. How a commander organized their forces, what their battlefield tactics would be—these were the primary elements that governed the outcome.

Today, the battleground might've extended into the third dimension, but the nature of warfare is essentially the same. Discover the enemy's strategy, disguise your own. Deploy your weapons to cause maximal damage, minimize your own vulnerabilities.

I don't envy Battlemaster Nedi's task.

Many of the Horizon's most agile warships travel in convoy with the *Dawn Skies*, ready to break and flee before the Empire gets too close. By the time of battle, they'll be dozens of light-minutes away; even if they may watch proceedings, they will play no part in our fight.

Of the warships that form part of the *Truthseeker*'s motley entourage, the vessels are rank-and-file craft, long in the tooth and in dire need of an overhaul. Every ship, civilian or otherwise I fear, will be part of the battle plan.

If there is a ray of hope, it comes in the composition of the UE splinter fleet that is chasing us. We will know its makeup more precisely in a couple of days when we're much closer to the opening exchanges, but even now we know it is only half the size of the fleet that goes after the *Dawn Skies*.

Battlemaster Nedi makes the exact point when he speaks to all the leaders of the sixty-three vessels that compose our ragtag flotilla. He ends his address with a rousing call-to-arms.

We will fight with faith in victory.

Such is the vast gulf that separates us from our enemy, the first shots will still not be fired for the better part of three days. That doesn't mean we have nothing to do. First, every vessel's military edges are sharpened like ancient blades honed on whetstones.

On the bridge of the *Truthseeker*, Battlemaster Nedi coordinates the transformation of our motley assembly of craft, an unending stream of remote calls with everyone from the engineers, who will prepare the craft, to the missile operatives who will discharge the weapons. They discuss ordnance systems and shield capacities, defensive formations and battlefield feints, communication protocols and a thousand other facets.

Watching from the shadows, I feel dizzy from the sheer complexity of the preparations.

The Overseer listens, interjecting occasionally where she has some guidance to give, but even her role is largely one of support and encouragement. Whereas many of the other Pilgrims who appear on the grainy feed give off an air of nervous tension, Liandra radiates confidence.

During a lull on the bridge, I corner the Overseer.

"They're afraid."

Liandra looks at me, tilting her head to indicate I should continue.

I turn and stare across the void at a couple of the nearest ships flying in formation. "I can see it in their eyes, hear it in their words. The color is drawn from their cheeks, and they play with their hands."

"It is not unexpected, is it?"

"No, it isn't," I reply. "I'm scared too. The United Empire are coming after us, and in three days we might all be dead—or worse."

"There is no shame in being afraid, Sewa."

"But you're not afraid!" I protest. "Battlemaster Nedi too, but he just seems focused whereas you seem the opposite of scared. Serene even."

"You think I'm not afraid?" she whispers. Right then, something changes in her expression, in her eyes. The mask slips and I see her fear. "Inside, I'm terrified."

Her face shifts again; any sign of the fear gone.

"All leaders must project confidence—even when they feel the opposite inside. Especially then." She smiles. "People will only follow those who give them belief, who they feel they can trust with their lives." She touches my arm. "You will need to learn this skill too. But let's keep this our secret."

"Yes, Overseer, but..."

"What, Sewa?"

"What you're asking of the Pilgrims. It's blind faith, isn't it?" I lower my voice, barely a whisper. "How is this any different to the faith in the Endless that the clerics demand?"

"The faith I ask—it isn't blind. It's earned."

As the next round of meetings begin, I realize that although the Overseer says little, her presence and demeanor is as important—if not more important—than the minutiae discussed. Belief as much as tactics will carry us to victory, and the Overseer is the fount from which this belief spreads. Understanding this, I stop hiding in the shadows, stand tall beside her, as calm and poised as I can muster. I'm beginning to *actually* feel confident, when one of the comms specialists approaches.

"Overseer, an urgent matter," he says, interrupting a discussion. "You'll need to accompany me."

"Carry on, Battlemaster," she instructs, before stepping to one side with the comms specialist. "Is this strictly necessary, Gwo?"

I join them, not wanting to miss the news.

Specialist Gwo glances between us, but Liandra nods her head. *Go ahead.*

Gwo drops his voice to a whisper, so that only myself and the Overseer are privy to his next words. "Analyst Tyjani needs to speak with you immediately."

My legs weaken.

It can be connected to only one thing.

The device.

EIGHT

⼿⼻⼚⼛⼅

"Let's make this quick."

Specialist Gwo begins leading the Overseer, and I move to follow, but she turns and shakes her head.

"You stay here, Sewa," she says. "Keep me apprised of any developments." She gives me a knowing look. "And you have other roles to play too."

A well of belief for the other Pilgrims.

A lookout for any mutiny.

I nod. "Yes, Overseer."

After they depart, I try to focus on the discussion, radiate confidence, but my nerves are shattered. At the side of the bridge, I watch Scriptmaster Artak and High Counsel Ito engage in a quiet, yet intense, conversation, but all I can think about is the device and what Tyjani might've discovered. Did we inadvertently stumble upon Empire tech? Did I endanger the whole arcology by bringing it aboard?

I wonder if I should confess that *I* found it—

"—Novice Eze!"

"Battlemaster?"

"I asked you a question."

The other Pilgrims stare with blank expressions.

"I'm sorry, Battlemaster," I say. "I was lost in thought."

He gives a disdainful look, turns back to the others and carries on the discussion.

Great. Far from giving them belief, I'm giving them doubts.

I focus on the conversation, stand tall, but I'm not consulted again. When Overseer Liandra returns, although she acts unruffled, I can see she's preoccupied.

"Battlemaster," she says, "I have other matters to attend. I leave further preparations in your hands."

Nedi nods, steely-eyed.

The Overseer lets her gaze fall on each of the other Pilgrims. "May the Endless protect you."

She departs and I follow.

"Sewa," she says as we stride through the *Truthseeker*'s sweltering heart. "A sensitive matter has come up. I think it best you return to the *Reverent* where—"

"It's the device, isn't it?"

The Overseer stops dead, spins. "Say no more."

A moment later we're standing in her makeshift quarters, a cramped workspace still bearing the previous occupant's possessions. She pulls the door shut, turns back to me. "What do you know?"

"I know it was found beneath the cometary surface," I answer. "And I know Cavemaster Kalad handed it over to Tyjani."

"Anything else?" the Overseer says impatiently.

"Kalad claimed to be the one who discovered the device—but he wasn't." I take a deep breath. "I was."

The Overseer narrows her eyes. *Go on.*

I tell her how Oba and I found the device while exploring the cave system.

"The Cavemaster claimed responsibility," I add, "because he knew Oba and I would be punished. The caves were supposed to be off-limits."

"For good reason," the Overseer chides. "Tell me, whereabouts in the caves did you find the device?"

"In a small, dead-end chamber," I say, "a few hundred meters into the system, fifty meters deep if I had to guess."

"And do you think that chamber would be accessible to any reasonably able Pilgrim?" she asks. "Think carefully, Sewa. You've been a caver more than half your life. How technical was that descent? Do you think *I* could've reached that chamber on my own?"

I take my mind back to the route.

The trek across the icy regolith, the narrow fissure into the subterranean realm, the frozen labyrinth leading into the comet's heart. All with only the faintest wrench of gravity.

Nothing too difficult for a disciplined mind.

"With planning and determination," I say, "I think most Pilgrims on this arcology could've made that descent."

The Overseer winces. *Wrong answer.*

"It's the near zero-gee," I say by way of apology. "Everything's easier when there's no danger of a fall. They would've needed good preparation—air supplies, footwear, suit, navigation aids—but otherwise they could've made a dozen mistakes during the actual descent and still been okay."

"Thank you, Sewa."

The Overseer stands still and silent, thinking.

Am I to be dismissed for bringing the device aboard?

"Oba and me," I say, "we weren't sure whether we should've left the device where we found it."

She says nothing, still thinking.

"Overseer?"

She purses her lips, studies me intensely. "What I'm about to tell you," she says, "is absolutely confidential. You must share this information with no one—and I mean *no one*. Do you swear on your life, your mother's life, and on your oath as a Pilgrim that you will speak of this to nobody?"

"I swear, Overseer," I say, trying not to rush the words, "on my life, on my mother's life, and on my oath as a Pilgrim."

My words are met with a solemn nod.

"Sewa," she begins, "it is no exaggeration to say that if it wasn't for your discovery of that device we'd likely all be blindly heading into United Empire hands."

"How?"

"The device was a sub-space beacon, transmitting our location to the UE hunter fleet." The Overseer shakes her head. "Because it was buried deep inside the comet under dozens of meters of rock and ice, its presence was invisible to us. Only when you detached the device did it stop broadcasting."

I freeze, understanding.

"They would've kept tracking us, edging closer and closer until escape would've been impossible."

"Exactly," the Overseer says icily. "When the signal disappeared they would've assumed it had been discovered—and so they acted."

That's when they came for us.

Then a colder horror grips me.

"The Empire," I say, "they didn't plant the device, did they?"

"Highly unlikely. We haven't encountered a single vessel, visited a habitable space, for more than eighteen months." Anger courses through her words. "The chances that an Empire agent managed to stay undetected for all that time seems inconceivable.

Every single one of us except a few of the elders who left Raia were space-born, Pilgrims from birth."

I need to say the words aloud.

"It was one of us."

"It was one of us," the Overseer echoes.

It doesn't make sense.

A Pilgrim selling out their own people to our mortal enemies, the United Empire. An empire whose yoke we fought so hard to escape half a century ago. There could be no greater betrayal. I shudder to think what might've happened if the entirety of the Horizon of Light had ended up in Emperor Zelevas' unforgiving hands.

"Why?"

"That's what we need to understand. Somebody among us despises this Pilgrim life so much that they are willing to betray us all. If we can understand why—and when and how—then maybe we can identify them."

Do they know that we're already onto them though?

Right now only a handful of people on the whole arcology know about the discovery of the device; the two of us, Oba, Tyjani—and Cavemaster Kalad, of course. After the UE's sudden course correction towards the comet, the guilty party might *suspect* the beacon's discovery, but they wouldn't *know.*

"We have to investigate undercover."

"Very good." The Overseer gives a guarded smile. "We must give the impression we know nothing of the beacon. Any advantage we can preserve might be vital." She sighs. "Besides, the last thing we need two days out from battle is word getting out that there's a turncoat among us."

I shudder. Pilgrims wouldn't be able to trust each other, everyone wondering if the kin they slept beside or the workmate they labored with was the betrayer. Suspicion would poison everything, eat us up from the inside like a cancer.

I can feel the first wave of that paranoia myself.

Is the traitor here, aboard the *Truthseeker*?

"Sewa," the Overseer says. "I need *you* to investigate."

"Me?"

"You are the natural choice. Choosing anyone beyond the circle who already know increases the risk of the truth getting out— especially if I select someone known for their scrutiny."

Outside, footsteps grow louder, then fade away.

"Let me talk to Oba, Tyjani, and Kalad." The Overseer lowers her voice. "Out of all of us who do know, as my understudy, your movement will arouse the least suspicion."

A tour.

I will need to flit between the vessels, hoping to find something—caving equipment where there shouldn't be any, unusual behavior or recent disappearances, long-held grievances. And that's assuming there *is* something to be found on this flotilla. Maybe the traitor is on one of the other two sub-fleets.

"What if they're not here?" I ask.

"My problem."

I nod.

So, why might I be paying a visit to every—

"I could be checking battle preparations."

"Sewa?"

"A justification for my tour around the flotilla." I grin. "I can give the appearance that I'm checking the battle readiness of every ship—when really I'm investigating."

The Overseer frowns. "Battlemaster Nedi is overseeing combat preparations… but you could certainly be a second set of eyes on my behalf." She nods, warming to the idea. "Tomorrow, liaise with his staff, procure all the relevant checklists for every vessel in our flotilla. When you have that in hand, we'll draw up our own shadow plan for your covert operations.

"So, you will do both: secretly investigate *and* ostensibly inspect." The Overseer gives a black laugh. "No appearances necessary. After all, we need every vessel on point if we want to win this fight."

We stand, unspeaking.

I think we both know that neither of us will be getting much respite over the next few days. The Overseer moves closer, smartens up the collar of my jacket, then lets her hand rest on my collarbone.

"Time to get some rest," she says. "Tomorrow will be a long day."

Life is strange.

Yesterday, all I could think about was becoming a caver. Now I am the Overseer's surrogate, and tomorrow I will be the beating heart of a frantic search for the Pilgrim betrayer.

"I will do my best, Overseer."

"I know you will."

That night I sleep a fitful sleep.

I wake early, sweaty and parched, the rough spun blanket of my bunk tangled around my body. Fleeting impressions of my dreams—a journey through twisted metal, smoke and fire—evaporate in the flickering light of Mother's votive candles.

She and Rina are still sleeping.

I'm careful not to wake them.

After wiping myself down with a semi-damp cloth, I get dressed into my official uniform. The fabric feels itchy against my skin and when I peer at myself via the wash cubicle feed, I can see that my face looks raw and red. On my jacket's lapel the breastpin signifying my new status as the Overseer's charge sits askew, so I neaten it up. I lift my chin, straighten my back, seeking a bearing of authority.

Let's call it a work-in-progress.

Oba's messaged me in the night. He looks distracted, asks if I've got time to see him today. I need to focus on my task, so I don't reply. I'll see him during my tour anyway.

I step out.

The hour's early and the ship is quiet. The living quarters of the *Reverent* are not unlike the original Raian ghettos where furtive Pilgrims banded together, three-storied facades facing one another across a gap so narrow that you can easily pass things from one side to the other. Of course, unlike in Empire territory, we don't have to hide who we are here. Many treat the walkway as an extension of their personal domains, and these sections are littered with housewarming trinkets—withered pot plants, hookah pipes, cavat boards, woven rugs, chai sets, upholstered stools and religious tomes.

No sign of the coming conflict.

Soon enough I'm back on the *Truthseeker*, where the war preparations are impossible to miss, the ship a hive of activity. After securing the battle checklists from my military contact, I meet with Overseer Liandra in the privacy of her makeshift quarters again. Sitting at her desk, she flicks through the digital dossier, making small grunts of approval.

"Battle preparations are thorough," she says, handing the tablet back. "Every vessel has detailed notes on everything from weapons to engine capabilities to the crew manifest. Checking everything will give you legitimate access to every ship in the flotilla, top to bottom."

"Perfect cover."

"Indeed." She peers up, thinking. "So, what should you look for?"

"First off, caving equipment," I reply. "Second, makeshift electronics, or digital workbenches. Whoever the traitor is, they needed to be able to get into the heart of the comet, and they had to rig-up that sub-space beacon."

"That's good. When you're checking system integrity, firewalls and the like, make sure you secure the ship logs with entry/exit data for the period we were stationed on the comet. That could be important." She nods. "Anyone asks, tell them it's for operational security, that we need to know who's had access to the vessel."

"Understood." I take a deep breath. "I was thinking, whoever planted that beacon, they're probably under psychological stress. And they might've been acting strangely over the past few days or weeks. Maybe expressed sympathies for the United Empire, however slight—"

"Or discontent with the Pilgrim way of life."

"Yeah, that too, perhaps."

"These are good lines of enquiry, but we need to be very careful." The Overseer drums her fingers on the desk. "Our military forces will be stretched thin across the flotilla. It'd seem prudent to check up on the mental health of all who'll play an active role in the hostilities, whether they're soldiers or not. That can be your angle."

"Checking they're ready for the coming battle."

"Exactly." She fixes me in the eye. "But don't push it. Nobody can twig what you're really up to."

"Okay."

"Now, I need to get back." The Overseer stands up. "And you need to start digging. Happy hunting, Sewa."

Feeling nervous, I head out for my first port of call: the *Draylus*, a small warship that'll be on the frontline.

Unsurprisingly, the *Draylus'* commander is none too pleased to prove his vessel's battle readiness to a tentative greenhorn, even if I am acting in the Overseer's stead. Clumsily I work through the checklist, out of my element both as a figure of authority and as an inspector. I realize, though, that his antagonism is useful for hiding my true intentions, and by the time I depart for the next ship I have delved into the *Draylus'* affairs in far greater depth than I imagined possible.

Not that I find anything.

No stashed caving equipment, no makeshift electronics, no unusual behavior beyond what you might expect as part of our strained existence, nothing but unalloyed loathing for the United Empire. The entry/exit logs I'll check later. What I do find is an uneasy, nervy atmosphere, only matched by a quiet determination to do whatever's necessary to eliminate the Empire threat. If the betrayer is aboard the *Draylus'* crew, they've hidden the evidence well.

Inspections of the support vessels *Sunrunner* and *Kalwraith*, and the warship *Pargesus*, follow the same pattern. Even if I don't glean much, each time, I feel a little less of a fraud, a little more competent at my work. The power I wield is a curious thing. A few days ago, I was happily destined to be a lowly caver. Now I can roam where I like across the flotilla, demanding answers from Pilgrims who've held their duties longer than I've lived. I think I'd be overwhelmed if I had time to digest everything.

Next, I head for Oba's family vessel, the *Eustatia*. I can't imagine any of Oba's kin being the traitor, but I do my duty in any case, diligently scouring and questioning under the guise of assessing the ship's preparations.

Nothing.

Afterwards I get some time alone with Oba, wedged in the *Eustatia*'s scullery. We sit on metal stools on adjacent sides of the small square counter where meals are prepped.

"I saw your message," I say. "Everything okay?"

"I couldn't sleep," he says quietly, his hands clasped together on the counter, fingers fidgeting. "I just want this thing to be over."

"We'll get through this," I say. "That's why I'm paying a visit to every vessel—to make sure everyone's ready."

"Not for any other reason?" His fingers stop twitching, his voice barely a whisper. "Nothing to do with that thing we found?"

I glance around, checking nobody is nearby.

"It's a beacon," I say. "Or rather, *was* a beacon."

"What?" His eyes are wide.

I tell him what we've discovered. "I'm investigating."

"And?" he asks, hungry for my words.

I sigh. "Nothing so far." I meet Oba's gaze. "You notice anything unusual? Anyone acting suspicious—either before or since we found that thing?"

He shakes his head.

"Who would want the United Empire to find us?"

"Maybe someone who hates this life."

"I don't know." He leans back, hands gripping the side of the counter. "You think someone would sell the rest of us out just because they found this life hard?"

"You think there's a deeper reason?"

Before he can answer, somebody calls Oba's name from the communal bay. A moment later, his uncle, Twako, appears at the entrance to the scullery.

"You're needed," he says to Oba, before noticing me. "Sewa, always a pleasure—" he frowns "—whatever the circumstances." His eyes linger on my insignia. "And congratulations. I know your father would be very proud."

"Thank you, Twako," I say, suddenly feeling emotional. Composing myself, I add: "Caving would've been my first choice, but at least this way I'll get to order this troublemaker around one day."

Twako laughs, leaves us.

"I should be getting on with my rounds." I grip Oba's forearm. "Don't worry. Soon we'll be safe and you'll be caving again in no time."

Oba grasps my arm back. "Stay out of danger, okay?"

As I depart from the *Eustatia*, something in Oba's words is disturbing me. *Who would want the United Empire to find us?*

And then I understand.

It can't just be for personal gain. It can't.

The scale is too big, the stakes too high.

That thought terrifies me.

I spend the remainder of the day assessing battle preparations and covertly investigating. Every ship is a dead-end, no sign of the traitor's handiwork or movements. Ship logs detailing entry/exit activity are a wealth of information, but all the data will need to be cross-referenced between vessels to determine if anybody stayed off-vessel for any unexplained period. I think back to our time on the comet, remember the well-trodden paths in the regolith. Hundreds of Pilgrims crisscrossed the surface every day, and many had legitimate reasons for staying off-vessel.

Disentangling the data is going to take serious work.

Worse than that, though, is the state of unreadiness I find aboard several vessels. Where the military ships are bastions of well-disciplined activity, some of the civilian vessels are scenes of chaos. Usually, they never take part in battle, keeping hundreds of thousands of klicks behind the frontlines, but with our forces stretched thin, this time they are going to have to be part of the action. On their bridges I find paralyzed leaders, while deep in the guts of the craft I find overburdened crew.

That night, I report back to the Overseer.

The connection isn't great, but even in her pixelated form I can see her skin is sallow, her eyes bloodshot. I'm guessing she didn't get much shut-eye last night. She wearily unfastens the top button of her officer's jacket. Where her collar has pressed against her skin, an ugly red line crosses her neck. "Tell me."

"I combed every vessel from top to bottom—"

"Give me the bottom line."

"No joy," I reply.

The Overseer cricks her neck. "Nothing?"

An edge of reproach.

"I've still got the entry/exit data to cross-check, but if the traitor's here they've hidden their tracks well."

"There's always a trail," she replies. "Any theories on how the UE are getting messages to the traitor?"

"No, Overseer."

She doesn't mask her grimace.

"And what about Cavemaster Kalad's ship?"

She can't suspect the Cavemaster, can she?

"Overseer?"

"Was any equipment missing from Kalad's inventory?"

Too late, I understand. Maybe the traitor stole a rebreather or other stuff. If something's missing it might be a lead.

"I didn't check," I confess. "Tomorrow, I'll—"

"Tomorrow might be too late."

The rebuke feels like a slap in the face.

"I'm sorry, Overseer," I say meekly. "I'll go back now—"

"No." She takes a deep breath, purses her lips. "Ignore me. I spoke out of turn. You're doing good work. We all must keep our faith." She touches the Overseer insignia on her loose collar. "Me especially."

I've let you down.

I try to find some appropriate words, something to give her some belief in me, but nothing comes to mind.

"Get some rest," the Overseer says, breaking the silence. "Tomorrow's going to be an even longer day. We're expecting hostilities to commence early evening." Her hand comes up, ready to kill the call. "Update me straight away if anything comes out of the cross-check. Now, unless there's something else?"

The preparations.

"Oh, you should know—many of the civilian craft are struggling to be ready."

"I am aware of the issue," the Overseer says. "The matter is in hand. Good night, Sewa."

The Overseer disappears, her image fleeing to a white dot and soon replaced by the Horizon of Light logo that spins with a placid indifference.

Next morning, I rise early, compile the data tight-beamed over from the other flotillas. In short time, my algorithms have completed their cross-reference of all the Horizon's vessels' entry/exit logs.

Eighty-seven names.

Eighty-seven suspects.

On 257 separate occasions these Pilgrims spent more than an hour off-vessel. The numbers are overwhelming.

I don't have time to investigate eighty-seven Pilgrims.

Especially when many aren't even on this flotilla.

I scan my eye down the list, hoping to find some easy eliminations, but the only names I can remove for certain are my own and Oba's. Many of the remaining eighty-five are repair techs from the *Fortitude* support vessel, probably engaged in genuine work on ship hulls. Until I know for sure that on each of their trips they *did* work though, I can't rule them out. If the traitor is a repair tech, it would be perfect cover for a quick detour into the comet.

How can I get the numbers down?!

I wonder if I should increase the off-vessel duration period to whittle them down. Ninety minutes is a more realistic period for the time it would take to hike to the cave entrance, descend, and return, but if someone's quick and determined they *could* do it in an hour.

No dice there then.

I need another piece of the puzzle.

For a while, I let my mind drift, imagining the guilty party leaving the safety of their vessel, and trekking alone across the barren cometary wilderness. They would've been tense, concerned with somebody noticing their departure. Does that mean they would've planted the device during our nominal "night" time? Fewer Pilgrims crisscrossing the surface. Fewer Pilgrims idly watching coming and goings from viewing galleries. Or would they have attempted to hide in plain sight? Wasn't there a small quarry in the direction of the cave system? Maybe they would've left on a rover, giving the impression they were heading for a job?

I don't know.

I'm going to have to do the legwork, laboriously examine each of these 257 excursions.

"Sewa," a small voice behind me says wearily, practically making me jump out of skin. "What are you doing?"

I glance over my shoulder.

Rina stands, swaying slightly, her night hair matted against one side of her face, her eyes still sleepy.

"Morning, Little Rabbit," I say shutting down the screen. "Just helping Overseer Liandra with some tasks."

You can't be too careful.

Last thing I need is Rina parroting something she's half read about the investigation to Mother, and then Mother gossiping to half of the *Reverent*.

Without invitation, she squirrels herself onto my lap, rests her head against my shoulder. "I missed you yesterday."

"I missed you too, Little Rabbit."

"Will you play with me today?"

"Not today, Little Rabbit." I smell her hair, choosing my words carefully. "Overseer Liandra needs my help with some very important work, and if I don't do it, nobody will."

She curls up, disappointed.

"There'll be time soon," I say. "I promise."

"You promise?"

"I promise," I say, knowing things might be out of my hands, depending on the outcome of the imminent battle.

Rina gives me a tight hug.

"Not much point being leader, if you can't do what you want from time to time, eh?" I hug her back. "Now, why don't you climb in with Mother—you're still half-asleep, Little Rabbit."

She obeys, and I give her a kiss on the forehead before slipping out. First, I should pay Cavemaster Kalad a visit. If any of his equipment's missing...

And then I get another idea.

Could the beacon's power source hold clues as to when it was planted?

I should pay Tyjani another visit too.

Even though we'll be engaged in battle before the day is out, I make to leave the *Reverent* if not in high spirits, then at least with purpose.

Then I hear the news about the *Dawn Skies*.

They didn't even try to capture it.

They destroyed it.

NINE

ᛉᚱᛉᛂ

Everybody knows.

A deathly silence like we're all in mourning pervades the *Reverent* as I make my way to the shuttle bay. Except it isn't only the silence of mourning—it's the silence of shock too. We all knew the *Dawn Skies* was lost as soon as the flotillas went their separate ways from our cometary refuge.

That's not the surprise.

The surprise is that the United Empire obliterated it, didn't even seem to give its capture the first thought, just turned it into so much heat and slag.

Did they know it was empty? Or set to self-destruct?

The rapid exodus of the accompanying warships might've clued them in, but to not even give the orbital a cursory inspection, to just fire on it from so many thousand klicks and damn any chance of acquiring any intel or prisoners?

That sends a message.

A message that strikes icy fear into every Pilgrim heart.

We're here to kill you, not capture you.

Tonight we must win the battle or there will be no tomorrow.

As I slip out of the *Reverent* into the starry void, I try to put the dark thoughts from my mind. In accordance with Battlemaster Nedi's plans, the flotilla has spread out, unfurled itself like a scorpion. The *Reverent*, with limited maneuverability and even less of an arsenal, is one of the vessels positioned furthest from the frontlines, but even it has some hidden fangs. As my shuttle accelerates away, I see the gleam of temporary missile batteries on its underside, reassuring in their heft.

With the flotilla stretched over thousands of klicks and the majority of our vessels' engines idle, I cannot spy any of our other craft, and I rely on the on-board nav systems to guide me towards Cavemaster Kalad's ship. As the *Reverent* disappears among the starfield, I experience an unsettling, prickly feeling. I am tiny, insignificant, a speck of dust in an infinite cosmos, cast adrift from my people.

I could be all alone in the universe.

If the engines failed I might drift forever.

I close my eyes, relax, and my unease shifts into a contented detachment as I imagine myself at one with everything. No division, only unity.

I open my eyes again, feeling at peace.

In deep space the heavens are magnificent, a swathe of innumerable stars, thickening along the galactic plane. Billions of suns in this galaxy alone. Endless know how many worlds circle those suns? Swollen gas giants with atmospheres thick as soup, arid rocky worlds burnt to a tinder, cloud-flecked spheres choking in a sulfuric haze, tidally locked planets with one side baking while the other freezes. Even if they're outnumbered by two, three, even four orders of magnitude, there's still a plenitude of more-or-less life-supporting worlds within the habitable zones.

Surely enough for both us and the United Empire?

But it isn't about space, is it?

It's about power. And vengeance.

Even fifty years later, Zelevas still loathes our very existence. We are an affront to his rule, his history, and in time will be an ugly blemish to his legacy. He wants to destroy us, eliminate us from the past and present.

And he cannot do that while we still have a future.

Shortly, I reach Kalad's vessel, no words exchanged as the docking procedure proceeds to a score of mechanized hisses and reverberating impacts. As I step aboard, I hear strains of classical music floating through the vessel, all strings in delicate but vigorous harmony. I enter the small bridge to find Kalad reclining in the bulky pilot's seat, his eyes on the starfield.

"The stars are wondrous, are they not?"

A rhetorical question, I think, and sure enough, Kalad doesn't wait for an answer.

"To think I spent so much of my life underground."

His fingers dance over the seat's controls located at the end of the armrest, and the chair begins to swivel.

Even though he's trying to hide it, I can feel his rage.

Like a white-hot sun behind thin clouds.

After his call to surrender to the UE became common knowledge, Kalad's stock fell. Now that the Empire has obliterated our capital vessel without a moment's hesitation, it will hit rock bottom.

Humiliation.

No one will be in any doubt that the Overseer made the right call when she ignored the old Cavemaster's advice. I want to ask him why he was so adamant we could trust Rachkov, but I know the wounds are too raw.

"We cavers," he says, "are strange creatures, aren't we?"

I hope that's an inclusive *we*, that he still sees me as a caver, even if my duty lies elsewhere now.

I shrug. "I guess."

"I sometimes think all cavers lack love," he replies. "We head down into the earth as far as we can so that the rock embraces us tight."

This is getting awkward.

Kalad's on a roll though.

"Some deep, fundamental desire to reprise our oldest, primeval memories... when we were entombed deep inside our mothers' wombs and had not a care in the world, our every need slaked by a wondrous umbilical of sinew and blood." He pauses, listens to a transition in the piece as the strings fall quieter before his next words. "Maybe it's unrequited love that sends us into the depths? Your father's disappearance for mysterious, inexplicable reasons must've been devastating."

His words cut deep, stinging.

How could I feel anything but unloved when my father upped and left and I never saw him again?

"And for you?" I ask, lashing out, not wanting to dwell on the hurt. "Who rejected your love?"

"I'm not sure. Even on Raia during the Pilgrim uprising, I had a happy childhood. The exodus was a great adventure for a young boy." He thinks. "Maybe my great unrequited love was the Horizon itself. I wanted to lead expeditions or repair engines or fly warships. I wanted to do anything for this great society we were building, but my education had been so disrupted that I had nothing but enthusiasm. I fell into a spiral of depression until one day the Cavemaster needed an extra pair of hands. I helped ferry equipment deep into the ruins of an underground Endless facility. After that I was a caver for life."

As he finishes, the orchestral music builds to a crescendo, a maelstrom of furious strings that abruptly falls to silence. For a while, we remain unspeaking, the quiet pooling like beads of liquid coming together in zero-gravity.

"I envy you," I say quietly.

The words feel like a confession, a betrayal even. My duty is elsewhere now, my adolescent wishes something I should leave behind like childhood toys and fairy tales.

"You shouldn't," Kalad replies. "The Overseer chose you for leadership, Sewa. Not caving, *leadership*. Instead of scrabbling around in the dark, one day you could be leading this arcology. One day you could steer the Horizon—steer the entire Pilgrim nation—towards a brighter future."

"A brighter future?"

"One not beholden to the Endless." He clasps his hands, thoughtful. "One that consigns them to history."

I gasp. Even spoken here, between two cynics, the words are treacherous, heretical. Our entire foundation as Pilgrims was built on our veneration of the Endless. Our very name invokes our desire to seek their fallen civilization, learn all we can from their relics and stories, and offer them the highest praise and worship. Even the Overseer in her latest address wasn't suggesting we turn our backs on the Endless but find a new purpose that unites this reverence with other ideals.

Instinctively, I lower my voice. "Why?"

Kalad massages his right knee. "You know why the Endless disappeared, don't you?"

"A civil war."

Every Pilgrim knows the story of the galaxy-shattering conflict between the Concretes and the Virtuals, two branches of the Endless with differing ideologies who fought a bitter, deadly war to mutual annihilation. Even in their destructive ferocity we idolize their power and wisdom.

"Exactly!" Kalad exclaims. "Their downfall came from within. Not without."

"And you think that's a danger for us? That we might sow the seeds of our own downfall if we learn too much?"

Is this the real reason he thought we should've surrendered?

Even I, a lapsed, or rather masquerading worshipper, know the doctrine of the dangers of forbidden knowledge—and its counter, of course. The Pilgrim priests argue that even if the Endless possessed profane knowledge or weapons capable of great harm, in the unlikely event that we could resurrect, or even understand, such instruments, we would never use them.

We are only custodians is the refrain.

"Not just our downfall," he says. "Every race's downfall."

We have only ranged one tiny backwater of the galaxy, but already we have met many others who are leaving behind the warming light of their birth suns, setting course for distant stars, and heading into the great darkness. Our United Empire forebears, of course, but also friendly, cerebral prodigies like the Sophons, all the way to nightmarish, half-mechanical monstrosities like the Cravers. With their farsighted sciences, the Sophons tell us that after millennia of silence in the aftermath of the Endless' demise the galaxy is suddenly blooming with spacefaring life.

Green shoots.

Could knowledge of the Endless' ways really threaten to trample all this new life, leave the galaxy dead and blackened again?

It seems unthinkable.

We worship them, but we are aware of their frailties despite their greatness, and most vitally, we are not them.

"Did you discover something?" I ask, curious. "A relic? Something buried in a wreck or a ruin that we should be worried about?"

"No. But I'm afraid nonetheless. And I only tell you that because one day you may lead this arcology." He studies me. "I'm not the only one who has these... heretical thoughts, you know. Once there was an underground movement seeking to repatriate the Pilgrims on Raia. Ito was one of the leaders."

"Ito? High Counsel Ito?"

"Not back then he wasn't." He pauses, smiles. "Come, forget these ramblings of a cantankerous, old apostate. You came to ask me something, didn't you?"

I think about pressing him, but hold my tongue. The clock's ticking. I explain the line-of-enquiry that theorizes the traitor might've stolen caving equipment from his ship, and together we examine his vessel's stocks. After finding some suspicious gaps in the stores, we cross-reference against the digital inventory and discover that a caving helmet, microfiber spool, and a pair of specialized boots are missing.

Finally, a decent lead.

"Damn," Kalad says, shaking his head. "Son-of-a-gun snagged the gear from right under my nose."

"You think they snuck in when you were off-ship?" I ask excitedly. I feel like I'm getting closer to cornering my prey. "If so, they'll show up in the entry/exit logs."

"Maybe." Kalad looks pensive, eyes scanning the floor before they light up. "More likely they grabbed the equipment during one of my outreach talks."

That won't help narrow down the suspects.

Kalad clocks my disappointment because he gives me a chin-up look. "Keep working, Sewa. I'm sure you'll learn their identity soon enough."

Disheartened but philosophical, I leave him, head straight for Tyjani's vessel. I get better news there: the device's remaining battery levels narrow down the timeframe for when it was planted, but as I head to the *Truthseeker*, any rekindled enthusiasm I have evaporates into a cold dread.

Tonight we fight for our lives.

Four hours later, the gnawing, sickly feeling in the pit of my stomach hasn't gone away, but I've pushed it from my mind as best I can, tried to focus on the investigation. Based on the new timeframe information, there were fifty-eight corresponding occasions when Pilgrims were off-vessel for more than an hour, and I've whittled down the list of suspects from eighty-seven to twenty-four. Many are still *Fortitude* repair techs, but several other names stand out: Artak, Ito, and Kalad.

Could the traitor be one of these men?

Given their status, even if they were witnessed crossing the frozen regolith, they wouldn't have been challenged. I feel queasy thinking that one of our leaders, one of the people most empowered to ensure our collective safety, might've sold us out to the United Empire.

No, it's just chance that they're still on the list.

For my peace of mind I resolve to first eliminate Kalad from the suspects, when Overseer Liandra joins me.

"Progress?" she asks, peering at my tablet.

I pass her the device. "I've narrowed it down to twenty-four individuals who were off-ship for sufficient time to install the beacon when we think it was placed."

"Hmm, some troubling names here," she says, handing the tablet back. "Focus on the highest-ranking Pilgrims first when you resume the investigation."

"Resume?"

"I want you back on the *Reverent*," she says, no hesitation in her voice. "Immediately."

"Overseer—"

"Our enemy shows no signs of slowing for the encounter." She grimaces. "They mean to drive a stake straight through our heart, take out our most potent vessels and learn what they can about the rest as they pass. The opening salvos will commence within two hours." Her voice softens. "Sewa, I've been impressed with your work, but there's nothing to be gained from you being aboard the *Truthseeker* any longer."

A flash of pride mingles with another wave of dread, but before I can say anything, Battlemaster Nedi has taken the Overseer to one side.

He lowers his voice, but I catch the salient points.

A small, nimble vessel has spiraled away from the incoming attackers' party, swiftly disappearing into deep space. Before I can learn more, Overseer Liandra dismisses me from the bridge, and minutes later I'm on my way back to the *Reverent*.

The waiting is the hardest thing.

The start of hostilities will almost be a relief.

Following the lead of many on the *Reverent*, I head to the vessel's great concourse, preferring to be among many Pilgrims rather than stewing in my family chambers.

Like Mother, many still huddle and pray in the privacy of their cramped homes, but most of the plaza's benches and shrines are occupied with pockets of Pilgrims exchanging quiet words. I feel bad for leaving Rina, but I couldn't face listening to Mother's pleas to the Endless one moment longer.

The only person who looks relaxed is Old Yaba, snoozing against one of the great trees, a near empty carafe of home-brew clutched to his chest. None of the stands except a few eateries are plying trade, and even they aren't doing much business. Nearby, the stewed rice seller, usually the epicenter of laughter and gossip, stirs her great pan of congealing food, wafting an aroma of pungent spices and cooked peppers through the air, but nobody's hungry.

War does that to an appetite.

More crowded are the shrines dedicated to the Endless. Even the small open-air chapel dedicated to the Raian old gods has a few believers offering prayers. A line has formed at the statue of Esseb Tarosh, the Endless traveler still thought to roam the galaxy dispensing wisdom, and Pilgrims are taking it in turns to approach and make devotions.

We learn of the outbreak of fighting not via the great screen that looms over the far end of the concourse—the Horizon of Light's spinning logo almost hypnotic—but by way of a young Pilgrim child running along one of the high gangways.

"Awad! Talanah!" he calls, scrabbling to peer over the balustrade. "Come, come! It's beginning! The lasers—"

His words cut short as he discovers hundreds of pairs of eyes staring up at him. He must've come from one of the observation decks. I imagine long streaks of crimson lasers lighting up the darkness, aimed upon invisible foes, followed by retaliatory slashes.

An exciting spectacle if you're young enough.

An eerie silence descends on the crowd.

The only motion comes from hands clasping charms and the palms of fellow Pilgrims.

The sick feeling tightens.

I can't breathe. My heart feels clamped in a vice. I'm back underground again, pitched into absolute darkness, choking. Then, in the periphery, I spy movement. Awad and Talanah break from their families, hightail across the plaza. Their motion shatters the impasse.

And so it begins.

Strangely, I feel relief.

I get up, wander through the reanimated crowds. Nobody looks happy, but I can see that many share my feelings of release, and an air of grim determination hangs over the *Reverent*. Nearly all are gathered with kin, from generation-spanning circles a dozen strong, to couples or trios newly entwined.

And here I am, alone.

I think of my father, lost or dead somewhere out in the galactic wastes, and my mother and Rina probably trembling with fright in our chambers. For a moment, I feel guilty for not being with them, but the feeling passes, replaced by... what is this... resentment? Yes, resentment.

Not at Rina. At Mother.

Why didn't you stop Father leaving?

And if you couldn't, why didn't you harden yourself after he left? Why couldn't you create a space where you could... heal... not become this grieving caricature? Most of all, why couldn't you help me, your little girl, who was lost in her own feelings of pain and confusion?

I know why.

She's weak.

Always has been, always will be.

And so I keep her at arm's length, terrified I might become weak too. Doesn't stop me feeling lonely now though.

The low grumble of the *Reverent*'s engines spooling up echoes through the concourse, a sound you can feel as much as hear, and everyone lurches a little as we begin moving. Nearby, an old woman has been sent tumbling by the sudden motion, and I help her back to her feet.

"Thank you, Sewa," she says, dusting herself off.

I'm surprised she knows my name.

"I was there in the gardens," she gives by way of explanation, smiling thinly. "The Overseer must think highly of you."

"You don't approve?"

"Come, sit with me awhile," she says, linking her arm through mine. "Help me take your mind off the fighting."

Help take my mind off the fighting?

From anyone else it would sound arrogant or condescending, but from this aging Pilgrim, so small she might pass for a child, it's a simple, undeniable kindness. With the *Reverent* still accelerating as per the complex choreography of the encounter, I carefully walk her over to the nearest bench, and ease her down. She pats the empty space beside her, and I join her.

Around us, I can hear others talking about the substance of their lives—confessions, regrets, promises for the future—like they don't want to leave anything unsaid should the worst happen. The old woman is no different.

"I was born on Raia," she says, her voice quiet but unwavering. "Long before anyone had any inkling that one day the Pilgrims might flee the world en masse."

Without any handwaving theatrics or verbal flourishes, her voice a steady tone, she relays the story of her early life. Through her childhood, she tells me, she always felt as an outsider as a Pilgrim. First shunned, and then ridiculed for their worship of the Endless, Emperor Zelevas eventually outlawed their religion.

"One day," she says, "when I couldn't have been more than eight years old, I snuck one of my family's priceless Endless relics into school. It was a splintered piece of tech, shiny and intricate and beautifully engineered, but its function was a mystery. I was so proud that my family owned this wondrous thing. I wanted to share its majesty with my classmates—and, of course, I wanted their esteem too."

She rubs her legs, bites her lip.

"And I got their esteem. I still remember them gathered around me, gazes trained on this piece of wizardry I held in my hand like I was cupping a rare butterfly. I was a magician in their eyes, a traveler from an antique land, a custodian of great tales and adventures."

Peering up, she loses herself in the memory.

"I knew what I was doing was wrong—there'd been an amnesty for Endless artifacts—but I didn't understand the gravity of it. To this day, I don't know who informed, but somebody did. That action set off a chain of events that still reverberates to this day."

I'm stunned. "How?"

"First, my teacher confiscated the relic. That was the last time I ever saw that piece... or any of the others my family had hoarded. The authorities were called. They questioned me, terrified me with their coldness, their rectitude, their threats and accusations. By the end of the day, my mother, father, and eldest brother, had been arrested, taken to an undisclosed location."

Her eyes are wet.

"I never saw them again."

I take her hand, squeeze, lost for words.

"Nobody did," she adds.

"That's... appalling."

She untangles her hand from mine, pinches the bridge of her nose. "I like to think that was the day the uprising truly began." She gives a sad smile. "Another vanity, I suppose, but one with a grain of truth. My family's treatment shocked all Pilgrims who thought their religion might be tolerated provided it was practiced behind closed doors. Zelevas' actions obliterated that hope. Most of all, it galvanized my father's sister, my aunt Deona Kryv. She saved us. More than anyone, she led the exodus."

I'm stunned, again. Before they've learnt to write, every Pilgrim knows her name, and before they've come-of-age every Pilgrim knows her story. Her words echo through us, bind us.

We will survive, we will seek, and we will prosper!

And to think this woman beside me is one of her last living kin. I gaze at her with renewed admiration. She lived through those terrors, helped shape the people who fought back, played a vital but unsung role in our survival.

She tells me how Pilgrims found sanctuary in the last of the Dukedoms that still resisted Zelevas' rule on a great island far from the mainlands. Twenty years later that Dukedom fell, but not before the Pilgrims had built the first starship and escaped into the cosmos.

She falls to silence, and we sit in quiet contemplation.

"Thank you for sharing—"

My words are interrupted by a cascade of thundering booms, the concourse shaking with each blast. We're firing the missile batteries, hammering deadly payloads into our enemy's flanks. The vessel stills again.

We must be deep in the fray.

My fear returns with a vengeance, my mouth dry, the pit of my stomach small and hard. We're a civilian vessel forced into the battle. A last resort. I imagine Empire vessels circling, deadly sharks stalking an aging whale, its only protection a dwindling school of snapper fish.

"Sewa," the old woman says, drawing me back. "Would you help me back to my quarters? I'd like to see my old stills before..."

"Of course."

I help her to her feet, and with arms interlocked, escort her across the concourse. Shortly, the missile batteries send off another barrage, and we almost topple in the tremors. I stumble towards a nearby tree, and it's lucky I do because an enormous explosion from the aft of the *Reverent* rocks the vessel, throwing Pilgrims like ragdolls. The lights die, pitching us into total darkness, and all I can see is the afterimage of people in mid-tumble. The screaming begins, a chorus of cries, some in horror, some in fright, and some in sickening pain.

Next to me, I feel the old woman still clutching me tight.

"Bloody Empire!" she shouts as the emergency lighting flickers into life. "Lucky strike."

In the dim, crimson-tinged illumination, I see the scene transformed, shell-shocked Pilgrims wandering or limping or crawling for safety. Despite my own rising panic, I marvel at the old woman's spirit.

Her strength fuels my strength.

I should attend to the injured.

"Are you hurt?" I yell over the screams.

She shakes her head. "Get me to the passageways. I can go on by myself from there. I expect you want to be with your loved ones."

I blink.

Do I?

I'm torn. I want to give them solace, especially Rina, but the idea of being in our family chambers doing nothing but waiting to die is too much.

"I'm going to stay here and help," I say, "but not before I've got you to safety."

"Come on, then," she says, smiling. "Help an old woman."

We weave through the carnage with stumbling steps, gruesome sights of cut, bruised, and broken-limbed Pilgrims looming out of the gloom. The low rumble of our missile batteries is near constant now, an ominous backdrop to the sounds of sobbing and howling.

I pray we're spared another direct hit.

"You know," the old woman says, perhaps trying to distract me from the terror, "for many of us on Raia, it wasn't Zelevas' crusade to eradicate our religion that spurred us on. As I grew older, I never had much love for the Endless and their monstrous civil war." She pauses, glancing at a toppled shrine. "What incited us, what drove us to expend such energies and make such sacrifices, was the belief that he wouldn't stop his purges until the mind of every single Raian had been bent to his will. No opposition, no dissent, not even the inkling of an incorrect thought. In his terrifying world, even the freedom to think freely needs to be crushed."

We come to the passage that leads to the living quarters.

"If we survive this night," she says, "remember these words, Sewa. The deepest, truest creed that unites all Pilgrims isn't concerned with the Endless. Our deepest, truest creed is our belief in freedom." Where she grips my upper arm, she gives it a squeeze. "I hope you do become Overseer one day, Sewa. You've got a good heart."

She leaves me, shuffles into the shadows.

I turn back to the chaos, muscles tight, heart thumping.

I might not be able to change the tide of the battle raging in the vacuum, but I can help those suffering here.

I start to move when I'm suddenly swept off my feet as another explosion rocks the *Reverent*. My head hits the ground with a fierce crack. Maybe I black out for a while or maybe the emergency lights stutter out right then, but the only thing I know is that when I next open my eyes I'm in total darkness.

Brushing the side of my temple, I feel a warm slickness, and when I bring my fingers to my tongue I get the metallic taste of blood. Around me I hear less screaming, more moans. I'm not really registering the situation though. Not even registering that this might be it, that any second I might be about to die. No, what's occupying me is cold, blind panic.

And a sliver of a long lost memory.

Tumbling through the dark, headlight beam flashing over slick, scarred rock—then the hard impact, the air knocked sideways from my lungs. Lying on the cold stone, gasping for breath. Beyond my awful rasping, the only sound was the creak of my headlight's shattered filament.

Absolute blackness, utterly shapeless yet somehow writhing.

"Faaaather!" I remember calling when I'd got my breath back, coughing. "Faaaaaatherrrrrrr!"

No answer.

In the inky black I curl up tight.

And you thought you might be a leader?

TEN

ꑄꑂꑥ

Later, I hear cheering.

My head feels groggy, my lips dry. I open heavy, lethargic eyes to find the world on its side. The cheers recede to silence. The concourse's emergency lighting has resurrected itself. In the attenuated halos of crimson light I see Pilgrims brushing themselves off, battered but still alive. Over the address system, I hear the *Reverent*'s commander speaking in determined tones. With one ear flat against the cold deck and the other still ringing I can't make out his words though.

I bring a stiff hand up to my head, brush the side of my forehead—and wince with pain. Examining my fingertips, I see the blood has dried into an ochre dust. I must've passed out. A conspiracy of exhaustion and terror.

I feel shame at my paralysis.

I must tell the Overseer I cannot be her ward.

Out of the shadows a silhouette approaches.

"Child," she says, offering a hand. "Are you hurt?"

I let her lever me up so I'm sitting on the ground. "I... I... cracked my head... during the second explosion," I say, groggily, probing the painful bruising around the cut. "The battle's over? We won?"

"By the grace of the Endless we emerged victorious."

Hardly, I think, but I'm too relieved to argue.

Through the structure I feel the *Reverent*'s engines firing, the gentle thrust of acceleration. She turns on a wrist-mounted torch, examines my injury with firm movements of her fingers. In the light I can see the raised collar of her gown, her hair pulled tight up by a golden band. One of Artak's Endless clerics. Across the concourse I can see several other bobbing torchlights; more clerics administering medical—and no doubt, spiritual—aid to the wounded Pilgrims.

She pulls a small instrument from her belt, and I feel a cold, stinging sensation as she dispenses a healing gel.

"There," she says, examining her handiwork. "All on the mend. You've suffered a minor concussion, but likely nothing serious. In any case, you should go to the makeshift medical ward in the Endless chapel."

I nod, thankful.

A blessing. An instruction not to return to my duties.

Not yet.

"And casualties?" I ask, thinking of the explosions that rocked the *Reverent*. "Did we lose anyone? Any vessels?"

She gives me a long, mournful look.

"I'm afraid so, child."

I feel numb.

"The unbelievers' fire burnt some of our holy number to ash and cinders on this day." Her jaw tightens. "Their sacrifice will not be forgotten, and we will pray the Endless shepherd their souls—"

"Wh-wh-which vessels?" I stutter, finding my tongue. "Did the *Truthseeker* survive? And the *Eustatia*?" I ask, remembering sitting with Oba in its scullery only yesterday. "Please tell me the *Eustatia* made it!"

"Child, child, calm yourself. The *Truthseeker* and our enlightened leader is still with us, but of the other I cannot say."

The edge of derision in the word enlightened is faint, but it is there nonetheless. I don't dwell on that detail, though, my mind elsewhere. I find my feet, swaying with the blood rush.

I must learn the truth.

"Child," the cleric chides, steadying me with a clamp-like hand, "you must rest, focus on your recovery. Go through—"

I shake off her grip. "Thank you, sister."

I leave her. Not in the direction of the medical ward, but for the stairs that lead up to the observation deck.

From the corner of my eye, I see her shaking her head.

"May the Endless protect you," she shouts, almost like she's goading me, but I don't look back.

Climbing the stairs renders me light-headed, and at the summit I lean on the balustrade, dizzy. Then I catch a glimpse of something in the starscape. A vast wreck burning in the darkness.

I force myself onwards.

Only twenty or so Pilgrims have come up here. Whether alone or in small clusters, all eyes are transfixed by the carnage beyond the glass. I am no different. Several shattered vessels drift in the void, some merely scarred and limping through the fray, while others have been torn into pieces. Superheated slag and the remnants of still-firing engines blaze bright, illuminating the destruction.

We edge through the battlefield slowly, watching for life.

As new sights reveal themselves, waves of whispers ripple through the islands of Pilgrims: excited voices when the blackened shells of United Empire vessels are seen; intakes of breath and then prayers when it's one of our own. Upon the appearance of the *Draylus*, a woman a few paces away howls with anguish. A great, catastrophic rift runs the warship's near-entire length, its innards spilling into the void.

Only yesterday, I think, I was aboard that ship.

As a tumbling section of the interior meets the absolute zero of the vacuum, I watch ice crystals forming on its surface, glinting in the starlight.

All dead. They're all dead.

Somebody consoles the sobbing woman, and her cries recede as she's led away to grieve elsewhere. I watch on, unable to avert my gaze from the terrible spectacle, desperate to learn the fate of the *Eustatia*.

Soon, a half-dozen rescue craft comb the field, docking with functional airlocks where they can, and lancing bright searchlights into gaping maws where they can't. They focus on Pilgrim vessels, occasionally veering away to examine the burning shells of UE ships, but I don't witness any boarding attempts. Even if she wouldn't welcome their presence given our strained circumstances, I'd like to think Overseer Liandra would offer shelter to any United Empire survivors.

Maybe I'm just naive.

Another Pilgrim vessel slides into view.

It's the *Eustatia*.

A rescue craft is already latched onto the prow airlock, but a perfect slashed line of scorched laser marks causes my heart to skip a beat. It's punctuated by a terrifying rupture whose ragged margins still glow white-hot.

Hull breach.

For a long moment I can't process what I'm seeing, my eyes locked on the monstrous rift. Then I'm stumbling through the onlookers, repeating the same question over and over, a question that only elicits shakes of the head or pitying shrugs.

"Where are they taking the wounded?"

Sometime later I find myself on the *Sunrunner*, the vessel designated as this flotilla's field hospital. I can't remember who gave me that information, or how exactly I came to be standing in the ship's main atrium, but here I am, a statuesque figure in a sea of motion. In contrast to the *Reverent*, the *Sunrunner* is a maelstrom of organized chaos, the bedlam playing out beneath the jarring blue of the false sky.

Not five paces away, an engineering gang checks their equipment, each member inspecting their stashes. Elsewhere, a uniformed Pilgrim leads a line of civilians across the atrium, each one bearing a crate or two of nutrition flash-packs.

The chatter is deafening, but in the snatches of conversation I overhear I don't discern any panic or hysteria, only people organizing and coordinating. The calm, purposeful atmosphere gives me strength, and when I spy a pair of rescue workers ferrying an injured Pilgrim through the throng on a hovering medical transport, I quietly fall in behind.

Please be alive. Please.

As I follow I catch glimpses of the wounded Pilgrim, the side of his face cracked and red with horrific burns. He makes a low moaning sound, and every bump elicits a pained cry. I don't know whether to try and make eye contact or avert my gaze, and end up half-heartedly doing both. I can't help it, but I keep thinking of Oba, keep imagining the worst. At the entrance to the field hospital, an older woman in medical fatigues directs the rescue workers straight through, before stepping into my path.

"Staff and patients only," she says, "unless you're first kin."

The field hospital has been set up at the margins of the Horizon's biggest medical facility, like a cancerous growth. Beyond the administrator I can see the hall has been co-opted into a recovery ward, visitors manning bedside vigils to convalescing family. Non-critical patients only. I can smell sickness mingling with the sharp tang of gauze and bleach. I crane my neck, seeking Oba, but I can't see him.

"If you're not first kin, you'll need to move along," the woman adds. "We're in an emergency situation."

"Obafemi Naia," I manage. "I need to see Obafemi Naia. He was aboard the *Eustatia*."

The name spurs the woman into action as she consults her tablet. "Are you first kin?" she asks, not looking up.

I shake my head. "No—but we're very close."

She stops tapping, peers over the top edge of the tablet. "I'm sorry…"

"Sewa."

No, no, no, no—

"I'm sorry, Sewa," she says, gently, and I'm ready to collapse with the most terrible news, my legs weak, but her next words are like warm sunshine. "I can only admit first kin."

My heart leaps.

"He's alive?"

"Yes—in a serious condition but alive."

Another pair of rescue workers get waved through, before the administrator gives me a hard-luck shrug.

No, I can't turn back now.

"That's all I can tell you," she says. "Now—"

"Please," I beg, stopping her from moving onto the tearful Pilgrim behind me. "Oba won't have anyone. His first kin were all aboard the *Eustatia* too. They'd be injured, or… or dead."

She gives me a long, hard look, then grits her teeth.

"Intensive Care, 7C."

"Thank you."

I move on fast before she can change her mind.

I weave through the makeshift recovery ward, then through heavy plastic curtains into the near silence of Intensive Care. Each bed is contained within a private, glass-walled cubicle, surrounded by a medley of machines. Oba's bed is at the far end. I see visitors in only a third or so of the berths. Like I imagined then. Unlike those outside, they're not in animated conversation. Most sit in silent watchfulness, clutching their loved ones' hands where they can and their own where they can't, the only noise the artificial hiss and electronic jabber of the machines.

"Oba!"

He's lying flat on his back, cocooned within a transparent cubic chamber, naked save for a loincloth. His usually flawless brown skin is covered with mottled patches of weeping scabs. As the glass door slides open, I watch his whole frame shake as he tries to raise his head, but the effort is too great and he collapses back again.

Closer, I can see his extremities have been ravaged—toes and fingers, ears and nose, all betraying signs of severe frostbite—and I feel tears welling up.

"Oba."

"Ess," he whispers. "I didn't… know we were kin."

A spurt of warm snot shoots from my nose as I snort at his joke. Despite his terrible condition, I can't help but smile.

"Only very distant."

I move to the side of his sealed chamber, where our eyes can meet without him needing to move his head. He doesn't offer another wisecrack this time, and I can see his hurt in his filmy eyes and trembling lip.

"The others?"

He slowly lifts one of his hands to the side of the chamber, plants it on the wall. I do likewise, acutely aware of the traumas inflicted on his hands.

"Everyone survived," he whispers, "everyone except Mama…" He closes his eyes, composes himself. "Mama and Leona didn't make it."

Oh, Endless above.

His mother and little sister.

Gone.

"I'm so sorry, O," I say, holding back my tears.

My words are inadequate, my grief inconsequential.

I want to pull him close to me, hold him, but this cursed chamber stops even the lightest touch.

I shake my head. "They didn't deserve this."

"No, they didn't." He takes his hand back, wincing with pain. "But we're going to keep dying at the hands of those fascists unless something changes."

I can see he's distancing himself from his grief, pushing it deep where he'll deal with it later—or perhaps let it fester, turn to hatred. Maybe it's too soon, but I need to show him I'm here for him.

"Do you remember that time we took Leona—"

"Why do they want us dead, Ess?" he asks, closing down the memory. "Before, they captured, imprisoned. Now they exterminate." He hacks out a long cough. "What's changed?"

Too raw. Later then.

I consider the question anew, try to imagine things from their perspective, but the only sane answer is the one I always unearth.

"Zelevas fears us."

"Why?"

"I don't know." In the next cubicle, I watch a frazzled physician checking her unconscious patient's vitals. "Maybe he thinks we're close to an Endless discovery that will transform us. Maybe he just thinks that after all these years of persecution, Pilgrims will never forgive the Empire, will always be seeking vengeance."

Oba grunts. "We should just leave this sector," he says, tense, his breaths shallow. "Every arcology, disappear, for good. The galaxy's a big place. We could ride the major slipways, travel thousands of light years, get to a nameless backwater where we'd never run into Zelevas."

I smile at his vision, happy to indulge in the dream of a reality where all Pilgrims were free of Zelevas' tyranny. An archipelago of shining, verdant worlds where we could seek whatever our hearts desired in peace.

But it is an indulgence; it is a dream.

The challenges would be formidable.

"A journey of that magnitude, Oba... The coordination we'd need between the arcologies, the resources we'd require—before we even left and were out there in the depths. Not to mention the unforeseen dangers. Collapsed slipways, unstable suns, swarm intelligences—"

"Nothing we can't overcome," he says, fist striking the inside of his imprisoning chamber, "if we have the will."

The chamber wall quivers, stills. Luckily, in his weakened state he's not been able to do any damage. I stare at his ravaged, belligerent face; he wears an expression that is daring me to defy his words.

A strange feeling flutters in my chest.

Holy Endless, he's right!

We can just run. Why not?

But a part of me already knows the answer.

"And the Endless?"

Oba closes his eyes, visibly wilts deeper into his bed.

He understands only too well what I mean. The myth of the Endless has held a stranglehold over us since our founding days. Zelevas hated our worship, tried to erase our religion, but it only fueled our faith—and our determination to escape his dominion. Even though we keep running, this little sector of the galaxy has come to be our homelands. We know its contours, its hiding places, its suns and its riches. What we barely know—what we've only just begun to discover—is its history and its secrets.

We know that long ago the Endless ranged across these skies, visited these worlds, constructed magnificent temples, technological marvels, even entire cities. The places are lost to time, swallowed by rock or vine or ocean, or simply forgotten, but we know they once existed. We possess theories and hypotheses, maps and legends, and a never-ending well of purpose and resolve.

These are our holy lands.

Asking the devout to leave this sector, journey thousands of light years to another part of the galaxy where we know nothing, and where the Endless might never have roamed?

An unforgivable sacrilege.

Many would rather die than run.

Oba sits up, eyes wide. "You can change things."

"Me?" I almost laugh. "How?"

"By taking a stand against those who elevate the Endless," he says. "By breaking the spell they have over us."

His belief in me is endearing. And hopelessly naive.

"What makes you think I have that power?"

"Ess," he says, for once no twinkle in his eye, no playfulness in his voice. "The mood is shifting. Belief in the Endless is waning. They might not say it aloud, but many Pilgrims are sick of this constant flight from the Empire. If a little less faith is the price of peace, they'll happily pay it."

I can see the truth in his words, just not my part.

"Things are moving fast." I sigh. "The faithful are trying to prop up their power."

"Which is why their opponents must act!" Oba cries. "Which is why you must act!" The physician in the next cubicle glances over, and Oba lowers his voice. "The Overseer recognized the waning influence of the Endless. And she recognized your potential. She chose you. One day you can be the leader of the Horizon, Ess."

"I can't," I whisper.

The memory of my terror, of my paralysis, during the attack comes surging back, frightening.

"What?"

"I can't be leader," I say. "I froze, Oba. When the *Reverent* came under fire I froze completely."

He shrugs. "When your life's in danger, you freeze, no? At least for an instant. Happens to everyone." His eyebrows furrow. "I saw it happen on the *Eustatia*. Felt it too."

"No, this was different."

"I don't understand."

"When I froze, when I was lying on the deck and the vessel was shuddering, I remembered something. My first bad fall as a kid. Alone. In the dark. Bruised and winded and terrified. I yelled and yelled and yelled, but no matter how loud I yelled Father didn't come." I stare down at Oba's ravaged feet, too ashamed to look him in the eye. "I can't be a leader, O."

He nods. "I get it. I think." He shifts in the bed, making himself more comfortable. "You need answers. When I'm on my feet I'll help you find them, I swear." He grins. "Then you'll have no excuse, Overseer."

I feel a smile coming to my lips. "Yes, Cavemaster."

"You better believe it!"

We enjoy the shared illusion for a moment, before I come back down to reality with a jolt. Us two kids in power on the Horizon? A fantasy.

Leadership isn't for me.

I need to let the Overseer know.

"Thanks, O," I say. "And anytime you need to talk, you know I'm here for you."

The fire in his eyes fades. "Sure."

I step away from the bed, take in the immediate surroundings of his cubicle for the first time. Sleek machines, bare glass, neon digitals. The soundscape is minimalist electronic beeps and hums. All very clinical, not very human. "You need anything just—"

"Yeah, I know."

He closes his eyes.

Part of me wants to tell him about the investigation to distract him, but I know he should grieve. Too late, anyway. The physician from the next cubicle enters, frowning.

"Sewa, isn't it?" she asks. "Sewa Eze?"

Does anyone not know my name now?

"Yes?" I ask sweetly, bracing for a reproach that I shouldn't be there, not being first kin.

"You're wanted on the *Truthseeker*," she says. "Overseer's orders."

I blink, her words still registering.

"Check your tablet," she adds, not waiting for any response, instead moving to Oba's bedside. "How's my fighter doing?"

Sure enough, when I check I can see I've been issued a priority summons. I wonder if she wants me back focused on the investigation?

"I'll be back, O."

"Sure," he wheezes.

When I don't know.

On the way to the *Truthseeker* I rehearse my words.

I'm sorry, Overseer, I'm not ready...

I'm sorry, Overseer, I can't offer...

I'm sorry, Overseer...

Outside, in the void, the debris from the battle has thinned out, a million pieces of twisted wreckage balletically expanding into the cosmos like a star going supernova. Millennia hence, most those pieces will still be journeying through the dark night, tiny clues to a violent battle fought eons past.

I resolve to tell her that I'll carry on with the investigation as needed, but after that I want to be assigned another duty.

She'll understand.

I hope.

"Sewa!"

On the bridge of the *Truthseeker*, the Overseer embraces me tight, unconcerned about decorum. Emotions I'd been keeping under wraps well up inside me, and I hug back, eyes stinging.

After she releases me, she grips my shoulders, gives me a long, hard look. "I'm so glad you're still with us," she says. "So many aren't."

This is the moment.

"Overseer—"

"Please," she interrupts, "let me finish. Right now I imagine you're a swirl of thoughts and impulses, but you need to know some things before you make any rash decisions."

I nod, wondering if she'd anticipated my cold feet. I shouldn't be surprised. That's what good leaders do, after all: read people. She leads me to a small antechamber off the bridge, where we can talk in private.

"We've identified the traitor."

I'm staggered. "What?"

"After you showed me that shortlist of names, I couldn't shake one from my mind: High Counsel Ito."

"Ito?"

"You wouldn't know it, but over the years Ito has been a quiet voice for Pilgrim repatriation on Raia. In private, he's always argued that the arcologies are not viable long-term, and that resettlement on any world in this sector makes us vulnerable to UE reprisal." The Overseer's talking at a fair clip, distant somehow, but she pauses to shake her head. "His belief was that the only chance of lasting peace was that if we returned to Raia where we would have a voice and influence."

"That's crazy."

"Maybe. Maybe not." She sighs. "What I can say is that Ito always leaned towards diplomatic solutions. It was what he knew, and it was what he believed. Military action was always anathema to him, a last resort. Ten years ago, he was caught attempting to organize peace talks between a Raian delegation led by Duke Lenastra and a secretive Pilgrim group he was part of known as True Peace."

"He wasn't punished?"

"Not directly, no." The Overseer frowns. "I was among a number of influential Pilgrims who argued that it would serve no purpose to judge and convict the True Peace hierarchy. We saw them as good Pilgrims pursuing a bad strategy. We kept it under wraps, broke up the group, and dispersed them across the diaspora." She gives a wry smile. "I brought Ito onto the Horizon, gave him a fresh start."

Even with this deeper insight into Ito's background, imagining him as the traitor feels wrong. I didn't know him well, but if there was one word I would use to describe High Counsel Ito it would be... gentle. I'm struggling to picture him being the instigator of all this devastation and death.

At least not intentionally.

"And now you think he kept on working for True Peace the whole time?" I ask. "That he was the one who installed the beacon?"

"I don't know if he was still working for True Peace, but yes, it looks like he was behind the beacon." The Overseer explains. "After his name came up on the shortlist I searched his quarters—and found a pair of specialized climbing boots. Lab analysis confirmed that microscopic residue on the soles could've only come from subterranean parts of the ice comet."

The pieces are falling into place.

"I bet they match the pair of climbing boots that were missing from Cavemaster Kalad's locker." I pace back and forth, thinking. "But why would he keep them in his quarters?"

"An oversight, perhaps? Or maybe he just didn't have time to discard them in a clean fashion." The Overseer shrugs. "Things moved pretty rapidly after we evacuated the comet."

I nod. "I guess we'll get answers when we question him."

The Overseer stays silent, her hand coming up to her mouth like she's upset.

What am I missing?

"Has he evaded arrest?"

Then the truth dawns, and I feel stupid.

He's dead.

"Ito was killed near the beginning of hostilities," she says, voice strained. She bites her lip, the closest I've ever seen her to showing her hurt. "I shouldn't be upset knowing what he did—how much suffering and sorrow he caused—but he was a person I was close to, somebody I cared about. I can't believe he intended things to turn out this way, I've got to believe something went wrong with his plan… maybe that he was betrayed—"

She cuts herself short. "I'm sorry. You don't need to hear this. Or my jumbled speculations."

"It's okay, I understand."

The Overseer smooths her uniform. "Anyway, as of the present moment, you can consider your involvement in the investigation over. I will follow-up all the loose ends."

"But—"

"You did fine work, but I need you elsewhere."

A wellspring of objections surface, so many questions still unanswered. Was Ito still working for True Peace? Who was his contact in the UE? What were his goals? I consider arguing the case, but the Overseer's tone tells me she's not for changing her mind. Besides, I'm curious as to the next job she has for me.

Please don't put me in charge of anybody.

"Elsewhere?"

"Yes. In a vital role." I must look nervous, because she gives a reassuring smile. "Don't worry, nothing you can't handle. Come."

She heads back out to the bridge, brings up the local star chart on the holographic board. The three splinter-fleets of the Horizon blink among a three-dimensional backdrop of stars. Zooming-out and panning, the galactic network of slipways comes into focus, and our three splinter-fleets coalesce into a single pulsing icon on the edge of the map.

"Once we regroup, we're going to enter the slipways here." The Overseer indicates a system on a major artery of the galactic network. "To minimize further UE threats, we'll head away from Raian space as far as we dare, head for the fringes of the sector."

I marvel at the map's scale—dozens of light years pinched in a span between thumb and index finger. My gaze dances over the major systems around the destination.

Most of the names are unfamiliar.

"Do we have the Dust reserves for such a jump?" I ask, both exhilarated and nervous.

"That is where you come in."

"Overseer?"

She couldn't mean… could she?

"Geophys have identified a mid-size moon orbiting a gas giant in the nearby Psarga system featuring all the hallmarks of natural reserves of liquid Dust." The star chart shifts again, focusing on a system close to our location, then arrowing in on a rugged ochre moon slaved to a swirling turquoise gas giant. "Dynamic tectonics, super-scale mountains, active volcanoes. Most important of all, there's no sign the Endless ever visited."

My excitement level rises to fever pitch.

"Virgin territory!" Luckily for us the Endless didn't discover every last drop of the magical substance. I say the next words tentatively. "And you want me on the expedition?"

"Not just me," the Overseer replies. "Cavemaster Kalad selected you personally for this mission. With a few of his usual team injured, or worse, he believes you can step up. And I'm in agreement." The holographic blinks off, and she turns to me. "This mission, Sewa... I can't overstress how critical it is to our future. The Horizon's on its knees. We need to find these Dust reserves and get out before more UE come sniffing. Our survival depends on it."

If she intended her words to have a sobering effect, it's worked. My focus on this descent is going to have to be absolute. We'll need to explore the cave system swiftly and efficiently, identify the most promising Dust sumps, and install the pumping equipment with minimal fuss.

I think of Oba. This would've been his gig.

"I will give everything to make it a success, Overseer."

"Make sure that you do."

I always wanted to be a caver.

Now I've got a chance to be one.

A real caver, on a real mission.

And if I screw up—if the caving team screws up? The Horizon of Light is going to become another sad footnote in Pilgrim history.

ELEVEN

⌇⊃⊱⊃⊰⊱

Three days later I'm standing on a strange windswept plateau under ochre skies. Monsoon season is coming, but long enough away to not interfere with the descent. Or so Horizon's meteorology division assured us. I hope they're right.

Mossy, tenacious plant life riddles the stony ground, and over the past few billion years the purple-leafed flora has produced enough oxygen to make a breathable, if unpleasant-tinged, atmosphere.

A sweet, acrid edge like charcoaled caramel.

Most of the six-strong team, including myself, are wearing simple filter masks to alleviate the smell. Cavemaster Kalad and the geologist, Dr Lasa, are the exceptions. Breathing hard, they've just arrived after hiking a few klicks from where they've hidden the interplanetary shuttle in a dry-bedded ravine system somewhere to the west.

One of the twins sits up from where he's been lying on a stack of climbing rope. Even with a headband, the wind whips his dark locks.

"What took you so long?"

"I persuaded Kalad to detour to the unusual geological formations on the ridge," Dr Lasa replies. "Yeah, I'm a rock nerd."

Gavi glowers, but doesn't say anything.

I don't know if he's irritable because of the delay or something else. Maybe he's just itching to get underground.

Out here we're exposed.

Gales, electrical storms, vicious wildlife, and, most improbably, but most dangerously, United Empire patrols. That's the reason we concealed the shuttle. Out here we're on our own, helpless against the enemy if they discover us. Once we're beneath the surface though, aside from our ride, there'll be no sign of any Pilgrims for a million klicks.

"Dr Lasa's insights into lunar geology are already proving invaluable for this mission," Kalad says, surveying the medley of equipment from food and medical supplies to simple autonomous robots and Dust processing units, "but now it's time to get subterranean."

Argo Vela, the Pilgrim super-athlete who's got as much a reputation for his volcanic ego as his physical prowess, stops dead in his press-ups routine and flips to his feet.

"Music to my ears," he exclaims. "Time we cracked this moon wide-open and found ourselves some juicy Dust!" He winks at Dr Lasa, his caving partner, who rolls her eyes, but can't help but grin at his childish enthusiasm.

Over the last few years, Argo and the rest of the team must've clocked up hundreds of caving expeditions, and they spring into action like clockwork automata. For me it's a different story. I might've caved dozens of times, but this is my first real descent in the wild.

I'm a bunch of nerves.

While the others load up, I stalk around the cave entrance—a thin scar in the desolate landscape, the rocky maw swiftly disappearing into pitch-black—feeling on edge. A faint breeze, dank and laced with organics, flows out of the darkness. I find it hard to imagine the subterranean realm as a sanctuary rather than a threat. Every other caving expedition I've undertaken has been in a well-mapped system or within a stone's throw of one of the Horizon's vessels.

Today we're on our own, heading into *terra incognita*.

I glance up through the faint ruddy skies, eyes locking on the enormous disc of the dominating gas giant. This is my first caving expedition on an actual moon rather than a Goldilocks-zone world, and the size of the gas giant is unnerving. Thick swirling bands stratify its surface, and in places I can even see the crackle of chain lightning.

"Alright," Kalad says. "Listen up."

The five of us gather round the Cavemaster, a motley crew united by our facility for descending into dark, claustrophobic labyrinths. Argo stands a little back from the tight circle, arms folded.

"I'll keep this brief. You all know why we're here. The Empire is still hunting us—but we're still alive and kicking. Before they find us again, the Overseer plans for the Horizon, or what's left of it at least, to flee far through the galactic network, travel dozens, if not hundreds, of light years down old forgotten slipways."

Kalad's bitterness isn't hard to detect.

"And to do that we need Dust. Lots of it."

He still smarts from his humiliation. He wanted to surrender, not fight. In the minds of most of the Horizon, he is exactly what Nedi branded him: a coward. He will be shunned.

And, when the need arises—like now—he'll do the Overseer's bidding. I almost feel pity for him.

He goes on. "We'll need to work fast, establish a base camp a klick or so deep, then split-up into our pairs and swiftly explore the most promising branches."

One kilometer descent. And that's just for the camp.

I've never gone so deep.

"Geological analysis suggests large Dust sumps should riddle the system from a depth of one and a half klicks, so we'll focus on securing a big score. Small reservoirs will be mapped, and only drained as a last resort."

"And other resources?" Dr Lasa asks, squatting in the brush and running her fingers over the dirt. "Minerals? Precious metals?"

"Not our concern," Kalad replies. "We focus on Dust. And let me be clear: we do need to find it. That doesn't mean any superhero antics, Argo, but it does mean taking our chances."

The twins glance at one another.

"What do you mean 'chances'?" one of them asks.

Amra, I think.

"I mean, don't be stupid, but be bold."

He looks up at the pastel skies.

"Ah, hell. I was going to keep this to myself, but maybe it'll help you understand." He scratches his stubble. "A few hours ago, an unidentified craft entered the far side of the system. Likelihood is, it's a UE scout, trying to pick up the Horizon's scent. Bottom line? Sooner we secure the Dust, sooner we can get out of here. By then, given where we're heading, detection won't matter." He grimaces. "If it finds us while we're still scrabbling around in the dark though, calls in the cavalry…"

He doesn't need to finish, the meaning clear.

Nobody responds, but I can feel the mood darken.

"Anyways, now you know." Kalad nods at each of his team. "Let's move out."

The autonomous robots descend into the maw first, large mechanical spiders that scuttle across the rock with equipment packs stowed on their bulbous backs. They're essentially our modern equivalent of pack animals; not very intelligent, but extremely useful for ferrying loads. Light from their torches crisscrosses the craggy surface, before the maw is all black again.

Next up the twins, working together in near silence.

Going first, they'll have the most difficult task, since they'll have no path to follow, and no anchor bolts to use. As they descend they'll drill bolts into the rock for the rest of us. It's slow, energy-sapping work.

I'm happy Kalad and I weren't up first.

They disappear over the lip without fuss, the only evidence they're still alive and moving the two taut ropes affixed to the anchor bolts on the nearby boulder.

Argo and Dr Lasa are next, but they're in no rush as they'll only catch up with the twins if they leave too soon. I can hear them joshing around while they wait. Playfully, Argo asks Dr Lasa what she'd do if they got word the UE had them trapped here.

"Nothing with you," she deadpans.

I look over to see Argo trying to laugh off the rejection, but his pride's been stung. A flash of hostility crosses his face as he sees me gawping.

I snap back to the contents of my pack.

A couple of minutes later, Argo crouches down next to me.

"Nobody teach you any manners?" he whispers, fierce-like but quiet enough that nobody else can hear.

"I... I... I'm—"

"Endless knows why Kalad even brought you on this mission," he spits. "Just stay the hell out of my way, maggot."

He trudges off, leaving me feeling like... well... a maggot.

Despondent, I watch him and Dr Lasa smoothly disappear into the cave system.

Why *am* I here?

The imposter-syndrome instinct is strong, but I tell myself I'm here because I'm a skilled caver and I can help with this mission. Kalad chose me because he could see my potential. Argo is just a huge writhing ball of neuroses and hang-ups.

Screw him.

I take a deep breath.

I can't afford to put one single toe-hold wrong during this descent. I can already feel the story of the mission taking shape should I get injured or put somebody else in jeopardy and we fail to secure the Dust. Inexperienced caver, Sewa Eze, imperils whole arcology when Dust-salvage expedition is abandoned.

"Relax," Kalad says, picking up on my anxiety. "You're gonna do fine."

I nod. "I'll do my best."

"All you can do."

He smiles. I feel some of the tension lifting from my shoulders. Not relaxed, but not stiff either. Kalad checks his equipment, gives a firm tug on the anchor bolts, then hoists on his pack.

"Alright, we're up, Sewa."

A few minutes later I'm hanging over the entrance lip, the rope taut between my hands. My backpack is a reassuring weight on my back, heavy but not onerously so. I can already feel some warmth in the cord from the friction. The vertical rock face, by contrast, feels cold against the heels of my thin climbing boots.

I descend, slowly, easing myself into the rhythm.

Darkness shrouds me. As my eyes adjust to the light I glance up, and the thin slash of visible sky now seems blood red.

Somewhere out there in the solar vicinity is a UE scout, searching. And the Horizon, laying low. One spells danger, the other sanctuary. They're playing a deadly game of hide-and-seek over a terrain of planets, gas giants, moons, asteroids, and any number of other astronomical odds and ends that can conceal a fleet's worth of ships.

I hope we win.

As I'm imagining the game, a dark shadow pitches me into near blackness.

Kalad, I tell myself. It's just Kalad.

The shadow shifts.

I hear him muttering a short blessing.

I fumble for my headlamp. An anemic beam spears the darkness, illuminating a nondescript patch of rock.

I shake my head and begin to descend again.

We descend, slowly, methodically, undertaking a war of attrition against the depths.

Anchor, rappel, regroup.

Survey, load-up, hike out.

Where the rock is still damp from the seasonal rains that wash down through the mountain, algal growths coat the surface in a pungent slime that is beyond slippery.

Sometimes the descents come thick and fast, the team finishing one vertical drop to find itself huddled together on a ledge no wider than two armspans. Other times we might come out of a drop and then walk hundreds of meters through cavernous fossil galleries or get down on our bellies and squeeze through a claustrophobic crawlspace.

Tether, wriggle, persist.

The journey is akin to descending a wild, paradoxical staircase one moment fashioned by a race of giants, the next made by a people no bigger than pygmies. We struggle onwards, planting our collective feet on the next step down, moving deeper and deeper into the earth. There is no escape from the never-ending darkness that surrounds us, nor the unyielding gravity that always tugs at us, but with our lamps and our bare hands we keep both at bay.

Rainwater, over millions of years, has fashioned channels down through this stone, and this knowledge gives us belief that we will likewise discover such paths. And our reward will be Dust.

Enough to fuel our escape.

"Let's take ten," Kalad barks as he rappels down onto the large outcrop where the rest of us are gathered. "I want to run a quick system check on the bots."

I am grateful for the robots.

Centuries ago, before such autonomous machines existed, a descent like this one would've taken weeks rather than days. The cavers would've had to ferry everything down themselves. For the first week or two of such an expedition—before they established a permanent underground base camp—they would've made daily returns to the surface for rest and resupply.

I can't imagine the bone-deep fatigue they must've felt, forced to ascend such heights at the end of each day. Even with ascending gear and anchor bolts minimizing the risk of deadly falls, climbing burns the muscles like nothing else.

I'm thankful that's no longer part of the gig.

Not that the bots are invulnerable—or omniscient.

They're just machines, slaves to complex algorithms. If they take a fall, get grit in their processor unit, damage a limb, they'll break down just as easily as a caver who twists an ankle. Unlike us though, they don't have the higher-level thinking that would enable them to undertake the entire excavation mission alone. No intuition, see.

The Pilgrims tried it, believe me.

After a number of failed runs, leadership slowly came to realize that the blend of skills necessary to navigate a deep cave system and pinpoint and extract a Dust vein was far beyond the capabilities of Pilgrim machines.

Hence the tag-team of humans and robots.

"Alright," Kalad announces, extracting a slender monitoring needle as he kneels beside one of the bots. "They're in pretty good shape, but Alpha's motor-control is flagging. We'll need to keep an eye on that."

He packs up the diagnostics kit, dispatches one of the bots to install the last section's thin, pliant pipework through which we hope liquid Dust will soon flow, and gives the order to move out.

Some people think caving is an extreme pursuit.

Heart-racing moments, adrenalin spikes, near-death experiences. That sort of thing.

They couldn't be more wrong.

For sure, the first time you step off a ledge above a sheer drop and let a razor thin cord bear your whole weight is hairy. And being pitched into darkness after forgetting to restock your carbide-powered headlamp? Even the most resilient caver's heart will skip a beat.

Yet... anyone who survives as a caver long-term, quickly comes to understand that caving is an activity best performed with somber reflection and cold, hard analysis.

Adrenalin junkies don't last long in this game.

A calm head is a much better asset than fast reflexes. And when the blood does get racing? Nine times out of ten it means danger—and bad choices.

So, slowly, methodically, the team descends.

As I rappel down the latest shaft, I try to stay focused, concentrating on each individual step, watching the light of my headlamp make a rhythmic sweeping triangle between the descender in my hands, the rock face under my boots, and the velvet darkness below.

It's hard to judge the distance down to the next caving pair, but from time to time I spot the beam of Dr Lasa's headlamp twitching out of the gloom and hear the gentle murmur of conversation between herself and Argo.

A tranquil contentment washes over me, and I find my thoughts drifting.

I think about the future.

I shouldn't, but I do.

After all, nothing is guaranteed about this mission.

Maybe there's no Dust here. Maybe there is, but the UE will find us before we extract it. Maybe we'll fuel up on Dust, but we won't reach the slipways before we're intercepted... but if we do?

I imagine being back among my Pilgrim brothers and sisters, all hundred-odd vessels hurtling through long forgotten passages to a sector far from the reach of Raia and Zelevas.

I would spend time with Oba and help him recover. I would help Rina outgrow her timidness. And I would try to build bridges with my mother, establish something… perhaps not a deep bond, but an understanding, a respect.

Maybe I would seek answers about my father.

Something the Overseer mentioned about the traitor, High Counsel Ito, comes to me.

He was part of a group known as True Peace.

Could my father have been connected too? The Overseer said it was ten years ago when Ito was caught—

I stop, suspended in the dark, the light of my headlamp playing across the descender and creating writhing shadows on the stone. Something's become painfully clear.

If I want answers, I'll need influence.

I'll need to stay under the Overseer's wing and slowly, inexorably accrue real power. If I pursue a life as a caver I'll stay close to powerless, just a small cog in someone else's grand machine.

Like Cavemaster Kalad, I think, glancing up.

I give a wistful shake of the head. Whatever happens, this will be my first—and last—official caving expedition.

The thought is a bittersweet one.

As I cast off, I decide I don't want to feel sorry for myself, so I go back to an earlier thought: *was* my father involved with True Peace?

Could he have been working with Ito, engineering an end to hostilities with Raia? Could the reason he needed to suddenly leave be because he was being sent as an envoy to an emergency meeting with a secret Raian delegation?

A chill skates down my spine.

I picture my father in shackles, led away by Zelevas loyalists who'd caught wind of the plot. Then years spent rotting in a Raian gulag in the world's wintry north.

"Sewa!"

"Sorry, klicks away," I reply, looking up. "Something up, Cavemaster?"

"Only that your technique's gone to pieces." The light from his headlamp dazzles. "Everything okay?"

I shield my eyes, thinking.

What have I got to lose?

"You knew my father, right?" I say, squinting between my splayed fingers. "Was he close to Ito?"

"Ito?"

"Yeah. I can't help but wonder if my father was caught up with

True Peace too. That he was doing something for them when he disappeared."

Kalad doesn't say anything, and I wonder if I've said too much. Below, I hear Dr Lasa curse, and I glance down, but the shaft is inky black.

Maybe Kalad isn't even aware of True Peace.

I look up again. "I shouldn't be dredging up the past. Forget—"

"True Peace," Kalad says slowly, unseen. "That's a name I haven't heard for years. Idealists. Misguided if you ask me. We all slept easier when they were disbanded."

"But Ito kept working to those ends. He—"

"—betrayed us all. I know."

I picture High Counsel Ito trekking across the cometary landscape, carrying the beacon. "I find it hard to get my head around the fact that it was him."

Ito had always been such a strong voice for the Pilgrims. Difficult to imagine he consciously chose to harm us.

"People," Kalad says somberly, "aren't always what they appear."

I shake my head.

"Anyway," Kalad says, his voice closer, "you wanted to know why your father left."

"Yes," I say, eager to hear his next words.

"By my reckoning," he begins, "your father wasn't involved with True Peace. Too proud a Pilgrim, too distrustful of Zelevas."

"Then why?"

"My hunch—and I have no hard evidence to back this up—is that Kendro suspected the Horizon, maybe other arcologies too, had been infiltrated by outside forces."

"Outside forces? The Empire?"

"Perhaps. Likely not though."

I frown. "Why didn't he take it to the leadership?"

"Probably because he thought the leadership had been compromised."

"So he took off to learn the truth."

"That's my guess."

A conspiracy then.

More speculation with as much credence as the theory Father left the Horizon for an edge-system lover. Nevertheless, I make a mental note to follow this up when I get back. Maybe Mother's been hiding something...

Thinking of compromised leadership, my thoughts drift back to Ito. *Something doesn't add up...*

I sigh.

Maybe I'll never understand what's bugging me.

I picture him descending into the comet's interior, moving through the low-gravity labyrinth, except—

That's it!

"Ito wasn't a caver, was he?"

Kalad is close enough now that I can see the surprise in his eyes. "You had enough of an old man's ramblings?"

While I'm carefully picking my next words, thirty or forty meters further down the shaft, I hear Argo and Dr Lasa exchanging rapid-fire words like they're having a full-blown argument.

"Sorry, I've heard those theories before," I reply, thinking we'll all hear the meat of the pair's disagreement later. "I can't shake the feeling we all missed something with Ito."

Kalad nods. "I understand. Sometimes we don't want to believe something even if it's plain as day." He descends a little more so we're now eye-to-eye. "As to your question, no, I believe Ito was only what we call 'a fair-weather caver'."

An old joke. Sunshine and caving never mix.

"Why do you ask?"

Before I answer, a sharp cry echoes up the shaft.

"Help me!" Dr Lasa screams, her words only too clear now. "I'm going to fall!"

I tense to rappel down fast, expecting Kalad to do the same, but the Cavemaster remains motionless.

"Come on," I implore, perplexed. "We can still help!"

"We're too late," he replies, chilling my blood.

As if on cue, Dr Lasa issues a spine-chilling scream that falls away as she drops. Too long, I think. The scream's lasting too long. It terminates with a slick, hard slap.

I feel numb.

Kalad orders the bot with the medical supplies to go to her, before we begin scaling down the shaft, determined but not reckless. I need to talk, put the horror from my mind.

"How did you—"

"Hindsight is a wonderful thing," Kalad says. "Let's just pray she's still alive."

I think back, realize I missed the same clues.

Kalad says, "You asked me if Ito was a caver. He wasn't, but that wouldn't have stopped him planting the beacon. Anyone can cave in near zero-gee."

Is he trying to distract me from the accident?

All I can think of is Dr Lasa lying in the dark, her life draining away. We must get to her, fast.

Every moment is precious.

"Yeah, you're right," I mumble.

"Come on, tell me," Kalad says, waiting for me to catch-up. "You had something. If you think Ito might not be—"

I hear myself answer. "Someone who wasn't a caver would've been slow—even in zero-gee. And their suit would've been scuffed up. They're both things we can check."

Kalad fixes me with a long, hard look.

Everyone wants to put that episode behind us, not dredge up matters we've moved past.

But we must be sure.

"Then we will," he says finally. "Then we will—when we're back on the Horizon."

Half-a-day later our exhausted, compromised, team is settling into a base-camp we've nicknamed the Dungeon. It's a long, low-ceilinged gallery with many nooks and chambers, perfect for creating a semblance of privacy. Far off, rushing water cascades down to unseen places with a constant white-noise hiss.

Dr Lasa lives.

Sedated by a cocktail of drugs, her broken bones held together by a scaffold of microfilaments, she occupies a side-recess while a small machine administers her care.

For now.

We're nearly two-klicks deep, but she'll need to be evacuated to the surface. Only the shuttle can provide the necessary medium-term care she requires, and in any case, the damp musty air and pitch darkness aren't exactly conducive to recovery.

Kalad and Argo will ferry her up tomorrow.

While Dr Lasa recuperates, the other five of us are sitting around the campfire, a thermal cook-square throwing out a dim-red light while nutri-packs slowly warming on the grid-line surface. Even through my sleep-sleeve that I'm sitting on, I can feel the cold seeping through my skin.

"I'm not staying with her," Argo says, not bothering to cock his head up from where he's lying. "I'll see her safe and settled in the shuttle, but then I'm coming back down with you, Kalad."

So much for the pair bond, I think.

Argo Vela looking out for Number One as usual.

My heart sinks.

The twins are like a finely-tuned caving machine, not needing any surplus parts. He'll join Kalad and me. And I'll be on the receiving end of his passive-aggressive personality for the rest of the expedition.

"No, you won't," Kalad replies. "We cave in our pairs, and we recover in our pairs. You'll stay with her."

Argo levers himself up to a sitting position. "Come on, Kalad. These aren't normal circumstances. The United Empire is close. We don't extract this Dust soon, then we're all torched." He snatches a nutri-pack from the cook-square, tips back his head and devours half. "You need me down here."

Kalad picks up a rock, tosses it up and down.

"Look," Argo continues, "medical care? I'm useless. And the shuttle can handle all of that anyway. But caving? I'm the best we've got"—he nods in my direction—"especially considering the company on this mission."

"No need to be a jerk, Vela," Gavi chips in. He turns his head to Kalad. "He's right, though. I know it's against protocol, but we need him down here, before it's too late."

Kalad catches the stone, hurls it into the darkness where it shatters with a loud crack. He's more on edge than I thought.

I guess he cares more for Dr Lasa than he lets on.

"Alright, you'll return with me," he says. "But then you'll go solo."

Solo? If there's one golden, inviolable rule in caving it's that you never cave alone. And not just for the companionship. The risks of catastrophe are just exponentially higher on your own. Especially two-klicks deep in uncharted territory.

"Fine with me," Argo says, breaking the silence.

The twins start speaking simultaneously.

"Are you nuts? Even in a trio—"

"Cavemaster, you gotta be kidding. Solo caving—"

Kalad raises his hand, cutting them both off. "As Argo says, we need to find the Dust fast. If he's adamant about coming back down, then three parties will be better than two. After all, this system branches off like crazy from here."

Argo nods. "That's settled then."

"Until we get back," Kalad says, "the three of you will limit yourselves to exploring in the vicinity of this base camp. Work out the most promising paths onwards from here, but don't go too far.

And stick together at all times." He stands up. "Am I making myself clear?"

I glance at the twins, and we all nod.

"Good. I suggest everyone get some shut-eye." He fixes each of us in turn, ending with a wistful look at me. "We've got a long way left to go yet."

As Kalad is settling in for the night in his little corner of the gallery, I approach him.

"Cavemaster?"

"What is it, Sewa?"

I lower my voice. "I keep thinking about Ito."

"Why? He's a traitor. Or was a traitor."

"That's the thing: what if he wasn't?"

Kalad's jaw tightens. "I said we'd check those other things out when we're back on the Horizon."

"I know. But it might be too late by then."

"Sewa." Kalad reaches out, places a hand on my shoulder. "I know it's hard to accept, but everything is only going to confirm what we already know. Ito was the one." He gives a final squeeze. "Now your focus must be on this expedition."

I nod. Kalad's probably right.

I'm about to go, but part of me can't leave it.

"Cavemaster... no matter the unlikelihood... I feel we still have a responsibility."

"What would you have me do?"

"When you reach the shuttle... send a message to the Overseer."

Kalad sighs. "As you wish."

I depart to my nook shortly afterwards, the sustenance giving me some relief from the cold, but it still takes me a long while to fall asleep. The black is so pure I can't tell if my eyes are shut or not. Phantasms play in the darkness. Oba recovering in the medical ward. Mother praying in the *Reverent*'s chapel. Rina at home pining for me. On the bridge of the *Truthseeker* I picture the Overseer pacing as she tracks the Empire vessel across the system. The one person who doesn't materialize is my father.

I have no idea what he might be doing.

I don't even know if he's still alive.

Where did you go, Father?

TWELVE

ㅈㅓㅌㄹㅈㅌ

The next morning I wake to find Kalad, Argo, and Dr Lasa already gone. The twins are squatting around a small camping stove, hands aloft seeking warmth, while the thin blue flame casts a steady yet dim light over the camp.

"Tea?" Amra asks, noticing me sitting up.

"Please," I croak, dry-mouthed.

She pours a cupful of simmering water into a metal mug, drops in an infusion bag, and brings it to my bedside. I smell wild berries and mint coming off the tea, warm and reassuring.

"Thanks," I say, taking the mug.

"Don't get used to it," she replies, "your turn tomorrow."

Maybe she's making a joke, maybe not.

"Of course," I say. "I'm not here to make up the numbers."

"Ignore Amra's tone," Gavi says. "She didn't sleep well."

Even in the low light I can see the fatigue in her face.

"I'm sorry to hear that."

"It happens."

She heads back to the stove.

"And you?" Gavi asks. "Sleep okay?"

"Aside from the weird dreams," I mumble, watching vapor eddy off my tea. "Yeah."

I blow and take a sip.

"Weird dreams?"

"I dreamt I was caving." I close my eyes, remembering. "I was somewhere deep, alone, in a labyrinth, but I was determined to push on. I couldn't go back. And then I found my father."

I snap my eyes open, embarrassed.

Too much information.

Both twins are staring at me, tongue-tied.

"Sorry."

Amra shakes her head. "No, no, don't be sorry."

"Yeah, absolutely," Gavi adds. "I can't imagine what it's like to lose your father so young. And so... abruptly... without knowing—"

"Gavi!"

"It's okay," I say. "I shouldn't hold it in."

We sit in silence, sipping our drinks.

"I guess I hope I still might find him one day."

Gavi nods. "You think he might still be out there somewhere?"

"I can hope," I reply. "I can't believe he wouldn't do everything in his power to let us know he was still alive though. That means he's lost or imprisoned—or dead."

"Not necessarily," Amra says. "Maybe we're the ones who are lost, and he just can't find us."

I smile.

I've entertained the same hope for many years.

I look down, smile fading, a sadness welling inside.

"I'm afraid that when we leave this sector, any last hope of reuniting with him again will be gone."

"That's a tough path you're on, kid," Gavi says, moving closer and gripping my shoulder. "I feel for you. I really do."

He pushes my chin up, so our gazes meet.

"I didn't know your father, but everyone who did always tells me how much you meant to him. Whatever he left for, it must've been for something important, something that was vital for all of us Pilgrims."

"Yeah," I say, half-heartedly, close to tears.

"You should talk to Ebo, he might have answers." I can see my pain reflected in Gavi's eyes, see that he's desperate to help me. "Ebo's a classicist. I know your father spent a lot of time with him discussing Endless science." He furrows his brow, thinking. "And, of course, our very own Cavemaster. They didn't see eye-to-eye, but there was something in their characters that drew them together. They were both outsiders, both freethinkers, in their own way."

Inwardly, I slump.

I try not to let my disappointment show.

Dead ends. Anytime I've even got close to the subject of my father with Ebo, he's shut down the conversation like it's dangerous talk. And as for Kalad, I've already quizzed him.

"Cavemaster's certainly unpopular now," I say, changing the

subject, not wanting to dwell on my despondency. I shuffle out of my sleep-sleeve, throw on my kit before the cold can get to me. "You and Amra known him a long time, right?"

"Nine years of expeditions," Gavi says, with a nod, like he senses I don't want to talk about my father anymore. He drains his tea and shakes out the dregs into the darkness. "And you get to know someone real well when you're in the deep together. You'll see that."

He treks back to the stove, begins packing up.

Amra purses her lips. "You know, he saved Gavi's life back in the day. It was a cave dive, three klicks down, long passage with no air pockets. Ice cold water, pitch-black conditions, and even with torches the kicked-up silt made it like we swam through an oil sump. Kalad went first, laid the guideline. I went next. Gavi followed. I was waiting on the other side, still catching my breath, when the line snapped." Amra shakes her head, still fear in her eyes all these years later. "Kalad knew something was wrong straight away. Strapped on his gear, went straight back in, no thought for his own safety. By some miracle he found Gavi a ways down the submerged passage, floating in the darkness, unconscious. Later we discovered that his rebreather had malfunctioned, hadn't been stripping the CO_2 out of the mix. Somehow Kalad hauled him back out through that black maze, brought him back to life on the cold hard stone." She pinches the sides of her nose. "Watching him come back from the dead... I'd never felt joy like it." She squeezes her twin's neck. "And I pray I never will again."

Gavi clasps his sister's hand, speaks.

"'Playing the hero is easy,' he'd often say. 'It's doing the unpopular thing that takes real courage.'" His jaw tightens. "Sometimes he had to make real hard choices. Choices that many others couldn't make, couldn't accept. When a cave-in trapped Elpha, he ordered the entire expedition back to base camp, said we might all end up dead if we attempted to rescue her there and then. I tell you, most of us wanted to kill him for that coldness—I did, for sure—but he made the right call. The whole sub-system collapsed, and instead of the whole caving team wiped out, we only lost one." He goes quiet, the hiss of the far-off cascading water the only noise. "Still, Mwepu could never forgive him for that call. Or maybe he just couldn't forgive himself for obeying."

"That's Kalad," Amra says. "Tough as rock."

"And almost as old," Gavi adds.

I feel my mouth creasing into a small smile.

Kalad's certainly showing his age these days. The scars, the half-limp gait, the lines of his weathered face. He can still navigate a system like a champion caver, though.

"Of course," Gavi goes on, checking his pack, "he's caved less these last couple of years."

"What?" I say, confused. "I thought he still led almost every caving mission."

"Oh, he comes on the gigs without exception," he replies. "Surveys the terrain, plans the descents, chooses the pairs—leads on everything except the actual caving. Mainly stays back on the surface, acting like a good homesteader."

I find it difficult imagining Kalad staying back at the nest, not grappling with the nitty gritty of a descent.

"Why?"

"Who knows?" Amra replies. "Fitness, fatigue, fear... maybe he just can't stand the idea of partnering with any of us." She grins. "We took bets on whether he'd get his hands dirty on this mission. I won."

"You called it," Gavi says. "Guess I underestimated how protective he'd feel towards the newest member of the team."

He winks, and I smile.

"What did he do up there while you were on a descent? I mean, some missions can last for days, if not weeks."

Amra answers. "He wasn't bored, that's for sure."

"Kalad is more than happy with only himself for company," Gavi continues. "He tinkered, he read, he hiked, probably was writing his life story too. And he kept an eye on the skies as well. Most the time we were in the UE's backyard after all. One system, if it was the right time of day and you got the right weather, you could see the Empire station orbiting one of the nearby moons."

"Scary."

"Not really," Gavi says. "They had no idea we were right under their noses. Needle in a haystack odds of them stumbling across us. And even if they did, majority of the time they didn't have the right assets to do anything about it. We're talking UE refueling depots, deep-space telescopes, autonomous science stations. The worst we risked was being attacked by a fleet of weather balloons."

I stifle a laugh.

"Not like that now."

"Nope, not like that now." Amra hoists her pack onto her back. "And that's why we need to get moving, locate some Dust sumps ASAP."

ㄱ

Through the "morning", we work fast, swiftly scouting the immediate environs of the Dungeon. Six paths splay out from the low-ceilinged camp, although calling them all paths gives the wrong impression. One is the long, arduous ascent back to the surface that Argo and Kalad are undertaking with their patient, Dr Lasa. Two are dead ends, ancient smoothed crawlspaces that dwindle to narrow horizontal fissures, where long-lost water channels once percolated down through the porous rock. The remaining three each offer potential, the first leading to more sheer drops deeper into the earth, while the second reveals a long, vaulting gallery that gently slopes downwards, the arched ceiling crowded with spectacular stalactites, while the ground underfoot is awash with breakdown, making it ripe for sprains and twists. The last route is a partially submerged passage, the still and cold water rising waist-high in places, the dappled ceiling only a hand's width above the head. Small crabs no bigger than a palm skitter across the lakebed, and the ones resting on the rock sides scatter to the vibrations of our footfalls with disquieting clicks.

The twins deem the latter the most promising, and we gear up for some cold swims. The thrill of the exploration is a visceral one, my intakes of breath at the wondrous discoveries equal to those I get when I wade into the ice-cold waters.

I'm in my element.

The only slither of disappointment is the fact that this might well be my first and last caving mission.

Resting on a rocky islet between expanses of black lakes, we squat down, take on some nourishment and water. The twins have barely said a word since we began the mapping work, no doubt knowing each other's routines and methods inside-out, but this time Gavi speaks.

"You feel that?"

His words startle in the immense stillness of our surroundings. I've taken their silences as signs of trust and confidence.

"A breeze," Amra replies. "Happy days."

In the light from our headlamps I see her grinning.

A breeze is a strong indication that this section of the cave system leads to an exit point at a lower elevation. It means we might be able to extract Dust there rather than needing to pump it all the way up to the highlands.

"Turn off your lights," Gavi instructs, killing his beam.

I place my canteen on the stony ground, and click off my headlamp. Amra does likewise, and after a few moments waiting for the afterglow of the headlamps to dissipate I find myself pitched into absolute darkness.

Except, now I notice it, the darkness isn't complete. Across the black waters of the lake I see something glittering. It's faint, but if I look carefully I can track the illumination.

"Is that—"

"Oh, yes," Amra says, glee in her voice.

I think they must be reflections off the lake's surface, but Gavi explains that it's motes of Dust drifting in the waters.

Dust.

I've heard stories of its wilder effects, stuff far beyond its use as a fuel or medicine, but these tales are near taboo in our society. For Pilgrims, knowing that the Endless used it to power their great civilization means the substance is almost as revered as those who mastered it.

Not many of us know its secrets.

And now I am close to a raw source!

I marvel at the twinkling motes, the movement of the waters making the Dust shimmer. I feel like a hunter, close to their quarry.

"Let's see the size of our bounty," Amra says, switching on her headlamp, extinguishing the light of the Dust.

We follow suit, pack up in a flurry of movement, and step back into the chilly waters. The icy feeling adds another level of anticipation, and we splash onwards with determined steps, no longer moving through the waters serenely, but half running.

Soon, even with the light of the headlamps, I spy the sparkling motes, suffusing the water in a golden aura.

Magical.

"Thank the Endless!" Gavi slaps the water before heaving himself onto a rocky lip, laughing with joy. "We've found the motherlode!"

Later, we discover the Dust lake goes no deeper than waist height, but at that first glimpse, its radiant expanse seems to stretch off to infinity. The ceiling of the space arches far overhead here, but the light of the Dust still bathes the roof in a warm glow, illuminating every nook and cranny.

Peering at the Dust sump itself is a mesmerizing experience, the fluid seemingly alive with constantly shifting shapes and hues like watching flames in a fire. Even though Amra assures me that it gives off no heat, it feels warm.

"Is it enough?" I ask, tentatively.

Gavi pulls out a small drone, gives it some commands, then tosses it upwards. Its blades whirr into life with a soft hum, stabilizing its position before it heads off, tracking the contours of the sump.

Less than a minute later it descends onto his palm.

"It's not vast," he says glumly, causing my heart to sink, "but it should be enough!"

He grabs his twin sister, grabs me, and we twirl and scream like lunatics, the noise reverberating through the gallery. Here, deep beneath the ground, on a nondescript moon in an unremarkable system, we've found the thing that will secure our survival.

My heart swells.

No, it's more than just survival.

Soon we'll enter the slipways, travel hundreds and hundreds of light years, further than we've ever gone before to reach a place beyond the clutches of the Empire.

Soon we will find a real home.

We head back to camp, buoyant.

We can't stop talking, now.

Which sector of the galaxy will we head for? What type of world will we settle? Will we still be nomads? What other species will we find? Will we still seek the relics and places of the Endless, or will the ancient civilization slowly, inevitably lose its grip on our culture?

Will we still be Pilgrims?

More questions still bounce around my head, unspoken. About my role, about Oba, about my father.

There are many questions, but few answers.

And that's okay. More than okay. The speculations feel liberating after living for so long as the hunted. One question above all others has dominated our thoughts for far too long: *Where next?*

Away, away, away.

We haven't been living.

We've been surviving.

And now that can end.

Before heads-down we set up the bots to rig together the extraction pipework. They'll work through the "night" and come tomorrow we'll be ready to drain the sump. Exhausted, I'm asleep before my head even reaches my sleep-sleeve.

THIRTEEN

ㅈㅋㅅㅿㅑㄷㅌㅌㅌ

I wake to raised voices.

Twisting in my sleep-sleeve, I rub my eyes to see the twins, Argo, and Kalad in lively conference, lit by a couple of weak halogens. Kalad stands to the left, opposite the twins, while Argo has placed himself between the others like an arbiter officiating a dispute.

Civil debate this isn't.

I prick my ears, trying to discern the nature of the disagreement, but they're all talking over one another. I shift a little, triggering a bout of coughing and the argument stops dead. Dazzling lights blind me as their torch beams turn in unison.

I cup a hand over my brow. "Morning."

The silence lengthens.

"Sorry for waking you," Amra says eventually, as she adjusts her headlamp, reducing the glare. "And sorry you had to hear that."

I clear my throat. "Actually, I didn't hear much."

"We were discussing—"

"Discussion over." Kalad grunts, satisfied. "We keep looking for another sump."

Over a strained breakfast I get up to speed through snatched whispers of conversation with the twins. First off, Dr Lasa's condition deteriorated during the ascent, and she was put into a medically induced coma once safely located onboard the shuttle. Second, messages from what remains of the Horizon hiding out in the Kuiper belt indicate that the small UE craft is now in-system, and is on a heading for the gas giant around which we orbit. Despite this, the Cavemaster is adamant that the volume of Dust we discovered yesterday isn't large enough.

Only a larger sump will satisfy.

Hence we split up, and head back out.

I worry for Dr Lasa, but I can't do much for her, two kilometers of solid rock between us. My more immediate concern is for the forthcoming descent. The twins will return to yesterday's sump, seek secondary lakes, while Argo will scout deeper into the vaulting gallery route. That leaves Kalad and I to tackle the path that leads to the vertical descents.

I must've drawn the short straw.

As I gear up, I realize an element of yesterday's euphoria came from the understanding I'd be ascending today, maybe even reaching the surface. Stars above, wind through the hair, even scratchy vegetation to run my fingers through. Now, we're going to go deeper. The rock above us... the millions upon millions of tons of stone that could flatten us... it doesn't just have a physical weight. We're not creatures that came from the depths. Over the eons we evolved on the surface, hiked mountains, sailed seas, basked in sunlight. Our double-helix sings of this tale, and the very fibers of our being rejoice in its telling. Too long underground... I am beginning to understand what cavers mean when they talk of falling under the spell of the dreaded heebie-jeebies.

Thousand-meter stares, paralysis, the shakes.

I'm not there yet, but they're in the post.

"You okay?"

Argo's words jolt me. He slaps me on the arm, his expression a decent effort at looking concerned. Maybe he's a good actor.

"Listen," he says, keeping his voice down, "sorry for being a jerk before. My meditator tells me it's part of my winning mindset. Anyway, I wanted to tell you you're doing great. Both Kalad and the twins have given glowing reports."

I drop my head. "I was hoping we'd be back upside by the end of the day. Especially given Dr Lasa's injuries."

"She's not in great shape, but she's stable. And she's a fighter. And let me tell you, first mission, everyone gets the chills some time or another. Even happened to yours truly."

"Thanks." I fix him square in the eye. "Apology accepted."

He grins. "That's the spirit." He runs his hand through his hair. "Once this is all over we should train. I'm sure I could still learn a thing or two from a new pretender."

Fat chance.

"Sure."

"Happy hunting!" he says, wheeling off.

I suddenly remember something I want to ask him.

"Argo?"

"What's up?"

He stands a few paces away, so I move closer, not wanting to be overheard. "Back on the surface," I whisper, "when Kalad sent a message to the Horizon... did he mention anything about Ito or his caving suit?"

Argo thinks. "No, can't say he did."

"And he only sent one message?"

"Affirmative," he scratches his chin. "I mean, we got some shut-eye... but I think I would've noticed. All our focus was on making Dr Lasa comfortable and then getting back here." He raises his eyebrows. "What's this about?"

"Nothing," I reply. "Don't worry about it."

Within the hour we've all headed our separate ways, the white hiss of the Dungeon already out of earshot. Argo picks his way through the debris field of the long gallery, while the twins glide through the chilly waters of the submerged passage. Kalad and I begin a series of sheer drops.

He isn't in a talkative mood, his attention lasered in on the repetitive actions of the descent. I want to know why he didn't contact the Overseer about Ito as he'd promised. I assume he'd just forgotten in his concern for Dr Lasa, but another part of me can't help but wonder if the oversight was intentional.

Why though?

Maybe he thinks the Overseer has enough on her plate already, without needing to worry about every last piece of evidence establishing Ito's guilt. Maybe he doesn't want another wave of paranoia sweeping the Horizon's command structure on the off-chance Ito wasn't the traitor. Or maybe he knows something, but still wants it pinned on Ito...

I shake off the stupid thought.

No, Kalad's not one for grudges.

We descend, two human corpuscles moving through an immense living organism of a cave system. A system with a bloodstream and respiratory tract, infections and infestations. We're two tiny pieces of organic matter, slowly being digested, and eventually—hopefully—being flushed out.

For the countless time today, I finish a rappel, my feet welcoming the hard pushback of stone. I unclip, twist, and examine the ground. Often these descents lead to tiny ledges above further drops, but this time I can see we've reached some kind of vast cave floor. A large phosphorescent lagoon stretches across most of the space, small rocky isles protruding from the surface here and there, while a slick shoreline disappears into darkness. Green fronds in the water cast an eerie glow upwards into the cavern, and I have the impression of many things moving above the lagoon.

"Bats," Kalad intones. "No bigger than your fist. Nothing to fear."

"That's... reassuring."

"Just watch out for guano on your hands," he adds. "A fungal infection can be deadly. Let's eat."

Despite his words, the arduous descent has built up my appetite, and after checking the ground for bat-shit I sit myself down and tear into my rations.

"How big a sump we looking for?" I ask, after a gulp of energy gruel. "Yesterday's one—"

"Wasn't big enough." Kalad crouches next to the water's edge, washing his hands of grit and dirt. "Overseer tasked us with bringing back as much Dust as we could muster." He finishes cleaning, shakes the water from his hands. "I know there's a bigger sump out there. One that could not only get us out of this sector, but set us up for years too."

"But the Empire... they're in-system, heading this way." I picture the craft arrowing towards us, bristling with malice. "Surely it's only a matter of time? We risk everything—"

"The UE vessel is a small one," he says, standing with his back to me now, carefully surveying the margins of the cavern, "likely incapable of military engagement. Worst case scenario, they become aware of our presence in a day or so. It'd take days before the message could reach any larger forces." He turns to me. "We have enough time."

"And Dr Lasa?"

He grimaces. "Whether Dr Lasa lives or dies will depend on her progress over the next day. Leaving now wouldn't change that. Her fate's in the hands of the Endless."

I give a small nod.

Please let her make it.

"Sewa, I know it's hard," Kalad says, "but she gets through tonight she'll be absolutely fine."

And Ito? I want to ask.

"Something else on your mind?"

He reads me too easily.

I take a breath. "Argo told me you didn't relay my questions about the traitor's caving suit to the Overseer."

"No, I didn't."

"Why?"

"Sewa, you know better than anyone that it's a very delicate time for the Overseer. Not everyone is onboard with our forthcoming exodus." The light of his headlamp momentarily dazzles me, before passing on. "Casting doubt on Ito's guilt can only destabilize things, provoke witch hunts, perhaps even lead to all-out mutiny."

Speculation.

Even if he's dead, Ito deserves justice.

"We should be as certain as we can."

"The case against him is overwhelming." Kalad's voice resounds off the hard stone walls. "Opportunity, motive, evidence. Ito was the one."

An uneasy quiet grows between us, the only sound the faint tremble of hundreds of fluttering bats' wings.

"Can you drop it, Sewa?" Kalad asks, finally. "For the sake of the Horizon's future, can you swear you'll let this matter lie?"

I stare at the stone beneath me, my gaze following the contours of the rock. I run a finger over a fracture line.

I have been chosen as Liandra's heir.

I am to be leader of the Horizon one day.

How can I abandon my principles before I even take up that mantle?

I can't.

I meet Kalad's gaze.

"I can't do that, Cavemaster." I get up, brush myself off. "Like you, I won't abandon my most deeply held beliefs."

He gives a wry smile that turns to a look of sadness.

"I can respect that," he says, "but whatever follows will be on you."

We scout the edge of the lake, discover a narrow fissure that leads further into darkness. Kalad instructs me to take point. I take a good look at the mesmerizing light of the phosphorescent lagoon, as if I can stockpile and draw on it later, before sliding into the gap in the rock face.

Behind me, I sense Kalad lingering beside the lagoon, perhaps taking in the sight before it's gone too, and then he joins me in the fissure, the light of his headlamp glancing off the hard walls and casting spiky shadows.

The fissure begins wide enough to easily accommodate us walking single file, but after a couple of dozen paces it steadily narrows until we're scraping through and I'm forced to turn my body and side-step onwards, shoulder first. I hear Kalad laboring close behind, his breaths heavy, the sound of his caving suit fabric rubbing against the coarse sides of the passage with a rhythmic grating noise.

Whatever follows will be on you.

His words haunt me.

I can be careful, I think. I won't send word. Once back with the Horizon, I'll simply investigate the suit and anything else I think of alone, discreetly. Anything turns up, I can bring in the Overseer then. Nothing turns up, nobody will be any the wiser.

Either way, Ito's guilt—or not—will be established.

The passage narrows further still at shoulder height, forcing us to crouch and then after a few more paces, crawl. The ground is cold and rough, rocky debris pressing into my body. Ahead, my light only reveals the crawlspace pinching further, inclining downwards, no relief for my growing feeling of claustrophobia. I think I'm going to have to call this path a bust soon. Mentally, I prime myself for the uncomfortable art of the reverse-crawl, when I notice that my light isn't exposing anything, instead lancing towards infinity unopposed.

Another cavern.

"It opens out!" I call over my shoulder.

Kalad doesn't reply.

I haul myself through the final section, then get to my feet, ditching my pack and stretching to loosen up aching limbs. The chamber is a large one, the beam of my headlamp revealing vast stalactites hanging from an arching roof, some at the periphery meeting their corresponding stalagmites. At ground level multiple passages lead away from the cavern floor.

Kalad is squatting by our entry point, catching his breath.

"Any idea which way's our best bet?" I ask. "I count at least seven other exits."

"Alright, let's get our bearings," he says, scrutinizing the upper reaches of the space. "First though, I should mark our path."

Good call, I think. I'd hate to get lost.

The vertical descents leave a whole host of markers to find your way back—ropes and bolts and the suchlike—but it's crazy how easy it can be to go astray when the trail goes horizontal.

Kalad slings off his pack, unhooks his small pick-ax. He drops to his knees, begins chipping away at the stone. I grab my canteen, wander to the middle of the chamber, and take a long draught of cool, refreshing water. Aside from a steady *tink-tink-tink* as Kalad works, the silence is absolute. Another of the galaxy's never-ending tombs.

I turn back to Kalad, about to ask him something about the geology of the moon, when my headlamp catches the markings he's just etched onto the rock. Three parallel slashes a hand's length long, so unassuming you might think them a natural feature if you didn't know otherwise.

Something about the pattern is familiar...

Still kneeling, Kalad notices me staring.

"Distinctive enough?"

Now I remember.

My blood runs cold.

I saw the same markings in the comet.

Where we found the beacon.

"Sure," I say, steadying my voice, "hard to miss."

He pauses, eyes narrowing a little, nods. "That's the idea."

He knows that I know.

My legs feel heavy as iron, paralyzing me. I think I might pass out or throw-up, dread coiling in the pit of my stomach.

Move, girl!

They're not my words. Somehow, from somewhere deep, I've dredged up Oba. His voice carries hope.

Now!

"I'm going to check out our options," I say, wheeling away, not waiting for Kalad to get to his feet. I wonder if he hears the tremor in my voice as clearly as I do. I don't run. Not yet.

But I don't dally either.

Twenty paces separate us... I pray it's enough. I can't go back, not with him blocking the way, but I can go onwards, head deeper into the system... as long as I choose the right passage.

The wrong choice and I'll hit a dead-end...

Think.

I stumble onwards, my torch beam illuminating outcrops rising from the stone ground, which swiftly morph into a field of tapering stalagmites. Beyond them I see the pitted walls of the cave—and, reassuringly, a diagonal cleft in the rock face, black and welcoming.

I glance back.

Kalad is swallowed in shadow, but the constant light of his headlamp bobs up and down, growing brighter. Panicking, I click off my own headlamp and crouch. I weave through the small forest of limestone spires.

"Sewa?" he calls. "You okay?"

If I answer he'll know where I am. If I stay silent it'll confirm his suspicions. *Damned if I do, damned if I don't.* My heart hammers in my chest, and I place a hand over it, as if I could calm its furious beating.

I force a couple of slow, deep breaths.

The light of his headlamp tracks back and forth, and I make myself as small as I can as the beam passes.

Maybe I could circle back, keep out of sight among the stalagmites that populate the periphery of the cave, then head back through the passage that leads to the lake? I'm on the verge of moving, when I remember the ascent.

I'd have no time.

Damn.

"Sewa?" he calls again, louder and with more urgency in his voice. "Are you hurt?"

No, but you'd like to hurt me, wouldn't you?

One hand on the pocked wall, I move as quietly as I can along the edge of the cave, eyes peeled for any details revealed by Kalad's roving head light. I come to the cleft I'd spied earlier. The urge to immediately head into its dark embrace is near overwhelming, but something gives me pause...

Wrong move and you'll be trapped.

There's no breeze.

This passage leads nowhere, the fissure a result of a stress fracture in the rock, not a channel cut by water.

Too close. Gotta keep my wits.

I keep moving, quiet as I can. In the darkness my hands find a second exit, but the passage is narrow and riddled with sharp rocks. Not this one. Kalad's light is closer now. Around me, shadows flicker to life. I pick up the pace, soon find myself at another passage.

The path is cramped, not high enough to stand fully. I run my hands over the ground, discovering a smooth undulating channel. Head bent, I shuffle inside and almost let out a gleeful cry as I discern the passage's gradual yet unmistakable downwards slope. Over millions of years, seasonal rains have washed down into this cave and carved out this gully.

Escape!

Still not daring to turn on my headlamp yet, I head onwards into the pitch-black, one hand raised to the passage's low roof, the other cast ahead clutching blindly at the nothingness. Pain suddenly jolts the side of my temple, and my lips betray me with a stifled cry.

"Sewa?"

I get down on all fours and scrabble forward.

"I know you're there," he says from somewhere in the cavern, voice muffled. "Something spooked you?"

Friction burns my knees as I piston onwards. If I can just reach a turn or a short precipice I might be able to get out of sight before he realizes which exit I've chosen.

Too late...

A faint light illuminates the passage, and for the first time I see the vague contours of the walls.

"Sewa," Kalad says, his voice louder, echoing off the rock. "This is foolish."

I turn, look back.

Far off, Kalad's headlamp blazes bright as a star.

My breathing is heavy, and not just from the exertions. I'm close to hyperventilating. I don't move, but he must see my silhouette clear as day. I expect him to barrel into the passage any moment, but he just stands there, watching.

"Come out," he commands. "Let's talk."

I grit my teeth, terrified.

The moment stretches, becomes unbearable.

"Sewa—"

"I know it was you!" I scream.

The accusation hangs between us, dividing everything we were from everything we will be. I can't unsay it, can't go back, but strangely, a wave of relief washes through me.

He moves—not into the passage, but away.

"I know it was you," I whisper, shaking.

I click on my headlamp and move on.

FOURTEEN

ᗩᐸᗞᎶᛕᛟᛟᕱ

Devoid of ropes, equipment, even the smallest refreshments, I head on, deeper and deeper. The total of my escape's arsenal comprises a headlamp, my caving suit, and my wits. I try not to think about my odds.

Stay sharp, stay positive.

Oba's words.

The fear has lessened, or rather not lessened, but… congealed. A cold, debilitating thing sitting heavy in my gut. White-hot terror morphed to a dank foreboding.

Not unlike the surrounding conditions.

The dry climes of the upper part of the system have given way to passages and tunnels slick with damp, vast galleries resounding with the steady percussion of dripping water. Every footstep is a potential slip, but at least I won't die of thirst.

Kalad though, he might kill me.

This whole venture—at least my part in it—was simply a ruse to put me at his mercy, away from prying eyes. And any hope of rescue. No wonder he insisted Argo cave alone after Dr Lasa injured herself. Three of us together wouldn't have worked for whatever he planned.

Maybe he hoped it wouldn't come to murder. Maybe he hoped he'd get a good read on me, gently persuade me to drop my digging if I seemed so inclined.

He should've known better.

Mother's always said I've got a stubborn streak.

Just like my father.

I knew I was stubborn, but I didn't know I was vain too. How else could I have overlooked Kalad's machinations? I can still hear

Overseer Liandra's words: *Cavemaster Kalad selected you personally for this mission… he believes you can step up.* My burst of pride at those words was dangerously misplaced.

Stupid, conceited girl.

If I come out of this alive, I swear on the Endless I'll get rid of my childish pride. And hopefully a little of my naivety too. Kalad should've been higher on my radar.

I just didn't want to see it.

He practically raised me… no, that's too strong. He *guided* me, a second father after my real one left the Horizon.

I trusted him the same way you trust family.

I couldn't entertain the possibility he might betray us.

That he might betray *me*.

I stop, cast my hand into the steady trickle of water that runs from this passage's porous ceiling. It feels cold, clean. I cup my hand, let the water pool, then splash it over my face. I'm thirstier than I realized, and my tongue seeks out the water in hungry licks. It tastes refreshing, crystal clear. I click off my headlamp, pitching myself into complete blackness.

I tilt my head and drink.

Satiated, I stand motionless in the dark, listening to the gentle susurration of the cataract tumbling onto the stone. I try to imagine that I'm somewhere else, hearing rains fall on a starlit surface, but I can feel Kalad coming. Relentless, determined.

Whatever follows will be on you.

I turn my lamp back on, returning to the monotone color of hard rock. I move on. Back in the cavern, when Kalad didn't come after me straight away I thought, for a moment, that I might've been wrong. Not about his guilt—but his intentions.

Maybe he didn't mean to kill me.

Not directly, at least. I thought that maybe his plan was to abandon me down here. Leave me to perish on an alien world, alone. A cruel death. He'd need to get back to the others, spin a tale that I'd fallen and died, my body irretrievable. Even if they swallowed that story though, they'd still need time to extract the Dust. Time for me to inconveniently rise from the dead.

That'd put some holes in his tale.

He wasn't going back though.

He was gearing up, commandeering my pack, and then driving me deeper into the system. Erasing any evidence that might contradict his later story, forcing me to a place that no matter how loud I might scream, nobody would hear me, and, should they later come looking, nobody would find me.

A few hours back, a light rain of grit on my head as I descended a shaft confirmed Kalad was on my tail. I killed my headlamp for a second and looked up. A flickering glow far above emanated from the darkness. I remembered Kalad telling me stories of tracking fugitives, long pursuits on harsh worlds.

There's always tracks, he said.

The stories always ended with him catching his prey.

My only chance is reuniting with the others before he corners me, but rather than discovering any double-back loops, so far the path has only led downwards. Maybe I'll emerge lower-down the mountainside, and then I can trek up to the landing site.

Maybe.

Ahead, the passage opens up, the rivulet of water that I've been following feeding into another underground lake. I track my beam across its placid surface, trying to get a sense of its underwater geography from any islands or rockfall on the lake's bed, but the water is a black, unbroken expanse. Casting my light over the low undulating ceiling I see that the entire cave is submerged, no exits above the water line.

I'm going to have to dive.

I feel the fear again, and I can't help but glance back.

No sign of Kalad. Not yet.

One thing I couldn't fathom as I hiked, crawled, and free-climbed down through those desolate passages was why he'd betrayed us. I couldn't believe any amount of riches or luxuries promised by the Empire would cause him to abandon his people. Was it the hope of immortality that enticed him? Rumors were rife that Emperor Zelevas had extended his lifespan many-fold. Could the Empire have tempted him with a similar offer? Or was it because he despised our culture, despised our worship of the Endless?

I couldn't believe it.

Not for such a betrayal.

Whatever his reason, it eluded me.

I turn back to the lake, shake off the thoughts.

After stretching and limbering up as well as I can, I slip into the black waters. Even with my specialized suit, the coldness has me gasping. I kick my legs, shake my arms, seeking warmth. The water is relatively clear, but without goggles and only a weak headlamp it's difficult to discern details. I make a swift reconnaissance dive, and my hopes lift as I find three underwater passages leading off from the lake.

A submerged crossroads.

Even the galaxy's best trackers would find it tricky following a trail underwater. Kalad won't know which way I've gone. It'll buy me some time. At least to begin with.

The first passage is a washout. Literally.

My lung capacity is good. Roleplaying oxygen-tank malfunctions during caver training through my youth ensured that, but the passage banks steeply downwards, no sign of any inversion. After a minute of exploration I turn round. If I go much further I won't be able to get back.

And I don't want to drown.

Bad as asphyxiation in the vacuum, some say.

I break the surface of the lake, fill my lungs.

My eyes dart for where I came into the cavern, panicking, imagining Kalad standing there, but the passage is a dark maw.

Still time, you still have time.

I try to calm myself, calm my breathing.

Then I fill my lungs and dive again.

The second passage is a different affair, rock-strewn and twisting, and after a few powerful kicks I spy above the pleasing spectacle of a mirror-like plane. The surface. I plunge through, shattering the water, and breathe in musty air. Pulling myself up onto a small stone shore, what I already know in my bones becomes clear.

It's a side-chamber, leading nowhere.

I waste no time, dive back into the water, barely inhaling.

I swim hard, desperate to get back, arriving back at the submerged crossroads with a violent crack and sending choppy waves up the chamber walls. Taking a breath, I spin again, orienting myself to where I originally came in—

My heart leaps.

The silhouette of a person is unmistakable in the glare of my light. They don't move. They've switched off their own lamp, only the merest hint of the whites of their eyes reflected in the light.

Am I seeing things?

I tread water, fighting the feeling of lead weights tied to my feet, waiting for a movement, a word, anything.

I daren't move closer.

"Sewa," the figure says eventually, Kalad's gravelly tones clear. "I'm getting too old for this."

"Then go back!" I scream, terror compressing my cry.

"I can't do that."

He clicks on his lamp, spilling light over his weather-beaten face. He looks tired, but determined. Dirt is smeared over his brow and his hair is matted, while he seems to have cut his jaw, a crimson slash marking his flesh.

He crouches. "You're making a big mistake."

More than anything I want to believe him, but his eyes betray his true intentions. They carry a coldness, a hostility, that I've never witnessed before, as if he's erased any feelings that he might've ever held for me.

"Liar!"

I inhale, exhale, then fill my lungs—and dive.

"This needs to end!" he shouts, his words distorted underwater, but still audible.

I kick, frightened, struggling to control my strokes and not thrash wildly. I must be calm, ensure I don't waste my oxygen, but then I feel him crashing into the water and my panic re-doubles. I want to kill my headlamp, not illuminate my whereabouts, but without any light I'll be blind. I keep it on, and with a fleeting sense of relief, I come to the third passage, glide onwards into its expansive girth.

This better lead somewhere.

Alarmingly, to start with, it angles downwards, the floor littered with smoothed rocks and boulders, and I swim on with an increasing sense of dread. I glance back, catch another light through the murk.

Come on, come on.

There's no going back now, my actions ragged, the air in my lungs depleted. I can feel a tightness around my chest, a darkness at the edge of my vision that isn't simply an artifact of the torch beam. I'm slipping away, lungs bursting, almost at the point of giving up, when I spy the telltale sign of a surface.

With a final push I reach it.

Stars spin above my head as I gasp air. Reaching out, my knuckles crack against stone as I try to survey the space as best I can. I tip my head back, revealing an unremarkable rock ceiling only an arm's length away. An air pocket. No escape here.

I feel like crying.

This world wants to crush me. Nothing would be easier than struggling no more, letting Kalad reach me. No more running, no more terror. Acceptance, then release.

Game over.

Like a hunted animal finally trapped by its hunter, there comes a point when the prey recognizes its defeat and no longer strives for life, but simply lies still, awaiting death.

I think of all the places I'll never see again.

All the people I'll never meet again.

All the words I should've said but haven't.

Confessions, pledges, absolutions.

I feel a twinge of anger.

I grab it tight.

The rage is swiftly overtaken by fear, but I don't mind. I embrace it, revel in its life-affirming impulses.

I take a deep breath and dive again.

Kalad is a mere arm's length away, and I buck left, evading his grasp. He doesn't give immediate chase, no doubt desperate for air, but he won't rest long. I kick onwards, heart racing.

The waters are dark, cold too, but I barely register that in my panic. Glimpses of the passage's mottled walls and craggy floor blink in and out of view in my haste, disorienting as much as helpful.

I click off my light.

Guide your damn self, Cavemaster.

Frantic, I blindly swim on, every few strokes a forearm or a knee or a finger crashing against stone as I pinball from side to side along the twisting passage. My only thought is to get away, keep pushing on. The tightness in my chest is strong, but not unbearable, when I surface.

I sense the light straight away. A faint golden hue illuminating the contours of a vast cavernous space.

I've seen this light before...

I haul myself out of the water onto a stony shore, not daring to believe I might be able to escape. With fast, shallow breaths, cold water dripping off my shivering frame, I look around. Behind, only the submerged passage, the cavern's roof emerging from the waters and closing off any egress that way. Ahead, I sense only a few paces of solid ground before it falls away.

Eyes adjusting, I edge forwards—and gasp.

I'm standing on a plateau above a gargantuan Dust lake, its glittering surface disappearing off to infinity, while far above, reflections of its magical waters cast undulating patterns on the cavern ceiling.

Somehow, this Dust lake is more potent than the other one.

I feel its power, an electricity skating through the air, tingling the tip of my tongue. Nothing much lives in these places and barely a whisper of a wind blows through these caves, yet the fluid is alive, writhing with an innate energy.

A miracle of the gods, some call it.

I'm beginning to understand why.

A tremendous crash somewhere behind jolts me back, and I twist round to see Kalad splashing and spluttering out of the waters. He doubles over, hands on knees, sucking in great mouthfuls of air.

While he recovers I run along the cliff edge, seeking an escape. On both sides I meet sheer rock, barring the way, while below a velvet black chasm separates this plateau from the underground lake.

"Dead end?" Kalad asks, still breathing hard.

He steps out of the water, not rushing.

I shuffle backwards until finally my foot only prods into thin air. The sensation isn't pleasant, and a wave of dizziness assails me.

End of the road.

Soon enough he has me pinned, then bound.

FIFTEEN

ᘔᐢᘔᐤᒉᘁᘁᒉᘁ

"I admire your tenacity, Sewa," Kalad says, sitting close by on a boulder. His skin glistens, still wet.

I'm sat on the scree-strewn ledge, propped up against a jagged rock that digs into my spine, facing away from the lake. My hands are tied behind my back, the rope cutting into my wrists. The light of the Dust gives him a golden hue, transforming his age-worn face into something more noble.

I would laugh if I wasn't so scared.

"Truly, I'm proud of you." He stares down at his upturned palms. "These hands helped raise you up, helped you become this strong woman I see before me. And now… I wish it could be another way."

His regret seems genuine.

A chink?

I clear my throat. "It can."

"It can't!" he roars, his words echoing across the cavern.

The violence in his words further tightens my stomach. Not moving, I scan the area, praying I've missed something…

Nothing.

"Please," I whisper, "I can keep my mouth shut. No one will need to know. It'll be our secret—"

"Silence!" He balls his fists tight, turns away.

Time! I need time!

There must be a way out.

This can't be the end.

I tremble. "Why?"

He turns, looks beyond me, studying the vista.

As he considers the question, with my hands tied behind my back

I feel for a decent-sized stone then brush it backwards off the cliff edge. I strain my ears, and count,

One, two, three, four, five—

"Yes." He nods. "You deserve to know."

—six, seven, eight, nine—

Impact. Faint, but clear.

Gravity's almost standard on this moon.

The chasm must go down nearly half a klick.

I wouldn't feel a thing.

"For you to understand," he begins, still staring over my shoulder, "I have to tell you a story. This goes back to before you were born. The galaxy was a very different place then.

"I was twenty-five years old, already a caver under the wing of a great Cavemaster named Anya Poora. Drifting wrecks, radiated worlds, anomalous sites—she took us everywhere. And, of course, Dust extraction, regardless of the risks. It's funny, without her work we probably wouldn't be here now.

"She pioneered so many new methods of exploration that during her watch caving became a respectable vocation among the Pilgrims. And not just on the Horizon. Word spread to the other arcologies."

As he speaks, I snatch a glance over my shoulder, trying to judge the width of the chasm. It's a large gap, but I think I could make it. The bigger problem is the drop. Even if I can get my hands free to help break the fall, the lake lies four or five meters below us, easily enough distance for a broken ankle or worse. Unless I can land in the lake itself. Assuming it's not just ankle-deep at the shoreline.

A lot of ifs.

With no other ideas, I start making tiny motions with my bound hands, delicately abrading the rope against the stone.

"Anyway, my point is," Kalad says, "she laid the foundations for more challenging work, whatever its nature. Extractions, recoveries—and, of course, digs. The Endless have always been a source of fascination to the Pilgrims, but her work allowed us to begin to move away from their *mythology* to their *reality*. At first, like everyone else, I thought this a tremendous thing."

His face lights up.

"We learnt more about the Endless in five years than we'd learnt in the last fifty. That their empire spanned a far greater extent of the galaxy than we'd ever imagined. That their understanding of physics was more akin to magic than science. That their lifespans stretched many times our own. Every discovery made them more wondrous, more exalted in our eyes. Until Samark."

Samark. Where have I heard that?

"Ah, I see you recognize the name."

I remember. A dark day in our history. Five cavers lost on a harsh, windswept world where some primitive civilization scraped an unremarkable existence in the depths.

A waste of life.

The memory chills me.

The Horizon's Cavemaster perished that day too.

I'd forgotten her name.

Now I knew it again.

Anya Poora.

"You?"

Kalad grits his teeth. "Do you know what we learnt about the Endless on Samark?"

I don't understand.

Samark had nothing to do with the Endless. It was a backwater world where the intelligent life only survived by scrabbling around in underground grottos.

I shake my head, snatching another glance at the drop.

"That's right!" Kalad cries. "Nothing! We learnt nothing about the Endless. Because of my actions."

I scratch my fingernails across the stone. I realize nothing I can say or do will deviate Kalad from his intention to kill me. If I'm going to get out of this, I need to escape. Even in my terror, though, I'm curious.

What did you learn on that world?

I feel sick asking…

"You killed five of your own," I whisper, wrists aching. "Not just Pilgrims, but cavers. Why?"

He looks to one side, remembering.

"Samark wasn't an Endless world, but they'd been there. Not that we could tell at first. We knew there were subsurface structures, but when we got beneath that hellish landscape all we found were primitive cave systems. Rudimentary tools, crude habitations, rough cave art. We named them the Hata. If it wasn't for the dust storms battering the surface we would've probably left with a few token artifacts, chalked it up as another minor civilization lost to history.

"But we didn't. We had time to explore deeper. And we found something gruesome, something that… demanded an explanation. You see, deep beneath the Hata's cave systems, far below any place they'd have any sound reason to go—no springs, no life, a barely breathable atmosphere—we found a mass grave, dozens upon dozens, if not hundreds of their dead. Well, not a mass grave. They weren't laid out, they weren't heaped upon one another, just their individual bones strung along a deep, descending passage that led nowhere, as if somebody had clicked their fingers and they'd all just died."

I shudder at the grisly image.

"We realized they'd been mining: crude pickaxes and hammers and the like were with the remains. The walls of the passage still had the residue of glittering ore. It still didn't explain why they'd all died *there*. We imagined they might've suffocated, maybe suffered a terrible explosion, but it didn't sit right.

"And then one of us, I can't remember who, unearthed something lodged into one of their skulls. It looked like a scuffed coin, which was strange because everything we'd seen about them so far suggested they had no need of any monetary systems. Up closer though, we saw these intricate lines etched the surface, and tiny, perfectly arrayed spines angled out from one side of the object."

My stomach drops. "Endless tech."

"Indeed," Kalad replies, empty-eyed, staring into the past. "Not that we knew it then. All we knew was that the Hata must've been enslaved, these exquisitely engineered devices driven into their heads, programmed to mindlessly excavate this precious ore for unknown masters. It was only when we found the mural, discovered the full horror of the Endless' involvement, recorded in stark, bone-chilling paintings like a child would draw, that we could be sure."

I'm careful with my words, not wanting to anger him, still wanting to understand. "That must've been... painful."

"It was. All of us were stunned, horrified, especially Poora. She'd always had an inner fire from her faith in the Endless. We all walked the length of that mural, came to our knees, shattered at the final painting. Our majestic, enlightened, benevolent Endless—our guiding lights—had committed something so foul, so evil. Some of us cried, others cursed.

"All of us were changed."

Kalad bites his lip, in turmoil inside.

"We argued about what we should do, of course."

Forty-odd years he's held this truth, forty years of being haunted by what he did, and now he gets a chance to confess.

"We knew," he says, "that if we brought this knowledge back to our brothers and sisters then the Pilgrim's reverence of the Endless would be shattered. Poora imagined that the blow would've been devastating, that as we lost our faith, we'd lose our way too. And maybe she'd have been right. You've got to remember, this was in the early years of the exodus. The worship of the Endless brought us together more than anything else, gave us belief that we could survive beyond Raia."

Kalad meets my gaze. "Poora wanted these revelations to stay buried, for us to vow to never speak of what we'd seen that day."

Behind my back, I feel my rope bindings weakening, but my wrists ache and my forearms burn.

"Not everyone agreed though," I say, gritting my teeth.

"No," he replies. "And I was among them—at least to begin with. We argued that nobody should be deceived as to the nature of the gods they worshipped, that knowing the truth was always better than laboring under a falsehood. We thought we Pilgrims would be resilient to the truth, that we'd forge a new, stronger conception of ourselves and our place in the galaxy.

"So, while we waited for the storms to abate, we found ourselves in deadlock. Whatever we decided, we all needed to agree on it, and to act as one unified voice. Everyone needed to make peace with whatever choice we made. We all understood that, either way, the choice would have huge consequences, so after hours of debate we took some time for reflection—alone.

"Things might've been different if we'd all come to agreement sooner, but we didn't, and so we went our own ways to think things over in the dark. And then Karuba discovered something more."

Kalad swallows. "Karuba was the youngest member of that expedition, born into a devout family around the time of the exodus. Free from the prying eyes of the Raian authorities, some Pilgrims' devotions became... all-consuming. In some believers' eyes, the Endless were perfect beings, incapable of sin, and any word spoken against them was heresy. Karuba grew up in such a family."

Kalad sighs. "The revelations hit him hard." He's silent for a moment.

"Even now," he continues, "I can still recall the confusion in his eyes. His world had been rocked, and he didn't know which way to turn. Should we be heralds of the truth or guardians of the lie? And then he found something. 'Come, come,' he cried. 'Cavemaster Poora, Kalad, everyone!' We came back together, followed him through the Hata's twisting tunnels, Karuba refusing to answer any questions as we followed. Over the centuries, millennia even, that the Hata had lived in these systems, they'd created paths—cut rough steps or handholds, widened passages, cleared rockfall—

so traversal through the caves was fast, but then Karuba had us squeezing through a cleft in a vast wall of rock.

"I remember edging through that fissure, suddenly feeling a change in the stone—it became smoother, colder, and when I cast my light on the surface it had a perfect metallic sheen, marked with geometric etchings that couldn't be natural. And then suddenly we were inside this artificial space, a long-dead crypt of the Endless. Even in the darkness, the place exuded an elegance, a philosophy, but most of all *control*. There was a portal-shaped threshold made of a viscous, reflective substance, but nothing we tried then or later could get us further into the facility. The scale and proportion of the space and its... furnishings—I call them 'furnishings', but none of us understood what they were—suggested tall, slim beings. We felt as if we trespassed on hallowed ground. Nothing in that room was comprehensible to us—except for one thing."

"What?" I ask, not wanting him to stop.

I sense Kalad is coming to the end of his tale, and I snatch another glance at the chasm and the Dust lake beyond.

Bad move.

The drop seems bigger than ever.

My stomach tightens.

I shouldn't look, just leap...

"A helmet."

"A helmet?"

"Well, more than a helmet. Karuba brandished it, held it aloft. He had that zealous look in his eyes. That's when the truth dawned on me: its function wasn't difficult to ascertain. Karuba yelled, 'An *Endless* artifact! One of the foretold gifts that will light our path to salvation!'"

I can picture Karuba's fanaticism, almost hear his words.

"The helmet—it was a device to be placed over the head of a Hata, wasn't it?"

Kalad nods, his face haunted. "With their elongated skulls, we could all tell straight away."

"It was an... imprinter?"

"We called it an embedder."

"They must've been terrified."

"Indeed." Kalad shakes his head. "That day I realized the Endless weren't gods to be worshipped—they were monsters to be buried."

"But the others, they didn't share your thinking?"

"Some did. Poora's faith was broken. And she wasn't alone. Others though? Karuba, for example. The artifact only deepened his belief in the Endless. He kept speaking of prophecies and destinies, the unknowable minds of gods and how this relic could transform our fortunes. They began talking about documenting everything, preparing inventories to bring back to the Horizon. I saw then where this path led. And I realized what I had to do."

I feel another wave of nausea.

"There must've been another way!"

"There wasn't!" Kalad shouts, his voice cracking. "Even if I'd destroyed the device, prevented it from being brought back to the Horizon, prevented any reverse-engineering, the idea would've been seeded. The Endless aren't just myths and legends, aren't just articles of faith, aren't just half-whispered glories from a galaxy-spanning empire long turned to dust. The Endless are still here, in their tools, in their ancient places, most of all, in their weapons. We'd never walked in their halls before, never held such diabolical relics in our hands. Our will to survive would have eventually trumped any moral considerations. We would've unleashed horrors.

"And if not us, then someone else." Kalad hangs his head. "The only hope was to kill the notion before it could infect more minds, preserve the received wisdom that the Endless were a long dead civilization lost to history."

He looks me square in the eyes again.

"After making preparations, I gathered the entire party in the deepest part of the system—the mass grave we'd discovered earlier—under the pretext of cataloging everything we found there. There was an excitement in the group, a sense they were going to make history, fundamentally change the Pilgrims' conceptions of the Endless."

I don't want to picture this scene.

"Please, you don't need—"

"I remember the stale air, the slight trace of something acrid in that passage, some remnant of the Hata's decomposition, maybe. I feared I might not go through with it if I gave them an explanation... or maybe I was just too cowardly, but in either case, I only whispered the words 'I'm sorry' to myself, and walked away." Kalad trembles, his eyes misting up. "I saw Karuba talking to Poora, trying to reassure her. Then I detonated the charges."

I feel numb, like this isn't real, like it might be a dream.

It isn't though.

A tear rolls down Kalad's cheek.

"The cave-in worked. Brought tons and tons of rock down on their heads and sealed them away forever. I like to think none of them suffered, that they died instantly. The most difficult part was making sure nothing remained of what we'd discovered." He rubs away the lone tear with the ball of his hand. "I shouldn't have worried."

"Everyone trusted me, swiftly accepted there was nothing they could do. They thought my survivor's guilt must've been a heavy burden, and they wanted nothing more than to leave that place of death behind as fast as they could. The guilt was real. But not in the way they imagined. I've always regretted that they never knew why they'd died."

Courage, give me courage…

"Tens of thousands of years have passed since the Endless disappeared, Sewa," Kalad continues, voice rising, more mechanical, like he's delivering something rehearsed. "Most of their cities, their vessels, their knowledge has gone, erased away by the sands of time, yet in the deep places, in the quiet places, remnants of their civilization remain. Some think the Endless left the galaxy, sights set on new realms, others that they ascended into planes of existence beyond mortal comprehension.

"I don't think either is true. I think their civil war spiraled out of control. I think they forged weapons of such destructive power that all their myriad possible futures collapsed into one single inevitable outcome: self-annihilation.

"The truth is, Sewa," he says, "our obsession with the Endless will not only be our downfall, it will be the downfall of the galaxy." He gives a small nod. "I will honor your name, tell them of your bravery. Be assured of that."

He gets up from the outcrop, legs stiff, and I give one last jolting push down, desperate. The last thread of the rope that's held me all this time snaps with a twang.

I spring to my feet, keeping low, ready to move.

"Why fight the inevitable, Sewa?"

I swipe up a rock, feint to charge at him. He braces for impact, but before I reach him I turn on my heels, and sprint for the edge as hard as I can.

This is insane…

I block everything out, keep my eyes fixed on the far side of the cavern, as my feet pound the stone.

No looking down!

The edge comes up fast. Not relenting, I plant my foot on the brink, push off, arms windmilling, legs pedaling, my fate in gravity's hands. I know I'm screaming, even if I'm not really hearing it, too caught up in a blur of motion, and the dazzling lake of Dust. Oba always loves to tell me that when you're falling, really you're weightless, and the only thing you need to worry about is the impact—

I'm gonna make it! I'm gonna make it!

Elation floods me as I hit rock, but before I can even give a celebratory cry, something crunches in my foot and a poker-hot lance of pain sees my scream transformed...

Lying splayed out, I grit my teeth, my right ankle feeling on fire, and look. My foot's sticking at an angle it has no anatomical right to be pointing. Adrenalin courses through me, giving me a chemical high, but my breaths still come in short piston-like gasps. The pain is intense.

Fighting it, I try to lever myself up onto my working leg, but it's too much, and I slump back to the stone.

"Your courage is formidable, Sewa," Kalad says, "though, ultimately, futile. You'll need a splint."

I glance back to see him standing on the edge of the cliff.

"If you're lucky you might find some shards of rock that'll do the trick, perhaps even some hardy weeds you can use as binding. Of course, climbing with such an injury, without equipment too, will be beyond you. While you scrabble around for an accessible path you'll get cold, hungry, probably feverish."

Shut up, shut up...

I turn back, seeking something... anything. The lake twinkles, its sparkling shoreline only a hand-span away. Nails digging into the warm stone, I drag myself forward, every single movement making me flinch with excruciating pain. Closer now, I let my fingers play in the golden fluid, the sensation not unlike pins and needles.

"It'll take you days to reach the surface—if you reach the surface—and by the time you get there, we'll be long gone."

Shut up! Shut up!

"So long, Sewa. Thank you." His voice is getting fainter, and I glance up to see only the weakening glow of his headlamp on the cavern walls. "Thank you for saving me the burden."

"You're still a—" I crash a fist into the lake edge, voice rising to a bloodcurdling scream "—murderer!"

The word comes out as more of a shriek than anything intelligible, another sharp jolt of pain sending me flailing. I empty my lungs with a long, primal scream, like I'm trying to expel all the anguish and horror in one vocal blast.

The effort leaves me breathless, wincing, curling up ready for the earth to swallow me. Hasn't it already? Soon I will cry. But first the enormity of the silence presses on me, heavier even than all the stone above my head.

Seeeeeee-waaaaa…

My eyes blink open. Did I imagine that?

Turning, I look up, follow a line of the cavern ceiling that disappears into darkness. I prick my ears, hold my breath…

"Seeeee-waaaaa!"

Argo!

He's faint, barely audible, but there's no mistaking his voice. Before I can cry out his name though, I hear a sudden patter of footsteps, a rush of wind—

Kalad slams into me, his whole weight crashing down on my small frame, his momentum rag-dolling my head into the stone. There'll be pain—awful, unbearable pain—I know that, but that'll have to wait…

Darkness descends.

Get up, Sewa…

I wake, panicking, trying to breathe, but no air reaches my lungs. A firm force presses the back of my head, and a heavy weight pins my body. I push against the pressure, trying to raise my head, but it's no good…

Kalad.

He's drowning me, his splayed hand clutching my skull, pushing me down into the lakebed. I struggle, desperate, try to shake him off even though my ribs and shoulder and arms explode with pain. I manage to snatch some air, but he hauls me further into the lake where it's deeper and presses down anew.

"Argo?"

Through the fluid, Kalad's bellowing voice sounds distorted. I can feel his speech through the tremor of his frame as he talks.

"That you?"

If Argo replies, I cannot hear his words.

I stop struggling, go limp, pretending…

"Sewa fell," Kalad shouts. "She's gone. No chance she'd survive the drop."

His lie enrages me, but I suppress the urge to flex and try to fling him off. I feel his grip relaxing.

Wait for it…

"No, don't come down!" Kalad cries, unnerved. "I need you elsewhere. I'll retrieve what I can."

Argo, please Argo. Don't believe his lies.

Gathering my strength, I push back with all my might, thrashing my legs. Kalad holds firm. I can't get any air, can't scream. My breath is spent. I cannot hold it any longer. The fluid surges inside. I can feel it coursing through me, filling my lungs.

"Trust me, I'd rather do this alone."

His words are getting quieter, like he's somewhere else. I think I hear something about the Empire being here. Even if I wanted to struggle I think I'd be too weak. Strangely, the panic is ebbing away, replaced by a deep relaxing feeling…

Kalad's voice is just burbling sounds now.

I feel myself losing myself.

My journey is ending.

A great warmth is washing over me, through me…

It is not unpleasant.

The last thing I remember are Mother and Father, young, happy, and full of love, cradling my newborn sister, Rina.

SIXTEEN

⊖⌐Ⱶᴋᴇᴇᴢ

Falling.

At least, the sensation of falling. No light to discern the downwards course, but a sense of weightlessness, a feeling the rest of the universe is moving past.

Moving out of reach.

Like sinking in a dark, viscous lake.

Is this death?

The waters darken, turn a blacker pitch.

Fear comes.

Yet, the velvet darkness reveals too. Motes of light so fine, so delicate they're almost invisible. They flit about at a distance, drifting upwards from this vantage, disinterested in the falling thing in their midst.

Some are curious though.

A few stop, unmoving as the thing falls past, while others seem to follow my path, gliding downwards before breaking away. Soon they come nearer, spiraling around in helical paths, their translucent structure shimmering in all its wondrous complexity. They dart so close the light is blinding.

And nourishing. And inviting.

A yearning stirs.

Deep and primitive.

Nothing is more vital.

Help.

A frenzy assails the nearest motes, quivering and pulsing with unknown energies. The mania spreads. More and more motes approach, bolder and bolder, the light getting brighter and brighter, a halo of white surrounding the falling thing.

Now they are both without *and* within.
Running wild, exploring, scrutinizing.
Shock... but not fear.
Soon acceptance.
Then serenity.
Like being with the ones you love.
All is light.
Cleansing, rejuvenating, illuminating—

I come round on a stony shore, gasping for breath.

Face down, cold waters lap against my weak limbs. Struggling, I lift my head, breathe. The sweetest thing, yet the air is musty, rancid.

With a great effort, I turn myself over, muscles burning.

I take a great lungful of air, greedy, feel the reviving effects spread through my stiff body. Then I tense, expecting him. I lift exhausted arms, ready to ward him off, but no blows come.

I open my eyes.

The cavern ceiling is lost in the darkness, but in the shimmering light of the water I can see the surface of the lake, the cliff from where I jumped.

Everything is still, silent.

Quiet as I can, I get to my knees, scanning. I retch, metallic-tasting waters leaving a bad taste in my mouth. I feel dog-tired but there's something else.

I feel different. I feel changed.

You almost died. Of course you feel different.

How long was I out? It can't have been long.

I tense again, straining my ears.

Kalad can't be far. Nor Argo.

I hear nothing, though.

No footfalls, no caving sounds, no voices.

Only the gentle susurration of the lapping waters.

A coldness assails me, more than that warranted by the chilly waters of the lake. They've gone. Somehow I know it deep in my bones. And I know something much more terrible too.

No, don't say it.

"Arg—"

My shout ends in a coughing fit, dirty water coming up, a burning feeling in my throat. I thump my chest, the feeling deadening.

"Argo!!" I slap my hands against the water, knowing he cannot hear me, knowing he is long gone. "Argo!! Come back! Please!"

No answer, not even an inkling of life.

For eons nothing has disturbed the silence here. Only a violent aberration to be erased, forgotten.

Now the silence is restored.

It is the easiest thing for this place.

No, don't say it.

I get up, pace along the shoreline, clapping my arms, trying to invigorate myself, trying to shake off this deep feeling of despondency.

"Kalad?"

I creep to the edge of the chasm that separates the lake from the cliff. A subtle breeze drifts past, reeking of the damp, algae, mineral ores. I'm surprised I can discern the different smells. The gap is immense, the drop greater still. I can't believe I made that jump. Then I remember the landing, the lance of white-hot pain—

How in the world?!

My ankle seems fine. I lift my heel, use the ball of my foot to work the ankle in small circular motions. No pain, no stiffness, not even a hint of soreness.

Dust.

There's no other explanation.

I gaze back at the shimmering waters. They look placid, but I'm not fooled. Not any longer. Be wary. Those motes can do far more than just power starship engines, more than just heal a broken ankle... I should know... I kick out in the shallows, creating an arc of fine spray.

"Kalad?" I repeat, louder.

The stone, the waters, the darkness—all are indifferent. I could be in a tomb. The silence is suffocating.

"You there, Kalad?" Speaking his name makes me feel defiled, so I imagine him listening while I taunt him. "You screwed up, old man! I didn't die, Kalad! I'm still alive!"

Except...

"Someone? Anyone?" I holler. "Is anyone there?"

The echoes of my cries fall to silence, as if my words were swallowed by something ancient, something immense that resides in the dark depths. Time moves differently here, deep in the subterranean realm. The usual markers are absent. No track of the sun. No wheeling of the stars. No shifting tides, no dawn choruses, no changing skies as the sun waxes and wanes.

How long was I out?

A sudden urge to climb assails me.

They might not be far ahead.

The next cavern. Maybe the one after.

I don't want to be alone.

I skirt the shore, seeking a starting point, ignoring the nagging voice telling me without ropes, without equipment, only a fool—or one with a death wish—would be so bold. It's not hard to pay no heed though.

Another thought gnaws at me, far more persistent.

A thought that says it doesn't matter whether they're still here or not. Why? Because I'm alone whether I find them or not. Because I could be back in the very heart of the Horizon, and I'd still be in absolute, abject isolation. Why? Because—

You died.

I stop, double-up, breathless again.

Shut up.

You died and something vital died too.

Shut up!

You died and now you feel nothing.

Shut up!!!

You're a ghoul, you're a zombie, you're an undead. Nothing can change that. I want to cry, but how can you cry when you're dead inside?

How can you live if you've already died?

Numb, I focus my energies on the climb.

You'll feel different when you're away from this place.

And there's another reason I should reach the surface as fast as I can: Kalad. He must be exposed as the traitor.

Word must reach Overseer Liandra. It must.

Who knows what he might plot should he get back to the Horizon with his secret intact?

I wade the periphery of the lake, examining the cavern's walls, focusing. A slick rock face, wet from the trickle of chilly waters wouldn't usually be my first choice, but something tells me this is the fastest route upwards. Despite my despondency, I feel alive to the cave system, its ebbs and flows, its rhythms. For the first time that I can remember, likening the system to a living organism doesn't feel so far-fetched. I plant a confident first step against the stone, push off.

The surface is slippery, but at every juncture, my fingertips find the right hold, my body the right balance, so I needn't strain or put undue weight on any single muscle. Rather than ascending straight up as I usually do, I zig-zag up the wall, happy to move horizontally, even downwards, to thread the optimum path. Even with the circuitous course, I feel like I'm climbing fast, and within a short time I find myself atop a ledge near the cavern's roof.

That was weird.

My breathing is calm, not quite resting pace, but still barely showing any sign of exertion, and when I go to clench my hands out of habit, shake out the lactic acid, I find no tension in my fingers or forearms.

This is really weird.

Normally even a short vertical climb would have some impact, require some short spell of rest, but here and now, I find myself refreshed and ready to go again straight away.

I peer down over the ledge, gaze over the tranquil, illuminating waters, the motes of Dust sparkling like precious stones, no sense of vertigo despite the drop. As I survey the site where my life was ended—or nearly ended—I can't shake the feeling of horror, but I'm disturbed to discover another very different emotion among the pain.

A sense of peace, perhaps even a sense of kinship.

Like these waters witnessed the act.

Like they know.

And they will always know.

I close my eyes, push away the terror.

In the darkness, the system feels more alive than ever. Below, I can hear the rustle of the lake. Elsewhere I hear an orchestra of winds, the low roar of tumbling waters, even the occasional groan of the rock. Smells come to me in a rich tapestry that I can pick apart with ease. Fetid waters, bat guano, breezes clipped with the taste of the tenacious, sage-like plants that grow on the surface, the remnants of the passage of humans.

Somehow, I know this system.

I'm alone, far in its depths, but I know it.

I turn back to the rock and climb again.

Sometime later I'm hauling myself out of the subterranean realm, up onto a hard scrub landscape under a shining vault of stars. The despair that's tracked me all the way up isn't far behind. Even though it's dark, only starlight for illumination, my eyes take a few moments to acclimate. For most of the ascent I climbed in pitch blackness, relying on my other senses to guide the way. Amazing what the mind can discern by sound, smell, and touch when the eyes are denied.

I lever myself down onto an outcrop, dizzy.

I breathe in, breathe out, muscles afire. The night is warm, the caramel scent of the brush lacing the air.

Rina would find it beautiful.

I can scarcely believe I've made the climb in one unbroken stint, only pausing to take water from a tumbling cataract or listen to the ceaseless whispers of the cave. Even though measuring time in the depths is a fool's errand, I'd judge my ascent took no longer than half-a-day, three-quarters tops.

Crazy fast.

And fatigue? Exhaustion? Not a hint, though now, sitting here under the stars, I feel absolutely drained.

No time to think what this all means.

I must search.

Now. They might still be here.

I get up, orienting myself.

My route out eventually led to the same paths we'd descended as a team, the metal bolts in the rock like pebbles marking a forest trail, so I know this is where we entered. That means the shuttle is a few klicks to the west in a dry-bedded ravine.

If they haven't left yet.

Locating a familiar twin-peaked hillock on the dark horizon, I set off at a light run. The despair is close. During the climb I managed to keep it at arm's length, finding solace in the intricacies of the cave, but here, exposed on this barren landscape, it is closer than ever.

I don't want to be alone.

I don't want to be left behind.

Most of all, I don't want to wait any longer to discover whether this gaping emptiness will go away.

Breathing hard, calves burning, I reach the ravine, skip down a course of boulders. A thin trickle of water winds along the riverbed, the first of the monsoon rains already arrived. I can smell dissolved minerals, the faint, acrid smell of fuel...

Above, the stars are a thin slash in the darkness, widening as I follow the canyon downstream, careful not to twist an ankle on the rocky debris. Soon the channel is wide enough for the shuttle, but I see no sign of the craft, no sign of any Pilgrims.

Another bend.

A little further.

I stop dead.

Underfoot, narrow, blackened marks scorch the stone. Looking across I spy a parallel slash not ten paces away. I already know what it means, already feel the sinking feeling, but I brush my fingertips across the sooty blemish anyway, bring them to my tongue. The taste of partially-burnt ion-engine fuel is unmistakable.

I must've experienced that tang a hundred times, but no memories come to me, my mind empty.

I am marooned.

I am alone.

Utterly spent, I lay down and sleep.

SEVENTEEN

⊖ᴇⴽᴇⴽⴿᴇᴇⴽ

"Wake up."

Coming round, I force my eyes open, the landscape of brush and stone slowly coming into focus, my dream shattering. *Did I hear that?* I'm lying on my side, the world tilted ninety degrees, half of my face pressed against the gritty rock. A bloated sun caresses the horizon, the skies colored a deep copper.

No sign of life beyond the scrub.

I remember.

I was left for dead.

And now I'm stranded.

And hearing things too.

I close my eyes tight, wanting to forget.

My body's stiff, back aching, every movement provoking twinges of pain, so I remain still, unmoving. My stomach rumbles.

What do I even eat—

"Come on, wake up!"

The voice is harsh, guttural—and very real.

Quick as a flash, I twist round, scrabble backwards.

A wide bulbous head, mottled cream and brown, looms over me, the lower part composed of half a dozen tendrils that pinch together to form a rudimentary mouth and nostrils. Their eyes, two perfect circles with horizontal slits that glow with a faint golden light, occupy the margins of their face, and beneath their tendrils, artificial linkages come together, acting like a clasp on a billowing cloak.

I scream.

Several suckered tentacles rise up from the folds of the cloak, undulating, their tips pointed to the skies.

"You're wasting your breath screaming."

Fast as I can, I crab-walk backwards, palms scraping against rock. *Something familiar in that voice…*

"S-S-Stay away from me!" I stutter, terrified.

"Stay away from you?" the alien asks in that jarring voice, gliding closer. "Stay away from you?! I don't think you want that."

One tentacle flicks backwards, pointing.

Beyond the alien I spy a spacecraft on the riverbed. The shape and livery make its origin clear as day. United Empire.

Comprehension dawns.

I know who you are. You're Zarva Rachkov.

Alien commander of the UE fleet.

I glance around, orienting myself, scanning the low sides of the riverbed canyon, the shadows long. Smells of the brush drift on a light breeze, and I can hear the distant howl of some wild animal. I can't see any other Empire forces.

Night is falling. I must've slept all day.

If I can make it to the cave entrance—

"I'm not with them anymore."

My gaze snaps back to the alien.

A Niris. Cephalopod species.

"With who?" I ask, playing dumb.

I wonder how fast a Niris can run.

"The Empire." The Niris keeps their distance. "Irreconcilable differences. We had to part ways."

Yeah, I'm sure it was all very amicable.

I don't know whether the Niris is telling the truth, but I do know that this creature standing before me, Zarva Rachkov, led the hunt for the only home I've ever known. Hunted us for two long, hard years, oversaw the destruction of the *Dawn Skies*. Most of all they were responsible for the deaths of hundreds of my people.

The Niris can go to hell, whatever their story.

I stand up, brush off the grit. I'm surprised I don't feel more afraid. Maybe that comes with being dead inside.

"You can tell your men to stop hiding."

"I don't have any men," Rachkov says, exasperated, throwing up a couple of limbs. "I told you. My days with the United Empire are over. I'm on my own now."

"Then what are you doing here?"

I scan the ravine's skyline, looking for tell-tale signs of Empire forces, but the craggy line of stone is still, no glint of scopes or flashes of color. The waning light paints one side a deep burnished flame, the other a bruised purple.

"We don't have time for this," Rachkov replies. "The Empire are coming. They might already be in-system."

"For Pilgrims, the Empire are always coming."

Rachkov nods. "Touché."

I wait, giving the Niris a chance to speak. They glance back at their thickset, squatting spacecraft, then up at the darkening skies. With slow, deliberate movements, they edge a little closer.

"I will tell you everything," they say. "Just... once we're safely away from this world."

"Even if what you say's true," I say suddenly angry, "what makes you think I want to spend one single moment more in your company? Don't you understand?" I get up close, unblinking as I stare at its slit-like eyes, its pungent, briny scent strong. "I despise you."

I spin, trudge away.

"That's why I want to help."

I stop, turn back. "What?"

"I want to right my wrongs," Rachkov says. "I want to atone for my sins. That begins with the Pilgrims. That begins with you—if you'll let me."

What do I care for your sins, Niris?

"Not interested."

I set off again, navigating over the rock-strewn riverbed, vaguely heading back towards the cave system entrance.

"They left you behind, didn't they?" Rachkov cries. "No one's coming back for you."

I ignore the words.

"Maybe you'll elude the Empire patrols, but you won't survive this world," the Niris shouts. "And if you do, what kind of life would you live? You'll become more animal than person."

Rachkov isn't wrong.

The world is deserted. No means of flagging down a passing interstellar vessel, no realistic hope of a chance encounter to get off-world. I'd likely live out my days scavenging, foraging, caving, my home some dank subterranean hollow.

Maybe that's fitting.

I'd cave to my heart's delight, master this strange new power that pulses inside, but Kalad? Kalad would go free. The Horizon would be at his mercy. Maybe all Pilgrims.

How can I take Rachkov at their word though?

Reluctantly, I stop, turn around.

"Why should I trust you?"

My voice echoes off the stony walls of the canyon.

Rachkov's limbs undulate in unnerving fashion before they answer. "You can trust me," they say, "because we share a deep bond, you and I."

I laugh. "I don't think—"

"I saw it in your eyes, Pilgrim," Rachkov cries. "Believe me, I was shocked, but I couldn't deny it. How it happened to you, I have no idea. But like me, you are touched by Dust."

I go very still.

I feel exposed... ashamed...

And, strangely, thankful.

Maybe I'm not alone.

Rachkov glides over.

"Call me Zarva." They gaze at me intensely, no evasion in their slit-like eyes. "I want you to know, I never gave any orders to kill."

I give a small nod. "I'm Sewa."

With no time to waste, Rachkov leads me back along the boulder-strewn riverbed, commands their craft's entry ramp to open before we've even reached the vessel. A moment later, we're inside the dim, cramped interior, the light dimming further as the entry ramp retracts, the scent of brush and stone eclipsed by smells of the engine and the ocean.

I hope I'm not making a terrible mistake.

Rachkov schleps onwards into the cockpit, tentacles flicking out to the sides of the narrow bay, while the entry ramp seals closed with a reverberating *thunk*. Strangely, there are few signs of Empire military in the craft's design. I later learn the Niris won the vessel in a wager with a Hissho mercenary on Raia. Everything feels claustrophobic. Outside the vessel hinted at spaciousness, but inside I can see near every available space has been given over to ultra-dynamic engineering concerns.

Maybe it's a good thing.

Fast and agile might be exactly what we need.

If this isn't a trap.

Rachkov powers up the craft, engines spinning with a reassuring hum as I arrive in the cockpit. As I sit down in the co-pilot seat the Niris gets us airborne with a sudden lurch skywards.

"Let's get on the dark side," Rachkov says, keeping us close to the sandstone landscape, while turning the craft away from the waning sun. "If there are any Empire forces about, we'll be harder to spot when we break atmosphere."

Below, the barren terrain hurtles past, growing more shadowed as Rachkov ups the speed and we head for the world's nightside. I follow the line of a ridge that climbs away into the lower slopes of a giant mountain range to the north, the upper reaches blanketed with a cover of pure white. I imagine the first snows fell whole ages past, that there might be things buried in that tundra from another era.

Things that no one will know. Ever.

Even though it was terrifying at times, I'm glad I carry a small shard of this world's story.

Once deep in the nightside, the ground below near invisible, Rachkov starts our ascent. A swathe of luminous stars fill the cockpit windows, heady and liberating, but as we climb higher and higher I'm also beset by a feeling of melancholy.

I might have died here, but I was reborn too.

A new life infused with a strange animating spirit.

In a sense this is my birthplace.

And I'm leaving already, barely knowing it.

"Be ready for evasive maneuvers," Rachkov says, interrupting my thoughts. "We might need to move fast once we've broken cover."

I shake away my contemplations, turn to the rippling form of the Niris. Suckered limbs flick out, simultaneously interacting with flight controls, navigation, scanning instruments. Rachkov's piscine stench fills my nostrils.

It catches me watching, glances back.

"Regrets?"

I turn back to the starfield, a wave of self-loathing washing over me. *How did it come to this?*

Hitching my fate to this alien who'd happily been Zelevas's lapdog, pursued us across the stars, overseen the deaths of countless Pilgrims— even if they'd claimed to never themself given any orders to kill.

And smelt bad to boot.

Who cared about our bond of Dust?

"Plenty."

Once we've cleared the atmosphere, Rachkov kills the engines, and we glide across the interplanetary gulf. The system gate is less than a day away, orbiting one of the gas giant's smaller moons, but the Niris is wary of hidden Empire forces. During surveillance operations, they tell me, hunter fleets often station small strike teams on planetary bodies close to gates.

We'll watch for the watchers.

I imagine Empire soldiers deployed on that icy moon, instruments trained on the heavens, burning away the time with idle chatter and games of chance.

"Why?"

The Niris stirs, flexing a couple of limbs. "Why what?"

"Why did you leave? The Empire, I mean."

"Working for the Empire... it wasn't my finest hour." The Niris's tentacles glide back and forth. "Capture and repatriate. That was my mission. Nothing more. As soon as I learnt different, I got out."

"Very noble of you." I shake my head. "Capture and repatriate? The Empire wants to destroy us."

"I see that now." They sigh. "Zelevas played me. He painted the Pilgrims as impressionable, wayward children. Impulsive souls that needed to be brought back into the fold, given love and discipline."

"Love and discipline?" I ask, incredulous.

"You know, on Raia," the Niris continues, "Pilgrims aren't held in very high esteem. Worshippers of false gods, thieves who escaped into the night with Empire jewels. I thought Zelevas was generous when he vowed to repatriate your people."

"More fool you."

"I guess I heard what I wanted to hear."

We go quiet. Across the void, the swirling clouds of the gas giant look majestic, peaceful, but I know that is a fiction, that these are storms of incredible savagery.

We all do that though, don't we? Hear what we want to hear.

Wasn't it exactly the same with Ito's guilt?

We couldn't stomach the idea that the traitor might still be among us, so as soon as a plausible suspect was identified we chose to believe in their guilt. And the result?

Kalad remains free to strike again.

"I want to get back to the Horizon."

"All in good time," Rachkov replies, eyes peeled on the starscape. "First, let's get out of this system."

For the next few hours we coast onwards, Rachkov keeping the engine's output minimal, our energy signature close to imperceptible. The ice-riddled moon and its orbiting artificial companion slowly edge nearer, though the pair remain nothing more a shining speck to the naked eye. The gas giant, by contrast, gradually comes to dominate the entire right half of the cockpit window, its churning atmosphere crackling with green-tinged electrical storms.

We detect no sign of the Empire—until we do.

"Shit," Rachkov mutters, cycling down the engines.

I scan the celestial vista but can't see anything amiss.

"What is it?" I ask, glancing at the instrument deck, wondering if they've seen something there.

One of its tentacles whips out, points at our destination.

Now I see it.

The moon is a speck of brilliant white, clearly distinguishable from the background stars by its slight lateral motion, but now I'm looking closer, I can see it's accompanied by a golden light that is growing brighter and brighter.

I sigh. "The gate's cycling up."

"Visitors," Rachkov confirms.

"Empire?"

"Likely. Dead-end system. Who else could it be?" The Niris punches in more instructions, and I feel the thrum of other ship systems winding down. The lights go out, leaving us in shadows. "We'll have a better idea when they arrive."

The roiling skies of the gas giant loom large, still millions of klicks away, but still impressively commanding. Without the engines running, we're just another inert mass, a gravitational plaything of this sun and its planets.

I can almost feel the pull of the bloated world.

I wonder if we're on a collision course.

"What do we do?"

"Play dead."

"And hope they leave?"

The Niris nods.

We watch the golden light of the gate grow brighter, a brief supernova of brilliance, before it fades to black. Any ships that arrived are too small, too dim to discern by eye, but that doesn't stop my grim knot of unease.

They're here.

Beside me, the Niris stiffens, and I see their suckers tense.

If this is a ruse—if Zarva Rachkov is still UE Commander Rachkov, and I'm about to be handed over to Empire agents—then they're playing their part superbly.

"What would they do to you?"

"They would…" The tip of one of their tentacles weaves lazy circles as the Niris chooses their words. "They would bury me in the deepest, darkest hole they could find, somewhere in the hinterlands, somewhere hidden. Then they would get to work."

I picture Rachkov strung up in a dank cell.

"And me?"

"Execution if you're lucky."

"And if I'm unlucky?"

"They'll squeeze you for intel. And if you're really unlucky," Rachkov says, turning its bulbous head towards me, "if they discover that Dust courses through your veins, then you'll spend the rest of your miserable life being picked apart in an Empire lab, piece by tiny piece."

I shudder.

"But don't worry," Rachkov continues. "I can make sure they'll never take us alive."

I blink, comprehension dawning.

Marvelous.

I turn back to the starfield, so serene, so entrancing, no inkling of the threat coming our way. On the right, the gas giant looms larger, our curving course towards its heart, unmistakable. The swirling atmosphere might provide sanctuary from Empire eyes, but there'd swiftly come a point where we'd get trapped in its embrace, quickly crushed by unimaginable forces.

The heat is rising too.

Rachkov must've switched off the cooling systems, hiding another of the emission signatures, but leaving no defense against the unrelenting solar radiation. I wipe my brow, the back of my hand already slick with sweat.

At least that's familiar.

Sitting in this sweltering tomb, I half-wish Rachkov hadn't rescued me. I'd be stuck on that moon, but I'd be safe. Maybe someone else *would've* come along. Maybe I'd have come across a secret Endless installation, commandeered one of their ancient craft, still flawless, still functioning despite the ages.

Rina would be impressed.

But I don't want to think about her.

Not now. Not like this.

"Why did you come here?"

"I was looking for someone."

"Kalad." I shake my head. "A day earlier you might've crossed paths."

"So, you Pilgrims knew."

"Only me."

The Niris doesn't say anything, inviting me to say more. I twist in my seat, getting more comfortable, the leather already warm to the touch.

"We thought we'd already found the traitor," I say. "Thought they'd died in the hostilities." A memory of the slashed stone comes to me. "I discovered the truth back on that moon."

The Niris nods, gazing at the stars.

That's why you got left behind. Kalad was giving himself a head-start—before you could get word out."

I remember the Cavemaster's hands on my neck.

"He won't run," I say. "He thinks I'm dead."

Rachkov's eyes snap onto me, confused.

"Thinks?"

"He left me for dead…"

The Niris nods, fixes me with a sympathetic look. "The Dust saved you."

So they know.

I wonder if they suspect that Kalad tried to kill me, wonder if they know the type of man with whom they conspired. I don't want to give life to those thoughts, though. Instead, I'm about to ask Rachkov if they experienced something similar in their own Dust transformation, when they notice something in the starfield.

I squint, not seeing anything. "Something happening?"

"Gate's cycling up again."

Peering closer, I can just see the soft golden hues getting brighter. Niris must have great eyesight.

"They're leaving? Already?" I give a tentative smile. "That's good news, right?"

I glance at the fast-approaching gas giant, the faintest trace of the upper atmosphere gently trembling our vessel. Below, roiling clouds race across its skies, in thrall to tremendous winds.

We'd be pummeled in short order.

"Good and bad."

Despite the growing heat and the buffering atmosphere, the Niris makes no move to restart our dormant systems or resurrect the engines. Sweat coats my whole body, my suit increasingly uncomfortable.

And I'm used to the heat.

"Why?"

"We're nearly in the clear," Rachkov replies, "but we're not out of the woods yet."

"Meaning?"

"They're not really leaving yet. At least not the entire force," they say. "A common Empire trick. A small surveillance craft stays, while the rest exit. Anybody laying low who fires up their engines after the gate goes dark gives themselves away."

"So we have to wait for the gate to cycle up a second time before me move again?"

The Niris grunts an affirmative.

"The fact they left so soon though," they say, "means they don't consider this a priority system."

I wonder if the oven-like conditions are worse for the Niris. Their tentacles look dry, no moisture in their suckers.

I shiver with the heat. "Guess that's something."

As our vessel cuts deeper into the gas giant's atmosphere, the craft shakes with the buffering, sending my teeth on edge. Far below I spy a massive cyclone cloud formation. We're on an intercept course.

"Assuming we see out this episode," I shout, over the turbulence, "can you get me back to the Horizon?"

Rachkov glances at me, but doesn't answer, focusing on one of the consoles.

"For your sins," I add.

"That won't be easy."

"They need to know about Kalad."

Above the starfield is dimming, the deep blacks of the night sky lightening. Every breath is getting painful from the hot dry heat, like we're trapped in some twisted sauna. We're also getting faster, firmly in the gas giant's gravitational grip.

"They'll know," the Niris shouts. "In time."

"But—"

"I know Kalad. He'll lie low."

"Really?"

"Listen, Sewa," Rachkov says, turning, his whole frame shaking, "you don't want to blow the element of surprise. Kalad thinks you're dead. You need to keep it that way. We'll regroup—"

"Where? Where will we regroup?"

I scream the words to be heard over the tumult. Above, the stars are gone, lost in the grey skies. Ahead and below, I can see the ferocious winds spinning lightning-wracked cloud banks around the calm heart of the super-cyclone. Right now it seems our final destination won't be the Horizon, a safe world at the sector's edge, or even the Niris's home planet.

It will be the hungry maw of the vortex.

And sooner rather than later.

Come on, come on, come on...

Something flickers on telemetry, a signal in the blizzard of data. Rachkov's tentacle whips out, booting the engines.

"Hold tight!"

Before I can properly brace, I slam forward into the restraining harness, the straps hot as anything. Reverse thrusters, full power, like hitting the brakes. The vessel groans under the stress, the thrusters swiftly reorienting themselves to give us lift. Like a skipping stone, we glance off the ceiling of the super-cyclone, and start a hard trek out of the gas giant's gravity well.

"Alright!" Rachkov screams, tentacles thumping the cockpit's roof.

"I take it they left?"

"They did, indeed."

I give an enormous sigh of relief, sinking low into the chair, welcoming the noise of the coolant pumps as they funnel chilly air into the vessel's interior. Soon, we clear the gas giant's atmosphere, the starfield cold and bright. We won't be in Empire hands tonight, but the feeling of relief soon slips into an uneasy foreboding.

I don't know this Niris.

I don't know their game.

And these days, I'm not sure I know myself either.

All I know is that, with Kalad free, the Horizon's in danger.

"So, what now?"

"Now, we go to the Academy."

EIGHTEEN

Six days later we drop out of the slipways at the edge of a nondescript system that houses a broken, half-obliterated world named Harrow. Any passing fleets would swiftly conclude the smattering of barren, rocky worlds—one a gouged-out ruin of a planet—offered nothing, and would be on their way within the day. Little would they know that if they had peered a little closer at that still-smoldering world, and if they had possessed sufficiently advanced detection tech, they would've spied a very unusual structure orbiting that ruined planet.

The fabled Academy.

At least that's the story that the Niris peddles.

Gazing across the starscape, all I can see is a dull red supergiant sun that must've baked its resident worlds into dry, dead husks a billion years past.

I shake my head.

Is this place a detour or a dead end?

Rachkov's told me the Academy is, first and foremost, a refuge for the galaxy's Dust-enhanced, or *misfits* as the Niris likes to brand the likes of us. Founded by a Vodyani named Isyander St Shaiad, here the Dust-enhanced can find acceptance, fellowship… and eventually, *purpose*.

I don't like the sound of that.

I don't need a *new* purpose.

My purpose is clear.

Locate the Horizon and see Kalad taken down, without tipping him off to my still very much mortal, if altered, condition. And that's the rub.

Without help, my chances of finding the Horizon are a million to one shot, and even if I do luck out through some underground gossip, Kalad is likely to get wind of my existence before I'm halfway there.

What would he do if he discovered I am alive?

That's a question I want to keep hypothetical.

Rachkov assures me Kalad will not act in haste. Not his style. The shock of the Empire attack would've thrown him. Not to mention the fact he was almost exposed in the aftermath.

No, he'll lie low, the Niris insists, lick his wounds.

And only then will he scheme again.

Turns out they got to know each other well while they plotted the Horizon's downfall.

"We needed to trust each other," Rachkov told me a couple of days back. "Over the course of a year, we came to a deep understanding of one another, our foibles, our secrets. Most of all we needed to have faith we'd each fulfill our end of the bargain."

I couldn't believe they'd conspired for so long.

The truth dawned. Every caving expedition under the noses of a UE installation... no wonder Kalad had hung back on the surface while the rest of the team descended.

He was exchanging messages.

"And the bargain?" I asked.

"Kalad would give me the Horizon's location, and I'd ensure no casualties and safe passage to Raia."

"So you screwed up your end, huh?"

"Zelevas didn't keep his word," the Niris said. "That's why I'm here."

Knowing what I knew, I'd been reluctant to ask the next question, but I had to know what the Niris thought.

"Weren't you worried Kalad was setting a trap?"

"At first, yes. But I came to trust him. At any time I could've blown his cover. That was brave." Rachkov looked at me. "Kalad sincerely believed the Pilgrims would be better off back on their original world."

I studied the Niris for any sign of deception or concealment, but found nothing.

So Kalad never mentioned the Endless.

Made sense.

More than anything else, he wanted them to be forgotten. And getting the Pilgrims back on Raia was the only solution he could see that would bury the Endless, while ensuring his own people's survival—no matter how squalid that existence.

The religion would've been forbidden.

With utter prejudice.

Zelevas would've seen to that.

The Niris gave me a curious look. "You think he had other reasons?"

"No," I answered, calmly as I could muster.

End of conversation.

And so, for now, believing I have a little time, my best option is the Academy.

Regroup, recuperate, and refresh.

Hell, I might even learn something about the Dust inside me, learn how to wield it, learn how to feel *alive* again.

That's if any of this is true.

Well, at least I'll know the truth soon.

The last few days haven't been easy.

I can feel the subtle changes that the Dust exposure has brought to my every waking moment. Rachkov assures me I have been revitalized, my senses honed, my synapses sharpened, but most of the time all I feel is my mind racing.

I am left agitated and exhausted.

My sleeping hours are worse.

Often I dream of being back on the Horizon, hanging out with Oba, or shadowing Overseer Liandra. They are familiar, comforting presences but there's an edge to these dreams too, a darkness, and sooner or later I always notice Kalad lurking in the shadows. I find myself wandering alone in some corner of the arcology—in hydroponics or the archives or the contemplation gardens—and soon enough he strikes.

Every time, no matter how hard I fight, he ends up subduing me, pinning me down. Sometimes he presses a forearm over my neck, leaves me choking, gasping for air that never comes. Other times his rough slab-like hand smothers my mouth and nose, suffocating me a different way. Other times I squirm enough to snatch a breath, but then he reaches for something out of sight and crashes it against my head.

By the third blow darkness descends.

I come to sweating, disoriented, heart hammering.

For an instant, the euphoria of escape briefly eclipses the overwhelming terror, but the feeling swiftly fades, replaced by a clammy unease that I can't shake for the rest of the day.

Then the cycle repeats.

Yesterday, the Niris asked about my Dust exposure. I told them I fell during a descent, cracked my head, and landed unconscious in a Dust sump. I don't know why, but I want to keep the truth to myself. I feel shame, but for what reason I'm not sure. Perhaps, perversely, I want to protect Kalad's reputation.

Is he really a monster, given what he thinks?

Maybe he had no choice.

Maybe this is all my fault.

I asked the Niris how their own exposure happened, wondering if it was similarly traumatic. Rachkov told me that after the Niris homeworld came perilously close to ecological collapse, the species decided that they needed to explore the stars and discover other ocean worlds that could support Niris colonies. A galactic hedging of bets, so to speak. Despite Rachkov's supple mind, they'd grown up in a grubby backwater (literally, given Niris civilization was all underwater) and their prospects were limited, so they'd volunteered for one of the passenger berths to a distant planet.

Unaware of the slipways that bypassed relativity effects and cut journeys down from decades to days, the Niris vessel opted for a slower-than-light jaunt across the cosmos, its residents safely ensconced in cryo-sleep chambers, oblivious to the world. Edging up to a cruising speed of 95 percent light speed as the vessel exited the homeworld system, Rachkov had expected thirty years of local time to have passed by the time they arrived at their destination. Of course, time dilation would mean almost a century would've passed on the Niris homeworld, severing the vessel's occupants chronologically as well as spatially from everything they'd known, but the ship had barely made it beyond the home system's Kuiper belt when disaster struck.

Not that Rachkov knew it.

Sometime later, the Niris awoke on Hekim, the Sophon homeworld. Strange hallucinogenic effects pulsed through its distributed nervous system, bewildering it as much as its compound-eyed interlocutors.

"Dust?" I asked.

"Indeed," the Niris answered, tentacles stilled. "Although, I had no inkling of the substance then and the only logical explanation I could find was that I must be dreaming."

Turned out Rachkov was the only known survivor of the ship's fusion engine explosion, a freak, million-to-one event precipitated by its traversal through a Dust cloud. The saving grace—for Rachkov, at least—was that the very same Dust that had caused the rupture, had infiltrated its cryo-chamber and preserved the Niris's life.

Years later, as the light and energy of the eruption rippled outwards from its point of origin, a Sophon observation post noticed the hail of cosmic particles and dispatched a scavenger vessel to comb the site.

"They found little of worth, including myself," the Niris said, half-joking, "but the Sophons assure me that without the tragedy, the Niris would've remained off their radar. That day, for better or worse, the Niris joined the galactic stage."

"So, you could've gone home, then?"

"And be an outsider, an oddity on a world from which I'd marooned myself in time? No. As soon as I learnt of the Academy, that's the only place I wanted to go."

I stayed quiet, digesting the Niris's choice.

It's different for me, I thought. Rina, Mother, Oba—everyone I know and love. All out there somewhere, right now, my disappearance a painful splinter in their hearts. Not something that happened years past. Something that happened mere days ago. Something still happening.

And then there's Kalad...

"Does anyone ever come out... unscathed?" I asked.

Rachkov grunted, understanding my meaning.

"Nobody, not even the greatest minds of the Academy," the Niris replied, several limbs curling in elaborate arabesques as was their wont when thinking, "have learnt how to reliably expose someone to Dust. Every successful uplift is a cosmic accident, an event so rare that across all the worlds of all the stars, every time it happens it is called a miracle, a wonder, an act of a capricious deity. Unlike our fates, most exposed to Dust die small and terrible deaths... or become half-things driven frenzied or mad. And the ones that survive, intact? They're changed."

"Traumatic, then."

"Of course." The Niris gazed at the starscape. "Yet, often this trauma leads to growth, mastery, even enlightenment. Like the old adage, in order to truly build one must first destroy."

This is the part where I'm in pieces, then.

"Chin up! You live!" the Niris exclaimed, sensing my deflation. "And, more than that, very soon you'll be surrounded by your kind."

Now, as we glide by the bloody red light of Harrow's ancient star, I keep coming back to Rachkov's words.

Who are my kind?

Am I still a Pilgrim? Or am I something else?

I feel torn, lost somewhere between my past Pilgrim self and another identity that's primal, coalescing.

From my bunk, I gaze through my cramped cabin's viewing portal, seeking a first glimpse of the striking geometry of the Academy that I've only heard Rachkov describe.

No sign yet.

Whatever's coming, I'll be glad to get off this poky bucket. Cabin fever is real. Every day the urge to cave grows stronger. I yearn for cold stone, pitch-black drops, crawlspaces and vaulting galleries. Even a cliff face would suffice.

"Sewa."

The Niris stands serenely at the threshold.

I swivel, sit up. "Rachkov."

They want something.

"Not long now," they say.

I nod. "About time."

The Niris grunts.

"Coming back here," I say, "it must stir up a lot of old memories."

"So, so many," Rachkov replies, staring into space. "This is almost a homecoming."

"Why did you leave?"

They sigh. "A loss of faith."

"In the Academy's mission?"

"Yes, in the mission."

"Which is?"

"You'll learn the *purpose* soon enough." The Niris fixes me with a wistful look. "Isyander always sees to that."

I doubt I'll care, I think, but I keep my cynicism to myself.

"So, what happened?"

"I was sent to Raia. On a job."

I give a look. *A job?*

What did Rachkov do in their past life?

What kind of outfit is this Academy? A galaxy-wide assassin's guild? A legion of Dust-enhanced spies? A company of thieves? To what end?

"The job's not important."

I find it hard to imagine Zarva Rachkov having faith in anything beyond their own narrow self-interests.

"This Isyander must have some messiah-level charisma," I say, "sending all you Dust-enhanced across the stars to do his bidding."

The name sparks the Niris to life.

"Isyander? Where to start with Isyander?" The Niris's tentacles twist through the air. "Prophet? Despot? Fraud? You'll have to decide for yourself. What I can tell you is that there'd be no Academy without Isyander. And whatever you think of him, when you meet him, you cannot be in any doubt as to the strength of his convictions." Rachkov glances at the starscape, sighs. "Anyway, the job wasn't important. What was important was that I was on Raia."

"How so?"

"Things *converged*." Rachkov gives a rueful shake of the head. "My waning faith… and an opportunity."

I sneer the name. "Zelevas."

"Yes, Zelevas." The Niris fixes me with those golden slits. "Even among the exalted company you find at the Academy, it's not every day you gain an audience with the leader of a galactic superpower—a leader with real power. We made a deal."

You promised him Pilgrims, he gave you a way out.

"What do you want, Rachkov?"

"To put it plainly, I need your discretion."

The freelance gig for the Empire.

I say nothing, wanting him to say it.

"The Academy is somewhat monastic at times… I've been away from the fold for a long time…" Across the Niris's skin patches of mottled crimson bloom and contract, while their tentacles come close to entangling themselves. "They can be very judgmental…"

"Out with it, Rachkov."

"Isyander cannot know I worked for Zelevas," they say quietly. "I'd be made a pariah."

I nod, as if I'm just digesting the request.

"So, the story is you just went off-grid for a few years, wandered in the Raian wilderness, found peace with yourself?"

"Something like that."

"That could work."

"This is a weight off my mind. Thank you, Sewa." The Niris relaxes. "Now, let me give you some space before we arrive."

I can hardly believe Rachkov thinks I'd be so accommodating. Even if they were duped by Zelevas, it is not my place to squirrel away their dirty little secret. They might've not given the order, but Pilgrims died under their watch.

Pilgrims I knew and loved.

"Rachkov!"

They stop, back to me. "Yes?"

"What you did, you did." I grit my teeth, steeling myself. "But if anyone asks, I won't be party to your lies."

The Niris goes dead still, save for the tip of one tentacle that traces tight circles in the air.

Careful.

"There's a simple answer," I add. "We reverse course, forget the Academy. And you help me find the Horizon."

"Out of the question."

"Why?"

"Listen, Sewa." One of the Niris's limbs undulates close, its tip coming to rest on my shoulder. I feel its suckers flexing against the fabric of my suit. "Right now, you're vulnerable. Coming to terms with your new... physiology, learning of Kalad's betrayal, being severed from your arcology... you need stability. And guidance. The Academy, despite all its faults, can give you that."

The Niris whips away their tentacle, suckers popping.

"Besides, the Horizon is long gone."

"Rachkov, I'm grateful for everything you've done for me. Without you, I'd likely be dead, carrion for whatever goes for scavengers on that moon." I roll my shoulder, still feeling the imprint of the Niris's suckers. "But my place is with my people. Not this Academy." I wave at the starscape. "If you won't help me, drop me at a hub world, and I'll go on my way."

Streaks of magenta flash over the Niris's skin.

"That old life is gone!" Rachkov bellows, before reining in their anger. "Sewa, you are not who you were. Dust has changed you. Irrevocably, yet potentially magnificently."

I don't want to hear these words.

Stop, I want to say, but remain silent.

"You are a chrysalis emerging from its cocoon," the Niris says. "You need protection, instruction, counsel. Let the Academy help you."

Something isn't right.

Why is the Niris so adamant?

And then it comes to me.

"I'm your ticket back, aren't I?"

"Sewa—"

"Why didn't I see this sooner?" I shake my head. "This personal escort to the ivory towers of the Academy isn't for my benefit, is it? It's for you. Zarva Rachkov's always been a hustler, always will be a hustler, and always will be looking out for number one."

"It's true we have mutual interests—"

"You came to that moon, hoping to find Kalad, hoping to find—what? A way into a Pilgrim arcology? Another job? Who knows? But Kalad had gone, hadn't he? You found his landing site, and then you got lucky, found a young Pilgrim left behind, strangely exhausted. You clocked the Dust coursing through my veins immediately though. You recognize your own kind, don't you?"

"Sewa—"

"I wonder, would you have rescued me had I just been... ordinary?

Then I'd have been a liability instead of the opportunity that you found, wouldn't I?"

"I'm not a monster."

"Maybe," I concede. "But you hatched a plan, didn't you? Bring in a Dust-enhanced—that's quite a gift to return to the Academy with, isn't it? That'll help forgive, or at least overlook, your... extended absence."

The slash of Dust in the Niris's eyes brightens.

"Yet," I say, "the interlude with the Empire needed to be kept under wraps. The Academy frown on—"

"What marvels of logical deduction," the Niris interrupts, two limbs impersonating a slow clap, making a disconcerting schlepping noise. "I'm only surprised it took you this long." The sarcastic applause stops. "Irrespective of my motives," they say, coldly, "the truth is the Academy is the best place for you. So, you will go, kicking and screaming if need be, and you will keep your trap shut, and I will—reluctantly—be welcomed back into the fold."

"And why will I stay silent?"

"Because I *can* lead you to the Horizon."

I'm stunned. "You know where it is?"

"Close enough," they say. "With my help I can get you near enough for a dead drop. Without me you'll be scouring the galaxy for the rest of your life."

So, it knows about Pilgrim dead drops...

"And in return you want my silence?"

The Niris gives a small nod.

Convenient.

"How do I know you're not taking me for a ride?"

"You don't. Ultimately, you'll have to trust me." Lidless eyes stay locked on mine, unblinking. "But you should remember I am a Seeker of the Academy, and I have many means and many contacts at my disposal. For example, I know where the Horizon last entered the slipways, and soon I'll know where they exited too."

Information I'd nearly kill to possess.

And they know it.

"And if I refuse?"

"Then I'll take my chances."

"Meaning?"

"I'll still bring you in, take the kudos, and should you bring up any Empire moonlighting gigs on my part, I'll call you"—the tip of a limb prods my chest, harder than I expect—"a lying fantasist."

I gaze out the viewing portal, and this time, to the vessel's fore, I see a weird shadow occluding the stars.

The Academy.

So it's real then.

I can't deny the anticipation I feel knowing we approach this ancient, majestic site, appetite more than whetted by the Niris's tales.

Rachkov's certainly done a number on me.

But then I remember the faces of those who must be grieving my death, and an incantation comes to me, equally powerful and intoxicating.

I'm going to find my people.

"I'll stay for one hundred days, no more."

"And I'll have your silence?"

Hating myself, I nod.

The cosmos will need to find another means of imposing karmic retribution on the Niris for their sins.

"And afterwards, you'll help me find my people?"

"You have my word."

Together, unspeaking, we watch the Academy materialize. The black silhouette shifts to a penumbra of twinkling annexes, before fully revealing its geometric splendor. A citadel of towers thrust up from a perfect disc, each paying homage to the colossal pyramid at their heart, while great radial spikes of differing lengths stud the disc's periphery, compass points to the heavens.

Rachkov wasn't lying.

It is truly beautiful.

NINETEEN

𐌔𐌓𐌄𐌊𐌄𐌄𐌓

An armada of knife drones, harmoniously spaced, accompany us on the last leg, sleek black shapes glinting against the starlight. Like cats, they're practically purring in their sense of preening superiority. Cutting-edge military tech, far beyond Pilgrim capabilities, they could slice us to pieces. Fortunately, Rachkov hailed the citadel and they're only on escort detail.

For our protection or to intimidate, I'm not sure.

Maybe both.

The reception wasn't exactly welcoming. Frosty, if I had to sum it up in a word. Once the Niris had established our identities, the Academy's comms operator fell to silence. After a small gulf of white noise, they issued instructions to land at a remote landing platform.

The return of the prodigal son, this isn't.

According to Rachkov, a pair of Dust-enhanced rocking up at the Academy's door happens less often than a two-star supernova. Unannounced too. No doubt our arrival is a bit of a wildcard, not something foreseen by even the Academy's most far-sighted minds. Serenity might reign on the surface, but underneath they'll be scrambling.

We have value.

But we're also a danger.

The Niris tells me they would've tracked our vessel as soon as we arrived in-system, only revealing their presence after we made contact. "Unsurprisingly, they're a little twitchy about uninvited guests." He glances between me and the closest knife drone. "It'll be fine."

Yes, but for who?

An old Pilgrim saying from the times our arcologies hid in the upper reaches of solar atmospheres comes to mind.

Out of the corona and into the fire.

I tremble, like I can feel the heat.

What really happens in this spired fortress?

Any present answers I have come from a Dust-enhanced Niris who bargains my life like a commodity, and until seven days ago, led a United Empire hunter fleet.

No turning back, now.

Like I have a choice.

Shortly, we're descending onto a landing platform high above the tip of the longest radial spike, as if we're being kept at arm's length from the heart of the Academy. Towards the hub, the tiered pyramid dominates the skyline, at odds with the skyscrapers and towers that nestle in its foothills. Its patterned surface shimmers with a different energy, and I spy four vast statues of humanoid figures carved into one of its faces.

The Endless, I whisper.

The pyramid, built eons past, feels timeless. The city, in contrast, must've risen in the galactic blink-of-an-eye, an archeological dig springing up around an ancient monument of a long-dead civilization. Beneath the disc that encompasses both old and new, I glimpse a craggy, subterranean realm.

It'd make a decent caving expedition.

We land with a jolt, shattering my flight-of-fancy.

As the engines cycle down the knife drones disperse.

Rachkov opens the landing ramp at the vessel's aft, lets a tentacle linger on the command console, then marches out.

"Come on, Sewa!" they thunder. "Time to make an entrance."

I follow, walking tall, but happy for the Niris to lead.

Stepping off our vessel, I shiver, the air cold and laced with a musty, rocky smell. Above, the invisible field that wraps the entire citadel distorts the stars, blue-shifting the light. From this vantage, the system's red supergiant appears a striking cyan color as if it's a vast icy ocean world.

Unsettling.

Behind us, bots scuttle onto our vessel.

"Standard protocol," Rachkov says, noticing my backwards glance. "Sanitization procedures."

At the rim of the platform a small welcoming party awaits us, still and silent. As we approach, I see only one, a Sophon, is flesh-and-blood, the others four droids standing in identikit poses, upright, primed.

"Damn," the Niris mutters.

I remember the first time I saw a Sophon. Elongated head, compound eyes, tip-to-toe clothed in a hard, synthetic carapace that gave the appearance it might be a machine too. I'd sat on Father's shoulders, gazing over the Horizon's crowds who'd come to spy the special visitor. Smart thinkers, he'd said, and told me not to fear their artificial suits, that they were flesh and bone just like us beneath.

"Not the reception you expected?" I ask quietly.

"Something like that," Rachkov replies.

The Niris raises four of their limbs, flamboyant.

"Ighszraaz! I'm honored—"

"Zarva Rachkov." The Sophon speaks the Niris's name like they're handling dung. "A rather unexpected visitor."

Not Seeker Rachkov. Just plain old Zarva Rachkov.

The Niris's stock has certainly dropped.

"Unexpected, yet welcome." Rachkov glances at the droids, who remain resolutely motionless. "I hope."

The Sophon says nothing.

"Anyway," the Niris continues, "Ighszraaz, please allow me the pleasure of introducing Sewa..." Rachkov turns to me, realizing they've never learnt my family name.

"Eze," I whisper.

For a moment, Rachkov stares at me.

"Ighszraaz meet... Sewa Eze."

"Welcome," Ighszraaz says, hands outstretched and turned upright. "The Dust... isn't always easy. May the Academy illuminate your path."

I nod, happy they recognized my transformation.

"Happy to be here," I say like an idiot. "I guess."

"Ighszraaz," Rachkov says, turning to me, "is instrumental in running Academy affairs—"

"Rachkov," Ighszraaz says. "You've been gone a long time. The Academy is not the same place you left."

"Isyander?"

I hear fear in Rachkov's voice.

All the Niris's plans fall apart without Isyander.

The Sophon ignores the question.

"Most thought you dead, Zarva. At best, languishing in one of Zelevas's hellholes. What else could explain your sudden disappearance from the face of Raia?" They move closer, their slender frame dwarfed by the Niris's stature, but they aren't intimidated. "And yet here you stand, hale and hearty, full of good spirits. As if the last years have been... invigorating."

Rachkov's head drops. "Ighszraaz, I lost my way—"

"I don't want to know." The Sophon turns back to the line of droids, who begin moving as one. "But I'm sure Isyander will be keen to learn your story."

The Niris's limbs quiver with relief.

So, he still leads.

Good news. I hope.

One of the droids approaches, addresses me.

"This way, please," it says, taking a step towards a staircase at the edge of the platform.

Another droid falls in beside it.

My personal escort detail, I guess.

"We're being split up?"

Rachkov, for all their selfish maneuvering, is the nearest thing I have to a friend in a hundred light years. My stomach tightens at the idea of being immediately separated in this vast place.

"That's right," Ighszraaz says. "First port of call, for you, is Acculturation. But not for Zarva."

"Chin up, kid." The Niris squeezes my shoulder with one of their limbs. "They'll take good care of you down there. And I'll drop by soon."

The four of them—Ighszraaz, Rachkov, and two other droids— march off to another staircase leaving only me and my own escort party. I take a breath, then start off too. The droids, despite having their backs to me, immediately sense my movement and begin walking in synchronized fashion, maintaining their distance.

Shortly, we descend.

The journey to Acculturation is a short one, but feels long on account of the heavy silence that falls over our little party. Small talk doesn't seem to be part of the Academy droids' standard protocol, and I don't feel like breaking the ice either.

Everything is spartan, pristine, functional.

We pass no others.

My unease grows.

After taking a turbo-lift that hurtles us down to the plane of the great disc, I'm escorted along several nondescript corridors, before being discharged into the trust of another droid.

"Follow me," it says.

We walk.

By my estimation we must still be near the tip of the longest compass point, far from the Academy's heart. Maybe that's why it's so quiet here—only the newly Dust-enhanced ever come to this quarter. I imagine the rest of the vast place brimming with life and color like the way the *Dawn Skies* buzzed before the Empire destroyed it.

At least that's my hope.

Otherwise the Academy is more mausoleum than city.

"What's your name?" I ask, breaking the silence.

"My designation is EF-247," the droid replies in the characteristic refined, high-pitched diction of most automatons, eyes ahead, then glances back. "But you can call me Anders."

Droids have little means of making facial expression, their visages largely fixed like porcelain masks, but I still detect a hint of mischief.

"Anders?"

"Darwin Anders is the daredevil anti-hero of the alternative space flick, *Galactic Raiders*, a Lumeris production that happens to be my favorite film." The droid drops its shoulders, hustles along, gunslinger-style, before twisting round, making a pistol shape with its hand. "I ain't playin', twinkle-toes!" It straightens up. "That's Anders' catchphrase."

I stop, nonplussed, suppressing a laugh. "I haven't seen that one."

The droid turns back, keeps walking. "I recommend watching in the original language if you can."

"No chance," I say, jogging to keep up. "I can't say I know any Lumeris."

"A shame," the droid replies. "I speak six thousand languages."

"Impressive."

I wonder how many of those Anders uses here, wonder how many species are found in the Academy sprawl. We fall back to silence, but this little island of light-relief has lifted my mood.

It's going to be okay.

We come to a high-ceilinged, circular hall, the vaulted arches conveying strength yet still elegant. Everything is minimal, but many decorative elements adorn the space. A meandering watercourse runs across the hall, splitting into small tributaries and side pools, over which simple arched bridges span. A few curved benches hewn from single pieces of stone are dotted here and there, their surfaces flawless. Delicate shrubbery and trees populate the banks, their branches and fronds carefully manicured. A droid tends to a plant with striking magenta leaves. Beneath the canopies, golden-scaled fish glide in the waters.

Acculturation?

These gardens would be relaxing if they weren't entirely devoid of people. Instead, their immaculate emptiness lends the place an unsettling edge as if any visitors had just vanished.

Or maybe nobody has been here for years.

Eerie, whatever the case.

Half-a-dozen doorways lead off the space. Anders doesn't break stride, guides me to the third one on the left. The doorway opens, revealing a small antechamber leading to a translucent, latticed screen.

"Your quarters," the droid intones, sliding across the screen. "It is customary to remove footwear."

I crane my neck, peek into the room beyond.

It is minimally furnished with a low wood-framed bed and a square wooden table that rises only a handspan above the floor. Simple, muted, calming. A nice change from a cramped cabin that reeks of Niris. I reach down, release my bindings, and kick off my boots.

"When on Hekim..."

The antechamber ground is hard and cold, but when I step up onto the raised level of the room itself I find a soft, pleasant mat flooring. Even the proportions of the space, the layout of the furnishings, feel pleasing, harmonious.

Maybe I'll get a good night's sleep.

"Please make yourself comfortable," Anders says. "Eat, rest, exercise, meditate—you'll find everything you need here. You are free to wander the gardens outside, but the rest of the Academy is strictly off-limits."

Like you wouldn't know.

"Sure," I reply. "And..."

And what?

Even though Anders is only a semi-autonomous droid, probably slaved to an external authority, part of me doesn't want it to leave. I could be in a tomb for all the life I've seen, and the thought of being left completely alone chills me.

I feel the hollowness inside, dark and hungry.

Anders waits for me to follow-up, but I stay silent.

"A mentor will come to see you soon."

It turns and leaves.

Soon, such a slippery word.

For a star on a nine-billion-year journey from hot bright thing to swollen clay-red supergiant, a couple of million years of its lifecycle could be reasonably described as *soon*. For an aphid, such as the ones who flit between the fronds of the plants in the hydroponic gardens, *soon*, on the other hand, is of a whole other order.

I'm not sure what qualifies as *soon* for myself.

There are no clocks here, but I would estimate several hours have crawled past since the droid departed. In this time, I've fully explored, inventoried, and utilized near-all aspects of my private quarters, from laying in several positions on the firm mattress, to sampling all the curious edibles, to standing in (but not filling) the barrel-shaped bathing tub in the adjoining washroom.

Of the gardens, I have sat at each of the five benches and still haven't decided which one is my favorite, attempted to engage the horticultural droid in small talk (unsuccessfully, this time), and determined that it is probably not a coincidence that the arrangement of bridges and islands is reminiscent of an old philosophical puzzle used as an introduction to topology.

My mood veers between boredom and dread.

The Horizon feels further away than ever.

I am standing on one of the bridges, leaning over its thick, red, wooden balustrade, mesmerized by the motion of the koi in the waters beneath, when I sense a nearby presence.

"Sewa."

I flinch, stunned that with my heightened senses, in this place of stillness and serenity, anyone could get so close. A few paces away, a figure with a long grey-white cloak and a masked visage leans over the bridge's balustrade as if they'd been there for ages.

"How did you—"

"I feel your pain, Sewa," the figure says, voice rich and melodious. They turn from the rail, face me, and place one of their gloved hands, fingers spread, flat against one side of their chest. "Deep in your heart, I feel a rift."

Such frankness, especially from a stranger, would usually provoke my defenses, but something about this figure disarms me. They have no face to speak of, just a curved, gleaming mask, but in that mirrored surface golden clouds swirl, tantalizing with a thousand visions.

I watch, transfixed.

"This rift isn't born of one trauma, is it?" they say. "I feel many layers to your grief. Estrangement from your people, of course. And the bewilderment that comes with the Dust, destroying your old self, remaking you anew. Every new arrival feels these things.

"Yet, you carry deeper scars."

They tilt their head, considering, the golden whorls in their mask agitated. My mind flares with painful moments I thought long buried.

Somehow, this figure knows me.

I drop my head, emotions long shackled welling inside.

"Something tender… still raw. A betrayal? Someone you trusted, admired even. It left you feeling dead and empty."

I look up, shocked.

Kalad's hands are on my neck, squeezing…

What sorcery is this?

"And burdened too," they add, puzzled. "Yet all overshadowed by something you've carried from your early years. A tear at the heart of your world. A loss. A death of someone close, perhaps?"

I close my eyes.

Father.

The last time I saw him springs up, vivid and powerful.

I thought I'd lost this moment, many times failing to recall how this played out no matter how hard I willed it, but here it is, near overwhelming. Father crouching, brushing my hair back behind my ear, caressing my cheek. *Be strong, my baby. Know I love you whatever the distance, whatever the days, between us.* He stands up, and I want to jump up, hook my arms around his neck, but he's turned to my mother who's standing, arms folded, fury radiating off her trembling body in great waves.

He caresses her swelling belly.

Then he's gone, and I'm sobbing in Mother's arms.

"It's still so real for you, isn't it?"

Enough.

I open my eyes, fix on the koi in the water.

"Who are you?"

I dare not look at that mask again.

"I am Isyander."

"Isyander," I echo, awe mixing with anger. "The Founder."

"Only those who have the luxury of hindsight would give me such a title," he says. "Believe me, at the time the reality was nothing so grand."

We stand in silence. I risk a glance, happy to see the golden swirls in his visage have calmed.

"I apologize," he says, "for any distress my words caused. Grief is natural, necessary even. But if it festers too long it can curdle, debilitate. Sometimes it needs to be drawn out like a poison."

I feel stripped bare, vulnerable—and still seething.

An urge to retreat to my quarters comes, but I resist. Isyander's aura is undeniable, hypnotic. Below, the fish glide through the waters, oblivious.

"How did you know those things?"

"Sewa, it's important you understand this," Isyander replies. "I wasn't in your head. I wasn't sifting through your memories. I don't know anything." He turns. "But I can *feel* a great deal."

I frown. "In your mask though… I saw things…"

"The mask is only a mirror, responding to your emotions, provoking your mind to delve back into the past."

I turn. "So, you don't know my secrets?"

"No, only the emotional contours of your life."

Thank the Endless!

My relief is tempered with an edge of disappointment.

My secrets are burdens, and I'd thought I'd finally shared their weight. Kalad, his betrayal, his furious attack, his apocalyptic prophecies… all still on my shoulders.

"Of course," Isyander says, "an individual's emotions can be pointers to their past. Like the loss I sensed you suffered—and still suffer." He turns. "What belongs to you though is yours to share as you wish."

I study the golden swirls in his mask, then look back to the rippling waters. "My father left us, left the Horizon of Light, years ago," I say. "It broke my mother, left me feeling hollowed out, left my unborn sister without a father. To this day, I still don't know where he went. And whether he will ever return."

Isyander nods. "Trust can be hard to recover when we're betrayed by our closest allies, by our own blood."

"It wasn't betrayal!" I cry. "He *had* to do something. For us, for all Pilgrims!"

"Still, deep down, for a young child," Isyander says, "it must've felt like that. I sincerely hope you are reunited with him one day, Sewa. Or at least find some answers."

I shrug.

Across the gardens I watch the droid pruning an ornate shrub, red laser light flashing out of its mechanical arm.

"Walk with me," Isyander says.

I clench my jaw, push off the balustrade.

We begin meandering through the gardens, the fragrance of blossoms and earth strong.

"I want you to know, Sewa," Isyander says, "that you're not alone. No matter the trauma, healing is always possible. The Academy's first concern, my first concern, is the wellbeing of all those who walk its halls."

"And if I want to leave?"

"You are free to go at any time," Isyander answers. "We would need to take precautions to protect the Academy's location, but other than that you would leave as you arrived. Nobody is forced to stay here."

"I see."

"Trust me, though, Sewa, there is no better place in the galaxy for those of your ilk. Here you won't be an outsider, you will be part of a community."

We come to the entrance of my quarters.

Isyander stops, turns. "And of the ravages and gifts of Dust… you will come to many understandings that would otherwise take you a lifetime to learn."

"And then what?" I ask. "My place is with my people, the Pilgrims. Maybe I don't want to become another servant of the Academy. Whatever its aims, its gospels."

"In time you will learn the reasons why the Academy came to be. But that is not for today. Or tomorrow." Isyander grips my shoulder, and I find his touch welcome, reassuring. "Whatever you feel is your calling, the Academy won't stand in your way. As I said, you may leave this place any time. In a day, in ten days… or in a hundred days."

A hundred days? Some coincidence…

Even as I speculate, I'm painfully aware that Isyander will be reading my feelings, already likely to be able to discern that something has thrown me…

He knows.

"You spoke with Rachkov," I state.

"I did."

Isyander waits, unspeaking.

For the first time his aura projects something other than complete benevolence and empathy. Deep beneath his cloth I can feel his immense power, and I begin to understand it can be used as a hammer to break as much as a shield to protect.

I say, "You know our agreement, then."

"I do." The golden whorls flicker and darken. "In one hundred days you will leave the Academy to look for your people. And Seeker Rachkov has vowed to aid you in your search."

Seeker Rachkov? Has Isyander welcomed back his long missing wayward convert into the Academy ranks already? Did he buy the Niris's wilderness years story?

"The Niris," Isyander says, "is a formidable tracker. No doubt it will greatly help your chances of reuniting with your arcology—should you decide to leave and take that path."

"My people think I died!" I say, hackles rising. "They deserve—"

"Indeed." Isyander lifts a placatory hand. "I don't dispute that. Like all of us who come to serve the Academy, you face a difficult choice." He drops his hand. "What troubled me, though, was why Seeker Rachkov would pledge to spend his valuable time helping you look for your kin—an endeavor likely to be long, difficult, and dangerous. Why would it do that, Sewa?"

Careful.

Of the Niris's work for the Empire, I gave Rachkov my word it'd have my silence. Yet Isyander will likely sense if I lie…

"There is a good reason," I say. "But Rachkov swore me to secrecy. And I won't break that promise."

Isyander's stance relaxes.

"A good answer."

"You were testing me?"

Isyander nods. "I know full well Seeker Rachkov led an Empire hunter fleet and reported directly to Emperor Zelevas. We have agents too, after all." He cocks his head, as if he's receiving a communication, before his attention comes back to me. "No, what I really wanted to know was how you would react when backed into a corner. It must've been tempting to betray the Niris's trust, reveal everything."

"It wasn't."

"A certain anger—a certain desire to see it punished too—wouldn't be misplaced considering Rachkov hunted Pilgrims, hunted your very own arcology."

"I gave Rachkov my word."

"And that's why I have faith in you, Sewa. You didn't break the Niris's trust. And yet you still spoke truthfully to me." Golden clouds drift across Isyander's masked visage, beguiling. "We have a phrase at the Academy: *there can be no trust without truth.* Over the next days you will begin to understand how that cuts to the heart of everything we do here. And I think it is a lesson you have already learnt."

I feel a swell of pride—mingling with unease.

"What will happen to Rachkov?"

"They will atone for their sins." Isyander clasps both my hands in his own. "Fear not, the Niris will be free to fulfill their pledge to you should you wish, after one hundred days, to seek your kin.

Atonement needn't mean punishment or incarceration. And I know Seeker Rachkov is most sincere in their wish to atone."

I shake with relief..

More than anything in the galaxy, I want to be among my fellow Pilgrims again, see Rina, Oba, and Mother too, see Kalad defanged…

"Thank you," I say. "I will keep an open mind, but my desire to go home isn't likely to change."

"That's all I can ask."

Another distraction captures Isyander's attention, the writhing clouds in his mask somehow opaque for once rather than evocative.

"Something wrong?"

"Politics." Isyander gives another squeeze of my clasped hands. "I must leave you now, but whatever path you choose, I hope this time here brings you peace and strength, Sewa."

He sets off, not looking back.

"Rest up, tomorrow your instruction begins."

TWENTY

ㅈㅌㅌㅌㅋㅋ

Over the next few days I slip into a habitual, if not entirely relaxed, routine. Acculturation's borders mark the limits of my freedom to roam the Academy, and although the gardens, the lecture theaters, the dining hall, and the rest, are pleasant and peaceful, I feel trapped.

Aside from the droids, I see no one else. At dawn, one wakes me, leaving a herbal infusion on my room's kotatsu. A little later, another leads me through a daily calisthenics regime, before another serves my nutritionally-calibrated breakfast in the dining hall. Next, I receive instruction from another, alone, in one of the lecture theaters. History, politics, economics... the subjects are varied, but, I suspect, all connected to Isyander's grand project. The droids have their idiosyncrasies, their nascent personalities, but it isn't the same as being around flesh-and-blood species.

After midday repast the majority of the afternoons are mine to occupy in any way I should choose, before the day is rounded out with a second spell of instruction.

Oba would find this hilarious.

Back on the Horizon, when all I wanted to do was cave I often complained about all the menial tasks a Pilgrim youth was expected to carry out, day-in day-out. Now that I have my every obligation met by an army of droids, when I do have some free time, I find myself itching for chores to occupy my mind.

Typical.

Caving's out, of course.

Despite the Academy rising from a huge chunk of rocky strata that hints at a wonderland of fissures, rifts, galleries, crawlspaces, and drops, that area, like the rest of the place, is strictly off-limits.

Instead, I brood.

Whatever my train-of-thought, whatever flights of imagination, my mind always returns to the plight of the Horizon. Where in the galaxy had they fled? Had they finally escaped the clutches of the Empire? And if so, had they found shelter and safety, or simply traded one crisis for another?

The Horizon is the only home I've ever known.

I yearn to walk its familiar halls, sleep in my real bed, joke around with Rina and Oba. I want them to know I am okay, that I've survived, that I came off that moon changed but still whole.

Most of all though, I fret about Kalad.

Even though thinking of him precipitates cold sweats, I can't stop obsessing over what he might be saying or doing or plotting. Destroying knowledge of the Endless. Sowing discord between Overseer Liandra and Scriptmaster Artak to undermine the church. Maybe even re-establishing contact with the Empire.

Is he really still trying to oversee the downfall of the Pilgrims? Is he really so wedded to his incredible thesis—that our reverence of the Endless could one day lead to galactic annihilation—that he'd happily see our entire culture shackled, or worse, obliterated?

The answer is always yes.

Long ago, he'd killed for that belief, and he would've killed me too if it wasn't for the Dust. No doubt, he'd kill again.

He needs to be exposed—and judged.

Nothing is more important.

And so, I agitate, fixate on the day I can leave this place with the Niris, a grim countdown that seems so far away, seems too long. Will the Horizon still be around at the end of my enforced exile? The days creep down, slow as continental drift.

Ninety-five, ninety-four, ninety-three…

And that's if Rachkov keeps their side of our bargain. Now Isyander knows the truth, what is my silence worth? Nothing. I just have to trust the Niris keeps their word. I wonder how they occupy their time beyond the monastic confines of Acculturation. Are they even still here?

My quarters are furnished with a terminal, discreetly embedded in the kotatsu so I can study while eating, but any messages I send to Rachkov through the limited comms go unanswered. The Niris is only one of the three recipients available in my sanctioned contacts, and I don't feel like troubling Isyander or Ighszraaz. After firing off a third message, I promise myself I won't send another until I get a reply.

I expect to wait a long time.

Maybe they're busy, incommunicado, or off-site, but whatever the reason, I pray the Niris isn't going to bail.

One day I catch sight of another novice.

At least, I assume they are, like me, another party newly touched by Dust. The four-armed marsupial-like creature (a Kalgeros, I later learn) keeps to themself, a silent presence always on the other side of the lecture theater, the dining hall, the gardens, the only clue they are likewise Dust-enhanced the golden hue in their soft eyes.

That and their incredible skills with a staff.

After my attempts at introductions are rebuffed, I decide I don't want to get into a spat with a four-armed master martial artist with introvert tendencies, and begin giving the Kalgeros an equally wide berth.

Instead, I seek sanctuary in my studies.

The morning sessions presently concern the Endless. Even for a Pilgrim, indoctrinated to venerate the cosmos's ancient conquerors, it is dry stuff. Archeological evidence, political speculations, mathematical models of their movement across the galaxy that situated Tor, the homeworld, in a sphere of space four thousand light years wide.

Only a hundred million or so star systems to search then…

Of course, the great problem is that the era of the Endless had… well… ended, many millennia past. And, according to the evidence, they hadn't dwindled out like a dying fire, bright flames gradually succumbing to glowing embers. No, they'd been extinguished in the galactic blink-of-an-eye, nobody around to bronze their legacy, ensure the annals of history remembered their undoubtedly mighty achievements.

A civilization cut down in its prime, well before it'd made plans for its dotage.

Little remained.

Just the metaphorical trunks of statues in a wilderness of sand, vitrified prints that confirmed their existence—but little more—on a broken chain of worlds across the galaxy.

The paucity of real, tangible artifacts meant the evidence was akin to the remnants of the pre-civilization cultures that existed in Raia's ancient past. Like discovering bone-carved tools, daubed cave art, skulls with life-shattering cracks, and then attempting to piece together their social fabric, their power structures, their day-to-day lives.

A fool's errand.

Everything was conjecture, speculation, a source of inexhaustible theses, debates, and counter-arguments… essentially, hearty grist for the academic mill, but little nourishment for the average galactic citizen who just wanted the abridged, officially-settled version.

Understanding their culture, their politics, their beliefs, and—the ultimate goal—their interior lives, was a gargantuan, perhaps impossible, task. Even something I thought might be a simple matter, like the cause of their demise, was anything but settled among the experts.

Had they, en masse, escaped the limitations of messy, dirty base reality and transcended to a higher plane of existence? Had a machine-plague rendered all their tech inoperable, triggering a dark age from which they'd never recovered? Or had they simply succumbed to their cataclysmic Dust Wars?

Whatever the truth, they were gone, leaving countless mysteries, conundrums, and a not inconsiderable smattering of curiosities in their wake. In a galaxy of four hundred billion stars, though, finding even one such trinket was like hunting for a pearl on a vast, unbroken beach.

I begin to see why this fluidity might've appealed to the precursor Pilgrims back on Raia, when they wanted to establish a mythology that unified and emboldened their cause.

Bold adventurers? Check.

Indistinguishable-from-magic technology? Check.

Dead and unlikely to rise again? Double-check.

Our reverence of them is, essentially, a crutch.

And I realize that the Pilgrim conception of the Endless, especially that promoted by the church, is a construct, a fiction, something shaped by a century of persecution and propaganda into our cultural bedrock.

Perhaps it *was* wholly true.

More likely it was very *economical* with the truth.

Kalad would certainly subscribe to the latter view.

Not that I feel aggrieved by this knowledge. In the galaxy, as in the evolutionary free-for-all of every biosphere where life does what it takes to win, survival is everything.

Whatever works, works.

Insect-machine menaces who sweep planets like swarms of locusts. Puny, scrawny things who pray at the altar of science for their protection. And some who find strength in the worship of a dead civilization shaped into an expedient ideal.

The galaxy sees all sorts.

So what did we know for certain of the Endless?

First, their homeworld was an icy, yet habitable, planet named Tor. Long lost to the mists of time, the Endless would've been a very different species when they first left their world. And a much more comprehensible one to the galaxy's current crop of eager, spacefaring races. Beyond a deep spiritual yearning to visit the birthplace of the Endless, this, of course, was part of the reason behind my people's burning obsession to find Tor.

Many believed, my mother among them, that the knowledge uncovered on Tor would provide a bridge, enabling us to not only deepen our veneration of this god-like race, but to actually become the Endless.

According to scripture, Tor promised apotheosis.

An apotheosis that would bring enlightenment, invulnerability, plenitude. But for someone like Kalad, Tor promised the opposite.

Annihilation.

Honestly, I had no idea who was right. The only thing I knew was that obsessions, whatever the flavor, usually led to dysfunction, and eventually collapse. And that went for civilizations as much as individuals.

The second thing everyone agreed on was that at some point the Endless had splintered into two distinct factions: the Concretes and the Virtuals. One lot had persisted as physically-based beings that, presumably, still ate and breathed and shat as they roamed the stars, while the other had foregone their mortal flesh for a more rarefied form of existence.

Earthly pursuits versus philosophical pleasures, you might imagine, thinking such a division could be frictionless. Wrong. Myriad evidence pointed to the Concretes strengthening their beliefs in ecological stewardship, while the Virtuals became the galaxy's hedonists, reveling in their newfound immortality.

Common ground eroded.

Then lacerated, trampled, and carpet-bombed. This resulted in the third well-established fact about the Endless: they fought amongst themselves in a biblical, galaxy-shattering conflict known as the Dust Wars.

Craver swarms, biological warfare, nuked worlds.

Nasty stuff.

By this era in the Endless' adventures among the stars, Dust had become a crucial resource for both sides. Whether it was fabricated, harvested, grown, mined, or otherwise acquired, is still a matter of lively debate, but what was known was that it was consumed in enormous quantities. The Virtualization process relied on a ceaseless supply of the stuff, while Concrete industrial worlds chugged it down like black holes swallow stars.

Dust was everything.

And while we're still backstreet conjurers, understanding its ways in dimly lit workshops like medieval alchemists, the Endless were master magicians, sprinkling the wondrous substance over all facets of their complex societies.

Not that it led to a happy ending. For either side.

Eventually, many worlds, even suns, lay in ruin.

And then the Endless simply vanished.

And that's the sum total of what we truly know. Interesting, for sure, but decidedly of the past. And the remnants of their civilization? So scattered, so buried, so esoteric to our eyes, that searching for them was surely a fool's game. They were tangential to the future at best, irrelevant at worst.

Ancient history. Literally.

Each day I hoped to learn why the Academy found them so captivating, but the reason remained shrouded, much like the Endless themselves.

Perhaps the Endless pyramid at the heart of the place holds the answers? Or maybe explanations lie in the vast caverns beneath the Academy? What's down there? Why did Isyander found the Academy here?

I'd be happy to be set loose for a marathon caving session in that craggy underworld... I can feel the Dust writhing inside me, impatient, desirous...

Thankfully, the lectures and exercises that round out my days, focus not on more dry Endless theorizing, but on Dust. A way more engrossing subject given my skin in the game. But one that messes with my emotions more than anything else I'm learning.

Although Dust was little understood in the established framework of biological, chemical, and physical laws that formed contemporary science and underpinned everything from space travel to genetic reconstruction, no place in the galaxy held a greater body of knowledge regarding its phenomenological characteristics.

In other words, like everybody else, the Academy had no idea what the stuff *was* exactly, but, more than anyone else, they knew what it was capable *of*.

And it wasn't all roses.

First, most scholars agreed that Dust, at some level, was best understood as being alive, even sentient. That creeped me out big-time. Something living, maybe even conscious, was inside me, feeding, ingesting, agitating, so inextricably entwined with my own nervous system that it could never be safely extracted.

Like a parasite in the gut.

For life.

Maybe that's how I'd been saved though.

Dust in the sump somehow recognizing my terror, recognizing something deep inside me that was worth protecting. Ninety-nine times out of a hundred, I was assured, no such salvation would've happened.

And that was the other thing with Dust.

Power stellar engines or industrial cores with the refined stuff, and it behaved consistently, reproducibly, reliably. Introduce it to a living, organic entity, even something as simple as a trilobite, and it was a whole other story.

Unpredictable, chaotic, inexplicable.

And dangerous.

Most organisms gave Dust a wide berth, evolutionary pressures teaching species that it wasn't worth the chaos. No wonder most civilizations kept it well away from their citizens, permitting it only for strictly controlled engineering processes like spaceflight and energy production.

Toxic was its middle name.

Of course, that didn't stop many experimenting...

For myself, I think of it as a friendly passenger; a guardian spirit that'd resurrected me, heightened my senses, and supercharged my natural caving skills. A force of good even if I've been warned Dust could be a capricious master. Many had been led down dark paths by its whispers in their blood.

Alienation, psychosis, paranoia. A whole psychiatrist's dictionary of mental illnesses. Yet, with meditation, exercises, guidance, I can keep it under control, bend it to my will.

And what is my will?

The Academy wants me to become its servant, but to what end I'm still in the dark. Soon, the droids tell me, you will learn this purpose. First, though, we must teach you how to live with Dust.

And so more instruction.

I learn that Dust-enhancement comes with other drawbacks. Although the substance slows the aging process in most subjects, allowing lifespans to be extended by dozens, if not hundreds, of years, most eventually experience some form of physical and cognitive degeneration.

Some rail against this dying of the light, experiment with Dust infusions and radiative therapies, or delve deep into Endless arcana and mythology in search of remedies. Others withdraw, venturing to see great cosmic vistas or returning to their places of birth in search of peace before the end.

One, a Z'vali, a brilliant chemist by all accounts, tried to stave off this decline by expunging the Dust.

They failed.

The attempts caused migraines, nausea, even scarring. The Z'vali's skin changed. Volcano-esque cracks riddled the creature from head-to-toe, glowing golden crimson, the once-symbiotic relationship between Dust and life-form wrecked beyond repair. Frail and half-mad, the Z'vali wandered the Academy's halls for the remainder of their days, a vivid symbol to all its brothers and sisters of the involuntary pact they'd made with Dust.

The droids tell me these stories, they say, so that I'm not deceived as to my nature, and to make the most of this gift.

I cannot lie.

Learning these things frightens me, but the droids' words only harden my resolve to aid my people. Inside, I'm thankful as much as afraid. Each day my respect for my mercurial passenger grows. I give my full and undivided attention to every aspect of my strange new life, well aware this time will soon end.

One evening while meditating, listening to the ebbs and flows of the Dust, I receive a message. Keeping my eyes closed, I instruct the terminal to read the communication aloud.

Sewa,

Excuse my brevity, but time is short and my tasks are many.

The pain of your father's departure from your life struck a deep chord with me, and I vowed to look into his disappearance. I had hoped some inkling of his journey or his reasons might give you solace, but alas, although Academy Intelligence managed to determine that he visited a Sophon waystation shortly after he left the Horizon of Light, they could find no further information regarding his onward destination or the burning questions that drove him. I attach some brief footage from security cameras on the waystation—

I snap my eyes open, hustle to the terminal. As I scrabble to get the footage playing, the voice continues.

Sadly, I am informed that due to the increasing Sophon-United

Empire hostilities of the time, this installation was decommissioned
shortly after his visit.

I hope this gives you some peace, however little that may be.

Your friend,

Isyander

As the grainy footage starts, I feel my heart thumping, hard and fast. The feed shows a nondescript corridor, somewhere deep inside the Sophon waystation. Dim illumination, grid-metal flooring, a haze of smoke. Two aliens are having a stand-off beside an arched entrance. In the foreground I see the top half of a nonplussed guard droid.

A bar or some such, then.

The door opens, spilling out a blaze of lights and a humanoid figure, closes again. The figure shifts past the arguing pair, low-key, then glances up and down the passage.

Is that Father?

Their head is shaved and the clothes aren't anything like normal Pilgrim attire, but there's something familiar in their slow, considered movement, their wiry build.

Let me see you.

They turn and tilt their face up to the camera as if they could hear me across space and time.

Father!

His guarded face speaks of struggles and secrets, but his eyes still carry the kindness I knew so well. He keeps his eyes locked on the camera, relaxes, and gives a small nod.

Then he swivels, disappears into the darkness.

The footage stops.

Staring at the message, I feel myself shaking.

Elation mingles with pain, happy times with the wretched aftermath. A memory springs up. I remember gripping his steely forearm with both hands, letting him lift me so far off the ground that we came face-to-face, his big beaming smile matching my own squeal of delight.

Where did you go, Father?

TWENTY-ONE

ᚕᚋᚓᚱᚲᚲ ᚛ᚌᚓᚌ

On the sixteenth day, as I'm making my way across the gardens to the lecture theater for morning instruction, I hear my name called.

"Sewa!"

I stop, stunned. Looking across the still, manicured landscape of ponds and foliage, I don't see anybody. I haven't heard a real voice since Isyander spoke to me on the first day, and for a moment I wonder if my mind's playing tricks on me.

"Over here."

Now I see her. She sits serenely on one of the simple stone benches, hands in her lap, a half-smile playing on her lips. With her ring of looped braids and striking facial tattoos there's no doubting her roots.

She's a Pilgrim. Or was.

"I wasn't expecting anyone," I say, standing a little away from where she sits. "Are you here for me?"

"I am." She pats the bench. "Come, sit with me."

"I have instruction."

"Not today."

I look across the gardens. Tranquility reigns, no sign of any disruption to the usual routine.

I remain standing. "This is the hard-sell bit, isn't it?"

Golden motes dance in her eyes.

The woman gives a wistful smile. "Clever. But, then again, everybody here is, aren't they?"

She pats the bench again, and I join her.

"It's so peaceful here… I forget."

So, she went through Acculturation…

For a while, we just sit, listening to the ebbing waters, the fish breaking the surface. I turn to her. "Which arcology?"

"The Faith Eternal."

"Not in your case, though."

That raises a smile. "Very good." She touches my forearm. "I like you. Come, let's walk. I have somewhere to show you."

She leads me across the gardens, and soon enough, out of Acculturation. I feel half-excited, half-anxious leaving what's become my home. We board a monorail, and soon we're hurtling towards the heart of the Academy. Going by the names of the stops it seems the rest of this wing is dedicated to preserving the history of the galaxy.

ARCHIVES – EARLY ERA

ARCHIVES – ENDLESS ERA

ARCHIVES – LATE ERA

Several droids get on and off, some alone, some accompanying (what I later learn are) Academy guests. I only see one other Dust-enhanced, an Amoeba floating majestically, its nucleus pulsing with an ethereal magenta light. As I learn the Pilgrim's story, I lose track of the stops and the passengers of the increasingly crowded carriage.

Her name is Oyita Nilfey. Forty years ago, she was an imaging expert aboard The Faith Eternal, disenchanted by the increasingly strident religious inclinations of her arcology. Transformed by an accident at an Endless temple that saw her showered by an intense hail of Dust, she vowed to discover all she could about this mysterious substance that she'd previously not given a second thought to.

For a few years she drifted, an itinerant wanderer skirting the edges of the galaxy's ambitious civilizations, struggling to not be consumed by the inner fire, fearful of being detained by the authorities while latching onto whatever band of misfits fitted her pedagogical bill. A most chaotic education in Dust. Some groups worshipped the stuff, some attempted to bend its vagaries to their will, some simply traded it.

All respected its power.

Later, a chance encounter with an Academy envoy led to an invitation to really learn its essence.

Oyita didn't need asking twice.

"This is us," she says, as we pull into a stop. "Stay close."

We file out with a dozen others, joining a tumult of movement. Beyond the throng, I catch a glimpse of the station name on a nearby wall: APEX.

We must be at the very heart of this place, beneath the pinnacle of the great pyramid. The passengers are a mix of droids and biologicals, many of one species I don't recognize. They wear muddy, hooded khakis and sport a breathing apparatus whose hose attaches to a bulky unit carried on their backs. Dust-enhanced are few and far between, but they aren't hard to spot, moving with a confidence and aura that sets them apart. A couple give me a knowing nod.

"The species with the artificial breathers," I shout, over the hubbub, "how come there's so many of them?"

"The Haroshem?" Oyita replies, glancing back. "They make up most of the workforce. They're peaceful, hard-working, and always discreet. And they seem to like coming here."

We duck into an ancillary passage, suddenly alone.

"They don't need the breathers here," she continues, lowering her voice, "but they feel more comfortable wearing them, so they keep them on."

So much life.

I've missed it.

"This place…" I say, running my fingers along the wall, "it's a thriving metropolis in all but name."

"That it is." Oyita smiles. "The Academy keeps a low profile, stays out of other civilization's affairs, but that doesn't mean it's drifting in the darkness gathering dust."

"Well—"

"No pun intended," Oyita adds. "The Academy employs workers in many industries and sectors, from the shipyards to the trade towers to the mining operations. As you might imagine, numbering fewer than a thousand, the Dust-enhanced don't stretch very far. We need the help."

We come to a set of ornately crafted doors, border framed by Endless script. Oyita waves her palm across a side panel, and the script illumines with a silver light. I hear the hum of machinery. An Endless lift?

"Are we going up?"

"Down actually."

We wait. As the lift arrives, the hum changes pitch. I hear voices on the other side. Rather than opening, the doors simply dematerialize. Two guards loom over me, their blood-red livery and distinctive steel-grey pauldrons, gorgets, and helmets clearly marking them as United Empire.

My stomach drops.

Please, no…

The voices stop. The Empire soldiers aren't alone. Behind the pair, Ighszraaz, the Sophon who met us upon arrival at the Academy, is flanked by another Empire individual in a very different garb—

black trench coat, high curved collar with the same blood-red color as the guards.

Unlike them, no helmet hides his hawk-like face.

An envoy, then.

"Well, well," he says, glancing between myself and Oyita. "We comb the hinterlands of the Empire for decades, rarely coming across a single Pilgrim soul, and then two show up just like that. And Dust-enhanced no less." He nods at Oyita. "Counselor Nilfey."

My heart thuds hard in my chest, but my fear is tempered with anger.

And we'll keep evading you.

He fixes me with a hard stare. "And one so young, too. Were you a recent arrival?"

Ighszraaz answers. "Riza has been with us almost a year."

The lie is startling, but I try not to show it.

I'm in a game I don't understand here.

Keep your head down, your mouth shut.

"What you were, what you might be," Oyita says, "is no matter here. We put tribal politics aside at the Academy, Envoy Zubkov. You know that."

She stands aside and I do likewise. The two Empire guards file out, followed by the Sophon and the envoy.

"A noble stance," he says to Oyita as he passes. "Yet very difficult to live up to in practice. Good day, Counselor."

They're followed by three security droids, diplomatic niceties resumed as Oyita and I step into the vacated lift.

"What an arrogant specimen, even by Empire standards," Oyita says, shaking her head. "I'm sorry, Sewa. That was an unfortunate encounter."

I take a deep breath, calmer. "Why are the Empire here?"

"Zarva Rachkov."

"They know the Niris is here?"

"No," Oyita says. "But they made an educated guess. They've made it clear that they believe Rachkov is a fugitive of the Empire— one who should be handed back should the Niris find itself under Academy jurisdiction."

For a death sentence... if they're lucky.

"That won't happen though, will it?" I ask as we begin to descend, the acceleration so smooth as to be barely perceptible.

"Not under Isyander's watch."

"You think differently?"

"Beneath the Dust, the Academy finery, I'm still a Pilgrim survivor at heart. And Zarva Rachkov served the Empire, did they not? Pilgrims died while they were in command, no?"

And I knew some of them.

I stare at Oyita, confused. Her facial tattoos that mark her as a Pilgrim look as vivid as the day she was inked.

What has kept you here?

Her jaw hardens. "Far as I'm concerned, the day the Niris signed up with the Empire, they lost the protection of the Academy."

"Zelevas manipulated Rachkov." It feels strange to defend the Niris, but I can't stay silent. "I believe they're deeply ashamed of their time with the Empire. I believe they want to make amends."

"Making amends." Oyita smiles. "Isyander used the same phrase. I'm a less forgiving animal."

The floor thrums with a near-subliminal energy, the only sign we're still descending. We must be kilometers deep, already.

I ask, "Did the Empire swallow the lie—that Zarva isn't here?"

"They're skeptical, but without evidence they have nothing." She shakes her head. "That's why Envoy Zubkov is getting the VIP treatment, by the way. A tour of the Endless ruins to indulge his vanities, give him a tale to tell when he returns to his dull little Empire world. The whole sorry episode will blow over." She glances at me. "That's the play anyway. The sooner Rachkov's gone, the easier the denials." Her eyes narrow. "You must never speak their name here. Understand?"

I nod.

The Empire won't stop hunting the Niris though, will they?

Rachkov knows too much, knows how the Empire operates. No doubt, knows a few dirty secrets too. Funny, it's like we've swapped places. Once I was the one hunted. Now it's the Niris's turn.

Maybe it's poetic justice.

My weight presses harder, dislodging my train of thought. Last stop approaching.

"One thing I don't understand," I say, as we come to rest. "After all this time, you still identify as a Pilgrim, still wear the markings with pride, still burn at every Pilgrim death, yet you remain here, a servant of the Academy. Why?"

Oyita nods, contemplating.

Regrets?

Like when we boarded, the door dematerializes, but this time there is no one on the other side. A cavernous darkness swallows the little light that spills from the lift.

A charred smell, faint and ancient, lingers.

Oyita snaps out of her reverie.

"Come, I'll show you why."

We're in the heart of an asteroid, a piece of rock hewn over billions of years, craggy and pocked and riddled with fissures and galleries, yet at every turn, geometric and physical oddities disturb the natural order.

The artificial gravity of the citadel above extends to this dark underworld, orienting everything into up and down, vault and earth, sky and chasm. Somehow, though, gravity is different here... more sensual... more alive... In some places it cajoles and aids, while in others it dissuades or obstructs. Engineered tunnels and chambers, slick lines and surfaces perfectly smooth to the touch, gleam with an ethereal light, studded with complex glyphs.

The charred smell intensifies.

Inside, the Dust coursing through my body flickers and surges, agitated like an animal sensing rain. Ancient machinery looms out of the shadows, labyrinthian sculptures of all sizes, all incomprehensible.

The work of the Endless.

We weave our way deeper and deeper, shifting between constructed areas and natural formations. The maze of passages, vaults, and crawlspaces should thrill, but instead I feel unsettled.

What's happening to me?

Oyita's only words are sporadic warnings.

Careful here.

Not that way.

That's the blood of the Hissho ambassador.

The place might be a trove of Endless artifacts, but it's also a deathtrap for the uninitiated. When they finally departed this realm, by accident or design, the Endless left it in a most dangerous state. Kalad would see it as another sign.

"Oyita?"

My guide is a dark silhouette, one arm raised, fingers brushing the cave wall. "Yes?"

"The Endless... do you think they're a danger?"

"They're gone, Sewa." The cave narrows, and she shuffles through a thin crevice, her words echoing off the stone. "At least, as far as we know."

"That's not what I meant."

Ahead, Oyita emerges from the fissure, turns back to me. "You mean: do I think the Endless' leftovers—their relics, their machines, their weapons—are a danger?"

I scrape through, joining her. "Yes, exactly."

We're on a small ledge above a vast, empty space.

Oyita steps to the edge, trembling. "And what you really mean is: if these things really are a danger, should we be getting our hands dirty? Wouldn't it be more prudent to ring-fence these places, erect signs that read 'Beyond Lie Dragons', or even better, destroy them entirely?"

I feel queasy, but not from the height.

Inside, I sense the Dust is inflamed, maybe even… *afraid*?

Where is she taking me?

I shuffle to the edge. I cannot see the other side of the huge chamber, the darkness rich and velvety, ever shifting, but in the inky black below I discern the silhouette of a dais.

"And?"

Oyita's stopped shaking, calming whatever vexed her.

"Civilizations," she says, "have always encountered forces that threaten their existence. Plagues, droughts, climate loops that turn idyllic worlds into icy tombs or sweltering furnaces, artificial intelligences who can bootstrap themselves into computational gods."

She flicks her head. *Follow me.*

"Embracing ignorance is never the answer," she continues, as we descend a rough stone staircase carved into the rock. "That only delays the inevitable, offloads the dangers to later generations who will be forced to confront even greater threats. And they won't look kindly on those who shied away from their responsibilities."

We come to the chamber floor, smooth and flat as a frozen lake. In the distance, the dais glimmers with a faint, chaotic light.

How did I miss that?

The Dust inside flexes and writhes.

"No, Sewa, we must be courageous." Oyita takes my hand, advances. "We must seek out the Endless and their relics, wield our curiosity like a torch cast into the darkness. And if we find monsters? We mustn't look away, but rather, keep our gazes fixed, unwavering, so in time they are fully brought into the light, divined and defanged."

And I'm going to learn first-hand, aren't I?

"Moreover," she says, "we have a duty to ensure that the moral arc of the universe bends towards justice. Mere survival isn't enough. Lizards survive. Cockroaches survive. Viruses survive. As enlightened, conscious beings, we must be held to a higher standard. No purpose is greater than acknowledging—and redressing—the wrongs of the past."

The marbled light of the dais crackles with violence, a lightning storm in miniature. In its illumination I spy a tall, gossamer-thin framework, like a gibbet cage for a vast being. My limbs pulse, conduits of the flailing Dust inside.

Each surge comes with an edge of white-hot fire.

"I don't want to go on."

Oyita grips my hand harder. "A little further."

The charred smell is gone. Or maybe just eclipsed by another. Something akin to ozone, burning metal.

The smell, I realize, comes from us.

I turn to Oyita, hoping she will see my fear.

"Please, no closer."

Her skin glows with a bright, golden hue, while her tattoos shine like sunlight, their shapes stark, unmistakable. I glance at my free hand, see that I luminesce with the same Dust-hued radiance. Whatever I'm experiencing, she is too.

And yet she seems calm.

At least on the outside.

"Come," she says, squeezing my hand. "You must truly understand what the Endless fashioned here."

We edge forward, two crazy souls heading for the heart of a storm. Great blazes of lightning leap from the dais, crackling through the cage overhead and dispersing across the vault. My skin burns.

"What do you know of the Lost?" Oyita shouts over the tempest.

The Lost?

Not much. A few obscure passages of Pilgrim scripture.

"Gods of the Endless' old religion," I cry, pained. "Mythical beings that died along with the civilization that once worshipped them."

"That's half right," Oyita says, grimacing.

Thankfully, she finally halts our progress, a dozen paces from the dais. Inside, the Dust thrashes around like a wild animal brought before a sacrificial plinth.

I want this agony to end.

"Half right?"

"The Lost were indeed the gods of the Endless' ancient religion." She casts her eyes upwards over the vast cage that looms over us. "But they were no myth. They were vast, ethereal creatures tinged with magic. They swam the galactic oceans, invaded dreams. They were real."

I follow her gaze.

An icy realization eclipses the fire.

This place... the Endless...

"They turned on their gods."

"Indeed."

I imagine a vast, delicate creature, trapped in this cage, in this cavern. "The Lost—they were vessels of Dust?"

"Not vessels. They *were* Dust."

I stand there frozen as the full horror dawns.

"They were harvested."

"Over and over and over again," Oyita says. "Not only here at this lodestone, but at many others. The Endless were ruthless."

The pain is near unbearable, but now I embrace it.

I don't want to forget.

"This is why you serve the Academy?" I ask. "To bear witness… to testify to the sins of the Endless?"

"That and more." Oyita nods. "We must atone."

What does she mean?

Before I can ask, she's dragging me away.

Exhaustion assails me, like we've just come to the end of a mighty battle. I use every reserve of strength to stay on my feet as we stumble back through the dark labyrinth. Round and round, one thought echoes through my head, strange and bewildering.

I carry the blood of dead gods.

TWENTY-TWO

ᚴᛃ�648ᚴ ᚴᛃᛈ

The expedition turns my world upside-down.

Over the next days, the exquisite pain and terror of the Endless' arcane machinery trying to wrest the Dust from my veins preys constantly on my mind. I can't imagine how much worse it must've been for the Lost all those millennia ago. Deceived by those who once worshipped them, lured into perfect traps, feeling the very fabric of their being unpicked.

Like skinning a beast. Head to toe, hide to organs.

Monstrous.

The Endless slaughtered a race of gods. Left them as little more than bloody remains on a galactic battlefield. I begin to understand very well why Oyita, like many others touched by Dust, had elected to stay with the Academy. I felt it myself. The story of this slaughter—this *deicide*—needs to be told.

Carefully, forensically, unambiguously.

This is who they were. This is what they did.

History has a responsibility.

I have a responsibility. The remnants of these ancient gods swim in my blood, a ceaseless reminder of their massacre.

I am torn though.

I am bound to Dust, but I am still a Pilgrim. Nothing can change that. The Academy needs me, but so does the Horizon. And that's even before I consider the matter of the Endless' atonement, whatever that entails…

Beyond my inner turmoil, my outward life is likewise transformed. Knowing the truth of Dust, I am now free, even encouraged, to explore this great citadel.

After instruction I wander its backstreets and thoroughfares, marveling at its life and grandeur. Situated on a mid-sized asteroid, the city is a dense maze of quarters layered like sedimentary sands, with the colossal ancient pyramid a striking landmark at its heart. Although I witness no squalor in its myriad districts, each has its own ambience, from the metronomic grind of the shipyards to the chaotic din of the commercial zones.

The majority of the inhabitants—workers, living or mechanical, untouched by Dust—stiffen or fall to silence when I'm in their midst. Not that they are ever anything but courteous. Maybe they've been instructed not to fraternize with those touched by Dust, or perhaps they are genuinely awed, but whatever the reason, I feel like an outsider.

Wherever I go, I feel like I'm being watched.

Despite this, I learn the rhythms of the citadel, the places where my counterparts congregate, and I come to make some, if not friendships, then at least acquaintances.

A cantina named The Jester is one place where a handful of Dust-enhanced can reliably be found most days. A rowdy place with a reputation for gossip and mischief, the first time I entered a garrulous Mavros challenged me to an arm-wrestle. Naturally, I didn't win, but in the cantina's energy and chaos I found a welcome diversion from my worries.

One table was always reserved for the Dust-enhanced, and this nightfall I walk in to find three sat in heated debate.

"Sewa!" Raudd, a grizzly Vaulter with a mischievous eye, shouts over the din. "Come settle a wager for us."

Raudd's a staple at The Jester who I've come to know during my daily excursions. On Auriga he'd razed many Necrophage nests, often fighting the deadly hive creatures in the darkness, and he liked nothing more than recounting tales of his bravery. He sits with a pair of Lumeris, one carrying a sculpted military bearing, the other a gargantuan belly that proudly spills over the table. They smell of the sea and spice.

"Jenhaestra, Iotar," Raudd says. "Meet Sewa, a survivor of the Horizon of Light."

"A pleasure," drawls Jenhaestra, the rotund Lumeris, as he twirls a barbel, the fleshy tendril beneath his mouth. "And deepest condolences for your loss."

"Reports of the Horizon's demise are greatly exaggerated," I say. "We lost our hub orbital, but the majority of the arcology escaped the Empire."

Iotar nods. "Well said, Pilgrim."

"So," I say, seating myself next to Raudd. "You spoke of a wager?"

Raudd grins. "Alright, no prompting—we want your honest answer." He strokes his beard. "Tell us, have you ever known a Pilgrim arcology to have enlisted one of us?"

I ponder.

Never. Is that so strange?

We are nomads, after all. Wanderers who keep to the shadows, hiding from our great enemy. Not that I'd necessarily know. Why are they talking about Pilgrims though?

Is it because of me?

"Well…"

The barkeep delivers my usual drink, a technicolor marvel that churns like a gas-giant's skies. I take a slow sip. Raudd and the others lean forward, anticipating.

"As far as I know," I say, "we Pilgrims have… never had that pleasure."

Raudd slaps the table. "I knew it!" He roars with laughter. "You two owe me a year's supply of Lumeris' finest!"

Iotar flicks his barbels, dismissive. "*As far as she knows.*"

He turns to his fellow Lumeris and the pair launch into a rapid-fire exchange in their mother tongue.

Raudd slaps my back, grinning.

I ask, "How did that come up?"

"Because you're the new kid on the block and everyone's interested in your story." His smile evaporates. "Kid, many here think the Empire have gone too far with the Pilgrims, that they're close to pogrom territory now."

I swirl my drink. "But the Academy can't intervene."

"Political neutrality bull."

I sink back in my seat, thinking of my little sister, living her life under the looming shadow of the Empire's hammer.

"But if the Pilgrims can commission a few of us," Raudd says, "the Academy *can* have an influence, help avoid the worst."

This is too depressing.

"What does the Academy get out of these assignments?" I ask, changing the subject. "It can't just be for the payday."

Raudd nods, understanding. "You're right. The Academy has far more profitable endeavors than contracting out a few dozen Dust-enhanced to a ragbag of galactic players." He scratches his chin, lowers his voice. "Should you stay, you'll learn this in time anyway… but no harm knowing now, I guess."

I lean closer, inhaling his gritty smell.

"The chief currency the Academy deals in?" He glances at the two Lumeris, still in intense conversation. "Knowledge."

"Knowledge?"

"No matter who you're with... Sophon geeks, Craver killing machines, even those creepy weirdos, the Riftborn... while you're on contract you dig. Historical conflicts, archeological sites, Endless myths. Every morsel comes back to the Academy, gets fed into the insatiable machine that paints the big picture."

No conjecture, no speculation...

"Isyander wants perfect knowledge of the past," I say. "The Endless' past. For the task of judgment. And atonement."

"Ah, the A-word."

"What does it entail?"

"I can't help you there, kid."

Just like everybody else.

I shake my head. "Nobody can."

I drain my drink, slump back, suddenly tired. All I want is to see a friendly face, somebody who isn't a stranger. Even the Niris would suffice.

"Hey, you know Zarva?" I ask. "Zarva Rachkov."

Raudd grabs my wrist. "Outside. Now."

We leave, fast but low-key. I rub my wrist, the indentations where he gripped me clear. "What the—"

"You were told to keep that name to yourself," he whispers, leaning in close. "Not to go mouthing it off—especially in a crowded place."

I glance over his shoulder, stare into the cantina. Boisterous chatter spills out and I can see silhouetted figures jostling at the bar, but there is no sign of anyone following us.

I massage my wrist.

"Are *you* watching me?"

"The Academy doesn't need a diplomatic incident with the United Empire, right now."

No denial then.

I wonder who else is keeping an eye on me, who else is observing me from afar.

"My lips are sealed," I say. "The Academy can rest easy." I look Raudd in the eye, belligerent. "Can I go now?"

The Vaulter casts an eye up and down the passage.

"Sewa," he says, "I know it's tough." He makes a fist, playfully jabs my chin. "Things will get easier, though."

I shouldn't be angry with him.

Just orders...

I nod. "I just wanted to see—"

"I know. I understand."

He clasps my hand, presses something into my palm.

"A long walk will see you right, kid."

He heads back towards The Jester.

"See you round, Raudd."

Not turning, he lifts an arm, waves.

Hand clenched tight, I meander away from the nightlife, find myself in a quarter of gleaming towers and polished boulevards. I keep walking, eventually coming to a small plaza where workers sit alone or in pairs on stone benches, contemplating or in quiet conversation.

I find a free bench, sit down.

Discreetly, I unfold the note.

It is a paper napkin, the name The Jester printed in a flamboyant font along two sides of the white square. In the middle, scrawled in a rough hand, is written:

Unit 17, Block 5B, Level 8, Hive F.
Memorize and destroy.

Night veils the citadel as I arrive at Hive F, only slivers of the starfield visible in the tangled heights. Tens of thousands of workers live in these twisted termite-like structures, half-built, half-grown. And, if Raudd can be trusted, one Dust-enhanced Niris too.

I pull the hood of my cloak tighter, head inside.

An earthy smell hits hard, mingling with aromas of exotic foods and sickly vapors. In the dimness and smoke, workers bustle around the food sellers, sharing jokes as their meals cook, or sitting at makeshift tables, eating. The ceiling is so low it magnifies the noise; if I reach up I could touch its rough-hewn surface.

Nobody pays me much notice.

For that I'm grateful.

The Dust-enhanced don't live here. And they rarely visit. If I'm seen word would get out.

Screw it.

The Niris shouldn't have ignored my messages.

Slipping through the crowd, I wonder if Rachkov gets out and about, or whether they've spent their entire time confined to their unit. In any case, they'll appreciate the company, I think, as I try to push away the sense that I'm trespassing.

I avoid the lifts, not wanting to get caught up in small-talk or be under the dazzle of bright lights, duck into the stairwell. I wait a little in the gloom, heart racing, half-marveling at the organic nature of the structure. Nobody follows.

At least that I can tell.

Satisfied, I start climbing, not too slow, not too fast. The levels tick by quickly, the squat levels meaning there aren't too many steps between floors. Everything in the hives isn't quite straight, isn't quite flat, a fight between nature and architecture. It feels a good place to lay low, hide.

Halfway, I spy a shard of rebar jutting from the wall. I snap it off easily, taking it as a sign I'm right to be armed.

A shiv is better than nothing.

As I come to the sixth level, the stairwell door jolts open, and suddenly I'm face-to-face with a wide-eyed Kalgeros. I slip past, saying nothing, not turning back. It mutters something in its native language, before I hear it descending.

Did my eyes give me away?

I feel the Dust stirring, heightening my senses.

Nearby, in the parallel shaft, I sense the lift hurtling past, its two occupants in a slanging match, drowning out the sound of the tinny public information speaker. Beyond, an orchestra of the faintest vibrations washes over me. Somebody washing, another chopping something, another waiting on their hot box to ping.

Banal, everyday, noises.

Familiar, reassuring.

Which is good.

Soon I'm on the eighth level, moving through a rabbit's warren of passages. Utility conduits snake across the walls, while underfoot I hear the gurgle of fluids beneath the grid-metal walkways. Entrances loom out of the darkness, their only light the dull clay-red numbers identifying each unit.

7, 12, 2.

I keep my eyes peeled for the magic number, wondering if Necrophage nests are anything akin to these labyrinthine hives. They'd make pretty decent territory for a caving adventure or two—aside from the presence of the insectoid menaces.

Maybe Raudd can give me a tour one day.

17.

No going back. I step forward, raise my fist—

Before I knock, standing in that dim, musty passage, I realize why I'm so tense. It isn't the smoke and daggers, the rule breaking, the threat of the Empire. They're a part of it, but the truth is much simpler.

I feel abandoned.

I've come to look Rachkov in the eye.

I knock, three slow heavy blows.

Across the passage, I hear an old flick playing. Beyond the Niris's door something shifts. Living or otherwise it's hard to tell. Could be the Niris, could be nothing.

I press the side of my head to the door, listen.

Silence now.

I knock again.

No answer.

I have to get inside.

I find the override panel, get to work. A hack from Kalad's little bag of tricks back when we combed the guts of space wrecks. Dead, malfunctioning, or obstinate doors could always be coaxed open. A pneumatic hiss and the door parts a fraction. I check the passage for passersby, then press my fingers into the thin gap and pull it open wide enough to slip through. *And I'm in.*

I smell the ocean, spicy meats, sea kelp. A neon sign written in the dense hieroglyphics of Niris script bathes the space in a dim electric-blue light.

Rachkov's pad, alright.

A scrabbling noise comes from the corner, briefly freaking me out, before I shake away the unease. An infiltration of vermin, no doubt. I've heard stories.

That or Rachkov's adopted a pet.

The place sure is a mess.

Even in the half-light I can see that. Food cartons, half-empty bottles, disassembled electronics, even old-fashion paper artifacts lie strewn about. The unit is small, but the clutter makes it feel smaller still. An alcove to the right houses a retractable sleeping rack that hasn't been folded-up in a long time, its top covered in detritus, its side shelves brimming.

No sign of the Niris.

I edge across the room, shiv extended, examining the shadowed recesses for any dead cephalopods, before ducking my head into the adjoining washroom.

The smell is bad.

As I stare at the grime-slicked walls and desiccated skin blocking up the shower drainage, I grimace, sickened. Niris hygiene leaves a lot to be desired. I pull the cubicle partition closed as best I can, flap my hand to disperse the stench, and survey the carnage.

Pretty sure this isn't a break-in.

No, this is just how Rachkov has lived since we arrived. I feel kinda guilty seeing this. Like I've seen a side they'd want to keep hidden. They'd be ashamed to see me here.

I drift through the room, using the shiv to pick through the debris, like I'm pulling back the curtain on their secretive, diminished life. Junk food, holo-games, eye-watering drinks. A real bucket list from the social misfit's playbook.

Some fall from grace.

Among the clutter I find many files on the United Empire, and not an insignificant number that relate to the Pilgrims. Diplomatic précis, military reports, strategic dossiers. Reflections on Rachkov's time in Zelevas' payroll, no doubt.

A weighing of its sins? Formulating a plan to help me find what's left of the Horizon? I can hope.

Maybe I should leave.

I've snooped enough. I could walk things back.

Rachkov needn't know.

I let my fingers play over the unit's door. Whatever thing skulked off from the corner is gone or silent.

Small mercies.

No, I'm staying.

I need Rachkov. And they need to know that.

One side of the prefabbed table that adjoins the galley kitchen faces the door, and I make some space before settling down onto its hard bench. No wonder Rachkov never sits here, I think, as I attempt to make myself comfortable. I push away the most pungent food cartons, place down the shiv, and rest my arms on the cleared area.

This could be a long night.

In the nearby units I can hear somebody in conversation with an absent party, someone solo-dancing to an electronica mix, and somebody else snoring with a very alien breathing pattern. Next to the hum of the fridge, the buzz from the neon sign, and the faint rustling in this unit, they're positively engrossing noises.

Damn vermin.

I try to meditate, relax myself, become oblivious to the slow passage of time, but I'm keyed up, mind racing as I turn over a hundred and one things.

Where is the Niris, for one?

Raising their very distinctive head above the parapet when Empire agents are abroad—or worse, cutting a deal in some dim underworld that breaks our own deal—wouldn't be cool.

Then there's their reception.

Rachkov's not going to be welcomed with open arms should they help me find the Horizon, that's for sure. Many Pilgrims won't forgive. And that'd be their right. We'd have to part ways, the Niris left to their own devices wherever the search might've taken us. Far from home, no doubt.

Whatever the Niris considers home, that is.

This place?

I wonder if a way back to the Academy will still exist for me, too, should I want to return. I reach for the shiv, cradle it between my fingertips. Something flickers in the crinkled reflection of one of the foil cartons. Reflexively, I jerk my head left as something whistles past, catching a brief look as it lands. Crab-like, skeletal, with a compact torso, chitinous limbs, and a spine-like tail.

What the—

It scuttles into the darkness, moving with sharp, rapid clacking noises. Snatching up the shiv, I bolt away from the table, circle towards the door. I brandish the weapon, but I've lost sight of whatever the hell this thing is, and I imagine it's too primitive to care anyway. Not taking my eyes from the corner, with my free hand I slap at the release panel. No luck.

I might be able to lever it open if I turn my back...

No chance.

The shiv trembles in my hand.

I can feel a stinging feeling on my face. I brush my fingers over my cheek. A trace of blood, barely a scratch. Yet, something's not right, a numbness already battling with the bite of the wound.

Poison. Ah, hell.

I don't have long.

Already, I can feel the toxin seeping into my bloodstream, spreading. I sense the Dust resisting, trying to derail the invader.

Across the unit, I hear the thing scurrying off.

I slap on the lights, harsh white light drowning out the neon blue. In the half-light the space had a laid-back, rebellious ambiance, but now, under the stark glare it looks like a sad, embarrassed shambles.

More movement at the periphery of my vision. A hint of the thing's tail disappearing close to the sleeping rack.

Damn thing moves fast.

I grip the shiv tight, wishing I had a firearm. Or an explosive. The entire right half of my face is numb. Maybe the Dust is fighting a losing battle.

This is on me.

I take a deep breath, focus.

It's waiting, bidding its time. And watching too.

Every second that passes is a second that tips the balance slightly more in its favor as its poison spreads. But if I turn my back to run it will strike.

I have only one choice.

Eyes fixed on the bunk, I hustle forward, grab a heavy tool from the workbench. I hurl it into the sleeping rack, before quickly loading up with another makeshift missile and firing away. I score a hit with the fifth or sixth throw, provoking an ear-splitting squeal. The thing breaks cover, scrabbling along the edge of one of the walls.

I move fast, blocking the route back, leaving the thing boxed into the corner. Some things lose their horror when they're cast into the light...

This isn't one of those times.

This thing—this bio-engineered assassin—is a horror of cartilage, limbs, and fangs.

I come out of this alive, Rachkov, you owe me big time.

Unmoving, save for its tail that flicks back and forth, the end punctuated by its lethal stinger, I'm glad I'm already a little numb to the world, I think darkly. I shake off the wooziness, switch the shiv into my good hand.

"Listen, you piece of Empire garbage," I spit as I edge forwards. "I don't know how you got here, how you found Rachkov, or how you slipped past Academy security, but now I'm going to end you."

Close, I smell its rancid stench, maggots and decaying meat. The thing's legs are bent, ready to spring. With my right foot, I feint a fast step—

And it comes at me.

My heart drops, its leap even more prodigious than I'd anticipated. Eyes on the stinger, I slash hard as it whips its tail back, the blade slicing satisfyingly through the second-last segment, viscera and fluid sloshing out.

The creature shrieks, but it's already on me.

We tumble backwards, my left-arm shielding my face from its blows. Beyond my arm I get the first terrifying glimpse of its underside. A round fleshy maw, lined with concentric circles of razor teeth, gnashing away so fast that they're a blur.

The thing's tail whips around frantically, still dangerous, occupying my other arm—and my only real weapon. I try to slice at it, but it's too fast, too slippery.

Then I make a mistake.

I stab at its torso instead, the shiv sliding into flesh, crunching against whatever this thing's made of, but doing little real damage. The tail whips around my neck double-quick.

It coils tight, choking.

Its grip is vice-like. I can't get any respite.

The world begins to darken.

The pain from the cuts start to recede…

Sewa! Fight!

Digging deep, I twist my right wrist, flick the shiv into a stabbing grip, and knife the thing. The blow hits my own shoulder. I'd scream if I could, but at least the lance of white pain is like a plunge into an ice bath, jolting me.

The second blow pierces the thing. And the third and fourth too. Again and again I attack, soon losing count, but each strike seems to have no effect.

Where's your damn brain?!

Fading, I summon the last of my strength, and stab hard and true. The end of the shiv bursts from the black heart of the thing's mouth, gore raining onto my own face.

Come on!

It flinches, but it keeps straining.

You've got to be kidding me.

Finally, I sense its whole body go limp, teeth included.

I wedge my fingers between the thing's limp tail and my neck, loosen the chokehold. Air seeps down my crushed windpipe, the sweetest thing.

Sometime later, the dead thing still resting on me, I wake to find Rachkov uncoiling the creature's lifeless tail from my neck.

"Sewa!" they exclaim. "You're alive!"

I clear my throat, each cough painful.

"Barely," I croak.

The Niris leans closer, hugs me tight.

Ignoring the discomfort, I squeeze back.

TWENTY-THREE

We leave the next morning.

No ceremony, no fanfare. Just the pair of us on a near-empty landing platform, a few auxiliary droids handling supplies, fueling, and the like. As we're about to board, Isyander glides out of the shadows. After a few private words with the Niris he joins me.

"I know you've been shaken."

I shrug, reflexively touch my bruised neck, knowing he'd be sensing the distress I still feel.

Golden whorls swirl in his mask.

"The failure of Academy security in this matter was most regrettable. That Niris owes you their life." Isyander steps closer. "Your courage was exemplary."

I snort. "I didn't even know what I was up against."

My voice is hoarse, cracked, each word painful.

"An Empire bio-assassin. State-of-the art." The clouds in the Academy leader's mask grow darker. "Zelevas grows bolder—and more capable—every year."

"Yeah, we've seen that on the Horizon."

Isyander nods. "Long may you, and all the Pilgrim arcologies, evade his forces."

Do you really care if the Pilgrims fall?

Isyander catches my dismissive sentiment, tenses, his instinctive anger hidden deep but not unseen. Even if my reads are a pale imitation of his own, he's not the only one with heightened senses.

Noticing that I've noticed, his posture softens.

Behind us, the droids finish their tasks, file away.

"Sewa, I want you to know," he says, fixing me with that golden-swirled mask, "you always have a home here. No matter what. The Academy would be honored to have you in our ranks. Our work is only just beginning…"

"Atonement," I whisper.

He nods. "Yes, the work of atonement."

I wait, but he volunteers nothing more.

"The Endless," I say, "they're gone, right? No trace of a single living one across the entire galaxy. So, how can they atone?"

"*They* can't," Isyander replies. "But that doesn't mean there can't be atonement for their sins. *We* can atone on their behalf."

"By doing what?" I croak, my vocal cords raw.

"Rest your voice," Isyander says. "They slaughtered *gods*. For this, there must be a reckoning, a rebalancing. When you return you will learn our true mission."

I go to speak, but Isyander raises a hand, silencing me.

"Sewa," he says, "the path you travel isn't an easy one. With persistence, with faith, though, I believe you will find everything you seek." He presses my upper arm. "And Sewa—when you're out there… think carefully about revealing who you are. Once your secret's out, there's no going back."

Half a system away, I still feel his hand's warmth. I sit up in my bunk, gently rotate my left arm, the lower part sheathed in a medical sleeve administering care to my shredded forearm. I feel a warm, tingling sensation, the pain gone, but the psychological scars run much deeper.

Every time I close my eyes I see the thing's frantic, gnashing maw a hand's width away.

New nightmares on old.

Ighszraaz speculated that the Empire party arrived with the incipient lifeform little more than a cluster of cells, too small to detect by traditional screening methods. After a few days' growth in a nutrient-rich environment like the waste system it would've possessed rudimentary mobility function, whereupon it would've begun searching for the Niris based on their genetic markers.

Devious *and* horrifying.

If I hadn't gone to the Niris's place, Rachkov would've been dead by the morning.

"Sewa."

Slowly, I lift my head. Rachkov stands in my cabin's doorway, a little less brash, a little less expressive, than the Niris I knew before our arrival at the Academy.

It seems half a lifetime ago.

I hope I can help them get their mojo back.

"Zarva?"

For a moment they look nonplussed, surprised I'd used their given name. "System gate approaching," they say. "Thought you'd want the heads-up."

"Yeah," I reply, getting up. "I'll come up front. Thanks."

"And you'd better take your eye-drops."

I peer at Rachkov, discern no trace of the golden hue in their pale blue eyes. Just an ordinary Niris, trekking across the galaxy.

Time to do likewise, travel incognito.

We're on a different craft to the one we arrived on, a slender needle of a ship better suited for long tracking missions. As well as more refined engines that leave less heat signature, the vessel is equipped with advanced hydroponics, hydrogen scoops, and copious fuel tanks. We can stay in deep space for near-unlimited lengths of time.

Not that I hope it comes to that.

Best of all, we each get our own cabin.

I pass Rachkov's on the way to the front. The smell of the seas, the tideline, drifts out, familiar and reassuring. Unlike their unit in the hive, the cabin is a lot tidier, although I can see it's stacked with several storage crates. A couple have already been cracked open, their contents liberally distributed.

Looks like they packed for the long haul.

That's good, I guess.

The deck is a halfway-house between a cockpit and a bridge, two throne-like flight seats and a vast console occupying the anterior, while the back end still has room for a small hologrid island. Rachkov stands behind their custom flight seat, transfixed by the sight through the cockpit screen that wraps around the deck, providing a one-eighty field of view.

"Always gives me shivers," they say, not turning.

The starscape is magnificent, a hundred million stars blazing in the darkness. The slash of the galactic plane with its bright churning heart and a few prominent stellar nebulae give shape and color to the vista, but the Niris isn't referring to these commonplace sights. No, what draws the eye, what holds the breath, is the perfect void, dead ahead. At first glance it looks like a region devoid of stars, but look more carefully and in the flawless square it becomes clear that something is blocking the light.

Something we're heading straight for.

The system gate.

A two-dimensional plane granting access to the galactic slipways, built by the Endless millennia past. As Pilgrims keen to avoid the Empire, we rarely used the gates, instead stealing into the slipways by ripping rifts in deep space.

Expensive but stealthy.

By contrast, the system gates afford entry to the galactic super-highway at minimal cost. Well, minimal Dust cost. The nerves certainly pay a high price. That's what comes from using the incomprehensible technology of a dead precursor race.

The square of inky black grows.

"Can you tell me something, Rachkov?" I ask, slipping past the hologrid and joining the Niris. "What does atonement mean?"

Rachkov slides into their flight seat, silent.

"You too?" I snark, teasingly. "At the Academy, everybody's happy to bleat on about the Endless atoning for their sins, but soon as you ask what that means they clam up."

"Atonement's a delicate subject," the Niris says, not taking their eyes from the gate. "Very delicate."

"How so?"

Rachkov sighs, peers hard at me. "You know, only true Pathfinders are supposed to know what atonement entails."

"Pathfinders?"

"Isyander's inner circle. Those sworn to uphold the Academy's most sacred duty."

"And, lemme guess," I say, "this most sacred duty is atoning for the Endless' sins."

Rachkov nods.

"Are you a Pathfinder?" I ask.

"I was close—"

"But you're not."

"I'm not."

"Hold up," I shout, excited. "You're not a Pathfinder, but you know what atonement entails, don't you!"

"Over the course of years—years!—of study, dedication, loyalty, I came to learn the truth from a Pathfinder who saw me as a kindred spirit." The Niris shakes their head. "Not after a matter of weeks."

"Pfft. Details." I laugh. "Loyalty? You ditched the Academy. You can tell me. I won't blab."

"I'll tell you." One of Rachkov's tentacles whips out, grabs my wrist. "But it's no laughing matter. Whole empires rise or fall on this knowledge. It needs to be kept under wraps. Even during my whole time with the Empire I didn't go near this. I'm serious."

I yank away my arm. "Then why tell me?"

"Because I know you'll keep digging—and that's more dangerous than knowing the truth." Rachkov gazes at the approaching gate. "More than that, though… I trust you."

I should feel happy, but I barely register anything.

The emptiness is still strong.

"I'm glad."

The Niris grunts, probably sensing my indifference.

"So, atonement…" Rachkov hesitates. "The Endless… the slaughter…" They press the tips of two tentacles together, go still. "I'll just say it: Isyander wants to resurrect the Lost."

"The Lost?" I stutter. "Resurrected?" I try to wrap my head around these words that feel like they don't make sense. "But they're gone… They're just… legends from an age that's long passed."

"They are." Rachkov nods. "Many even dispute whether they ever really existed. Many civilizations invent gods, after all."

No disputing the horror of the lodestone, though.

That was all too real.

I shiver, remembering the pain and terror in the Academy's subterranean depths as the ancient machinery tried to prize out the Dust in my veins. I shake the feeling away.

"Do you think they're real, I mean, *were* real?"

"Oh, they were real," Rachkov says. "Ask the Nakalim. Visit the archives. But you needn't delve into ancient history to find the Lost."

Does he mean…?

"They're still alive?"

"Likely just a handful. And scattered across the galaxy. But we have strong suspicions that's the case." Rachkov lowers their voice. "This, of course, is the Academy's most closely guarded secret. Even Isyander never speaks of these surviving Lost."

I ponder the Niris's words.

I feel some comfort in the knowledge they're not completely gone, that the Dust that courses through me is still connected to its living incarnations, but also apprehension.

Am I a thief? Are these ancient gods—no matter how few, how desperate their straits—plotting its recapture? Might I be harvested?

"How do you remake gods?"

Rachkov strokes a barbel on the side of their mouth. "As far as I know, nobody knows the answer to that question. Among the inner circle there are theories... obviously Dust is at the heart of the ideas."

"You're not scared?"

"No, I'm not scared." Rachkov chuckles. "We're the foot soldiers of Isyander's masterplan. Without us, he has no army. Besides, the Dust that we possess is but a drop in the ocean next to what's out there." The Niris gets more serious. "No, what worries me, though, is word getting out."

"To the empires?"

"Yes, to the empires. Can you imagine... the Sophons, the Vodyani, the United Empire... all the rest getting wind that the Academy sought to bring back the Lost? There'd be chaos. Dust wars, and then... Not many things frighten Emperor Maximilian Zelevas—and I should know—but the resurrection of a race of ancient, vengeful gods who were once hunted to near-oblivion? That would terrify him."

"Who knows what the Lost would do?" I say, shaking my head. "Nobody would want that genie to come out of the lamp." I join up the dots, the bigger picture coming into focus. "The Academy would become a target."

Rachkov nods.

"Even if Isyander convinced them this was just an ideology, a unifying vision, a north star that could never be reached, the very idea would unsettle the galactic order."

"They'd be attacked."

"From all sides."

The gate is closer now, a large square of dead space.

"So," I ask, "what's the answer?"

"The answer is not letting word get out and hoping Isyander's dream sours."

"That likely?"

"Isyander's determined but not insane." Rachkov gazes at the approaching gate. "If he learns that resurrecting the Lost is impossible he'll move on..."

"You don't sound sure about that."

"With Isyander you can never be sure." The Niris glances at me. "But that's my feeling."

With a chill, I recall the first time I met the Academy leader, stared into his golden-swirled visage. Beyond the mask, the cloth, he carried an otherworldly aura, like he was different to other mortals, even other Dust-enhanced.

"That why you ditched the Academy?" I ask, shaking off the memory. "Isyander's project not to your taste?"

"Not really," Rachkov replies. "The Academy just felt suffocating. I'd wanted to get away from that rock for a while when I caught wind of what Isyander really meant by *atonement*. I didn't take it seriously, thought it would fizzle out."

"But it didn't."

"Coming back," the Niris says glumly, "I've learnt that Isyander's more determined than ever."

A deep groan emanates from the rear of the ship, half noise, half vibration, trembling my bones and putting my teeth on edge. Hyper-engines spooling up.

"Anyway," Rachkov says, "that's atonement. Not your problem though, so now you can forget all about it." They smile. "Easiest way not to talk about it too."

The groan from the engines settles down, becomes a more pleasant hum.

"Now we focus on finding the Horizon," they add.

For an instant I let myself imagine reuniting with Rina, picking her up, telling her she's grown.

"This ever go wrong?" I ask.

"Sure." Zarva turns. "But, don't worry. We'd be ripped into a billion pieces before we even knew it."

"Reassuring."

"I think so." One of the Niris's tentacles rises and falls. "We'll be fine. You're only in trouble if your hyper-engine is damaged. Or missing. Never enter a gate without a working hyper-engine. That's the golden rule."

"Gotcha."

Ahead, faint silvery lines mark the edges of the gate, exotic alloys half-a-klick thick. Nobody's been able to reverse-engineer the gates, so they remain as unchanging testaments to the Endless, still defining the hub systems and major thoroughfares of the galaxy. Within the web, backwaters are numerous, vast swathes of space where the Endless didn't venture—or at least, didn't lay down roots. Only way to reach these isolated regions is to rip your own entry and exit holes into lesser traveled slipways.

And that costs.

Which means they're good places to hide.

Ahead, the perfect square of inky black gets larger and larger, soon dwarfing our modest vessel, eclipsing all but the very edges of the heavens. Even a Pilgrim hub orbital would comfortably fit within these gates. Undeviating, we head for its heart, the darkness relentlessly devouring the stars.

It feels like we're falling into oblivion.

The eyes begin to play tricks.

Shapes dance in the velvet black.

Visions, memories, night terrors. Yet it's not all tricks; the surface does have its own intrinsic texture. Like a viscous black fluid rippled by unseen forces.

An electric zing fills my nostrils.

And then we're sliding in.

Black tendrils lance up from the surface, entangling our vessel, crisscrossing the viewing port before pulling us in, slingshotting us onwards.

For a split-second the magnificent starscape surrounds us again, before every point of light begins fleeing along crisp lines for a single brilliant dot on the horizon, an inverse supernova attenuated by the screen's brightness algorithms. We move beyond light speed, space and time and geometry made anew.

All is dark except for the lone, incandescent star.

The lone star that is the whole universe.

"We didn't die!" I cry, trying to distance myself from the disconcerting sight. "Woohoo!"

"Woohoo, indeed."

"So, where are we heading?"

Rachkov sighs. "We left the Academy earlier than anticipated. Way earlier. I'll need to run the sims again."

I can feel their weariness.

"Hey," I say, touching the end of one of their limbs, "I'm glad you're here, helping me."

"I owe you more, so much more." Rachkov turns to the hologrid. "The least I can do is get you home."

"That's enough."

"Is it?"

"For me, yes," I reply. "You got other wrongs to right, other karmic balances to repay, you can redress them later. You owe me nothing more."

The Niris turns. "You could've run, you know."

"And let that thing kill you? No chance." I smile. "Who's going to give you a hard time about your Empire days?"

"You joke with me."

"You're right." I nod. "I did what I needed to survive. Nothing more."

"Well, I'm grateful, regardless."

"We do what we need to survive."

Zarva turns back to the void.

"We do."

Dead still, they gaze out, lost in thought.

"You're a real survivor, Sewa," they say, eventually. "I'm going to do my damnedest to get you back to your people. Believe me."

And they did.

Do their damnedest, I mean.

Over the following days, as we barreled through the slipways, darting from one system to another like a wild cat on the scent of prey, I watched the Niris spend every waking moment working tirelessly to my cause.

Chaos enveloped their quarters as they synthesized a flotsam of data and attempted to track the Horizon's bloodstained trail. My insights into Pilgrim operations, Rachkov said, were likely to be key, so I stayed at hand, ready to give answers. Hiding strategies, water replenishment routines, important dates on the Pilgrim calendar. Rachkov's appetite for details was voracious, unpredictable.

Between slipways, as we trekked across the fringes of systems, they'd contact the locals, hoover up whatever information they could get their tentacles on. Market activity from trading posts, gossip from passing flotillas, even bone-dry data collected by unmanned observation stations.

We never stopped, though.

Everything was harvested at a distance, anonymously.

By and large, we stayed away from colonized systems, Rachkov deeming the chances of the Empire's presence too great to risk. I knew the Niris was well-connected—diplomatic associates, system governors, corp directors—but their not-so-little black book of contacts remained firmly closed.

Not that they seemed too unnerved that their name was near the top of Emperor Zelevas' hit-list and Empire assassins were scouring the galaxy for their hide. I think I was more twitchy on that account. Even though I wasn't the target, I didn't want to be anyone's collateral damage.

Not before I could expose Kalad, at least.

And see the Horizon safe.

And learn my father's fate.

So, we were on our own in this hunt.

Beyond a few basic principles, Rachkov could no more articulate their tracking methods than I could explain my supercharged caving skills.

That was the nature of Dust.

Most of the time we worked on feeling, instinct.

"One of these systems," Rachkov says, gesturing at a trio of stars in the hologrid, "is where they're hiding."

Unlike the Niris's time hunting Pilgrims, where they commanded a large, noisy throng in the open, now we are only a lone, near-silent stalker in the hinterlands. No longer a pack of wolves tracking across an empty steppe, but a solitary jaguar creeping through a dark forest.

Watching and listening for the faintest hint of its prey.

In each system, we seek signs of my people.

We land on barren worlds and moons, looking for the telltale signatures of Pilgrim landing craft, freshwater collection, limited strip mining. We skirt the edges of gas giants, hunting for evidence of hydrogen harvesting in their heavy, swirling atmospheres. We hide in the broken shoreline of distant planetesimals where the system's sun is nothing more than a bright point in a starry sky, our eyes peeled for the slightest flare of ion-engines.

A game of hide-and-seek on a galactic scale.

Nothing. Not even a hint.

It's discouraging, but we remain positive.

We leave a marker to our own presence, a secret symbol that can alert arcologies to the existence of other Pilgrims in the vicinity. Every Pilgrim learns how to make this marker before they come-of-age, a last-ditch method should they ever find themselves sundered from their home.

Like me.

So, on each of the three system's largest rocky worlds, in the dead heart of their largest continents, we carve out a simple pattern in the earth or brush or ice that can be easily seen by any craft flying past overhead.

Seventeen days after we began, we return to the final one.

From the skies I can see the pattern in the ochre ground, distinct slashes that would provoke curiosity but little more in any other observers.

My heart sinks.

No additions have been made to the pattern that would indicate other Pilgrims' presence.

They're not here.

Or if they are, they're staying hidden.

We hit another region, start over. Rachkov is despondent, but puts on a brave face, immersing themself in the ocean of data again with renewed vigor. Despite their determination, I can't but feel defeated.

They're gone.

Worse still, I can feel the Dust in my veins craving their next adventure, itching to do anything but restart this hunt. A break might do us both good. With my wounds well healed, I badger Rachkov to let me go on a caving sortie in one of the nearby systems.

"Hankering for some cold, dank cave action, huh?" Rachkov asks, attention on the hologrid.

"I can take or leave the cold and dank." I scan my eyes over the smattering of systems flickering on the grid. "As long as there's caving."

Rachkov smiles. "Maybe we *should* have a time-out."

"I think so."

"Alright." Rachkov nods, looks up. "Next system, there's a world I wanted to visit—"

"Something on the Horizon?"

"No, something else."

I wait for the Niris to offer more, but they remain reticent. Could be anything given their past. I don't pry.

"Anyway," they say, tentacles gripping the sides of the hologrid, "that world should have some prime caving spots. We can kill two birds with one stone."

"Then what are we waiting for?"

TWENTY-FOUR

ㅋㅅㄷㅋㅏㅆ ㄱ◁ㆆƐ

We land in the world's northern hemisphere, pitching down on the margins of a rocky plateau that overlooks unbroken rainforest, a sandstone island in a ocean of green, the rising sun casting the treetops in a thin golden light. Stepping off our vessel, what's striking is the absence of noise from the trees, no trill of birds, no susurration of insects, no call of primates, nothing except the occasional rustle of leaves on the gentle breeze.

A festering, damp smell laces the muggy air.

Gazing out over the upper canopy, I can't help but notice signs of decay, many leaves blotched with a grey sickness, the tips curled and yellowing.

"What is that?" I ask, cupping my brow. "Some kind of blight?"

Rachkov approaches the edge of the plateau, flicks out a tentacle, breaking off one of the fronds. The Niris studies it.

"Dieback," they say, tossing the leaf.

"So, a disease?"

"Uh-uh." Rachkov thinks. "A lack of balance."

Lack of balance? Like what? A drought?

"That why it's so quiet?"

"Maybe."

I want to ask if this is connected to their mission here, but I know I won't get anything out of the Niris. Instead, I skirt the cliff edge, getting my bearings, struggling a little against the heavy gravity of the planet.

My calves are going to suffer.

I stop, catching sight of structures on the far side of the plateau. "What's that?" I shout, gesturing.

Rachkov joins me. "Let's take a look."

As we make a beeline for the area, the Niris delves into their cloak, proffers a dark, angular object.

A handgun. Long square barrel, hefty grip.

"As a precaution," Rachkov says.

"You expecting trouble?"

"No." Rachkov brandishes the firearm, encouraging me to take it. "But you never know."

I take the gun and the belt, holster it on my hip.

Gonna take a while to get used to this.

We carry on, and a short time later the hazy structures come into focus. A sleek, mid-size spacecraft sits amid a haphazard collection of shipping crates, the site messy like it was abandoned in a hurry. It looks deserted, but we take no chances, scurrying closer with our guns drawn.

Nobody greets us.

Satisfied we're alone, I give the vessel a better look. Although the design is elegant, the ship has seen better days, its large round main section coated in a patina of green fuzz, while the two long fins that hold the engines show signs of corrosion. At first glance, the deep red decorative color might be mistaken for Empire livery, but the hue is slightly different, and this craft is nothing like anything from Zelevas's armada.

"Lumeris?"

"Nakalim," Rachkov answers, seeming aggrieved.

"You mentioned them before," I say, remembering. "I can't say I've heard of them."

"Few have." The Niris glances around. "They're an ancient people, but, by and large, they've lain dormant for millennia."

"And now they're awakening?"

Rachkov eyes the decayed vessel that looms over us.

"We shouldn't dwell here." The Niris's gaze moves to the surrounding rainforest, still deadly silent. "You scratch your caving itch and I'll get... where I need to go." They nod. "We'll meet back at the ship. Wait for me if you're back first. Understood?"

I nod.

"Am I going to run across Nakalim?"

"I doubt it. I think they've gone." They study the site again. "Remember: you've got heightened senses. Stay alert and no one's getting the jump on you."

If the Niris's words are meant to reassure me, they fail.

"You stay alert too," I reply.

I'm about to take off, when Rachkov calls again.

"Wait up!" They skim over, delve into their cloak. "Something I've been meaning to give you for a while."

They offer a tentacle, a small, gleaming object clutched in its tip. *A data crystal.*

With reluctance, I take it.

"All my correspondences with Kalad," Rachkov says. "For when you're back. Cast-iron evidence of his guilt."

And yours.

I close my palm, stow away the crystal.

"I'll see you at the ship, okay?"

Soon after, I've scaled down to the rainforest floor, a thick, tangled landscape of roots and tubers, gnarled trunks weaving upwards in wild patterns. A perpetual twilight exists here, only rare beams of sunlight spearing the canopy. Like from above, something feels amiss, the forest deadly still and silent, laced with decay.

Inside, the Dust is on edge, watchful.

I creep through the undergrowth, rustling leaves, snapping twigs, anything but quiet despite my efforts. Following a descending incline I soon pick up a fault line in the ground, and after trekking what must be less than a klick from the plateau, my instincts lead me to a fissure in the earth.

I gaze at the black scar, feeling like I'm being watched.

Aside from the uneasy feeling though, I can't find any evidence of others in the dense undergrowth.

A slight breeze issues from the subterranean realm.

Still waters, rich minerals, *my scents.*

I leave the surface, happy to head into the depths.

The cave system is vast and diverse. Sheer drops, twisting galleries, crawlspaces, and submerged sections populate its innards. I couldn't ask for a better playground for my caving fix, mind and muscles well exercised, but for the entire session I have a nagging feeling that saps my enjoyment.

We shouldn't have come here.

We should be searching for the Horizon, not wasting time on side missions, and definitely not getting entangled in whatever messed up shit that's led to this world's current state.

I'm annoyed with Rachkov, more annoyed with myself.

Every day away from the Pilgrims is a day Kalad plots.

I hike back to the plateau in a funk, the heavy gravity sapping now, hoping to find the Niris ready and waiting to go, but upon scaling the bluff, I find our ship deserted.

Sooner we leave, sooner we can be back on track.

I sit and massage my burning calves, stare out over the silent rainforest, but it's not long before I'm heading back to the Nakalim landing site where we parted ways.

Same story there.

No Rachkov, still no sign of life.

The Nakalim craft towers over the site, dazzling in the midday sun. I give it a cursory inspection, seeking a way inside, but the vessel is sealed tight. If the Nakalim crew their vessels in similar fashion to the Pilgrims, I estimate this ship might've held forty to fifty of their number.

Where are they now?

Did they leave on another ship? Apart from the lack of maintenance, this one doesn't seem to have suffered any damage. *What would I know though?* The hyper-engines could be crocked and I wouldn't have a clue. The unkempt nature of the site suggests whatever happened they left swiftly…

Maybe they're still here.

For what purpose though?

A religious breakaway? Survivalists rejecting the spacefaring age? Are they dying along with the planet too? Or maybe they're the reason for the dieback. I wander between the crates, wishing I knew more about the Nakalim, what might have brought them to this virgin world.

Under the shadow of their vessel, seeking respite from the muggy heat, I crouch. I close my eyes, let the slight breeze caress my face. Beyond the festering, dank miasma of decay, I can just about smell Rachkov, a taste of its piscine reek coming from the jungle to the north.

There you are.

At the plateau edge I scan the forest. A few hundred meters away I spy a thinning of the trees, maybe a clearing. I breathe deep, Rachkov's scent stronger. The Niris went there.

I know it.

And, I swiftly discover, it wasn't the only one.

After descending to the forest floor, limbs weary, I soon find a trampled path through the undergrowth, vegetation underfoot flattened, fronds and branches snapped and hanging limp. Not just the trail of a few, but dozens, probably hauling equipment and supplies too. Looking closer, I see new plant life sprouting from the trampled ground.

An old trail then.

Near the clearing, scorch marks disfigure the gnarled bark of a vast trunk. I stop, brush one streak with my fingertips, bring the ashy residue to my lips. Acrid taste, carbonization. Following the invisible trajectories of the lines, I find foliage punctured by cauterized holes confirming my misgivings.

Laser fire.

I'm suddenly glad Rachkov gave me a gun. I feel its reassuring weight against my hip, enjoy its cold, angular heft. I draw it.

Stepping into the clearing, the first thing I notice is the squat, black edifice. From its hard, angular construction to its etched, glimmering surfaces it stands at odds with the natural wilds of the rainforest. A wide threshold leads to a shadowed interior, and my skin hums from the odd energy emanating from the structure.

Or maybe that's on account of the bodies.

Two creatures lay splayed in the brush close to the edifice, while a third lies prone on the threshold. I shuffle closer to the pair, scanning the surrounding forest, gun gripped tight.

Even with their full-body attire—dark khaki fatigues brimming with equipment, loose fitting cowls hiding their faces—I can see they're dead. The breathing hose that runs from mask to back marks their species clear as day. The third corpse is the same.

Haroshem.

The species most chosen as servants of the Academy, known for their quiet restraint, their loyalty.

A coincidence? I don't think so.

The Academy was up to something here.

Did they come into conflict with the Nakalim?

Calming myself, I step over the corpse, enter.

The interior is dark, yet a faint energy crackles off the walls, throwing a golden light over everything. I gasp. Somehow, despite the outside of the structure occupying a space no bigger than my quarters at the Academy, the inside is immeasurably vaster, and the black vault above twinkles with stars. Even without the imposing, tessellated sculpture of a humanoid figure towering over me, I would know who built this.

The Endless.

I suddenly feel like a trespasser.

They've gone, I tell myself, but I don't know if I believe it.

How can such a civilization simply end? I let out a nervous laugh. We're truly like children next to them. Blind, stumbling runts squabbling in the gutters of their magnificent ruins. No wonder we Pilgrims have elevated them to the realm of the divine.

Heart thudding, I wonder if this vast cavern is real or illusion, but if it is a simulacrum I can discern no sign of the trick. Casting my eyes down from the starscape, my eyes alight on an opening at the base of the statue.

A staircase into the depths.

I glance back at the oblong of light where I entered, the greenery and stillness of the rainforest beyond a surreal sight. Even in its decay it calls to me, offering sanctuary from whatever's in this place…

What is this place?

I step forward, start off down the steps.

The air cools. Cerulean crystals in the walls issue a dim flickering light. Far off, faintly, I detect the smell of smoke, timber, something like camphor—and something altogether more acrid. Like something burnt in a fire, singed beyond recognition. Something malevolent.

The Niris too.

These ruins are far from abandoned.

Any urge to call out for Rachkov ebbs away.

After descending for what feels an age, I come to a long, empty hallway, several arches on either side leading elsewhere. Even though this place was built eons ago it has a timeless air, the glyphs and decorations on the walls near pristine. Only the occasional intrusion of the rocky crust, breaking off chunks of the friezes gives any sign of elapsed time. Keeping to the shadows, I head through the first arch on the left…

The site is vast, like an underground city, yet full of precipitous drops, empty caverns, geometries that make little sense to the naked eye. The deeper I go, the more the natural geology encroaches, a comforting salve. Long, long ago the Endless must've inhabited this place, but discerning their existence, their daily habits, from this maze feels impossible.

The Nakalim's ways, on the other hand, are easier to fathom. *They* are this subterranean realm's current inhabitants and there are many signs of their presence. Small cairns, shrines, old campfires. A makeshift slaughterhouse where animals from the world above have been butchered for meat. A chamber near the foot of the first staircase stacked with lengths of timber. A small plaza where their dead have been laid out.

Twelve bodies, four on one side, eight on the other, each covered with a thin muslin cloth.

I can't help but peek beneath the fabric.

The Nakalim are slender, dark-skinned humanoids, all twelve with their heads shaved. Curiously, the four are still dressed in an elaborate attire that might be military dress, while the eight wear much simpler garb. Some kind of embalming ritual has preserved their mortal remains, but many among the eight show evidence of terrible burns. Strangely, despite what I imagine might've been agonizing, fatal wounds, many of their faces are set in beatific rather than horrified expressions. *Stranger and stranger.*

Sometimes I hear the living, but I'm careful to remain unseen, swiftly backtracking or staying hidden while they pass. Slowly, methodically—listening, watching, following—I zero in on the location of their settlement, until I find myself on a ledge overlooking their primitive camp.

They've chosen one of the deepest recesses, the passages and caves more natural rock than built edifices, the air chilly. Crude abodes made of laced timber and torn insulation—lean-tos really—are arrayed in a rough circle. A small fire, more embers than flames, sits at the camp's heart, and a few Nakalim are planted around it, engaged in murmured conversation. Like the corpses, all have shaved heads. Even if I understood their tongue I wouldn't know their words though, so softly do they speak. Beyond the camp, almost lost in the shadows, I can see the silhouettes of more Nakalim, standing where the cavern slopes away.

Based on the dwelling, I estimate twenty to thirty live here, and as I look carefully, I spy several scattered about, sitting alone in unmoving reposes.

Why are they here?

They came from the stars! Yet nothing about the site suggests this is a military or scientific expedition, no archeological digs, no hardware crates, no sense of outward activity or purpose. Only half-joking I imagine that they might've been infected with some parasite that's addled their minds, turned them into these strange, lethargic creatures.

From one of the grander lean-tos a figure emerges.

The Nakalim go quiet.

My stomach drops.

Is that Rachkov?

In the half-light it takes me a moment to register that they're just another Nakalim, one dressed in thick robes and wearing an elaborate headpiece. I breathe out, relieved, then pull myself in tighter, still watching.

Is this their leader?

The Nakalim approaches the fire, circles slowly, keeping themself outside the ring of others. They stop behind one, speak, voice confident, authoritative. From the cadence of their words it feels like they're asking a rhetorical question, and the addressed Nakalim stays silent, head down, like they've been shamed. Not moving, the robed figure turns their head, repeats their words to the next Nakalim—but louder.

Same result.

Across the camp I can feel the tension rising, others turning, getting up, congregating.

Before the Nakalim can address another, one of the sat number leaps up, confronts the leader with fierce words, a hair's width away. The leader doesn't respond, letting the angry Nakalim say their piece, but before they've finished another barrels out of the surrounding shadows, shoves the speaker back.

Within moments, a melee ensues, a dozen Nakalim on their feet pushing and shouting, close to blows. The scrum spirals about, some interposing themselves between warring Nakalim, others screaming with a visceral intensity. The leader raises their arms, seemingly appealing for accord, when an eerie, demented screech echoes through the cavern, silencing all.

They stand like statues, fixed in their poses, only turning their heads towards the blackness, and I feel the hairs on the back of my neck rising.

What the hell is that?!

Right then, someone grabs me.

My instinctive cry is snaffled as something is planted over my mouth, and a sudden icy horror envelops me.

No, no, no, no…

Unthinking, I struggle against the sinuous, iron limbs, but they've got me bound tight. I'm in half a mind to bite whatever's over my lips, but my mouth is clamped, so I focus on breaking out, trying to roll this away and that. My captor's saying something, but another terrifying shriek resounds through the cave, louder this time, swallowing their words.

I go limp.

Something about that cry frightens me far more than my current predicament.

"Sewa! It's Rachkov!" my captor growls, and this time I hear the words. "Rachkov!"

Now I can smell the Niris, I wonder how I didn't notice its presence. Relief floods me.

"Easy, easy now!" they whisper. "I'm going to let go."

The tip of Rachkov's tentacle falls away from my mouth, other limbs relaxing and releasing me from their grip too.

I give my jaw a rub. "The hell, Rachkov?!"

"We need to go," the Niris says, livid. "Now."

Their gaze is not on me, but looking out beyond the Nakalim. Most, I see, have fallen to the ground, taken up poses of supplication towards the depths, foreheads against the stone. Only the leader and a couple of others remain standing. From the darkness, a faint pallid glow flickers, growing brighter…

"Now!" Rachkov repeats, hauling me to my feet.

"What is that thing?" I ask, as we skitter off.

Rachkov scrambles over the stony ground, their tentacles a blur of motion. "Our end if we don't move."

I glance back to see some shambling, glowing horror emerge out of the depths, stop before the leader and the rest of the prostrate Nakalim. I can't help but stop, transfixed by the sight of this malformed creature, easily twice the size of the Nakalim. It's like it's aflame, but the flames don't look like flames, the wrong color, the wrong shape, and more than that, the matter that forms its body shifts and writhes too, so it's difficult to know where it begins and ends.

A thing from nightmares.

I'm wondering if it has *any* comprehensible physiology, when I get the sense of its anatomy shifting again—myriad eyes coming to the fore.

It sees me.

And not in a simple visual sense.

A sudden coldness runs through me, my insides burning, and the creature issues another ear-splitting shriek, so vehement it feels like it's coming from inside my own head. I watch it barrel through the Nakalim, eliciting cries that I can't tell are made in agony or ecstasy, before Rachkov slaps my cheek, drags me onwards.

"Never look back," they admonish. "Never!"

I feel light-headed, but also terrified.

We run, faster than ever, careening into walls, leaping across crevasses, the geology of the deeper regions slowly giving way to the Endless' artifice as we ascend. The gun smacks against my hip, then clatters loose as I bump against an outcrop.

I don't even think about grabbing it.

My lungs burn, my calves too.

I feel the creature closing the gap, its sickly light spilling over us. The urge to glance back is near overwhelming.

"It wants you to turn!" the Niris shouts. "Resist!"

We reach the vast entrance hall, only the last long staircase between us and the surface, but the thing feels so close now, chilling me. *We aren't going to make it.* I glance at Rachkov hoping for some strategy, some hope, and the Niris reaches inside its cloak, pulls out something. It glints in the monster's light. Rachkov manipulates it, and the object suddenly radiates a golden light.

Dust? It must be.

Nothing else glows with such an aura.

The creature screams, a depraved craving.

The Niris pulls back a languid tentacle, hurls it deep into one of the side passages. The creature's light recedes as it swerves after it like a dog distracted by a stick.

"Don't let up," Rachkov says. "That morsel won't go far."

As we bound up the ancient steps, I understand why it's after us. The creature hunts us for our Dust. That's why the Nakalim didn't interest it.

Only we possess the rarefied substance.

A wretched scream reverberates up the staircase, distant, but not far enough to relax, and we push on, harder. We don't stop to marvel at the absurd, space-time twisting entrance, nor offer the dead Haroshem in the clearing any last rites, but simply scramble on through the rainforest, aiming for the dark heft of the plateau where we landed.

A short time later, barely in our seats, we lurch away from the jungle world, breathing hard, hearts hammering, sweat and dirt and brush still coating us, still more in shock than relief.

Once I get my breath back, I turn to the Niris.

"What the hell was that thing, Rachkov?"

TWENTY-FIVE

ㅈﾘ∈ﾝㅏ⅄ ㅓﾘ∿ﾝㅌ

The Niris stonewalls me.

Anytime I ask anything about the episode, they grow angry, tell me that I nearly got us both killed, that everything I saw on that world isn't my concern, that it's better if I don't know.

It doesn't stop me speculating, though.

Why had the Endless come to this world?

What were the Nakalim doing there?

Most of all, why did the Academy get involved?

No easy answers come, but one thing's clear: that creature was desperate, frenzied even, for our Dust. It wanted to *feed*. I shiver recalling my terror. Was it composed of Dust as well as matter? The light had the wrong luster, a sickly pale imitation of the golden sheen that emanated off the true substance, but was that some reflection of its diseased nature? Could this creature, I pondered, have been some lesser species of the Lost?

Was that why the Nakalim worshipped it?

They saw a reflection of the magnificent gods of old that they'd once revered, had misguidedly chosen to devote themselves to it, living in the shadowed ruins for their beliefs. Then when the Academy had got wind of the Nakalim's discovery, they came to see for themselves. And ended up coming into deadly conflict.

Maybe that's how it had played out.

I shake away the thoughts.

Whatever that creature was, whatever the Academy's involvement, Rachkov's right. It's not my concern.

The Horizon is.

٦

"Can I come in?"

Lying in my bunk, I lift up my head to see Rachkov standing stock-still in my doorway. Less than a day has passed since we left the Nakalim and the monstrous creature, the system gate getting close now.

I shrug. "Sure."

"You okay?"

I don't move. "Not really." I glance at the starfield. "It feels hopeless. Like we'll never find them."

They move closer. "I got your hopes up."

I can smell the tide, seaweed. Where once I might've turned my nose, it's now familiar, reassuring.

"No… well, maybe."

"I'm sorry. I really thought we were close."

"And now? You think we'll ever find them?"

"I don't know."

I exhale. "Damn."

Are they gone? Forever?

I don't want to feel this now.

Beside me I can sense Rachkov thinking, several limbs undulating. "There is another option."

That gets my attention.

"What do you mean?"

"I know someone," they say. "Someone who might know where they are. At the very least, might have contact with another Pilgrim arcology."

Am I hearing this right?

"Why didn't you say this earlier?" I sit up, clenching the bed covers, trying not to go ballistic. "Like, why have we been scrambling around all this time when—"

"They're on Raia."

"Raia?"

"Yes, Raia."

This is crazy.

"Then why are we even talking about this?" I get up, pace. "Raia? We'll be in shackles before we even make landfall."

"Maybe. And, I should add—" Rachkov says, brushing down its cloak "—this contact, they won't be easy to find, and they might not want to help either."

"Then why?" I spin to face the Niris. "I want to get back to the Horizon, believe me, but not for a hundred-to-one shot in Zelevas's backyard!"

Something's off…

"There's another reason…" Rachkov says, softly.

"Another reason? To go to Raia?" With a cold clarity, I suddenly understand. "It's to do with that monster, isn't it?" I shout, hackles rising. "I'm playing second fiddle to Academy business now, aren't I?!"

"No, you're not." Irritation colors Rachkov's words. They close their eyes, take a breath. "That's not it."

"Then what is it?"

"I was going to keep this to myself… if we'd found the Horizon…" Rachkov mumbles, before clearing their throat. "This isn't going to be easy to hear, but you deserve to know."

I steel myself, afraid. "Tell me."

The Niris takes a deep breath. "It's your father—I crossed paths with him. On Raia."

"What?"

You went to Raia, Father?

I feel dizzy, sick.

"I didn't know he was your father—not until we reached the Academy and I heard your family name: *Eze.*"

My mouth is dry as sandpaper.

I already know the rough shape of the likely answer to my next question, but I want to hear it in the Niris's words. "And you waited until now to tell me because…?"

"Because I betrayed him. Because I gained his trust, then saw how I could turn him in and gain Zelevas's trust." Rachkov hangs their head. "Without my betrayal you might've seen your father again."

The room is spinning.

A white-hot fury rises from deep inside.

"What happened to him?" I spit.

"I don't know."

I turn away.

"Get out," I whisper.

"Sewa, I'm sorry."

"Get out!"

The Niris obeys, no more words.

The tears come soon after.

I feel dirty, shamed.

Like I, *myself*, have betrayed my father for associating with this wretched Niris. They *hunted* Pilgrims. Hawked out their services to the highest bidder, Maximilian Zelevas, without a second thought for the consequences. I shouldn't be surprised they happily traded my father's freedom for a chance to win favor with the Emperor.

Oyita wouldn't be.

Like her, maybe I should've been less forgiving.

I want to ditch this vessel, ditch this slippery Niris, get dropped off at the nearest hub-world as fast as I can.

I could lay low, think, plan my next move.

All without the traitor skulking around.

But, but, but…

I shouldn't be hasty.

If I burn my bridges with the Niris, I might never get the chance to discover what happened to Father. He could still be alive, wallowing in a gulag at the heart of the Empire, or eking out a miserable existence in one of Zelevas's work camps at the frozen edge of the Raian system.

Or beyond.

And then there's the Horizon.

Walk away from the Niris, and I walk away from this ever-so-slender lead they dangled in front of my eyes. A mysterious figure located on Raia who acts as a messenger between the arcologies.

It's plausible.

Many were left behind at the time of the exodus.

Most got rounded up by Zelevas's squads, but some survived at the margins of Raian society. They practiced their religion in the dead of night, in the empty places, in the more tolerant zones, but some hunkered for more. Every Pilgrim has heard the whispers of an underground resistance on Raia.

Less a military force, more a political operation.

Working in the shadows, encouraging freedom of thought, artistic and religious expression, even civil disobedience. And, most importantly, undermining Empire efforts to eradicate the arcologies. Go-betweens, information brokers.

So, plausible.

And maybe that's what Rachkov's banking on.

Maybe after some downtime at the Academy, the Niris isn't too excited about the thought of another stint under Isyander's command. Maybe they prefer the Empire lifestyle. Maybe they think if they bring me in—not just a Pilgrim, but a Dust-blessed Pilgrim, no less—they'll get reinstated into the upper echelons of the Empire.

Bait and switch.

Privileges restored. Death warrant revoked.

Two birds with one stone.

Maybe this wild-eyed hunt we've been on is pure theater, a ruse to convince me to trust enough to go to Raia. Talk about black comedy. Wouldn't it be a joke of the darkest shade if the Niris delivered two generations of the same family to Zelevas?

If they even did shop my father.

Of course, there is one way out of this paranoid spiral of distrust. Walk away, cut ties. Now.

Forget about the Horizon.

Forget about my father.

Forget about Mother and Oba and Rina.

Listen to the whispers of the Dust in my blood, and fully embrace my Academy identity.

This, then, is my state of mind, as we drift through this desolate backwater of the galaxy. I veer between extremes, one moment happy to sever myself from the past, the next certain my fate lies on Raia. I will not choose in such a frame of mind.

We keep to ourselves.

I hear the Niris shuffling around, monitoring the telemetry data, still seeking signs of the Horizon. Whatever choice I make, they tell me through the locked partition to my cabin, they will honor.

They give me a day to decide.

I grunt so they know I heard.

They are the only words we've exchanged.

The revelations have torn down the barriers between past and present. Before it was straightforward. First there was the past. Life on a Pilgrim arcology, running free, the one dark blot the hole where my father should've been. Then, there was everything that came after that caving mission. A new life, surrendered to the Dust, hightailing around the galaxy with a wily cephalopod.

Now it's anything but straightforward.

The Niris straddles my past and present, entangling everything so I feel like tearing my hair out.

Caution be damned.

I will never trust the Niris…

I leap from my bed, march out of my cabin. The ship feels strange, alien. The Niris's pervasive smell fills me with revulsion. I find Rachkov in the pilot's seat, lost in the starfield.

"Take me to Raia."

I don't wait for a reply.

TWENTY-SIX

ㅈㅅㅌㄹㅅㅅ ⊖ㅅㅌ

Under a slate grey sky, the rain falls in a barrage of ceaseless, windswept sheets, chilling me to the bones. I wear a grimy poncho, purchased from one of the shanty town's cheap clothing stalls, but the hood is busted, and the rain spatters my freshly shaven head.

I feel exposed.

We've come to Rustal, a bland moon of the Raia system's sixth planet, where only two things happen. The first is the excavation of the moon's plentiful stocks of a valuable silicon oxide by a mining workforce that is inexperienced, poorly paid, and very eclectic in its demographics. The second is the daily processing of thousands of Raian-bound hopefuls, looking for a fresh start at the heart of the United Empire.

The two are not unconnected.

Only a third of the migrant hopefuls gain entry-visas to Raia, and many of the failed applicants lurch straight into the moon's chaotic mining industry such is their desperation. If our cover's blown, though, Rustal's mining operations will be a summer camp compared to where we'll be sent.

No point dwelling on that.

I pull the collar of my poncho tighter, rivulets of icy rainwater still running down the gaps. Through the deluge I can just about make out the silhouette of Rachkov further ahead in the line, the shallow, angular dome of their head distinctive against the more humanoid races.

I swallow back my bile.

My contempt for the Niris has only deepened, but this is no time to get agitated. Heading through separately is a sensible safety measure should either of us get collared, but being alone is making me feel vulnerable.

The line shuffles forward, the gates just opened.

Each day, prospective immigrants begin queuing around dawn, ready for when the processing counters open their shutters a few hours later. Nobody sleeps out overnight, the harsh, freezing downpours discouraging even the most hardy souls—not to mention the Empire patrols who move on any stragglers or campers with extreme prejudice.

The ragged line to the immigration block runs along the spaceport wall, a towering, monolithic grey expanse that looms upward, perpetually darkened by the rains that always seem to come from the west. I imagine some Empire bureaucrat designing the layout of the site exactly so that no shelter is offered to the huddling masses seeking entry to Raia.

Asshole.

On the other side of the line, the sprawling shanty town that surrounds the spaceport spills out, a chaotic maze of avenues defined by where the market sellers set their stalls. Here, beside the line that forever crawls forward yet never ends by the time the shutters close at nightfall, it is mainly food sellers preparing hot and spicy dishes for the hopeful.

I can smell tamarind and chilies, garlic and chestnuts, roasting meats of unknown provenance. The rain patters on corrugated roofs and lean-tos, while great saucer-like cooking dishes sizzle with steam as errant raindrops hit the pans. As the line worms its way forward, queuers duck over to the food stalls seeking their favorite dish like moths chasing a flame.

I'm hungry, but my stomach is knotted up.

I'll chow on something on the other side.

If you get to the other side.

Among the line there's a camaraderie, a gallows humor, families teasing one another, people sharing stories or food, a sense of fragile community despite the high stakes and terrible conditions.

I speak to no one though.

Around me, the chatter dies as we draw near to the counters. Documents are readied, stories silently rehearsed, blank faces primed.

Each hopeful will face the Empire alone.

Through the mist I watch Rachkov beckoned forward.

With the state of Raia's oceans, popular wisdom has it that Niris find it easy to gain entry on account of their natural expertise in underwater operations like salvage missions, seafloor surveys, and rig repairs. Rachkov's more pressing concern is not being IDed as one of Zelevas's most wanted.

"This is the last place they'll expect me," they told me as we wandered the shanty town yesterday.

Let's see.

The Empire official waits stony-faced, reaches out for the Niris's faked papers. Unlike the makeshift waterproofs most of the hopefuls are wearing, the official sports a military-grade black trench coat with an elaborate head-covering. He looks warm, comfortable—and dry. On his hip I can see a stun-baton on one side, and a stocky firearm on the other.

They engage in a rapid-fire back and forth.

No niceties, I imagine.

Vital fluids are sequestered, loaded into an analyzer. Rachkov assured me these devices are not sensitive to Dust, instead simply seeking to establish the absence of illicit pharmaceuticals in the bloodstream.

I pray that's still right.

They talk as they wait for the results. Then the official goes still, cranes his neck, scanning the line. Our eyes meet...

No, please no.

I might've run if I wasn't rooted to the spot.

Rachkov turns, says something as they wink.

The official breaks into raucous laughter, before switching his attention to the device in his hand, still shaking his head.

I relax, still trembling.

False alarm. I'll quiz the Niris later...

Rachkov gets the green light, heads on for the security lane, the most difficult hurdle passed with flying colors. Soon after, a young girl, no older than ten, gets dispassionately rejected by the same border official. Too shocked to cry, she stands statuesque beside the line, pale as winter. I can't help but think of Rina, but as I pass, I just give her my best *stay strong* look.

Now I'm up.

At the front of the line, hopefuls fan out into one of four open lanes, and I get shuffled towards another official.

"Next," the woman barks. "Step forward."

The last hopeful, a burly Gnashast, has been refused entry, but is still arguing their case. They're up in the official's face, blocking my path. I can smell their fetid breath.

The rain drums on the shelter.

"Deeee-nied!" the woman says, drawing out the word, while pushing them back with the tip of her stun-baton. "Move along! Now!"

The order only further infuriates the Gnashast, who keeps arguing, louder, closer.

Bad idea.

The stun-baton crackles to life with electric menace.

The Gnashast's legs give out, their whole frame shuddering from the terrible jolt. They spasm on the floor, before being swiftly dragged away by a pair of Empire soldiers.

"Papers," the woman demands, nonplussed.

I pass my ID card and entry-permit application.

"Name?"

"Akri Belram."

The woman studies my ID, eyes flitting between the card and my face. "Why do you seek entry to Raia?"

"To earn money for my family," I reply, wiping my rain-sleeked forehead. "The droughts on Tarak V destroyed my parents' crops. Without money they and my younger brothers and sisters will starve."

I hold the woman's gaze, trying to show I have nothing to hide. Her look is flinty, unsympathetic, like she's heard this story a million times and can no longer summon any empathy.

"Tarak V? Whereabouts?"

"Sixty klicks or so north of Hope's Landing," I say, not missing a beat. "Not the best soil, but beggars can't be choosers."

I've never even been within ten light years of the entire system, but I've studied the world intensely these past few days. Colonized only twenty years past, Tarak V is the runt of the litter, long passed over for the more verdant lands of the system's other inner worlds. Empire presence is rudimentary, administrative records not yet integrated.

That's why we chose it.

But it cuts both ways.

Empire officials pay extra attention when in-bounds claim to hail from such worlds.

Her next words throw me, though.

"That accent—don't hear it too often these days."

Damn. Thought I'd masked that.

"Yeah…" I mumble. "The cross I bear."

I'm unsure how to go on, but a commotion from the next lane—a family being pulled apart—gives me a chance to get my composure.

"That's why my parents left Raia," I explain. "They got sick of people accusing them of being Pilgrims."

"No sympathies, then?"

"They hate that stupid cult."

"And you?"

"No love lost here," I say, thanking the stars I was never inked after the ceremony. "Only caused me trouble."

The woman smiles.

Right answer.

After that, we move onto safer ground. Labor skills, plans for Raia. The drugs test comes back clean too, no hint of the Dust. My sense of excitement grows, but I try to stay calm.

"Alright, you're approved." The woman stamps my papers. "You'll be an asset to the Empire."

I nod, take my papers, move on.

I'm letting out a long breath, when she shouts.

"Hey, Belram!"

I stop dead, turn, try to stay casual.

"Something else?"

She swings her stun-baton, nonchalantly.

"You must know that crazy Amblyr. What's his name, again? Runs the space docks in Hope's Landing? Thok. That's it. Torvald Thok."

Torvald Thok?

The name is familiar, a piece of jetsam in my head. I dig deep, thinking. Yes, he *is* the boss of the space docks, but I sense a trap...

What though?

"Sure, I know Torvald," I reply slowly. "Not well though, more by reputation than anything else."

The official raises her eyebrows.

That's it! Trick question.

With as much calm as I can muster, I say, "Surprised anyone would mistake a Lumeris for an Amblyr, though."

She shakes her head, almost disappointed.

"Slip of the tongue," she says, holstering her baton. "Safe travels, Belram."

"What did you say to the official?" I ask, keeping my voice low. "Just before he started eyeballing the line, I mean."

With thousands of others, Rachkov and I have been herded onto a massive passenger liner. We sit in the cavernous, dimly lit canteen, wedged opposite one another at the end of a table we share with a family of three generations of Z'vali.

"You assumed the worst?"

"Can you blame me?"

Rachkov grimaces. "Just wanted a little distraction. Told him I thought I'd seen Rhync Raggiodri further back in the line."

"Who?"

Rachkov glances across the canteen.

"Wow, you Pilgrims sure live sheltered lives," they say, playing with the last crab stick on their plate. "Rhync's one of the most wanted individuals in the entire galaxy. Ripped off a series of corps with some high-tech heists back in the day."

"Never heard of him." I wonder if the Niris is feeding me some more old bull, but I'm happy to hear the story. "Go on."

"Rhync ended up with the nickname 'The Photobomber' after folks realized his calling card was getting snapped on the periphery of the places he was fleecing."

"Bad idea for a master criminal, no?"

Rachkov waves around its crab stick, before it disappears into an unseen orifice.

"Some," they say, "crave fame more than wealth."

The din of the canteen grows, more and more passengers filing in to grab some grub before take-off. Everybody's excited, happy to have been granted access to Raia, their dreams a little closer to reality. Fame and wealth await. Or not. Probably, for a few, this'll be the high point of their Raian adventure.

"Anyway," Rachkov says, "a highly lucrative market developed for genuine images of Rhync outside the places he'd swindled. Security camera footage, tourist snaps, media shoots. Everybody scoured their clouds as soon as word came out that Rhync had pulled off another job. One good pic could see you set for life."

What a mad world.

"So this border guard thought you might be giving him a heads-up to a very profitable photo op?"

"Exactly."

"No wonder he scanned the line."

"Indeed," Rachkov says. "At least until I pointed out that the most valuable enterprise in the vicinity was a well-attended burger shack."

I smile. I can see why the agent would laugh.

"The distraction worked then?"

"I'm here, aren't I?"

Even though part of me is glad, a bigger part still loathes being in the Niris's presence. "You are."

They reach out a limb, touch my forearm.

I shake it off, irritated.

Forgiveness isn't something I can offer.

Not now. Maybe not ever.

"I know I betrayed your father," Rachkov says. "But I won't betray *you*. I swear."

TWENTY-SEVEN

ㅈㅖㅌㅅㅅ ㅇㅌㅋㅌㅋ

A month later—a month of squirreling through the underbelly of Raia's capital, Silny, following tenuous leads—Rachkov has kept their word.

At least, as far as I know.

Maybe they're playing a long game.

Today we've come forty klicks north to one of the old abandoned shipyards that dot the continent's eastern seaboard. I've scaled one of the tallest cranes, a cakewalk compared to ascending a slick, smooth-worn cave wall deep underground, and have clear views over the entire site.

Useful for clocking uninvited guests.

The shipyard occupies a vast tract of land, largely open space, with a smattering of sheds, warehouses, and corporate buildings. Plenty of places to lay low and hide should our planned shindig get gatecrashed.

Thin clouds mask the glare, and a gentle breeze comes off the ocean, carrying the smell of the sea and industry. Several giant vessels have been left to decompose in the adjoining harbor a little up coast. The endless play of the elements has, slowly yet inevitably, eroded their metal skins, revealing their corroded innards to the sun.

Every now and then I catch a whiff of oil, plastics, harsh chemicals, a reminder of Raia's seafaring past. Nowadays, the Empire's sights are on the vast ocean of stars, the seas of its homeworld charted, stripped, and scrubbed of most life.

I wonder if the same fate awaits the heavens.

Above, if I squint, I can see one of Raia's orbital shipyards, the occasional flare of ion engines. Far beneath me, Rachkov loiters among a maze of cargo containers, keeping out of sight. Unlike the swaddling comfort you get in the pitch-black of a cave, the drop is stark and constant.

Stop looking down.

My earpiece crackles.

"Any sign?" Rachkov asks.

Crouched at the end of the crane's jib, I lift my spex with rust-red hands and scan the horizon again. I take it the Niris is asking about our informant rather than any interlopers but, in any case, I do a complete three-sixty sweep.

"Nothing."

In all likelihood, the informant will arrive along one of the two roads that connect the shipyard to the north and south. Any interlopers, on the other hand, could arrive from any direction—and by any means. Jeep, drop-ship, powerboat, hell, they could even scuba dive in through one of the canals that link the ocean to the shipbuilding yards.

Even with an early warning, Rachkov would be hard-pressed to escape should the Empire turn up. As for me, my whole exit strategy would be to wait it out, hope they don't spy the lookout. Foolhardy or brave, I don't know.

All I know is that we're desperate.

Or rather, I am.

I shuffle along to the jib's trolley and sit down, legs crossed like I've come up here for a spot of meditation.

"You still think he's coming?"

"I don't know," Rachkov replies. "Might've got spooked. Might've shopped us in." I can hear the Niris's tentacles drumming against the metal floor of the container as they pace. "Or maybe he's en route. Let's give him another hour."

The earpiece goes quiet. Seawards I can hear the gentle lap of the waves, while closer the crane creaks and groans in the breeze. Out here the skies are clear, but if I cast my gaze back at Silny, a haze obliterates most the skyline, only the largest, starkest structures of the capital visible through the smog.

The gargantuan city has fascinated and appalled.

Its squares and monuments are testaments to Empire authority, its waterways are supplicant to the gods of industry, and its dark heart houses the seat of Emperor Zelevas, yet it is also alive and vibrant, even free, in ways I could never have imagined.

By day, grand cafes with high, peeling ceilings resound with the noise of conversation, the clink of glass and china, while at night entire districts pulse to the sound of deep, primal music, the air electric with potential. Night or day, older citizens play ancient games wherever they can set up their dust-worn boards, talking softly, sometimes furtively, while they sip on one of Raia's more acquired tastes—a throat-burning alcohol made from an especially ugly tuber.

There is misery, but, more often, there is light.

For the first time, I see the Empire is not simply the monster of Pilgrim stories we are led to believe.

Somewhere in that den of graft and fire, Rachkov assures me, is a man named Osiris. Osiris is the Pilgrim go-between, the one man who might have reliable word on the plight and whereabouts of the Horizon. Everything I know of Osiris has come from Rachkov, who tells me that he was born to a Pilgrim family on an arcology a few years after the exodus.

At least that's the story.

The Empire, like everybody else, knows next to nothing about this mysterious figure.

"A long-lived thorn in the Empire's side," Rachkov once told me. "One the Emperor longs to draw out, even if it means bloodshed. Some, though, claim the man is a fiction. A handy, enduring bogeyman used to scare the rank-and-file into accepting a perpetual police state."

Maybe he is a fiction.

After all, Rachkov's efforts to make contact have stalled, whether through flesh-and-blood messengers sent into suspected Pilgrim ghettos, or anonymized codewords left on dark net servers. Or maybe Osiris is very real, yet doesn't feel inclined to meet up with the Niris who was once Zelevas's personal Pilgrim hunting dog.

I wouldn't blame him.

In either case, for now, we've exhausted our options. Any more digging for Osiris and the Niris is likely to come to the attention of the Empire's agents.

If they haven't already.

So, we've turned our attention to the other reason we're here. My father. Even though I still have no idea what he was seeking, I'm glad I can roam the same places that he would've walked all those years past.

It's not much, but it's something.

I picture him in the central square, shaking his head at the grotesque immensity of Zelevas's statue, while delighting at the disheveled performers scratching a living under its watch.

I wonder what he made of Silny, of Raia.

Entertained? Amused? Unsettled?

A little of all, I suspect. Certainly not disgusted or enraged like many Pilgrims of a more pious persuasion would be. Father always saw the best in people, strove to never judge them, or blame them for circumstances beyond their control.

That's what I remember, at least.

Most of all, though, I wonder what fire burned so fiercely inside that he risked coming here, into his enemy's backyard, leaving behind his family, leaving behind me.

The lure of ancient knowledge? A desire for vengeance? A lover?

I glance again at the vast metropolis.

Could he still be out there somewhere? A drifter watching the world go by… somehow released from Zelevas's thrall, yet still rooting for answers among the detritus…

But surely, he would've returned if he was able to, wouldn't he? Maybe he's trapped, living a half-life somewhere, alive, but denied full freedom, unable to leave.

I can hope.

I tap my earpiece. "Do you think he's still out there?"

"I don't know," Rachkov replies, knowing full well who I mean. "I hope so. What I do know is that we're going to do everything we can to find him."

I stare at the city.

"What was he looking for?"

"I don't know that either, Sewa." It's masked, but I can hear the frustration in their voice. "I told you what I know."

"Tell me again."

Birdsong breaks the silence, seabirds nesting among the upper reaches of the abandoned shipyard.

"There must be something," I add.

Rachkov sighs. "First I heard of your father was when we heard there was a man knocking around on Raia asking questions about the Academy. Like I said, I'd become jaded with Isyander's project, so I volunteered to go, double sharp. I was more than happy to get out of the citadel, help assess if this guy was a threat or opportunity."

Below, I catch a glimpse of the Niris skulking in the shadows.

"Your loyalty was still with the Academy."

"It was then," Rachkov says. "I thought I'd get some perspective, come back refreshed."

"But your head got turned."

"Raia opened my eyes to the other lives I could've been leading. We have the blood of gods coursing through our veins, Sewa! I thought 'Why should I waste my time slaving away for an institution led by a half-mad prophet obsessed with the ancient past?'"

"And my father offered an out?"

A long time passes. "He did."

He trusted you. Just like I did. Like I am.

"It took a while," they say, "but, eventually I found him. Even though he disguised it pretty well, I suspected he was a Pilgrim from the off. The Dust. You must feel it too. Sometimes it's like a sixth sense."

Or a passenger who won't shut up.

"What was he like?"

"Calm. Resourceful. Cagey."

"And you never got a sense of what he was after?" I ask, thinking of the countless times I'd scoured his possessions back on the Horizon, learning nothing. "Was he looking for someone? Was he after relics? Was it just information?" I lower my voice. "Could he have been seeking vengeance?"

"I don't know. And that vexed me." Rachkov sighs again. "Like I said, he was cagey."

I smile at that little victory.

Chalk one up for the old man.

"So, I showed him my hand early," the Niris says, voice echoing against hard metal walls. "I revealed I was with the Academy, hoping to get him to open up, but he stayed guarded. Said he'd only talk to Isyander."

"And that meant a stalemate."

"I said I needed to know more before there was any chance of that. But he wouldn't give me anything more. So, we shot the breeze instead."

"You mean," I say accusingly, "you tried to gain his trust."

Rachkov's terse. "I hoped he'd open up, let me in."

"So you could deliver him to the authorities."

"No," the Niris snaps. "That idea hadn't crossed my mind, yet. I was still acting for the Academy. I just needed to know what he wanted."

"What did you talk about?"

"Everything. Nothing."

"No clues what he was after?"

"We talked about Raia, its past, its wars, Zelevas's rise to power, the expansions into space. We discussed the galaxy's main players, tensions and allegiances."

You knew so much, didn't you, Father?

"On the Horizon, Father was a historian." I gaze over the

landscape, tilt my head to the skies. "Well, more than a historian. An antiquarian. An archeologist too, when the chance arose."

"He was very knowledgeable," Rachkov says. "I enjoyed our long meandering conversations immensely."

"Not enough to not betray him, though."

I hear steel cables gently flapping in the wind, giving off a low whistle.

"No, not enough."

Why couldn't you see the Niris's true colors, Father?

I shake off the bitterness, thinking.

Maybe I'm thinking about this wrong.

Maybe his quest wasn't personal. Maybe he was doing this for his people. Seeking a discovery, an ally, a sanctuary that could transform our fortunes...

"And he never confessed to being a Pilgrim?"

"The Pilgrims only came up in passing," Rachkov says. "I think he thought that I was in the dark as to where he was from, and he was keen to keep it that way."

That was Father.

Our safety was always paramount.

"I thought he'd open up eventually," Rachkov says, "give me something. But he didn't. And the longer it went on, the more I resented him, resented the Pilgrims. They were free, where I was trapped. I didn't want to go back to the Academy like a failure, empty-handed."

"You could've gone your own way."

"I could've," Rachkov says. "But I didn't want to start from scratch. Not then."

I get up, stretch my legs. The sea glints in the sunlight.

"So you threw your lot in with the Empire. And the price of entry was my father's freedom." I kick off a rust-caked piece of paintwork, raining flakes onto the containers beneath. "Maybe his life."

Silence.

No words, Rachkov?

On the road to the south I spy a vehicle approaching. A part of me hopes it's the Empire. I could lay low, let them seize the Niris... it would be a fitting symmetry, wouldn't it? Rachkov turns my father in, then, years later, I turn in the Niris.

"I can't... I can't..." Rachkov stutters, takes a breath. "I can't change the past."

I can feel the pain in its words.

Is this pity, I feel? Dammit!

"All I can do," they say, "is try to make amends."

I pick up the spex, glass the road. A battered pick-up is weaving along the dirt track, a plume of dust trailing in its wake. Not very Empire, although it could be a ruse.

I'm not sure I'll ever forgive the Niris, but maybe one day I can stop being their judge, let the stars decide their fate.

"Somebody's coming."

Rachkov composes themself. "What are we talking?"

"Pick-up on the southern road."

"Sounds like our guy. Occupants?"

I magnify on the windshield, but the sun's reflection obscures the interior.

"Unknown. Too much glare."

"Anybody else approaching?"

I do a three-sixty sweep, paying close attention to the nearby scrubland and the long wide arc of the flat ocean. Nothing. Dropping the spex, I scan the skies by eye.

All clear.

"I don't think so."

"Alright, we're on. I'll leave the channel open so you can hear. Unless there's anything else…?"

"Nothing else, just… stay safe, Rachkov."

"You too, kid."

I track the vehicle into the compound. It crawls along, the growl of its engines growing louder. As it disappears into the site, the noise muffles one moment, then amplifies the next, the sound conveyed along corridors of steel and concrete.

A squeak of brakes, then the engine cuts off.

Silence, then a door slam.

Only one.

I picture the man scanning the site, wary, peering up at the cranes that crisscross the skies. Faintly, I hear boots crunching against gravel. The rap on the container doors—three hard strikes—comes through the earpiece before the real sound hits my ears.

"It's open," Rachkov says.

I hear the door creak open.

The patter of footsteps.

"Nobody here but me," Rachkov says. "Aside from my lookout, of course."

The Niris told me he'd be upfront about my presence, but I still feel a jolt of exposure hearing the words.

"And you?" Rachkov adds. "You came alone?"

"Maybe." The man's voice is thick, ugly. "Didn't know I was selling secrets to a damn Niris."

"That a problem?"

"Doubles the price."

"Double?"

"More risk my end. I get caught?" The man spits. "Plus, I don't like aliens."

I can hear Rachkov's breaths, slow, angry.

The man goes on. "I can walk if you don't like it. Figuring this might be more hassle than it's worth, anyway."

"Really? With your debts?"

"What do you know about my debts?"

"I know that you like spending a lot of time in the *sims*—the expensive, illegal ones. And now you owe a lot of money to the kind of people who aren't, shall we say, patient."

The man grunts. "You gonna pay? Double, like I said."

"I'll pay—when I see the goods."

I hear an unbuckling noise, the rustle of paper.

Please, let it be legit.

Rachkov speaks. "A full year of records—from the date I gave you?"

"Yep, a whole goddamn year's worth," the man replies. "Wasn't easy getting hold of this."

"But you found a way," Rachkov says. "Amazing what a man can achieve with the right motivation."

"Are we done?"

Everything is still and quiet.

The silence grows, and I'm on the verge of saying something when Rachkov speaks again.

"Money's been transferred."

"I can see that." A muffled thump. "Good doing business."

I hear footsteps growing weaker, then a sudden rush across the container floor.

"What the—"

I can hear a scrabble, but two arms and two legs are no match for eight limbs.

What the hell is Rachkov doing?

This wasn't part of the plan.

"Shut up and listen," Rachkov growls. "Any word of this—the records, our meet, your haul—gets out, and you're a dead man. You understand?"

"I... understand."

"You keep your mouth shut."

Another shuffle, the slam of the container door.

I hear footsteps again, this time not through the earpiece. I look down to see the man careening through the containers back to his pick-up. The engine revs high, tires screech, and the vehicle hightails out of the compound.

"Was that necessary?"

The Niris steps out of the container into the sunshine, a saddle bag raised up in one of its tentacles. They start moving towards the foot of my crane tower.

"Give them free rein, and guys like that can't help but spill the beans. One night he'd get drunk, brag about this episode to anyone who'd listen. Too much ego."

"Guess you'd know."

"Now, though," they say, ignoring my jibe, "with my little pep talk, he might stay quiet. At least for a while."

"Buying us enough time to follow any leads without unwanted attention."

"Exactly." Rachkov turns, beckons me down. "Come on, kid. We've got some reading to do."

TWENTY-EIGHT

ㅈㅅㄷㄹㅆ ㅗㅅㄱㅊㅏ

A couple of hours later we're back at our digs, a barely furnished apartment in one nondescript block of many on the edge of Silny. Unskilled workers and their families live here, scratching a living as best they can. Many are aliens, winding up on Raia on account of the world's labor shortage, and, no doubt, other, more desperate reasons.

Most of the time I can sense an uneasy peace across the blocks, but sometimes when there's strife it falls along native-versus-alien lines. No surprise given the way Zelevas and his media lapdogs stir up discord. Not enough to put off-worlders from coming, but more than enough to make them feel like second-class citizens when they arrive.

We fit right in.

"Alright," Rachkov says, slamming the stack of paperwork on the ramshackle table at the side of the main living space. "We do this slow and methodical, okay. We don't want to miss anything."

Slow and methodical. Gotcha.

Shaking a little, I peel off the top half of the stack, move it to my side of the table. Before I begin, I head over to the sink, run the cold tap, and pour myself a grimy glass of water. It tastes of the pipes, metallic and gritty.

I sit back down, opposite the Niris.

I turn over the cover sheet. "Let's do this."

The print is small, grainy, machine-like, row upon row of names filling the page, each one accompanied by banal yet incriminating supplementary information.

I read the first line.

HAGY LASZLO, 69, RAIAN, NO FIXED ADDRESS,
5 YEARS, SILNY PENAL INST.

Instead of moving on, like I should, I pause.

I wonder what happened to Laszlo. I imagine a homeless man, long ago caught up in some protest against Zelevas. We've passed the prison in Silny, a hard, brutal, towering fortress of stone, but Rachkov tells me that its proximity to the masses means that it's one of the less harsh places to be incarcerated in the Empire.

Less harsh, but it's all relative.

Five years means Laszlo should have served his sentence and been released by now, but I've been warned that these prison terms are often extended.

Maybe Laszlo is still behind bars.

Maybe he's dead.

KOROK ULA, 27, RAIAN, 27 ANATOV PLAZA,
REYARCH, ████, ████

I can't help myself.

Maybe she's a terrorist. Implicated in a plot to assassinate Zelevas or one of his subordinates. Her sentence is indeterminate. Still rotting away on a labor camp at the icy hinterlands of Raia.

PORO NINPERE, UNKNOWN, KALGEROS, UNKNOWN, 23 YEARS,
BORASTAN DETENTION CENTER

Contraband smuggler.

Accused of bribing party officials.

Shivved while imprisoned and suffered life-changing injuries resulting in his transfer to a decaying prison hospital…

My eyes slide down over the names, not reading them, just recognizing their existence, recognizing each is a real life, suspended in time. Each one found guilty of political crimes, each one incarcerated in grey, inhumane facilities somewhere on one of Raia's sprawling continents. Forty, maybe fifty people per page, hundreds of pages, and this only a single year's worth of imprisonments. A small subset of the hundreds of thousands who are locked up at Zelevas's pleasure every year. Not to mention the millions more on secret police watchlists.

"You can't dwell on the names."

Rachkov stares across the table.

I can see that they're already on the third or fourth sheet of their pile, marking their place two thirds down the page with the tip of a tentacle.

I rub my temple. "How can you do that?"

"The same way you shut out all the pain and misery in this apartment block, this district, this city." The Niris glances at the little light intruding through the shuttered blinds. "You look the other way."

I wonder how many times the Niris has scanned lists like this across the years. "And that's right?"

"I don't know if it's right." They meet my eyes again. "I just know it's necessary."

My fingers dig into the sheet, crumpling the paper. I can feel my eyes tearing up.

"My father might be on this list!"

"And if he is we'll find him."

"And if he's not?"

"Then we'll keep looking."

With angry swipes I rub my eyes with the heel of my hand. *They're not names. They're just marks on a page.*

I have only space for one name.

My father.

Kendro Eze.

He's not here.

The knowledge rests heavy, like an iron ball in the pit of my stomach. I don't know if I'll even be able to stand on my own two feet. I feel numb, empty, lost.

No sign of the Horizon.

No sign of my father.

I lay against the table, arms folded over my head, my cheek resting on my half of the pages, my ribs pressed against the table edge, still sitting in the same place. My legs feel dead, my feet like they belong to someone else. Outside, through the slats, I can see it is night, only a thin actinic glare of the block's strip lighting.

We went through the list twice, swapping over our halves of the stack, double checking each other's work.

Maybe, third time lucky?

Tomorrow, I will cast my eye over the names again—just in case, just for the faintest chance we missed him somehow—but right now I am exhausted, or rather, not exhausted, but defeated.

I don't think I could take a final blow.

I need to regroup, then rally.

Of the Pilgrims I still feel hope.

They're out there somewhere, of that I'm certain. They're survivors, wily operators, laying low until the storm passes.

I might not find them soon, but I will one day.

As long as Kalad doesn't hit the self-destruct button.

My father, though, my father is another matter.

He's one man, one man swallowed by an immense bureaucratic machine, lost on a world that isn't his own, his existence near-completely erased. No allies, no friends, no family.

Apart from me.

I might never know what happened.

I... might... never... know... what... happened.

The words hit hard, a punch to the gut.

This not knowing, it might kill me.

Father, where are you?

I get up, afraid, knocking my chair to the ground with a loud clatter. The bottom half of my body has no sensation, while my top half only aches. Rachkov is still seated, staring at their half of the stack, barely noticing my commotion.

"I'm crashing," I say, forcing my legs to move.

The Niris grunts.

I wake thirsty, slowly remembering where I am, what we're doing here. Everything's dark, the night not yet over. I want to go back to sleep, but my mouth is dry, my mind whirring again.

Damn.

I turn, sit on the side of the bed, clutch for hair that's gone, feel only the rough stubble of its remains.

A dim light is coming from the living area.

Stiff-legged, I get up, shuffle to the door, and shoulder my way into the other room. Rachkov is still sat at the table, poring over the list of names, a desk lamp casting long shadows across the floor and walls.

Have they not stopped all night?

"Rachkov?" I croak. "You still looking?"

They look pale, exhausted, but their eyes shine.

"I think I've found him."

My legs go weak, and I rest my weight on the back of the chair opposite. The Niris gestures for me to sit, and I ease myself down into the chair, heart hammering.

"When I was a… When I was with the Empire," they say, speaking softly, gazing at the list, "I heard a rumor about political prisoners. I heard for some of the most sensitive prisoners they'd sometimes use codenames."

"Codenames?"

"They'd swap the real prisoner's first and last names, then create an alias using the first letters of the rearranged name. Your father is Kendro Eze. So, his codename would have the initials EK."

I glance at the list, seeing it in a different light.

"I found four individuals named EK. One was female, while for two of the others I found they really existed after cross-referencing with other sources."

"And the fourth?"

"This is the fourth." The Niris lifts the top page off the stack, flicks it one-eighty so I can read it. "Here."

KAZAKOV EVGENI, 35, ███████, NO FIXED ADDRESS, 8 YEARS, YARPOL RE-EDUCATION CAMP

Is this really you, Father?

"How old was your father when he left, Sewa?"

"Thirty, I think. Maybe thirty-one."

"Which would make him around thirty-five at his arrest."

The room is spinning. "This is him?"

"Everything fits," the Niris replies. "His Pilgrim identity would be kept secret, and I know he had no stable address. And then there's where the sentence is being served."

I whisper the words. "Yarpol Re-Education Camp."

"Many Pilgrims wind up there."

Our history is full of tales of Zelevas's camps, places where Pilgrims were broken, re-constituted as upstanding Raian citizens. Unless they couldn't be broken.

"What is it like?"

"Harsh. Cold. Faraway."

My heart sinks, knowing his fate.

"Eight years though," I cry, grasping for any chink of light. "He'd be halfway into his sentence. We must go there."

"We will," Rachkov says. "And we'll find him. I promise." The Niris collects up the sheet, places it back into the stack, returns the whole pile to the saddle bag. "But, Sewa, I want you to understand… the re-education camps… they can change people… if we find him, he might not be the person you remember."

I nod. "I'm going to pack up."

I get to my bedroom door, turn.

"And Rachkov, my father?" I say, belligerently. "On the Horizon everyone told me there was nobody tougher. He won't have cracked."

The Niris gives me a wistful look, but stays silent.

TWENTY-NINE

"That's the place."

The snow is hardpacked beneath me, the cold seeping deep into my skin. In the valley, all I can see through the gently falling sleet is the faint outline of a half-dozen buildings, maybe a boundary fence. From the corner of the site a thin cord of smoke meanders upwards into the slate grey skies, drifting slightly from the chill breeze.

I reach over, my gloved hand trembling.

"Let me see."

Rachkov passes the spex, the metal casing of the instrument cold to my touch even through the insulated fabric of my gloves. Pine needles dapple the soft, powdery snow around us, the trees tall and straight and dense, and I can smell their scent mingling with the earthy aroma of the unseen fire.

I glass the camp.

Even with the magnified view, the place is fuzzy, difficult to parse, but I can still discern its rough layout. We're overlooking two sides; one that houses the camp's main southerly entrance, the other the featureless western wall. Low, squat guard towers loom up from the walls, regularly spaced, and outside the walls I can spy a chain-linked fence topped with razor wire.

It could house thousands.

The camp is still, no sign of life aside from the smoke.

Another false hope?

"Tell me this is still an operational facility."

Rachkov shivers. "Switch to thermal."

I twist a dial. The view transforms, the buildings becoming stark, angular greens in a sea of deep blue, but it is the speckles of reds and yellows that most vividly draw the eye. *People.*

Or more specifically, guards.

They're lone fireflies on the walls, clustered at the main entrance, and manning the guard towers.

Despite the dangers, I feel a frisson of excitement.

Are you in there, Father?

"Can we get in?"

"Maybe." Beside me, the snow crunches as the Niris shifts their weight. "But getting in, locating your father, and getting out with him? No chance. That'd be suicide."

I zoom-in on a guard trekking between watchtowers, then realize there are two distinct heat sources, the latter one close to the ground, leading the other.

"Guard dogs."

I shiver. I've never felt comfortable with the creatures, no animals permitted on the Horizon.

"Indeed," Rachkov says. "We're lucky the wind's towards us."

"We shouldn't push our luck."

"No, we shouldn't."

Just a little longer…

I glass the buildings, wondering which one is the prisoner dorms, which ones the workhouses, which one is the refectory, and which ones are the classrooms—if re-education is dispensed by such means. If he's still there, that'd be close to the sum total of his movements these days.

"You think he's in there?"

"I don't know." Rachkov shuffles backwards, deeper into the treeline.

I power down the spex, crawl back too, near breathless from the cold. Under the cover of the dark canopy, we both get up, clap the snow off our fatigues.

"What next?"

"I've got an idea." Rachkov turns, striding into the trees, swiftly disappearing in the shadows. "Come on," they shout, unseen, "we've got a long hike back."

No one comes to Yarpol on vacation.

The town, ten kilometers from the re-education facility via a gravel road that snakes up through pristine pine forests and glacial lakes like a grey, twisted umbilical cord, wouldn't exist without the camp.

Everything is harsh, utilitarian, built solely to serve the needs of the facility—from the stripped back railway station ferrying workers and materials from the lowlands, to the retail outlets selling basic commodities of food, clothing, and hardware. Rachkov tells me it was constructed in a whirlwind fifty years past, when Zelevas's purges were at their most vicious, an architectural snapshot capturing the old mood of the Empire.

Call it the High Brutalism period.

The drinking house, despite its rough-planked, sawdust floors and machine-hewn tables and benches, is probably the most lively and colorful establishment in the entire town. The long row of optics behind the bar is far more eclectic than the usual five varieties of spirits you'd normally expect, and instead of bare walls, the whole place is plastered with amateurish, yet heartfelt, posters for gigs and other entertainments. Alone on my table in the corner, I sip on my murky beer, trying not to wince.

Outside, it's dark, the sun long gone, only the glare of vehicles' headlights breaking the black beyond the rattling windows. No streetlights illuminate Yarpol's frosted roads. The day shift at the camp ended an hour ago, and every other minute another knot of workers barges through the steel door, accompanied by a blast of frozen air.

Most are in high spirits.

I pull up my collar, discreetly study the newcomers.

Almost all arrivals are still in their work clothes, so it's relatively easy to discern their roles once they loosen their winter jackets. Maintenance crew, kitchen staff, administrator—

"Who are you?"

A woman stands over me, her two drinking companions already slipping into the free spaces at the other end of the table. Her face is rugged, frostbitten. She takes a swig of her drink, waiting for me to answer, and I see her nails are caked with dirt.

Grounds staff?

"Nobody," I answer.

"Suit yourself," she says, and slips in beside me, but turning away to talk to her friends. Her jacket smells of packed earth and old ice. I think I may have misjudged her frankness for animosity. Maybe she was just being friendly?

Perhaps I could build a rapport…

No, stick to the plan.

The place is filling up, pockets of patrons forgoing tables to remain standing in their small clusters, but I can still see Rachkov nursing a drink at the bar. A thick, dark cloak hides the majority of their tentacles, but even from this distance there is no mistaking that they're a Niris, the mottled back of their bulbous head, and the lone serpentine limb cradling their tumbler dead giveaways.

Few aliens come to Yarpol.

More drinkers arrive, bringing in another icy blast.

They file in, solemn, unspeaking, the last of the five accompanied by a muzzled guard dog, the chain-link leash wrapped around its master's hand, shortening the lead.

Guards.

Our marks.

They stop in the middle of the establishment, and the whole place quietens. They're about to turf off a couple of lowly workers from a table near the bar, when one of them spies Rachkov. He nudges another of the guards, flicks his head in the Niris's direction.

"Well, well, well," the ringleader says, getting the whole bar's attention, "what do we have here?"

"Gavran."

"Not talking to you, old man."

I crane my neck.

The old man is a wiry, chicken-necked Raian sat alone at the end of the bar, wearing dark grey coveralls. He puts his hands up in mock surrender. "Whatever you say, Gavran."

Gavran steps forward, stabs a finger into Rachkov's shoulder. "Hey, I was talking to you."

The Niris twists round. "I don't want any trouble."

"Then maybe you shouldn't have come here."

My hands itch, wanting to get involved, but Rachkov warned me this might happen. Warned me that I shouldn't get caught up in any confrontations. In fact, they told me, this sort of encounter could play into our hands.

Rachkov drains their drink. "I can go if it's a problem."

"Where you going to go, squid?" Gavran says. "You see, that's the problem, isn't it. You come to Raia, looking for work, but instead of heading to the oceans where you might be useful, you come up into the mountains. A squid in the mountains—that make any sense to you?"

Without warning, he grips Rachkov's shoulders, hauls them to the ground. I fight with every fiber of my being not to react, remembering the Niris's own words.

I can take care of myself.

Rachkov doesn't cower, but they don't move either.

"God, you smell bad," Gavran says, exaggeratedly fanning his hand. "Let me make something clear. We don't *need* squid here! We don't *want* squid here, either!" He towers over the Niris, enraged. "You understand?"

I hear whispers of endorsement, even some outright hollers of approval.

Still prone, Rachkov nods.

They get up, faces their tormenter.

A Niris at full height stands a hand taller than most Raians, and Rachkov is no exception next to this bully.

For Gavran, it's a humiliation.

I see it in his eyes.

His voice shakes with his next words. "I see you again in this town... you better run, squid."

Rachkov stares down at the guard, then brushes past and disappears out into the night, the steel door clattering in its frame. Slowly, the hubbub of conversation returns, but the talk is muted, unfinished business in the air. Gavran's still agitated, pacing, scratching his stubble, engaged in rapid-fire exchanges with his little crew. They eye the door. The one with the leashed dog grabs Gavran's wrist with his free hand.

Gavran doesn't like that.

He sneers, shakes off the restraining grip.

Next moment he takes off, three of his goons following in his wake, only the older one with the guard dog remaining.

Watch out, Zarva.

The mood in the place lifts.

Violence is abroad, but these drinkers are happy to turn a blind eye. I want to track the men, step in should they corner the Niris, but I'd be wasting the opportunity that Rachkov's already engineered. Instead, I head for the bar.

The last guard has installed himself on a bar stool near the end, so I wedge myself between him and the patron on the next stool, eyes on the barkeep like I want to get served.

I hear the old man speak. "That kid—"

"I don't want to hear it, Adrik."

I steal a glance down the bar, see the old man nod, silenced. Beneath me, I feel eyes on me, and look down to find the dog watching me.

The dog growls, bares its teeth.

I can smell its slobber, meaty and fetid.

I hate dogs.

"Fyodor doesn't like strangers." The guard pats his dog's neck, and the animal stops snarling, settles.

"Me neither."

"Meaning?"

I catch the barkeep's attention, order a drink.

"Meaning," I say, turning back to the guard. "Raia's getting overrun with fucking aliens."

The words leave a bitter aftertaste.

The guard gives a wry smile though, sizes me up.

I take the opportunity to do likewise. Slab-like build, muscles like iron weights. His hair is short and cropped, but it still cannot hide the flecks of grey marking his advancing years. On his thickset neck I catch what looks like the upper part of a Sheredyn crest, and everything comes into focus.

Ex-military elite.

Nobody embraces Raian patriotism more than Zelevas's personal guards, the Sheredyn. I hope my shaved head, thousand-yard stare, and casual xenophobia conveys a similar ideology. Eventually, the guard clinks my drink.

"What I don't understand, though," I say, "is why you held your boy back? You gotta soft spot for squid?"

His jaw tenses.

"Watch your mouth," he says, glancing around. "Nah, I just prefer to do things more... effectively."

"Effectively?"

"Gavran likes theater, but this kind of thing can backfire. With aliens, a thousand cuts are better than one heavy blow. You know what I mean?"

"Right, don't let anybody feel sorry for them."

"Exactly. That squid turns up as a frozen corpse in the morning, we'll have alien rights' activists out on Silny's streets by the afternoon."

Staring at my glass, I say, "Still one less alien though."

The guard doesn't say anything.

I twist my head to find him eyeballing me.

"What do you want?"

Something's not adding up for him. I don't know what it is, but I need to give him more if he's going to trust me. Something real. Something more than we planned.

"I'm looking for my father."

I feel brazen—and vulnerable.

"And your father is?"

I glance at the old man down the bar who's minding his own business, then lower my voice.

"His real name is Kendro Eze."

No sign of recognition from the guard.

"But you might know him as Evgeni Kazakov."

The guard shrugs. "Who is he?"

"A political prisoner. He came to Yarpol around four years ago. I need to know if he's still here."

The guard takes a quick look over his shoulder. "You should write to the authorities."

"Officially, he doesn't exist."

I can see I'm losing him.

"Please, I can pay."

In his eyes I see temptation, but also fear.

He stands up. "I can't help you."

I grab his wrist. "He's a Pilgrim."

The guard narrows his eyes. "But you're not?"

"No, I'm a Raian," I snap. "Born and bred."

He settles back into his seat. "Keep talking."

I sip my drink.

Keep it as close to the truth as you can.

"I never knew my father growing up," I begin. "Mother would never talk about him, just said he was a bad seed and that he wasn't ever coming back." I close my eyes, half-acting, half-digging out the painful feelings. "Then a couple of years ago I learnt he was a Pilgrim. Twenty years back, he'd come to Raia undercover, somehow got involved with my mother. I guess I was an accident. I don't know where he went when he left us, maybe back to the arcs, but at some point he got collared by the authorities. I like to think he came back to Raia to find me."

I wipe my eye with the heel of my hand, turn to the guard. "Now I want to find him."

"See why you hate outsiders." The guard rubs his jaw, torn. "Ask me, you're better off without a screw-up like that in your life."

I say nothing.

"But," he says, "I know where you're coming from. My old man walked out on my ma, left her to raise me and my three brothers all by herself. I was the oldest. Five years old. I hated him. Still do." He exhales. "But, if you told me I could see him tomorrow... I wouldn't think twice."

"You'll help me?"

He nods. "For a price."

"I can pay ten thousand," I say. "Half up front. Half when you give me something concrete."

He nods once more. "Give me those names again."

"Evgeni Kazakov," I whisper. "Real name, Kendro Eze."

He gets his device from his pocket, thumbs it out of sight beneath the bar, then tilts the screen in my direction.

I make the transfer.

"Meet me at dawn at the old chemical plant." He stands up to go. "I'll find out what I can."

After he leaves I can't help but notice the old man still sitting at the end of the bar, quietly sipping his drink.

I leave soon after, hands trembling.

THIRTY

ᚥᛉᛁᚾᚲᚲ

Rachkov isn't at the safe house when I get back.

I feel both giddy and sick. I want to tell them that we're so close now, but I can't help but fear the worst might've happened to the Niris. Sleeping is impossible. I pace, but it's little respite, my imagination throwing up gruesome spectacles of Rachkov bleeding out in the cold and dark.

The Niris might be a stone's throw away.

I head out to search the streets.

I wander aimlessly, crunching through hardpacked snow, shivering with every gust of the biting wind. I check alleyways, refuse sheds, children's play yards, calling Rachkov's name when I think nobody's within earshot, but find no sign of the Niris.

Few are out on the streets, anyway, and the ones I spy are usually walking fast, wrapped up tight, heads down against the elements. Sometimes I see something that gives me pause, but it's always nothing: a tarpaulin over logs, a snowdrift, something caught in the trees.

I return, demoralized.

The safe house is still empty.

Where are you, Zarva?

Time crawls.

I keep the lights off, lest I draw attention.

I lie in bed, wide awake. I sit at the table in the kitchen, cupping a mug of steaming hot water, watching the whorls eddy up. I stand at the window, straining my eyes at the shadowed buildings, the streetlights long switched off.

Sometime in the early hours, I hear a noise outside.

Next moment, the door creeps open, admitting a stream of bone-chilling air. A cloaked figure slips inside.

"Zarva!"

The Niris leans back, lets their full weight slump against the door, shutting off the chilly blast.

"Are you hurt?"

Sticking out from the foot of its cloak, I can see its tentacles, frosted and shivering.

They pull down their hood, revealing their very pallid head.

"N-n-no, just damn c-c-cold."

A short time later, still in the dark, we're sat at the kitchen table, the Niris wrapped in blankets, their eight limbs bathing in a hodgepodge of saucepans, buckets, and other receptacles filled to the brim with hot water.

In the time taken to get the Niris comfortable, I've already learnt that after leaving the bar, they scoped out some of the town's administrative buildings, before nearly running into Gavran's merry band of xenophobes. After that near-miss they laid low in some woods at the edge of town.

"And you?" they ask, sipping a honeyed infusion. "Any leads?"

I smile. "That guard at the bar, the one who stayed—"

"With the dog."

"Yeah, him." I nod. "I got talking... I'm meeting him at dawn. He's going to find out what he can."

"Not out of the kindness of his heart, I assume?"

"No." I glance at the window, and the shaded streets beyond. "And there's something else..."

I trail off, unsure how to say this.

Rachkov's going to be livid.

The Niris goes still. "What?"

"He knows the man we're looking for is my father."

The Niris throws up a pair of tentacles, knocking over a cup. "How the hell would he know that?"

"I told him." I get up, avoiding a slick of steaming water flowing to the table edge. "I had to, Rachkov. He was going to leave without giving me anything. I spun a story, something to pull the heartstrings, and it worked."

The Niris moves to the window, gazes out.

They turn back. "And what if that story doesn't add up?"

I try to keep the edge from my voice. "I kept it simple."

"You don't know what they know."

"Listen, nobody knows we're here together."

"Don't they? This town doesn't see many strangers. Then two show up on the same day? People will suspect."

"I need to know what happened to my father!" I kick the table, raging. A glass bowl falls to the floor, shatters. "And you should need to know too! You put him there!"

Silence envelops us.

Somewhere in the darkness a dog barks.

"Okay, okay," Rachkov says, eventually. "I get it."

I say nothing, still shaking.

"What's done is done, we can't change that."

The Niris is talking about my indiscretions, but all I can think of is their betrayal.

"But," they say, "I need to know exactly what you told him. Tell me everything, starting from the top."

I start picking up the shards of glass, composing myself, when there's a knock on the door.

What the—

Rachkov slips to the other side of the door.

"Find out who it is," they whisper.

Have we been followed?

The Empire wouldn't knock, so at least there's that. I move up to the door, place a hand on the cold wood.

"Who's there?"

"I was at the bar." The voice is labored, coarse. "I heard you talking to Pachka."

My mouth goes dry.

He must mean the guard.

What did he hear?

I glance at Rachkov, see the dread in their eyes.

I crack the door open, give the man a quick once-over. He's draped in shadow, nervously scanning the street, but I recognize him as the old man who sat at the end of the bar. Beyond him everything is still, the first hints of dawn swallowing the stars.

"I've come alone," he says, with small puffs of breath.

I step back, pull the door a little wider.

Before the man is even half inside, Rachkov has dragged him into the room, got him jammed up in the corner.

"How did you find us?"

One of the Niris's tentacles is across the old man's neck, half choking him, while a couple of others pin his arms. His eyes are wide, full of fear and panic.

"Easy," I say, gripping the Niris's limb that's doing the choking. "He can't breathe."

A little more color comes into the man's cracked cheeks.

"I followed her," he rasps, nodding at me. "After she left the bar. Then I waited to the early hours. I didn't know you'd be here as well, I swear."

I wasn't careful enough.

"Why?"

"Because I knew her…" He looks over at me, wistful. "Because I knew your father, Sewa."

I feel my legs weaken, and suddenly feel faint.

Rachkov releases the man. He doubles over, coughing, massaging his throat.

Because I knew your father, Sewa.

If that means the worst, I don't want to know, not yet.

I take his arm, escort him over to the table where I help him sit. I run the tap, fill a glass with cold water, then give it to him. He takes it, sips a little.

"Adrik, isn't it?"

He nods, smiling. "Sharp, just like your father."

Rachkov takes me to the side, whispers. "This could be a trap."

"I want to hear what he says," I reply, not lowering my voice.

My father, my call.

I go back to the table, sit down. "How did you know him?"

He takes another sip of water, like he's steeling himself. He's taking a big risk coming here, I realize, a risk that could see him executed.

"Up at the camp, I'm one of the groundskeepers. Longest serving one, truth be told, though I ain't in charge. I like to keep to myself, you know, so my work usually takes me beyond the walls. Maintaining the paths, cutting wood, keeping the pests at bay, you know." He glances at Rachkov, who's pacing. "Anyway, first met your father one winter, a few years back. Prisoners earn privileges for good behavior, and one of those privileges is work detail outside the camp. Not everyone wants to go beyond the walls what with the snowstorms, the cold. And they have to be vetted, of course, check they ain't a flight risk—not that I know anyone who'd survive more than night out in the wilderness in those fatigues."

He sips his water again.

"Kendro was one of those selected for work detail. Came out once a week with a few others and a couple of guards. I had them chopping wood, clearing trails, sometimes more backbreaking stuff like hauling rockfall off the road. He never complained, always just got on with the job, and I could tell these handful of hours outside the camp were a blessing for him. The way he gazed at the frost coming off the peaks, how he crouched in the snow and rubbed the pine needles between his fingers, how he identified the constellations when night had fallen and we'd be trekking back to the gates. I'd never talk to the men, only give instructions, but one shift that changed.

"A blizzard had come in, unexpected—winds that bit through to the bone, snowfall so thick you could barely see the man beside you. The forest became a twilight zone so I led the men to a cave that I knew was nearby. A miserable little dank hole, but shelter to ride out the storm. The others grumbled, chewed on their rations, eyes glued on the cave mouth waiting for the blizzard to relent, but your father, he did none of that. He delved around the cave, used a flint lighter to light up the nooks and crannies, spent that whole time engrossed, while the rest wallowed in the misery and cold. My curiosity got the better of me. Afterwards, out of earshot of the others, I had to ask him what he was doing. I still remember his words to this day. 'The signs of the past,' he said, 'are all around us. You just need to know where to look.' That was the start of our friendship."

I smile. Even incarcerated, he still sought answers.

"You got to know him well?"

"Well enough." He taps the table with his thumb. "Whip-smart was your father. He taught me a lot. History, geology, archeology. I tried to return the favor. Hunting, tracking, surviving in the mountains. We both knew what it meant."

My heart flutters.

"That he planned to escape?"

"Never outright said it, but I knew. Our unspoken secret, I guess. I knew he was a Pilgrim too, even if he kept that to himself. Many suspected as much. He often talked about you, how bright you shined, how much energy and life you had. He called you his little caver." He takes a sip of water. "He said how hard it had been to leave and how every day was painful. He wanted to do everything in his power to get back to you."

I can feel emotion welling inside.

"He ever tell you why he came to Raia?"

"That, I can't tell you." He clenches his jaw. "I know he was searching for something, but what I don't know."

Early dawn light is seeping in, the Niris no longer just a dark silhouette at the window. The day's first rays delineate the surrounding peaks, skim over the rooftops. Silence envelops us, save for the rhythmic drip of water and the odd crack of ice.

I build up my courage, brace myself.

"And did he?" I whisper. "Escape, I mean?"

Adrik hangs his head. "No."

My mouth is dry. "What happened?"

"Someone caught wind of his escape plans, ratted him out to the authorities." He gives me a sad look. "Situations like that? They like to make examples. I never saw him again."

"Solitary confinement? Relocation?" I hear the panic in my own voice. "Where is he now?"

Adrik picks up his hat, stands up. "Come."

Everything feels on rails after that, like I'm a passenger.

Slipping my pack on, crunching across the hardpacked snow in the early-morning gloom, listening to Rachkov question Adrik about patrols, schedules, routes out of Yarpol.

Near the bar, we get in his pick-up.

We all sit up-front, Adrik driving. I shift along so I'm squeezed in the middle between the other two. He drives slowly, keeping the engine to a low growl, keeping to the backstreets.

Rachkov's tentacles twitch, nervous.

We leave the housing district, head for the edge of town, passing industrial sites that are beginning to stir. Signs of Raian activity thin, until we're crossing a stark, white wilderness, distant hillsides dappled with brooding evergreens. Lift your eyes from the road and you could be on a virgin world.

We turn off the main highway onto a small branch road that weaves upwards and becomes a rutted track, climbing between thick banks of ramrod straight pines. Clearing the treeline, we emerge into crisp dawn sunlight, the landscape a blanket of undulating snow, here and there webs of tenacious weeds poke up through the white. In the valley to the left I can see the arrow-straight train tracks of the line that brought us to Yarpol.

Shortly after, Adrik pulls off the road, kills the engine.

A little way off I see a cabin, well, more like a shed, really, and briefly I entertain the stupid, childish thought that my father might be in there, waiting.

Adrik's words come to me, shattering that hope.

I never saw him again.

We get out, the cold air taking the breath away, the hot metal guts of the pick-up flexing and making a rapid *tink-tink-tink* sound. Above, a hawk circles, searching for prey.

Adrik leads.

I'm confused, though.

He doesn't head for the shed, but walks out into the wilderness, his footfalls breaking the pristine ground. Snowdrifts have created small sculpted peaks in places, and elsewhere I see jagged rocks jutting out.

He stops at one.

"I'm sorry, Sewa."

I drop to my knees.

They are unmarked graves.

This is a cemetery.

Father is here.

I'm never going to see him again.

Never going to hear his voice.

Never going to be lifted into his arms like the little girl who loved to be cradled all those years ago. I feel a hollowness, and I know— with absolute, crushing certainty—that this feeling, this loss, will stay with me until the end of my days.

With all the strength I can muster, I edge forward, dragging my knees through the unspoiled snow that glimmers in the sunlight. The top of the grave is fringed with snow, and a light dusting, half-ice, half-snowflakes covers the rest. Staring closely, I can see it isn't unmarked, a crude darkened metal plaque beneath the frost, bolted into the stone.

I wipe off the ice.

KENDRO EZE

His name is hand-engraved, but the workmanship is excellent. At a glance you'd think it machine chiseled. I touch the indentation of the "K" the cold sharp, then brush my fingers across the rest of the letters.

"I love you, Father," I whisper, welling up.

I turn my head, hiding my face from the others.

The distant landscape is beautiful, hills and forests and mountain peaks unsullied by Raian hand. Above the range to the east, the sunrise paints the crest in warm hues of yellow and orange, while higher up the sky is a cool blue.

I wipe away my tears, turn back to the grave.

"Maybe one day I'll forgive you," I say. "Rest in peace."

I stand up, take a moment.

"Why didn't he wait?" I ask, not turning. "A few more years he'd have served his time."

"Never works like that for people like your father," Adrik answers. "The sentences are always extended. He knew that. Escape was his best chance of freedom."

I scan the inhospitable landscape.

"He would've survived out here."

"I don't doubt that."

I turn. Adrik and Rachkov stand a few paces apart, the Raian holding his hat in his crossed hands, the Niris standing tall, the hood of their cloak down, exposing their head.

"What he wasn't so good at," I say, icily, "was recognizing signs of betrayal. He always saw the good in everyone."

"And," Adrik says, "by my reckoning, if he got to live it all again, he wouldn't want to change that."

Even if it cost him his life.

Yeah, that's probably right.

I wonder if I can live like that.

Adrik puts his hat back on. "I've got some things for you."

He starts off for the shed.

Rachkov approaches.

"Sewa," they say, "I'm truly sorry."

They look wretched.

"Thank you," I reply, struggling to keep the anger at bay. "We all have to live with this now."

They stare at the grave. "We do."

"What will you do now?"

I can see the question takes the Niris aback.

"I thought... I'd like to..." They flail for the right words. "Let me help you find the Horizon."

"I don't know, Rachkov."

Adrik has opened the shed. I watch him pottering around inside. "I'm going to need some time. Alone."

"Of course," they say, crestfallen.

I walk past the Niris.

I have no idea what's next.

All I know is that I just need to be by myself.

Maybe I'll stay on Raia, find a deep, dark cave system...

"Here," Adrik says, passing me a small, tin box as he steps out of the shed. "A few of your father's things."

The box is light, but it weighs heavy. I'm in half a mind to squirrel it away, but the need to see, touch, and feel things that he held is overwhelming. Opening it, I see the first item is a photograph.

Me and Father, wrapped in one another's arms. We're in our family chambers on the *Reverent*, in front of the double-bunk, the vantage point low, tilted upwards, so the underside of the bunk's ceiling is visible.

Mother must've taken the picture.

My head is thrown back in joyful abandon, while Father, crouching, is laughing at the camera. In his eyes though, I can see a sadness.

He knows he's leaving soon.

I slip the photo back into the box, close the lid.

"Thank you."

"Least I can do."

I turn to the gravestones. Now I know this is a burial site, I spy twenty or more graves in the empty expanse.

"Are they all off-worlders?"

"The majority."

"Executed?"

"Some." Adrik locks up. "Natural causes, most."

"However they died, they'd be thankful for what you do," I say. "As would their families. As I am."

"Souls need to be laid to rest." He claps his hands for warmth. "Now, you two need to be leaving. People will be looking for you. And I know the perfect means."

We get back in the pick-up, carry on away from Yarpol on the winding backroad across a desolate landscape, the snowfields glistening in the sun. Sometime later, my thoughts lost in the wilds, Adrik slows up, carefully checks his rear-view mirror, then pulls onto a side lane that can't have seen a vehicle for days, if not weeks. We bounce along, even the snow-chained wheels having difficulty finding purchase on the icy ground, come to a small yard flanked by a couple of open-sided storage shelters and a vertical silo.

Nobody else is around.

"On foot from here," Adrik says, climbing out.

I can feel Rachkov scanning the buildings, uncertain.

"I trust him," I say, quietly. "Come on."

The air is cold, each of my exhalations accompanied by a plume of breath, but I don't feel much, numb to sensation. He leads us between the shelters, and out across an empty field that descends towards a dense, gloomy forest. By the time we're almost at the first trees, each of our steps sees us plunging into snow up to our knees. We step into the cover of the forest and the going gets easier.

Adrik stops. "This is as far as I go."

"Where have you led us?" Rachkov peers into the shadowy forest, shakes their head. "I thought you were helping us escape."

There is no sign of any obvious path.

"Ahead, not far," Adrik says, making a chopping motion, "you'll come to a train track that cuts through the woods. The line runs heavy goods trains to-and-from Yarpol before joining the mainline twenty klicks further on."

"We're jumping on a moving train?"

"That you are."

Adrik breaks off a sprig of pine, rubs it between his fingers.

"Sewa," he says, "I don't know what your father was searching for, but I know it would've been something that wasn't just for himself. That's who he was." He tosses the sprig. "I also know he wouldn't have wanted you spending your life following his obsessions." He gives a small nod. "Goodbye, Sewa Eze."

He turns, not waiting, twists back through the trees.

"Take care, Adrik," I shout, at a loss for words.

We head on, just the two of us again.

The groundskeeper's as good as his word. A couple of hundred paces on we find a narrow channel cutting through the forest with a steel track underfoot. The line climbs out of Yarpol on a long ascent, and we walk a little way along the track to find the apex where the goods train will be slowest. We wait a long time in the cold and still and quiet, sitting in the forest a dozen paces back so that we're not spied by the driver. Eventually we hear the rumble of the train, the high-pitched whistle of the trembling steel, and soon its locomotive engine chugs past, pulling a tail of cars that stretch far down the hill.

I launch myself at a rusting iron ladder on the side of one car, jerking into motion as the momentum tugs my shoulders, but holding firm. I climb up, stand on the top of the car, the trees gliding past, the breeze already colder. Rachkov clambers up the side of the next car, which I can see is open-topped and holds long sections of white-barked trunks.

We can lay low here.

I jump across the gap, before carefully walking along the curved trunks. As the train picks up speed, I find a small recess, then lie down flat on my back and gaze at the endless expanse of sky, the forest already gone. The firmament is a vast brilliant blue, except for some gathering clouds to the south, where we head.

THIRTY-ONE

ᚴ ᛉᛀᛂᚲᚲ ᚴᛂᛂ

"Wake up."

I open my eyes to a blistering light, close them again, grasping for my rapidly fragmenting dream. I was with Father, back on the Horizon long ago, just hanging out, joking around.

And now he's gone.

I slump inwardly, remembering.

Nearby, I can hear a high-pitched grinding wail, and feel my weight pressing into my feet. My back is agony, like I've been sleeping on a rocky beach, and then I realize that isn't so far from the truth.

The escape, the train, the car of chopped trunks acting as our private sleeping berths. I shield my eyes with the crook of my elbow, force them open. Rachkov's looming over me, looking concerned. They help me up into a sitting position. We're coming to a standstill. Fast.

I glance at the surroundings.

Barren, featureless plains peer back, ambivalent to the drama, the snowy wilds of the far north gone and replaced with thin grasslands.

"Why are we stopping?" I croak.

My throat's dry, my lips gummy.

"I don't know," Rachkov replies. "Next stop shouldn't be for ages."

Despite the warmer climes, I feel a chill.

"Something on the tracks?"

I ask more in hope than expectation.

The more likely reason is obvious. *We've been found.*

"I doubt it." Rachkov helps me onto my feet. "Let's keep out of sight. And keep our wits about us."

Before we've reached the front of the car, the train comes to a halt, rocking us. The motion almost sends the Niris tumbling as the tree trunks jostle into a new equilibrium, but at the last moment they whip out a tentacle and steady themself.

We crouch low, watching and listening.

The smell of hot metal drifts up from the tracks.

From the front of the train I hear terse instructions. Any hope this isn't a military operation evaporates.

"They've found us."

I scan the plains, searching for some refuge or hiding place—a few boulders, tall grasses, even a drinking trough.

Nothing.

My stomach tightens.

"We need to hide." I turn to Rachkov. "Any ideas?"

Before they can answer, movement over their shoulder catches my eye. Mouth agape, I watch four or five riders, each astride a strapping beast, haring across the plains towards the rear of the train, dust billowing in their wake.

"What is this?"

For a second I think we might've got caught in the middle of a piracy operation, lowlifes from the badlands hijacking a goods train for its most valuable commodities.

A leather-clad man hauls himself up onto the locomotive at the front, begins stepping along the train, hammering on the first car with a metal stick, and I know that's not the case.

"Zarva Rachkov!" he cries. "We know you're here."

In the distance, I can hear the thunder of the beasts' hooves on the dry, parched ground. The man steps across to the second car, peers over the edge.

"We can protect you," he shouts.

"They're not Empire, are they?" I whisper.

Rachkov shakes their head.

"And that's good news or bad?"

"Hard to say."

Behind us, the riders have reached the back of the train, the furious stampede falling to silence as they begin examining the cars to the rear. They must be working together with the group at the front, I think. One or two forcing the train to stop before overwhelming the driver, and a larger, mounted group hiding out of sight before approaching from the back.

And we're trapped in the middle.

"Let's get under the train." I watch the man skip across to the third car, then disappear as he jumps down into its empty interior. "Now!"

As I leap from one side, I sense Rachkov moving too.

My ankle twists as I hit the loose gravel embankment with a crunch, but as I push off, I can feel it's just a mild sprain. I quickly scrabble into the darkness. The Niris squeezes in from the other side, breathing hard. Around us, I smell fuel and metal.

Did anyone see us?

"You head for the front," Rachkov says, looking at me intensely. "I'll head for the back."

I look up and down the cramped channel that runs beneath the train, the light at the ends occluded by boxy protrusions and dangling cables. No sweat for me, a lithe caver, but for an eight-limbed cephalopod it looks a miserable passage.

"And then what?" Before I finish the question I already know the answer. "No, Rachkov."

"We can't both escape," they say. "But I can give you a decent shot."

A car or two away, metal strikes metal like a tolling bell.

"Empire forces are coming, Rachkov!" the man cries, his voice attenuated, belying its proximity. "And I guarantee you're better off with us than them."

I shake my head. "We get out together," I whisper fiercely, "or we get caught together."

"No!" Rachkov grips my shoulders, angry, twisting me towards the front of the train. "Now go!"

I plant my hands against some machinery on the channel's ceiling, stubborn, not wanting to be coerced into flight.

Then understanding dawns.

If I'm caught it'll break the Niris.

They would rather be caught, even die.

Without waiting, I scrabble along to the underside of the next car, briefly exposed by a slice of daylight. Before I can get any further though, I hear the heavy thud of hooves and long, coarse breaths. The beast stops beside the car.

The rider dismounts.

Panicking, I haul myself up into a makeshift alcove among the machinery, hoping I'm out of sight should the rider crouch down and look. I still my breathing, muscles burning. Something hard and angular pokes into my ribs.

The beast snorts.

I can smell its fur, smell its meaty breath.

The man atop the train calls again, his voice sounding like he's passed overhead now. "Osiris is waiting, Rachkov!"

Osiris? The Pilgrim go-between? He's real? Or is this a trap?

A commotion breaks out a few cars back. Upside-down, I crane my neck, look back the way I've come, see Rachkov getting hauled out into the open. Beside my car, the rider jumps back onto their mount. I watch the beast wheel back the other way.

This is your chance! Go!

I relax stiff fingers, fall to the ground with a painful thud that knocks the wind out of me. I twist onto my front, scrabble away.

I'm one car away from the engine when I hear Rachkov.

"Sewa!" they shout. "Come out! They're with Osiris!"

The darkness, the claustrophobia, the sense of the great weight of the train pressing down from above, are familiar, comforting. If there was a crack in the earth here, I'd probably crawl into it, take my chances underground.

There isn't though.

I crawl out into the light, brush off the dirt.

A rider is already heading towards me.

"Climb up," the woman says, leaning down, offering an arm over the side of the great, muscular beast. "We need to get moving."

I grip her forearm, and she hauls me up. I swing my leg over the beast's vast flank, settle into the gap between the rider and the mount's head.

"You're with Osiris?" I ask over my shoulder.

"We are." The woman loops the thick reins over her hands. "Now, keep low and hold tight. Getting tossed from a kharva isn't on anyone's bucket list, believe me."

I want to ask if she has news of the Horizon, but before I can get the words out, she snaps the reins, and we thunder off, the wind howling through my hair, the juddering worse than any drop-ship turbulence.

I keep my mouth shut, lest I bite my tongue.

Soon. Soon I'll have answers.

We ride for what seems an age, heading into the hills and keeping to forest trails, winding mountain passes, moorland with gorse so thick and high we're hidden from sight.

The only time we spy Empire forces is when we're climbing through a deep, shadowed canyon and somebody spots the triangular silhouette of a scout craft through the thin clouds. We huddle under an outcrop, the beasts' breaths mingling in the chill air, and wait in silence until we can no longer hear the craft's muted but recognizable engines.

For the rest of the journey we see no other signs of the Empire, no sign of anyone. This hinterland of Raia was stripped of its subterranean riches long ago.

By the time we approach a smattering of industrial, blackened structures nestling into a scree and brush mountainside, my backside is so sore I worry that I'm going to struggle to walk when I dismount.

I'm not wrong.

In a building co-opted into makeshift stables for the kharva, I slide off my mount, the whole lower half of my body stiff and aching. Heaps of drab black rocks still occupy some of the stalls that have otherwise been cleared for the animals. The stench of the beasts' dung mingles with the smell of their feed and an unfamiliar gritty smell.

"What is that?" I ask the woman, gesturing at the drift of black stones, while I flex my legs.

"That?" the woman asks, incredulous. "That's coal."

"Coal?"

She bursts out laughing, startling her mount.

"Pilgrims," she says, shaking her head while she soothes the animal. "You gotta love them."

I stand there, mystified.

She must feel sorry for me, because she begins explaining that this place is an abandoned coal mine. I feel like an ignorant kid as she tells me coal is a natural resource found underground that was once exploited as an energy source in earlier eras.

"Dirty stuff."

I turn to see Rachkov dismounting.

"A few worlds came a cropper burning too much of the stuff," they say. "Runaway climate change. Not pretty."

The Niris coils and uncoils their limbs.

Whatever else the Niris is, they're certainly a knowledgeable soul. A lifetime of experience.

Unlike me.

So much I don't know.

And if these last few months have taught me anything, it's that I still have so much to learn. I realize with a start that I don't want to cut myself off from this gruff, smelly, double-crossing cephalopod. Even though some part of me hates them, will probably always hate them, nobody knows me better. Not even Oba these days.

And they've got my back. I know that now.

I fiddle with my hands.

"I'd like to learn more someday, Zarva."

I see the deepest relief in their eyes. "And you will."

"Osiris wants to see you both."

The speaker, a resistance fighter who wasn't with the ambush party, stands in the stable entrance, silhouetted against the late day light.

"Straight away."

Before we leave, I give the woman I rode with a nod of gratitude, but she doesn't respond, just gives me a stony look.

I guess we're not exactly welcome guests.

The fighter who leads us doesn't say anything else, either, the only noise he makes the rattle of the rifle that's slung across his back. We wind through the brooding structures of the abandoned site, nothing in the rusted machinery or broken, grimy windows to suggest the place is anything but dead. We duck into a factory building, full of vast crushing machines and wide conveyor belts, a patina of coal dust coating all the surfaces.

"Up there," he instructs, stopping at the foot of a metal grid staircase that leads to a mezzanine level overlooking the factory floor. "First office."

Rachkov goes first. I follow.

Halfway up, I whisper, "I don't want them to know."

"Know what?"

"That I'm… like you."

Rachkov turns back. "Okay. Our little secret."

When we enter the office, a woman is standing by the window, gazing out over the factory yard. Unlike the other resistance members dressed in standard combat fatigues, she's wearing Pilgrim military attire, the distinctive ribbed collar emphasizing her position of command.

Is this Osiris?

"Zarva Rachkov," she says, not turning. "One time Zelevas's favored attack dog. Now the Empire's most wanted. A spectacular fall. I would shed a tear, were it not for your butchery."

"I assure you, I oversaw no butchery."

"I suspect those mourning the Horizon of Light's dead would disagree with you." She turns. "Wouldn't you say, Sewa Eze?"

My heart leaps.

She knows about the Empire attack. This *must* be Osiris.

Maybe she knows where the Horizon is too.

"They might," I answer. "I know I did. And I have more reason than most."

Osiris's hair is up and braided in the traditional Pilgrim style, and an angular, golden tattoo runs down the side of her face and neck.

No wonder she's a myth on Raia.

She must keep to the shadows religiously.

I step up beside the Niris. "But I also know *that* Rachkov is dead, and *this* Rachkov means to atone for their sins."

Osiris gives me a long, hard look.

"You should know, Sewa, I am not a devout Pilgrim. I wear these clothes only so my soldiers remember who they are fighting for, nothing more." She eyes the Niris. "Only the survival of my people matters. All the piety, the rituals, the Endless worship? Not my concern."

"Then we are alike."

She considers that, but whether she believes it, or whether it pleases her, I do not know. I wonder if she knows about the lurch towards zealotry on the Horizon, or if she has any inkling of Cavemaster Kalad's deranged ideas, but these are not subjects to idly toss into conversation, so I hold my tongue.

Rachkov breaks the silence.

"You have our thanks," they say, building bridges. "We've been searching for you since we arrived on Raia."

"Like I don't know that." Osiris shakes her head. "Your clumsy attempts at contact haven't gone unnoticed by many in the Raian underworld."

"Our plight was desperate—"

"Let me be clear," Osiris snaps. "We have no interest in you, no need of you. Once a snake, always a snake. We only got interested when we learnt of your association with a Pilgrim."

Osiris shifts her gaze from Rachkov to me.

"I was curious. Why, I wondered, was a Niris mercenary, once of the Academy, once of Zelevas's inner circle, aiding a lost Pilgrim youth? And on Raia of all places?!" She holds up her palm so she can finish. "Call me cynical, but I couldn't swallow the idea this was a purely altruistic act."

Right and wrong.

"Whether you believe it or not, it's the truth," Rachkov replies. "After the attack on the Horizon—an attack I neither ordered nor condoned—I realized I'd been duped by Zelevas. That's when I left the Empire. While lying low, I found Sewa marooned on a nearby moon. I decided to help her find the Horizon again."

"Very noble."

"Not really." Rachkov hangs their head. "Soon after we met, I learnt that she was the daughter of a man I'd been instrumental in having incarcerated on Raia. Guilt drove me."

"Kendro Eze."

"Yes."

"Without Zarva, I'd have likely died on that moon," I add. "And never learnt the fate of my father, either."

I can see Osiris is still suspicious, but there's enough truth in the Niris's words that the omissions are not missed.

"I'm sorry, Sewa," she says. "From what little I've gleaned of your father, he was an impressive man."

"He was my father. That's all that mattered to me."

I step past Osiris over to the window, not wanting to show my hurt. Dark clouds hang heavy in the sky, and the light is waning.

"Anyway," I say, "we're not here to dwell on the past." I steel myself, turn back. "Can you help me get back to the Horizon? Do you even know where it is?"

Osiris gives a grudging smile.

"You know," she says, "we picked you up because our hands were forced. With all the heat, Empire agents would've likely cornered you within a day or two on your return to the capital. My responsibility—my mission even—is to see the Pilgrims stay free. I had to step in for you, Sewa."

A small island of Pilgrim resistance right in the heart of the United Empire's backyard. I feel pride. Zelevas isn't quite the invulnerable foe we sometimes imagine out in our arcologies in the dark between the stars.

I want to be part of that fight.

"And you have my thanks."

"Mine too," Rachkov says, "for what it's worth. But you didn't answer her question. Can you help her get back to the Horizon?"

"We can."

Two simple words, but they precipitate such joy.

I'm going back!

I'm going home.

Then Osiris adds, "In theory."

Rachkov takes the words right out of my mouth. "What do you mean *in theory*?"

"In normal circumstances, I wouldn't know the location of any of the arcologies that make up the Pilgrim diaspora. Years can pass without contact, and messages that come in can be relayed via dead drops." Her face darkens. "The reason we have had recent contact with the Horizon—"

My stomach drops. "They're in trouble."

"Unfortunately, yes. A seemingly empty system where they planned to regroup turned out to be the home of a massive Craver hive. Fighting off converging swarms, they issued a plea for assistance."

"And?"

"Two other arcologies in the sector responded," she says. "The current status of the fighting is unknown, but the Craver response leads us to believe the system possesses an important hive with an active Queen."

"Cravers will do anything to protect their Queens," Rachkov says, shaking their head. "They won't stop coming until the threat is eliminated—or the Queen destroyed."

"Indeed," Osiris agrees, momentarily distracted by something over my shoulder beyond the glass. "If retreat is impossible, the only course is a ground operation to destroy the Queen."

More like an underground operation.

Darkness, claustrophobia, and endless twisting passages crawling with insectoid killing machines.

Osiris steps closer, caresses my cheek, sympathetic.

"I know you want to return immediately, but we need to wait and see how things play out—"

"No, I need to be there! I can help!"

Osiris is unmoved.

I look to Rachkov, seeking backup.

"Tell her," I plead. "No one can navigate those Craver tunnels better than me."

Rachkov gives me a long, hard look.

I'm not sure if the Niris is going plead my case or tell me that she's right, but before they can speak, Osiris steps over to the window.

"Ah, hell," she says. "The Empire's here."

THIRTY-TWO

ㅊㅋㅏㄷㄴ ㅊㅓㅅ

While Osiris scrambles for her rifle, I scan the dull, craggy skyline beyond the mining facility's gates, wondering what she's seen, when a soldier bursts into the room.

"We're under attack, Commander!"

"I can see that!" she barks, livid.

Someone messed up.

"Issue the evacuation order," she says, snatching up a device on a table. "Everyone to the hangar."

"Yes, Commander!"

The soldier ducks out.

"You two, with me," she says, passing us each a sub-machine gun. "We've got two stealth-copters—if we're lucky, between the darkness and the terrain we'll get out of this."

The gun is cold and heavy in my hands, nothing like the laser firearms we're trained with on the Horizon. Still, the principle remains the same.

Point and shoot.

We rush down the stairs, out into the mine's yard. In the half-light I can see resistance soldiers spilling from the other buildings. A streak of light flashes past overhead, a supersonic Empire fighter on a reconnaissance pass.

"We find out you have anything to do with this attack, Rachkov," Osiris shouts, glancing over her shoulder as she runs, "we will kill you."

The Niris looks angry but holds their tongue.

Somewhere not far off, enemy ground forces are approaching, but for now they remain unseen. My stomach tightens, my tongue bone dry. The gun feels like dead weight in my hands. Hard to fight a foe you cannot see.

At that moment, a slash of light blazes down from the heavens, pierces the structure we're sprinting towards, causing a terrific explosion. Time and space are mangled. The light hits me first, a blinding supernova, followed by the whistle of the missile's trajectory and the deafening crash.

Like a hammer blow from the skies.

Then, a scorching wind, hot as the sun, knocks me to the ground, and I feel a hail of debris arrow past.

Nobody in the hangar's surviving that, I think, dazed.

Next thing I know, Rachkov's getting me to my feet.

My ears are ringing, my eyes still dazzled, and I get the feeling I'm bleeding somewhere. We hunker down.

"Are you hurt?"

The Niris's words come to me like we're underwater. The strained tones aren't just down to my ringing ears, though. A deep cut has almost severed the tip of one of their limbs.

"Ah, that's nothing for a Niris," they say, noticing where I'm looking. "We regrow limbs for fun."

I have no idea if that's true, but Rachkov's joking insulates me from the battlefield horror enough to get myself together. I check myself over. My fingers come away bloodied from my temple, but it's only a nick, and aside from a bruised hip, I've got off lightly. "I'm fine."

"Good."

Near us I can see Osiris limping back and forth, in shock. She reaches for the radio on her chest, but she doesn't know what orders to give, just gapes, lost.

"The mine!" I shout. "We can survive in the mine."

"There's no way out," she cries over the sound of gunfire. "We'll be trapped."

"No, we won't. There's always a way out. And I'll find it." I grip her forearm, meet her eyes. "Trust me."

The exchange of gunshots intensifies, nearer. From the obliterated hangar, a hot mangle of metal, stone, and flesh, I watch thick, black plumes drift upwards. Even at this distance, I can smell the smoke, rich with oil and chemicals and other odors I don't want to consider.

Osiris nods.

"Fall back to the mine!" she barks into her radio. "Staggered retreat! Now!"

She turns to me.

"I'm trusting you, Pilgrim," she says, fire in her eyes. "Now, get to the mine! I'll be right behind."

Rachkov doesn't wait for a second invitation, grabbing my arm, and hauling me in the direction of the mine shaft tower. Shortly, we barrel into the large, corrugated shack at its foot, almost colliding with another soldier who's guarding the entrance, firearm pointed into the twilight.

He waves us on.

We come to the shaft entrance, a few soldiers already milling around the fenced-off central area that leads to the depths. The maw is dark, with taut, quivering cables arrowing into the black. Nearby machinery grinds and whirrs.

The platform's missing.

"Where is it?" Rachkov asks.

A soldier standing at the rugged console answers. "Coming up. Two klicks down."

I feel sick.

"How long?"

"A few minutes?"

A despairing look crosses the Niris's face. "We'll need that long again to keep the Empire out."

I understand. Even if we start descending before they reach the shaft entrance, we'll be easy pickings until we reach the bottom. They could cut the cables any time... Looking around, I can see every soldier has already understood the deadly calculus.

The atmosphere is heavy, rebellious.

"Why wasn't it here?" I ask the soldier at the console. "It doesn't make any sense to be down, unless—"

"—somebody fled into the mine," he finishes, deadpan. "If we're lucky we might find out who."

Another soldier, sat against the wall, firearm across his lap, speaks. "We shouldn't have fallen back here."

"Damn straight," another adds, "what was Osiris thinking?"

"It was my idea," I say, addressing the last soldier.

"Your idea?" A flash of anger crosses his face. "I don't even know why we risked our hides for you."

Beside me, I sense Rachkov tensing.

I'm not getting into a fight.

"We need to focus," I say evenly. "We can survive in the mine. Down there we can regroup, then find a route out that the Empire won't expect."

Can we, though?

The only noise comes from the spluttering engine pulling up the platform, but the shaft remains resolutely black.

I need to make them believe.

I need to believe.

"Out there," I say, "we've got no chance. We're outnumbered, outgunned, and outmaneuvered. One or two might escape into the night, but the rest will die. Or worse."

I let that sink in a little.

"Here though," I say, turning about, "if we're smart, if we work together, we can all come out of this alive. We owe that to the ones we've already lost."

Outside, a gunfire exchange rattles across the site, nearer than ever. More soldiers pile in, the relief on their faces swiftly switching to confusion at the tense atmosphere.

The soldier who confronted me steps closer.

"I'll gather some supplies," he says, grasping my shoulder. "The barracks aren't far."

As the soldier slips off, Rachkov gives me a nod.

Well played.

The Niris beckons me over to one side, away from the other soldiers. "You okay?"

I realize I'm trembling. "I'm scared."

"We're all scared," Rachkov says.

They glance over to the shaft, but the platform is nowhere to be seen, the rattle of its steel cage still faint. The Niris sinks inwards, before collecting themself, standing tall.

"Sewa," they whisper, "I need to tell you about that world."

Straight away, I know which one they mean. I can still smell the decomposing air sitting heavy in the rainforest, feel my stark fear as we fled the underground ruins.

"The Nakalim?"

Rachkov nods.

"They didn't come alone," they say. "There was only ever one party. They came united, but what happened on the world led to division."

They were brought there.

"The Academy."

The Niris nods again.

A dark secret is being unwrapped before me, but I sense that's not the worst thing about this.

Why are you telling me this now, Rachkov?

"Tell me in the mines."

They shake their head.

"Zarva—"

"Listen, the world held a lodestone. That thing, that creature? It was a failed resurrection... a monster, an abomination, made by one man's hubris." The Niris lowers their voice. "Isyander has begun the next phase of his grand project, Sewa."

"Bringing back the Lost."

Rachkov nods. "I thought it was a fantasy, until..." They trail off, start again. "The galaxy will not survive his designs. The disruption to the balance will be too great. I see that now. Worlds will be leached of Dust, whole biospheres will fail. Monstrosities will be unleashed. Even if they're not malformed, not unhinged, they will not sit idly by this time. Civilizations will be crushed, countless trillions will suffer."

Too much.

"What can we do?" I ask meekly.

"Isyander's project must be stopped. At all costs. *You* must find one of the original Academy Pathfinders. Kinete Muldaur. She's ex-Empire. Tell her what you saw, what I've just told you. No one else must know." Rachkov grimaces. "No one else can be trusted with this information, Sewa. Isyander has many disciples, but not Kinete. Not anymore."

Standing in the midst of these frightened soldiers—with the Empire closing in, with Rachkov's demands fresh—I can barely take it all in, overwhelmed. Sweat and fear mingle with the coal dust in the cold air. A loud clank echoes from the shaft, and I catch the platform cage rising from the darkness.

The soldiers begin stirring.

The Niris, I realize, is not coming with us.

"Where are you going?" I whisper.

I already know though.

"Say her name," Rachkov says.

"Kinete," I say. "Kinete Muldaur."

"Good. If you're lucky you might still find her at the Academy. She was still biding her time last time we spoke. Otherwise, that's where your trail starts."

"I'm still going home first, Rachkov."

"I know." They nod. "Just don't wait too long."

Osiris staggers in, still limping, face laced with perspiration.

"Yara, Leandro!" she cries, as the platform cage finally arrives, grinding to a halt with an ears-splitting squeal. "Get to the entrance. I want suppressing fire, now!"

Using their numerous limbs, Rachkov helps make a path through the throng for the pair, and I stay close, hugging the Niris's side.

As the chain-link hatch is hauled open, the two soldiers hustle off, unslinging their weapons. The rest of the soldiers begin filing onto the platform, fast but orderly. Noisy bursts of machine gun fire echo through the chamber. My ears ring with the cacophony. I can smell burnt metal shells, hot steel cables, the diesel of the engine.

"Sewa."

"Zarva, let's go," I shout, denying reality, starting for the platform as I grip one of their limbs, but the Niris stands firm. "Come on."

"They know where we are," they reply, leaning in. "And they're close. Without a… diversion, the platform…"

No, Zarva. No.

"We can rig an explosion," I stutter, words jumbling over one another, "cave in the entrance, buy time—"

"We're out of time, Sewa."

"No, Zarva." I touch their face. "Please."

Their skin is warm, not clammy.

"You've given me so much," they say. "Where I was… who I was… I couldn't ask for more." They unfurl the limb that's holding me, let go. "Now time's up, kid."

I press myself into the Niris's flank, opening my arms wide to hold as much of them as I can. I don't want to forget these sensations. The press of their body, the shape of their eyes, the pungent smell of the sea.

"We did okay, didn't we?"

I nod, the words too painful.

I wipe my eyes, detach myself.

"I won't forget you, Zarva."

"Farewell, Sewa."

And like that the being who knows and understands me better than anyone now, slips away. My mentor, my protector, my betrayer. I stumble onto the platform, only half hearing the soldiers' shouts. Strangers' bodies press tight, everything earthy and intimate. I can smell their dirt, their sweat, their breath, even their blood, but nothing stirs me.

I feel numb.

The pair who were laying down the suppressing fire rush in, breathless, their voices joining the hubbub, but I'm barely listening. Then the platform jolts into life, a final passenger joining the throng, before the hatch is heaved closed.

Besides the machinery, all is silent.

We descend, darkness gradually enveloping us, the only light coming from the soldiers' HUDs and flashlights, above the square of light rapidly diminishing. I don't look up myself, but around me I sense faces turning upwards, sunflowers tilting towards the sun.

Whispered voices emerge from the shadows.

A prayer, an angry exchange, somebody cursing.

We can't have gone a hundred meters when I feel it.

Like in a thunderstorm when the lightning's about to strike and the hairs on your arm snap to attention from the electricity on the wind. Except for me, the feeling's inside, and I know instinctively it's the Dust.

A resonance.

Not unpleasant, but… disconcerting.

Then for a split-second we're bathed in a golden white light. The soldiers flinch, turning their heads away from the top of the shaft where the illuminance originated.

The air shifts.

An explosion rocks the mountain with a mighty clap.

The strata trembles and rockfall spills onto the roof of our cage, while the platform nearly shakes itself to pieces. I don't fall, though, the wedge of bodies keeping me on my feet.

Zarva.

As the afterglow fades, we find ourselves in pitch-black, all the electronics cooked in the electromagnetic wash. The only motion, the only noise, comes from the lift and its mechanisms, still delivering us to a fate at the foot of this shaft.

In the silence and darkness, I cry with shuddering gasps.

I bring forth memories of our times together, and I feel a tinge of joy mingling with the overwhelming sadness.

Somebody close by presses something into my hand.

A piece of cloth to wipe my eyes.

"Thank you," I whisper between sobs.

"We won't forget its sacrifice."

We descend.

I hear the soldiers' breaths, each one keeping their thoughts hidden. A remembrance for the fallen.

That or they're simply afraid.

Here, now, we're vulnerable.

So, so vulnerable.

A few thin, taut, steel cables are the only thing preventing us from plummeting hundreds of meters to our deaths. Should a single Empire soldier reach the shaft head…

We crawl downwards.

Someone has got their flashlight working again, and I can see the strata of the rock passing by, agonizingly slowly, but also reassuring.

This is my domain.

I wipe my teary eyes. I will grieve later.

I need to be ready for when we make it. If we make it. I brought these people down here. And I will do everything in my power to bring them back out again.

After what seems an age, the platform begins to slow.

Through the gridded floor, slices of torch beams cast light on the foot of the mine shaft. A cheer goes up, more relief than celebration, but before we reach the bottom proper the lift halts with an ugly squeal.

Panicked voices shout out.

I twist round in a tight shuffle.

Sheer rock face stares back beyond the chain-link, no chance of escape that way even if we opened the gate.

"There's an escape hatch," somebody cries from the middle of the scrum. "We can jump down. It's not far."

Near me, bodies press harder as the soldiers clear some space, and I hear the first man thump onto rocky ground.

"Clear!"

Two... three... four soldiers have escaped, when the lift jolts upwards, and I hear a cry of pain as the fifth soldier lands.

They're bringing us back up!

Not fast, but fast enough.

Leaping will soon lead to much worse than twisted ankles.

Gunfire bursts out, staccato flashes in the semi-darkness. Soldiers aiming for the cables, but their shots are bad or ineffective. Angry shouts follow, before Osiris's voice rises above the commotion.

"No shooting!" she commands. "Keep exiting while we can, soften the landing. And I want someone on the cage roof to jam the gears, halt the ascent."

Her fighters spring into life, a soldier swiftly thrust up through the cage's roof hatch. Within a few moments they've rammed something into the mechanism, triggering a flurry of hot sparks. The platform jerks to a stop.

"Where's Sewa?" Osiris calls.

"I'm here," I answer. "Near the gate."

"Get to the escape hatch—I want you out ASAP."

She doesn't say why, but the reason's clear.

I've got to lead these soldiers out.

As I thread through the thinning-out platform, distant gunshots echo down the shaft.

Enemy fire.

"Go!" someone orders.

I hustle down a section of chain that's being used to shorten the drop then jump into darkness. The fall's terrifyingly long, and I bend my knees at the last moment as the ground suddenly rears into sight.

No breaks.

Somebody drags me away, before another soldier crashes into the vacated ground, but this woman's landing isn't so lucky. The crunch of one of her bones breaking is audible, even more so her subsequent scream.

We pull her away, no time for assessment.

Above, one of the cables snaps with a ping, and the lift lurches down, before holding steady.

They're cutting the cables.

Somebody throws in some tarpaulin sheeting to the landing zone, and aside from what sounds like a broken ankle, the next few jumpers escape with nothing more than sprains and bruises.

I hear another whiplash ping.

Two cables down.

With each jumper I look out for Osiris, before I realize she's saving her escape till last. I must've helped haul off a dozen soldiers, when she finally lands. As we pull her out of the shaft, the platform comes crashing down, missing her feet by a hair's width, and coating us all in choking dust.

Osiris grips my hand, eyes closed.

"Now get us out of here."

THIRTY-THREE

ᚵᚴᛁᛌᛘᚴ ᚴᛌᛚᛖ

The mine is dark, musty, long absent the sounds of industry and camaraderie. *I must focus.* I push everything from my mind, sweep away all the distractions that will only hinder me. I am the difference between life and death for these men and women.

All that exists is us and the mine. No different to a hundred other descents. Except this time the Empire's closing. And we're seeking a route *out*, not *in*.

Yes, that's different.

I'm different too, though.

Every choice is fraught with new perils, dangers I usually needn't consider. I must give them due thought, yet still instill the soldiers with belief. I remember an old motto that Kalad always muttered before we entered a cave system.

Trust must be absolute.

Whereas I am invigorated by the idea of the labyrinth, I can feel the soldiers' fear, cold and real. Their trust won't be easily earned, but it is vital. I dust myself down, step into their midst. Lances of torchlight cut the darkness, illuminating the surrounding figures. Most are standing, but a few are squatting, tending the injured.

"Listen up," I say. Several torch beams zero-in on me, dazzling. "Coming down here was my idea. Up there we would've been slaughtered. Down here, if we're smart, if we work together, we're safe—"

"For how long?"

"Long enough to get out."

"You know that?"

I turn slowly, let every soldier see my belief, my determination.

Beyond them, the inky black passages carry the scent of coal on the faintest breeze.

Fissures back to the overworld.

"I do," I say. "I learnt to cave before I learnt to read. I've descended into—and come back out of—everything from underground cities on Endless jungle worlds to geological mazes on methane-frozen comets."

"And what about Raian coal mines?"

I turn. My interrogator is a grizzled veteran with a proud, fulsome beard, but here, in this mine, I can see he is afraid. Between the dark, the claustrophobia, the great weight of rock over our heads, the subterranean realm spooks.

I need to get him onside.

"If you listen to me, I'll get you out." I meet others' eyes. "All of you."

I haven't swayed him, but no dissenting voices greet my words this time. I have their attention at least.

"Sewa," Osiris says, stepping up next to me, "you have operational command. Tell us what you need."

The next hour is a blur as I organize the thirty-six soldiers that make up our forces. We set up a small staging area close to the shaft. Aside from a dusty office where the shift foreman would've overseen the working miners all those decades ago, there are a number of side chambers that hold supplies. Mining equipment, explosives, first aid, spare clothing.

Our first priority is preventing Empire soldiers from following us. We discover two auxiliary shafts used to ferry ore up to the surface, and I have two of the group's best climbers hustle up to plant incendiary devices. I'm standing in the passage outside the second, when rifle shots ricochet down the shaft.

"They're abseiling down!"

The soldier crunches to the ground, flings himself out of the line-of-fire. He pats his neck, thinking he might've been shot, but he's okay. A close shave.

"Detonate the charges," I order.

He opens his saddle bag, revealing a half-dozen unused explosives. "I only laid a few."

"No matter," I reply. "We'll ferry more material by hand afterwards."

He fishes inside the bag, finds the detonator.

A moment later an explosion rocks the mountain. A heavy rain of debris tumbles from the shaft, piles up at the ground.

A good start.

"Now grab a few more soldiers," I say, "and make that shaft impassable."

He nods, disappears into the shadows to find help.

The other ore shaft is more straightforward, the full complement of explosives laid and detonated before any Empire interference. Several tons of hard stone crashes down, billowing rock dust into the passages and provoking a chorus of coughs.

Nobody's getting through that.

Not for a long while at least.

Satisfied the enemy has been repelled, I retreat back through the swirling dust to the foreman's office. With the injured being treated, another party securing caving equipment from the stores, and a third group scoping out the nearby tunnels, it's time to plan the escape route.

"You find anything?" I ask.

Osiris nods. "We've got plans of the mine system, plus a topological survey of the mountain range itself." She rolls out the map on the dented desk, secures the corners with several specimen rocks that glint in the torchlight. "You need anything else?"

I stand over the desk, brush my fingers across the thin lines that mark the tunnels on the brittle paper. The mine system is vast, a complicated grid of passages that span multiple levels. I flick through the survey too, a brick-thick volume dense with small, technical print and rich, annotated diagrams.

Too much information.

And deep down I already know the path, anyway. Soon as I got out the shaft, I could feel the Dust working its magic, assessing a hundred thousand subtleties of geology, wind, and Endless knows what, into an escape plan.

"Sewa?"

"No, this is all I need."

I study the map, cross-reference it with the survey.

Give the impression you're working this out.

They get a sniff that I'm going on gut instinct they'll either lose faith or know I'm graced by Dust.

Neither is acceptable.

"Sewa, I wanted to say…" Osiris clears her throat. "I'm sorry… about the Niris."

"The Niris had a name," I reply, eyes locked on the map. "Zarva Rachkov." I grit my teeth. "Zarva saved us. Just remember that later."

"I know," she says. "And I'm sorry I questioned their loyalty." She clutches my hand. "That's how we stay alive, though. Pilgrims can't afford to trust outsiders."

Sometimes we can't trust insiders either.

I withdraw my hand.

"Give me your word you'll get me back to the Horizon." I meet her eyes. "I know I can help defeat the Craver swarm."

And expose the Cavemaster should he still be alive.

"Alright." Osiris gives a wry smile. "You get us out of this, and I'll get you on the first shuttle off-world. You have my word."

Home!

For a moment I am transported back to our family chamber, braiding Rina's locks. I can almost hear her yelping as I pull too hard, smell the scent of her hair…

Not here. Not now.

There's work to do.

I give my attention back to the map, trace my finger along slender lines, attempt to rationalize what I've already intuited. The more I study though, the more confused I become. I can't explain my instincts, and worse, the more I glean from the records, the more I doubt those very same instincts.

Head deeper into the mountain rather than climbing for the surface?

I consider ditching my original divinations for the cold, hard facts on the table, when a soldier bolts in.

"Commander! Empire forces are drilling through the bottom of the shaft," the soldier says, his trembling voice betraying his nerves. "They'll be through in no time. We need to go."

"Alright, assemble everyone," Osiris instructs calmly. "We'll move out ASAP. But do it quietly. I don't want the enemy thinking they're close when they break through."

The soldier nods and leaves.

Osiris turns to me. "Time's up."

Rachkov said the same words, not long before…

Bad omen.

"You set?"

I roll up the map, unsure.

Osiris grips my wrist. "Trust your gut."

Does she know?

I nod, saying nothing. She takes the map, slides it into a cylindrical tube that she straps across her back, then squirrels the thick survey away into her saddle bag.

"I'll take these."

We head into the passage, the soldiers lined up in silence like statues in a tomb. Nearly all carry thick loops of rope, helmets, waists draped with climbing paraphernalia. *Good.* A muted whine of metal grinding into stone comes from the ore shaft.

I close my eyes, still my thoughts.

The way is clear.

"Let's go," I say as I snake through the soldiers. "And don't march in-step. That'll make more noise."

We move out into the darkness, a ragtag army led by an off-world Pilgrim girl. Some wounded, many scared, all desperate to bask in the light of the sun again. Long ago miners would've trudged these tunnels, gossiping and joking, but we walk in silence.

The early going is marked by many forks, many crossroads in the underground maze of tunnels, but I don't hesitate at the junctions. Far off I think I hear the sound of voices. Sometimes we follow two-way train tracks in wide low tunnels, other times we're squeezed single-file as we proceed through narrow connecting passages. We cross an underground station of sorts, rusting containers and handcars scattered along the multiple spurs. A welcome smell of clammy rocks and dark moss grows.

Our target is gaining entry into the vast natural cave system that sprawls beneath this mighty mountain range. If I choose our exit point carefully, it'll seem like we've vanished into thin air. Then all we'll need do is climb out.

All we'll need do…

I say it like it's trivial, like we'd only be a hop, skip, and a jump from freedom, but compared to the danger we're in now, it will be the easier half of the equation. We've got good supplies, fresh water, capable men and women used to digging deep. We could take our time, scout the easier paths, choose a route that takes us up into forested slopes where we could escape under cover of darkness.

"Sewa," Osiris whispers, breaking my thoughts. "What about our tracks?"

She's absolutely right. I glance down, cast my torchlight on the tunnel floor. The ground is uneven rock overlaid with a layer of grit and dust. Undisturbed for half a century or more, our thirty-strong party's passage must be like a stampede through a field of wheat. In the dark it might be hard to spot—

Bright lights thrum into life, momentarily blinding. Further down the passage the lights flick on, one after another. I spy some small animal scurrying away.

Dammit!

I turn back to see the soldiers blinking in the sudden glare. They look nervous, exhausted, and many are looking over their shoulders. I walk through their ranks, keen to see what signs of our passage we've left.

Not good.

Where we've marched I can see a shallow, but clear, furrow in the dirt, even some clear footprints. I think back to our route, trying to figure if we crossed any smooth ground where we wouldn't have left a trail. Maybe in the station, some of the gridded tunnels. At best it'll only slow the enemy's pursuit…

The soldiers near me clock my concerns.

"They'll be onto us soon," one mutters.

He's right. We can't go back now though.

I sense we're only half-a-klick or so away from the cave system, but we're going to need to erase our next set of tracks to stand any chance of throwing them off. If only we could levitate… zero-gee would be a blessing, I think, unhelpfully…

Then I have an idea.

"Osiris!" I hustle back to the front of the group. "The map, quickly."

She unslings the cylinder, pulls out the map, gets a couple of nearby soldiers to keep it unfurled on the ground. I drop to my knees, begin tracing my finger across the stenciled lines.

That's where we came in…

That's the station…

That's where we're headed…

My heart leaps as I spy the nearby, parallel tunnel that carries an underground track.

"Here," I say, stabbing the paper. "We need to get to this rail passage. We can walk on the sleepers, hide our tracks, before we cut back across."

We move out again.

Under the bright lights I feel naked, exposed. I yearn for the darkness of the cave system.

I don't think I'm alone.

Soon enough we cross a connecting passage and reach the rail tunnel. Thankfully, ahead, I can still discern the subtlest signs of the damp breeze coming from the cave.

"Everybody, listen up," I say, keeping my voice low. "We're not far now. From here on out, though, we make zero tracks. Walk on the rails or the sleepers. The enemy must not know where we've gone. Understand?"

I get a sharp assent.

Before we start off, one soldier offers to create fake tracks in the other direction and another volunteers to help her. I glance at Osiris, but she offers no instruction.

Your call.

"Good idea," I say, even if I'm not sure it is. "Move fast. And don't get lost. We'll be turning off this tunnel three or four hundred meters down the line."

They head off, trampling across the ground around the train tracks with heavy footfalls, while the rest of us start off the other way. We walk single file. I focus on each footstep, determined not to displace a single speck of rock as I step onto each new sleeper.

Behind me the soldiers creep along in silence.

Sometimes, above the constant hum of the actinic lights, I think I can hear distant shouts. We come to the side tunnel which leads back to the other passage where we'll escape into the caves. It's a narrow corridor, no wider than the span of my outstretched arms, the walls rough and pockmarked.

Easy bouldering.

Which is lucky because the floor of the passage is covered with a fine sediment of rock dust. Even one single soldier walking through would leave easily visible tracks.

"Get me more rope," I call over my shoulder, as I estimate the length of the coiled bundle already slung across my back. "Two more loops."

"Stay here," I tell Osiris. "I'll set up a rope traversal so nobody need touch the ground here on out."

"They'll be on us—"

"Trust me."

She looks at me like I'm crazy, but holds her tongue. I turn away, briefly study the nearby wall, then leap. I hear a collective intake of breath from my captive audience, but my landing is flawless, not even a hint of a slip.

I can hear mutters of disbelief as I scuttle along the wall, but I pay them no heed, just focus on the work.

Let them have an inflated sense of Pilgrim climbing skills.

Every few meters, I fire in the bolts to the stone, one at my ankles, one at my shoulders, and soon enough I have two parallel tracks of rope running along the entire length of the passage. Once at the end I double back, tightrope walking along the new path, checking everything is well secured.

Perfect.

Osiris shakes her head.

"I've never seen anyone boulder so fast."

"I told you I was good."

My hands are burning, though. I turn them over, my fingertips ragged with cuts and scrapes, bleeding in places.

Behind her eyes I can see curiosity, even awe.

A muffled shout, far off, breaks the moment. This time it isn't just me who hears it, many soldiers' heads twisting to gaze back the way we've come.

"Get everyone moving onto the rope lines," I say. "I'll go ahead and finish the route."

I don't wait for a reply, scurry back along the path I've just installed, and get to the main tunnel. The smell of lichens, stagnant water, and loamy earth is strong, the entry to the cave system very close. In the shadowed clefts on the other side of the tunnel, I can practically feel the breeze.

Wasting no time, I free climb across the passage roof, securing a couple more bolts in the ceiling as I go, before fastening another line of rope. A moment later I find the crevice that leads into the caves, a near invisible scar of shadow deep in the passage wall.

No one's seeing that, I think, happily.

As long we leave no signs.

I wiggle through the narrow channel to find myself in a pitch-black chamber, my torchlight illuminating a cavernous space of natural formations. I doubt any living soul has ever stepped foot here. *Terra incognita.*

I cast around my beam, spy several paths out.

This will do nicely.

As I'm heading back, I hear gunshots responding to the screech of laser fire. I get back to the main group as fast as I can, relieved to see that the gunfight is still far off, only involving the pair who went off to lay false tracks. The rest balance on the line that runs along the connecting passage wall. The ropes are taut, the strain on the bolts great, but rather than moving they've come to a halt.

I can hear fierce, whispered talk.

They want to go back and help.

"You can't help them," I shout as loud as I dare. "A single one of us jumps off the line, makes marks in the dirt, then we're all dead."

"They need us!"

"Others do too," I cry. "Others who can't protect themselves from Empire brutality. Besides, alone, as a pair, they might still make it if they're smart."

The mutterings continue.

"But, if they don't," I say, "don't make their sacrifice mean nothing."

Osiris chimes in. "She's right."

Grimly, they obey.

I give them instructions to get to the cavern, tell them to wait for me there, before I boulder along the opposite wall in the other direction. Occasionally I meet the eyes of the soldiers I'm passing. They look at me with cold, dead gazes.

One has tears in her eyes.

After the last soldier moves off the first section of the line, I start dismantling the route, recovering the bolts, before carefully winding the excess lengths of rope over my shoulder.

No sign of our passage must remain.

I'm halfway done with the clean-up operation, when the sporadic exchanges of gunfire coming from down the train tracks fall to silence.

What it means, I don't know, but I work faster.

I come to the main passage again, every muscle burning. Sweat soaks my clothes, and the saddle bag of equipment weighs heavy on my shoulder.

One more push…

I rest a moment, watch the last soldier wriggle into the channel that leads to the cavern, feel a flare of hope. Our escape route is a marvel, hidden from all but the most attentive eyes. Like the soldier just merged into the stone.

Behind, I hear boots thumping on hard slabs; maybe our stragglers running along the sleepers of the track—or maybe Empire grunts. I imagine them jogging along, laser rifles gripped tight, eyes peeled.

Keep going…

I haul myself up to the passage roof, excavate the first bolt, but when I get to the second it doesn't want to come out. Come on. Re-gripping my tool, I attack it from another angle. Then another. My knuckles are scrapped raw, my fingers on fire.

No movement.

Nothing.

I have no choice but to leave it, praying it'll be lost in the glare of the overhead lights…

As I'm removing the final bolt from the wall beside the cleft, I hear the enemy. They've stopped at the other end of the side passage opposite. Two voices in a tense back-and-forth, before one starts moving nearer, boots pounding on the ground.

Too late!

I take a last glance at the remaining bolt in the passage roof, then slip into the darkness of the crevice. Moments later the Empire soldier stands a dozen paces away, breathing hard, utterly unaware that nearby thirty-odd Pilgrim sympathizers huddle.

My heart drops.

On the passage floor, not a hand's length away, lies a keychain. It must've been hanging on someone's pack, snagged on the narrow sides of the crevice. The urge to reach out and grab it is close to overwhelming, but I stay my hand.

Lodged in the shadows, I can't see the soldier, but I can hear every crunch of his footsteps, every rustle of his fatigues. I picture him turning about, gazing one way down the tunnel, then the other.

Gotta pick the right moment…

Time slows to a tortuous crawl.

I stare at the dull lump of shaped metal that might be our downfall, unable to discern its likeness. Every beat of my heart sounds like a blow on a bass drum.

"Andrei," the soldier shouts. "No sign."

His voice sounds quiet, like he's facing the other way.

He carries on talking, relaying his next steps, but I'm only half-listening. Poking my head out, I check he really is facing the other way, then snatch up the keychain.

I dart back into the darkness, go still.

Just in time…

The soldier crunches past, laser rifle tight in hands, before setting off into a light run.

Breathing out, body quivering with relief, I turn the keychain over in my palm and can't help but laugh. A stalking tiger. A mascot from one of Silny's big lazball clubs.

I close my fist, keep moving.

With my torch, in the darkness of the cavern, I can see the silhouettes of the men and women I've led here, some crouching, some standing, a few splayed out on their backs, all silent.

"Any lazball fans here?" I ask.

The question elicits confused mutters—and a loud curse.

I step over. "Think you dropped this."

I press the keychain into the man's hands.

"Damn, this could've sunk us. Where—"

"It doesn't matter."

"Thank you. I owe you." He squeezes my hand back, hard, not letting go. "All of us do."

THIRTY-FOUR

ㅈㅋㅅㄥㅏㅏㅋ ㅋㅁㅋㄥ

We rest up, take stock.

I consult the maps, get a better idea of the system, before scouting the best path out of this cavern. Occasionally, we hear boots passing in the tunnel. As a precaution, we move into another, smaller chamber a little distance away, up an easy but well-hidden climb. A couple of the badly injured struggle, but between the pain relief and the assistance, they make it up the short hike.

The chamber is cold, permeated with a loamy smell.

Huddling in the dark, the soldiers' fears are palpable.

Before I head out, I go round the whole group, calming nerves, offering reassurance, ensuring people are warm and comfortable. A few are hostile, the dark or the claustrophobia overwhelming, but they still know I'm their best bet. I do what I can.

"The worst is over," I say, often.

Most believe me.

Nobody speaks of the lost.

Several hours later I'm back, flush with adrenalin, and in possession of something priceless: the path out. Between that and the natural high of my caving adventure, I'm practically bouncing off the walls as I seek out Osiris. I need to rein it in a little, but not too much.

These people need some good news, after all.

"Sewa?" Osiris's voice floats over from a huddle of soldiers near the middle of the chamber, uncertain.

"I found it." I crouch next to her, a grin on my face. "We're going to escape."

"Thank the stars."

A ripple of excitement spreads through the soldiers as the news filters out, and I see shadowed figures getting to their feet, punching the air, embracing one another.

I lean closer to Osiris, lower my voice. "Any sign of the Empire in the caves?"

"Nothing," she says, then turns to me, concerned. "Why?"

"They'll suspect we've gone deeper into the mountain when they don't find us in the mines." I pick up some dirt, let it fall through the bottom of my clenched fist. "But they won't know where, and they'll definitely think twice about following us in with any sizable force. They'll probably fall back to the surface."

Osiris grips my wrist. "But you found a path out that emerges in the taiga, right?"

"I did."

I close my eyes, recall the cold air, the piney smell of the boreal forest. A cauldron of bats, flickering among the trees. It was still daylight, but the thick, snow-covered canopy made it seem like dusk. "I scaled a tree," I say. "And the taiga stretched unbroken as far as I could see."

Osiris's eyes sparkle.

I nod. "Still, we'll need to be careful. The Empire will be hunting us."

"There we have an advantage."

"Why?"

The soldier beside her answers. "Empire boots on the ground will be limited," he says. "Zelevas's war on the rebellion has always been a covert one. He can't afford to be seen fighting—and losing against—us."

"Then we should be good."

Osiris nods. "Alright, what's next?"

Shortly afterwards, Osiris, another soldier called Hakim, and I load up with equipment and head off. The mood in the camp is jubilant, the hum of excited conversation following us upwards as we secure the first ascent's rope line.

As well as acting as pack mules, Osiris and Hakim will road-test the path out, ensure nothing is too tricky for even the most inexperienced soldier.

Plus I get some company.

After spending part of a day alone, hiking and climbing, crawling and squeezing through pitch-black passages, shafts, and galleries, it's probably good for me, even if the going is tortuously slow...

"I thought I was in good shape," Osiris gasps, as she climbs over the cliff lip, joining me on a small ledge halfway up one of the longest ascents. "But you're on a whole other level."

She crouches, catching her breath, unfastening her ropes so that Hakim, far below, can begin the climb.

"Technique goes a long way," I reply, hand already searching for the best grip on the next section. "We had a straight-up fistfight? You'd deck me."

"I'm beginning to doubt it," she says, still blowing hard.

She gives the rope two sharp tugs—the signal for Hakim to climb. I'm on the verge of pushing off, when she speaks again.

"Wait."

I turn back from the wall.

My torchlight illuminates Osiris's crouching form, causing her to shield her eyes. Shadows dance across the stone ledge, before getting lost in the darkness beyond. Far off, I can smell the faintest trace of the guano of roosting bats.

We're getting close.

"You've impressed me, Sewa," she says. "No, more than impressed me. Astonished me. Without you, we'd…"

Astonished? Is she hinting she knows?

I decide to play it straight.

"Without me, maybe none of this would've happened."

"We made our choices," she says, eyeing me. "Anyway, we can argue that later. What I mean is… the resistance… we could do with another fighter like you. Smart, determined, capable. Most of all, a true Pilgrim who understands the stakes."

"That's very flattering—"

"Every arcology lives under a death sentence while Zelevas stays in power." She stands, moves closer. "Pilgrims will only be truly free when his reign ends."

"I know," I say. "But I need to go back—to the Horizon. They think I'm dead. That's not right."

"We can send word you're alive and well."

"Can you also send a message to my mother," I ask, "letting her know the father of her children is dead?"

"Like I said, we all have hard choices to make."

"And my choice is with the Horizon."

Osiris gives me a long, hard look, then nods. "I pray you're not too late. The Cravers—"

"Sooner you can get me back, sooner I can help."

Help take care of Kalad too.

She nods, softens. "I believe you."

"You promised you'd get me back if—"

"I know. And I will."

"Alright."

"Just think about it though, okay?" she says. "Needn't be tomorrow, needn't be next full moon. This war isn't ending anytime soon."

I nod, adjusting the thick loop of rope hanging across my chest. "When things with the Horizon are... settled, I'll give it careful consideration. I promise."

"That's all I'm asking for."

Except, there are other matters too.

Father's pursuits.

Rachkov's revelations.

I turn back to the wall, leap.

The next twenty-four hours are a blur of shadows and rock, bone-numbing fatigue and snatched sleep. Once I get them to the surface, Osiris and Hakim scout the vicinity, coordinate an airlift for once everyone's topside.

For me, it's another swift descent, followed by the grueling task of leading the rest out. The route is fully roped now, but most of these soldiers aren't natural climbers, and they're tired and hungry too. At times, a couple of the most badly injured need to be hoisted.

The challenge is less technical, more motivational.

By the time we do reach the last climb, my throat is hoarse, my fingers ripped to shreds, and my stock of rousing encouragements fully exhausted.

Just like my body.

Never has the stench of bat piss been more welcome.

As we hike through the dark forest, footsteps crunching on the hardpacked snow, I'm running on empty. The only thing keeping me going is the elation of our survival.

Near every soldier who went in, came out.

I barely remember reaching the evac point, barely recall the whirling blades of the stealth-copter or the sudden lift of takeoff, nor the transfer to an off-world shuttle, but they must've all happened as sometime later, bleary-eyed, I watch one of Raia's moons glide past.

At long last, I'm going home.

Whatever home looks like.

THIRTY-FIVE

ㅈㅋ ㄷ Σ ㅏㅅㅋ ㅋ ㅏ ㄱ ㄴ Є

Even using the gates, jumping between far-flung systems like a stone skimming over water, the journey back to the Horizon takes days. I want to be there now, helping see off the Cravers, but galactic realities don't care for my wishes. The pilot, Tibor, is an old veteran. He's not one for small-talk, and honestly, knowing we'll part ways once we reach the arcology—assuming it isn't so much slag and ash—I'm not feeling sociable either.

Calisthenics helps me burn some of my nervous energy, but the cramped shuttle isn't big enough to stretch out properly, so mainly I'm trapped in my head.

I think of the Niris often.

Not that long ago, I was a surprise passenger in their vessel, slingshotting across the stars. It feels a lifetime back. An eager young Pilgrim, simmering with resentment that an Empire conspirator had saved her skin. Now, with everything that had happened, everything that Zarva had confessed, everything that they had sacrificed, I just feel a hole in my life where the Niris should be.

We still had unfinished business.

I hadn't forgiven them, but I hadn't condemned them either. I needed more time, much more time, to understand how I truly felt about everything they'd said and done. Like my father, I loved and hated Zarva Rachkov, and the fact they too were gone, meant I might never get past that duality.

Had Zarva truly changed? I liked to think so.

Before they'd acted out of selfish interests, pursuing a life of power and privilege, nailing their colors to Zelevas's flag. Later, back on Raia, they'd sweated and hustled and bled for me. And I couldn't forget some of the last words we'd exchanged.

The Academy threatens the future of the galaxy.

The Pathfinders are the foot soldiers of this peril. They must be opposed. Zarva intended to work with others against Isyander, despite the dangers, because they believed it was right.

And they wanted me to join the fight.

The irony was, the place where Zarva had come to rest, philosophically-speaking, wasn't so different from Kalad's outlook. Both viewed Endless artifacts as potential catalysts for galactic annihilation, and both were prepared to act on that belief. But whereas Zarva wanted to build consensus, come together with like-minded souls, Kalad acted furtively, alone in the dark, willing to sacrifice—even kill—his own people to achieve his aims.

He might've been right in his beliefs, but the method mattered. The ends might justify *some* means, but that didn't make *any* means acceptable. Once I trusted Kalad as much as I trusted my own blood. But however much I could sympathize with his beliefs, he was an unrepentant murderer.

Kalad was a danger and needed to be stopped.

And then he needed to face justice.

I'm too late.

The battle is over.

Through the starlit darkness, the blackened shells of vessels—some Pilgrim, mostly Craver—drift towards oblivion.

I've seen a scene like this before, when we repulsed the United Empire attack, but the aftermath I'm witnessing today has settled, gone cold. Among the dead vessels, no fires burn bright, and no rescue craft comb the wrecks.

This deadly encounter ended days ago.

We must've lost people, yet I feel strangely detached.

Is it because I'm intruding onto others' grief? Or am I simply no longer a Pilgrim?

I don't know, but I shouldn't feel like this.

Rina and Mother might be among the dead.

Oba too.

And maybe Kalad.

We head deeper towards the ground zero of the battlefield, towards the densest part of the system's asteroid field, located in a gravitationally chaotic zone between two of its mighty gas giants. Craver territory. The bigger of the two gas giants dominates the view, a vast green eye of storms peering back from its swirling atmosphere.

"Beautiful," Tibor remarks. "But sinister."

I'm glad I'm not seeing this alone.

The good news is we won.

We learnt that as soon as we arrived in-system through the interstellar gate, immediately asked to identify ourselves by the neutral tones of a standard security algo. If the Cravers had won, we wouldn't have even been asked.

We would've been incapacitated.

Then boarded.

After that, I don't even want to imagine.

We receive instruction to land on one of the largest bodies of the asteroid field, glide onwards through the carnage. Somewhere deep inside that rock lies the dead Queen, dispatched by a brave fire-team who, no doubt, experienced countless horrors in the darkness.

Horrors I need not witness.

For the first time since I learnt of the Craver threat, I let myself feel relief. Descending into the heart of the lair will not be necessary. As we land on the asteroid's hard, undulating surface, nestling between several familiar vessels, my mind turns to the people I've not seen for so many moons. Oba. Mother. Most of all, Rina.

And Cavemaster Kalad.

Except Kalad, I pray they're still alive, that I'll meet them again soon, perhaps even here, somewhere among the craft perched on this rock. Suited up, we drop towards the asteroid, the gravity gently dragging us down onto the hard stone. With no atmosphere, the starfield is bright, the horizon a stark line separating heaven and earth.

A memory of trekking across the ice comet where we found Kalad's beacon springs up in my mind.

The day of the Ceremony of Duties.

Everything changed that day.

It feels so long ago.

As we hike towards the capital vessel, we step over slain Cravers, twisted masses of sinew and steel, fearsome even in death. Near a fissure that leads underground, I spy a whole massacred platoon, the mechanical insectoids obliterated by Pilgrim missiles as they swarmed out of the nest.

The fighting must've been intense.

Pilgrim drop-ships descending onto the asteroid. Counterstrikes by Craver infantry streaming out of the subterranean realm.

Not far off, I see a felled craft, the rear half of a Craver soldier sticking out of the smashed cockpit. Pilgrims must've been among the fallen too. They're only absent because they've already been ferried away by clean-up crews. Above though, I do spy one, pinwheeling through space, trapped in an elliptical orbit around the asteroid. For a moment, I wonder if they might still be alive, but as they pass overhead I can see their shattered helmet, a ghostly pale visage within.

A grim satellite.

Then I spy something worse.

I stop dead, blood running cold.

Cavemaster Kalad's craft, the *Mestaphos*. A little worse for wear, but still flightworthy. *Doesn't mean he's still here, but—*

He could be on there, right now.

"Familiar vessel?" Tibor asks, his voice crackling over the comms. "We can swing by—"

"No," I bark, too abruptly. I get moving again. "Capital vessel first. We're expected."

They don't know that I'm coming. Not yet. Only that we're with the resistance on Raia. I thought that prudent in case Kalad *was* still around... wouldn't want him sharpening his story or taking off before I had a chance to share word of his murderous duplicity.

I glance back at his vessel, shiver.

At least I'll have the element of surprise.

Granted access to the capital ship, we proceed through decontamination, slip off our helmets. Pilgrim vestments hang in the small vestibule. I robe myself, pull the hood tight. Breathing deep, I inhale the faintly aromatic air that's laced with scents I'd almost forgotten—burning votives, script parchment, holy oils. Not my favorite smells, but they still bring a smile to my lips.

I'm really, truly home.

Someone steps from the shadows...

"Overseer!" I cry, surprise turning to joy.

"Sewa?" she holds my face with both hands, staring deep into my eyes. "Is that really you?"

I want to ask the same.

She looks pale and drawn, worry lines etched deep.

"It is."

"Thank the Endless!' She pulls me into a fierce hug. "I thought we'd lost you."

I hold her tight, emotion welling.

Beyond her, I can see a cavernous hall where the Pilgrim dead have been laid out in neat rows. The light is dim, the main illumination coming from the flickering flames of the candles placed around each fallen. Clerics are attending the dead, reading scripture in low whispers, but I'm also disturbed to see a bare-backed Pilgrim standing over one of the fallen, administering self-penance with a birching branch.

I've never seen such a sight before.

Birching branches were always symbolic.

As we stay embraced, I hear Tibor excusing himself.

"What's happening, Overseer?" I ask as we extricate ourselves, gesturing at the scene from the hall.

Before she answers, she leads me into the shadows.

"Sewa," she whispers, severe but low, "things are different now." She drops her head. "I'm no longer the Overseer."

I blink, dumbstruck. *I don't understand.* I haven't been away *that* long. Liandra's leadership wasn't due for Council consideration...

"How?" I stutter. "Why?"

"Sewa—"

"It's Artak, isn't it?" I ask, already knowing the answer. "He's Overseer now, isn't he?"

Liandra nods. "After the Empire attack, Pilgrims sought refuge in their faith. Artak used that to his advantage, wrested control."

"That's treason!"

"No, I stepped aside."

"Why?"

Liandra sighs. "I could only give the people hard truths. And they needed more. They needed hope." She watches a cleric kneeling beside one of the dead to administer last rites. "Artak gave them that."

I stare across the hall of the dead.

This is still my home, but not the one I knew.

"What does that mean for the Horizon?"

"It means we have peace, not civil war."

A grave thought strikes me.

"And the Endless?" I ask. "Will Artak pursue their relics with even greater fervor? Will he seek to find Tor?"

"Sewa, you are a revelation." Liandra shakes her head, tears coming to her eyes. "I barely recognize this bold young woman standing before me. How did you survive? Cavemaster Kalad said... said there was no hope."

"Kalad?" I feel his hands around my throat, his face up close. "I saw his vessel... he's still with the Horizon?"

"Of course," Liandra replies, puzzled. "The Cavemaster was one of my most vocal supporters. Everyone knows he's never been fond of the more religious elements of the Horizon, but in the past he always held his tongue. This time he didn't hold back."

He still fears the profane knowledge. With the lurch to religious fundamentalism and faith in the Endless renewed, he might be feeling emboldened to act.

"But his voice didn't carry much weight."

"Not enough," Liandra says. "Now he's more of a pariah than ever."

Emboldened *and* desperate.

"Where is he now?"

Liandra gives me another puzzled look. "Why all these questions about Kalad?"

"Because—" I close my eyes, tighten my fists. "—because Cavemaster Kalad tried to kill me on that moon."

Liandra gasps, attracting the attention of a nearby cleric, who gives her a severe look before returning to her devotions. She gapes at me, stunned. I feel so exposed, so vulnerable.

Does she believe me?

She has to believe me.

"What... Kalad... I'm..." she stutters, before getting her words together. "Cavemaster Kalad tried to kill you?"

I nod.

"Why?"

I take a breath. "You remember the beacon? In the comet."

"I can hardly forget it."

"It wasn't planted by Ito," I say. "Ito was framed. By Kalad. Cavemaster Kalad was the real traitor." The moment of truth looms back, cold as ice. "And I only realized that when we were on that moon. When it was just me and him."

Liandra shakes her head.

"You believe me?"

"Why would you lie?"

It's not a ringing endorsement, but I'll take it.

Liandra paces, examining the angles.

"Why did he give us away to the Empire?"

"The Endless. Kalad believes that the pursuit of the Endless will lead to obliteration. For everyone. Pilgrims, the Empire, every—"

"Who are you conversing with, Novitiate Liandra?"

The voice from the hall is stern, the question accusing. I see it comes from a Script Herald, one of the most pious ranks of the religiously inclined. She looks ready to pounce.

"One of the new arrivals," Liandra answers. "They sought guidance. I offered it. I will escort them onwards."

She ushers me along the edge of the hall.

"They'll know it's me, soon enough."

"I know. But we must not let word get to Kalad that you're here. He might run—or worse. Let me think."

We huddle in the shadows, like sinners avoiding the light.

I'm home, but I feel more vulnerable than ever. Until Kalad is apprehended, I must stay hidden, maintain the advantage of surprise, keep my identity secret.

No one must know I'm back.

I could be on Raia again.

"I've got an idea," Liandra says.

She taps on her cufflinks, hails someone. No answer. As I'm about to speak, she holds up her palm, calls again.

"Vela?"

I don't hear his reply. The last time I saw Argo Vela, climber extraordinaire, was on that moon, all jokes and arrogance, oblivious to the viper in our midst.

"I'm looking for Kalad. You seen him?"

Liandra's eyes narrow.

"In the nest? Why?"

She frowns, worried.

I feel the same.

"Alright, thanks Vela."

As she kills the call, I speak.

"Kalad's gone down there alone, hasn't he?"

"He has." She looks puzzled. "How did you know?"

"When he's up to something, he doesn't want prying eyes." I think of the riddle of tunnels, dark and musty and littered with the dead. "What did Vela say he's doing down there?"

"He just said Kalad was curious—wanted to get first-hand experience of a Craver nest. Only set out a short while ago." Liandra glances across the chamber. "I know someone in security. Someone I can trust. We can seize Kalad when he comes back."

"No."

"No?"

"We can't risk that," I reply. "He might be planting something again."

Or bringing something out…

Liandra grimaces. "We'll go in then. A small team."

"No, I'll go alone."

"Sewa—"

"Please, trust me." Across the makeshift mortuary, a couple of clerics have come together, staring at us. I lower my voice. "On my own I can track him, fast and silent."

I want to tell her more, tell her I'm not the same girl who left, but something holds me back. Everything changes the moment my secret's out. There'd be no going back.

Later, maybe later.

I try another tack.

"Besides," I say, "the more of us head into the nest, the more chance word gets out."

"I don't like it." Liandra gives me a long look, then shakes her head. "But I'll help."

She tells me to keep my hood tight, then hustles me away from the chamber and deeper into the vessel. Dimly lit corridors and circumspect Pilgrims help, but the atmosphere's oppressive, disturbing. In a nondescript passage she glances over her shoulder, then pulls me into some small living quarters.

"You live here?"

The space is cramped, devoid of personal belongings. The only color in the room comes from the religious robes.

Liandra nods. "I'm a warning for others who might think of crossing Artak. Look how the mighty have fallen."

"This is messed up."

"It is what it is. That's why the other arcologies didn't stick around after the battle. Gave the pretense it was for strategic reasons— never congregate—but really they couldn't stomach the Horizon's newfound religious mania." She sighs. "We have peace though—and we're together. That's the most important thing."

Who are you trying to convince, Liandra?

Now's not the time though.

"What are we doing here?" I ask. "I need to find Kalad."

Liandra turns her back, delves deep down the side of bunk, fingers reaching into the wall space.

"I hope you don't need to use this," she says, "but I don't want you to hesitate if you do."

She turns back, places the sleek object in my hand.

Cold, weighty, engineered with deadly, beautiful precision. An old weapon made on Raia before the Pilgrim exodus. Short, stocky barrel, electromagnetic accelerators, encrypted firmware.

I imagine this gun has a few stories to tell.

Maybe it'll have another one soon.

"I want to bring him in alive."

"I know."

"There's plenty of evidence," I say, "once you know where to look. Conviction should be easy."

"I believe you. But..."

"What?"

"Nothing. It doesn't matter." Liandra grips my upper arm. "I know you'll do the right thing."

I tuck away the gun, wondering.

What were you going to say? That I should kill him if I get the chance? That he might escape punishment if he's brought in?

I leave my doubts unsaid.

Instead, I pull out the data crystal that Zarva gave me.

"This contains every correspondence between Kalad and his Empire contact, Commander Rachkov."

"Rachkov? The Niris?"

Zarva's final words echo in my head. *Farewell, Sewa.*

"Kalad wanted to see us repatriated to Raia. Commander Rachkov was negotiating terms on behalf of Emperor Zelevas." I pass her the crystal. "With this, Kalad's guilt will be irrefutable."

"How did you get this?"

Where do I start?

"It's a long story."

We hug.

Not long after, hidden in the vessel's long shadow, I'm back marching across the stone, my path set towards a distant canyon that leads into the asteroid's dark heart.

Whatever you're up to, Kalad, I'm coming.

I just hope I'm not too late.

THIRTY-SIX

ᚠ ᛋ ᚾ ᛐ ᚴ ᚴ ᚦ ᚾ ᛐ

The nest is far from dead.

Unlike the gritty iron smell of the coal mine and the clammy lichen odor of the caves, the place reeks of a dry, yeasty stench. In the darkness I sense the low thrum of heavy machinery and the distant scrabble of claws on stone. The Queen might be slain, her fleet scattered, but the nest carries on through its hopeless rhythms.

That's the thing with Cravers.

They never give up.

The Bishops have gone. Most of the rank-and-file remaining are simply witless insectoid machines who'll follow their programming long after their oblivion is assured. Industrial lines will keep churning, workers will keep toiling, but without fresh younglings, this place is certain to become a graveyard.

Hopefully one without my tombstone.

Weird to be combing an asteroid without a helmet, that's for sure. Usually these interiors are hard vacuum, but Cravers seal up every orifice of their astronomical bodies with a thick, mucus-like substance so they can maintain a breathable atmosphere inside. The barriers are self-repairing, so Cravers—and invaders—can come and go as they like, even if the experience isn't entirely pleasant for outsiders.

I listen, untangling the orchestra of sounds, seeking signs of another like myself among the tumult. Clicks and burrs, piston-hisses, the rumble of industry. I can hear my heart too, its beat strong, its tempo raised. If Kalad is making any noises, they remain unheard.

I click on my headlamp, illuminating the passage wall with a spear of white light. The rock is ancient, riddled with pockmarks and undulations, formed eons ago when the universe was in its infancy.

Glancing down, some of the remnants of the web-like material that seals the nest from the vacuum clings to my suit, and, even though it's harmless, I brush it off with a shaking hand.

I must be insane coming here.

I brush away the thought, check myself over.

Oxygen levels adequate.

Helmet secured on my hip.

Gun holstered.

Now I just need one of the dead. Fast.

I don't need to go far to find one.

A little down the passage, a Craver soldier lies sprawled, bled out from a gaping wound. It frightens even in death, a hulking amalgamation of sinewy muscle and hard engineering, two of its four arms still clutching a heavy hand cannon, one clawing the stone, while the last one grasps upwards like a stunted tree. *Now, Raudd, where were the glands?*

I crouch, delve into the thick tangle of mechanisms and cabling beneath its neck. As I search for the pheromone glands, I keep half-an-eye on the Craver's cold, dead eyes, half expecting them to flare red.

There.

Gripping the leathery gland with one hand, I reach for my blade with the other, and soon enough, richly scented pheromone fluids are sluicing out. I cup my hands, douse myself with the liquid stench, careful to rub the stuff everywhere.

The things you learn in bars…

Satisfied I'm slathered in the fluid, I move on.

The passage descends, a winding path that slowly heads deeper and deeper into the asteroid. Many tunnels branch off this main passage, but unlike most space vessels' interiors, the offshoots care not for any established sense of up and down, forking off the path in every direction. With the nest hale and hearty, swarms of Cravers would hustle down these tunnels, their six powerful limbs making easy work of the twisting geometry.

For now, I only pass the dead.

Sometimes I see evidence of Pilgrim incursions—a punctured helmet, a lost rifle, a scuffed-up boot that's cleanly sliced across the ankle. I can't help but let my torch beam linger. I jerk away, assailed by a cold horror, but the image is already seared deep. A clean cross-section of crimson flesh and white bone. The stump of a Pilgrim foot.

I shake away the vision.

Raudd better be right about these glands.

Dust-enhanced or not, if I'm attacked, I'm dead.

Soon, I come to a vast chamber seething with Craver workers. They scurry over a mammoth production line of machines that occupy the entirety of the space like a gigantic intricate maze. I shouldn't be surprised. Cravers, once the killing machines of the Endless, are utterly unlike other spacefaring races with their rich cultures and tangled histories. No religion, no science, no iconic figures who span the ages. Cravers have no memory, no sense of progress, no conception of a future that isn't unending conflict. What they do have, however, is the knowledge, the instinct, of how to build a ceaseless, efficient war machine.

Deadly weaponry, cybernetic soldiers, monstrous warships.

Again and again and again.

Here, a starship engine. But I'm only guessing. The Endless' technological legacy is a far cry from Pilgrim engineering.

I give a small, bitter laugh.

Kalad's here, scheming, yet all around him—as he sees it—lie the deadly fruits of Endless technology. Exactly the kind of knowledge he'd like to see consigned to oblivion. Maybe he's planning on vaporizing this nest. At my laughter, a nearby drone stops in its tracks, mandibles twitching. I go still, but the creature has already sensed my uninvited presence.

It edges closer, curious.

Once next to me, it roughly manhandles me, mandibles and feelers gliding across my suit's contours. Deep down, it knows something isn't right. I keep my mouth shut, not breathing. I'm terrified it'll detect something amiss in the miasma of scents on my breath. The feelers reach my face, the thick hairs on their tips tickling my skin. Then the mandibles are crawling up my chin, across my mouth…

Back off!

I want to scream the words, but I hold my tongue. The examination goes on, jaw to crown, ear to ear, glacial-like, time slowed to a crawl. Then I feel a sharp pain from my left-cheek. Like a paper cut. Before I can react, the drone has gone, scuttling away with its precious cargo.

Did I get the all-clear?

I brush my cheek with gloved fingers, the tips coming back darkened with blood. My stomach drops. Am I marked for execution? The scent of my blood drifting through the nest until it comes to the attention of a soldier?

Like a drop of blood in shark-infested waters.

Then I remember something else Raudd told me.

Cravers sometimes enslave captives as menial workers, disseminating chemical markers in the slave's bodily fluids around the nest so that they're not attacked on sight.

I pray that's the case here.

I don't have to wait long to find out.

On the other side of the factory chamber I pass a Craver soldier, a clear head taller than the scurrying drones, statuesque in comparison to its nest mates, but it pays me no heed.

I'm part of the nest.

I head on, encouraged, but tense.

As I head deeper, the chambers become busier still, hundreds if not thousands of workers still going about their tasks. In one I spy the construction line of the Cravers' distinct shoulder-mounted weaponry, in another drones harvest bioluminescent fungal pap that grows across every available surface, while in another—a vast hollow that stretches further than my light can reach—I witness a specialist sub-species mining gleaming ore with ferocious intensity.

Every part in service to an insatiable war machine.

The absence of the soldier-class is readily apparent, only a smattering of the taller, bulkier, armed Cravers crossing my path, the majority no doubt already slain.

Beyond my nerves, I feel something close to pity.

They didn't choose this life.

They were born into servitude, and they will die in servitude. Tiny cogs in a vast machine of which they have no comprehension. I wonder if they mourn their dead, or if they're even aware their siblings have fallen.

Who knows?

Outside our jurisdiction, as Oba would say when confronted with theological conundrums. I shake away the distracting thoughts, close my eyes, and stop and listen for the hundredth time.

Familiar sounds now.

A ceaseless, urgent refrain of pattering and rustling and scratching as the Craver work-gangs go about their tasks. The low boom of their distant machines. And the haphazard shrieks of the gang masters. Every time I hear one screaming orders at one of its underlings, my skin crawls.

Yet, this time, there's something else.

A tiny thread of reverberations that don't fit.

Lighter, the cadence different too—slow and hesitant next to the Cravers' furious vibrations.

Footfalls.

And not Craver ones.

I close my eyes, concentrate, follow the thread of sound through the labyrinth. Not too far. Only a couple of passages and a chamber away. Given his caution, I could be on him in no time. I reach for the gun. Its cold, hard presence reassures. It'll be a long walk back, escorting Kalad out, but nothing I can't handle.

I move on, upping my pace but keeping as quiet as I can, gliding smoothly through the low-gravity environment. The yeasty scent is still strong, but I've got used to it now, and between the warm air and the wide passages, this would make a pleasant descent... if I wasn't in the heart of an active Craver nest, chasing down a sociopathic killer...

Sometimes, I hear him muttering. I can't make out his words, but I can sense his emotions. Half horrified, half awed. The brutal magnificence of this place fills him with existential terror. The Cravers, an enduring creation of the Endless, are dedicated to the singular goal of galactic destruction. With the Pilgrims' fanatical faith, he would see a cautionary parallel, and beyond his admiration and fear, I can sense *his* determination too.

His own faith in his mission is frightening.

Entering high up, I come to a wide chamber, teeming with movement as if the ground itself were alive. Peering down, I see that's not far from the truth. *A nursery.* Craver young, a quarter the size of the adult specimens and bereft of their cybernetics, swarm across the chamber floor, feeding off fungal pap, climbing ancient columns, fighting each other. Looming over them I catch sight of grotesquely shaped brood mothers, part feeding machines, part nursery wardens.

No wonder Kalad was afraid.

I wade through the throng, easing off a couple of exuberant younglings who grapple me, relieved when I find myself in a quiet passage on the other side. A foul odor hangs in the air, growing stronger with each step. Occasionally, a drone passes, steering a fresh youngling towards the nursery.

I stop, listen again.

Kalad is very close now, lingering in the next chamber.

Unlike the nursery behind, it's near deathly silent, save for the careful clicks and taps of a few workers—

What in the world?!

My blood runs cold.

Something—or someone—else is close.

They creep with preternatural skill, whisper-quiet, their traversal utterly at odds with the uninhibited rhythms of the rest of the nest. Cold, intelligent, malevolent. Whatever it is, it's stalking Kalad, not me. I click off my headlamp, let my eyes adjust to the near darkness. A faint purple light suffuses the tunnel, emanating from patches of a tough, long-stalked grass. I edge onwards, ultra-careful. If they hear me, I'll run. Until I know what they are, what they want, I can't risk confrontation.

Kalad, by contrast, is a whirlwind of noise, crunching on the littered ground, issuing excited proclamations, shifting his framework backpack. Coming to the threshold, I spy him, crouched, his torchlight spearing the uneven topography.

A sea of eggs.

The hatchery.

The shells of old embryos litter the ground, and an overwhelming stench of birthing fluids and decaying chitin hangs heavy. I dry retch, cover my mouth and nose to escape the worst of the smell. With the Queen dead, these are the last embryos. Soon the whole chamber will be a wasteland. A twisted graveyard and a sad monument to a dead nest.

Is Kalad securing unhatched eggs?

He holds up an embryo, studies it in the light of his torch. A small one, oval-shaped, riddled with thick veins that spread up from the base like tree roots. Beautiful if you didn't know the horror that grew inside.

Except, for Kalad, it *is* an object of desire.

Dotingly, carefully, like he's handling a priceless ornament, he places it in a cradle lattice. He repeats the trick several times, moving around the chamber, only selecting small embryos that meet some quality threshold.

I shiver.

He's picking the eggs based on their vigor. And their markings. One of the subspecies. Soldier-class? Worker-class? Only thing I can be sure of is that he means to bring them back to the Horizon.

Why though?

I realize I can no longer hear Kalad's stalker.

I go still, letting only my eyes move, praying I haven't been sensed. My gaze darts over the flickering shadows of the hatchery, but of the stalker there is no sign. The only movement comes from Kalad, ferreting around the embryos.

It must be waiting, watching.

Get out! Get out!

I psyche myself up, ready to flee—

From the far side, a blur of razored limbs rushes Kalad, knocking him to the ground before he even knows what's hit him. The attacker reaches down, pins him. Kalad lifts his head, stunned. Terror mingles with confusion in his eyes.

This is no ordinary Craver.

Only Bishops should demonstrate this level of intelligence, but this specimen is clearly not of that ilk. Scuffed, gunmetal-grey weaponry glimmers on one shoulder, while its rippling, fibrous muscles are protected by robust armor plates.

A soldier, then.

At least once upon a time.

Maybe I won't need to deal with Kalad.

Maybe I won't have a choice.

It leans closer to him, pulls him up by the scruff of his neck—and speaks!

"Who… are… you?"

The words are harsh, guttural, but clear.

"K-K-Kalad." He can barely speak, such is his terror. "M-m-m-my name's K-K-Kalad."

The Craver turns its head, scrutinizing the lattice of stolen embryos. Studying it, I realize that it's been in a terrible accident, one half of its torso and head bludgeoned and burnt. The exposed flesh glitters with a golden hue.

When I check the eyes, I see the telltale signs…

Dust exposure.

"You attacked the nest."

"No, no, no, I didn't," Kalad pleads, still held like a rag doll. "My people did, but I didn't."

"We do not… understand this distinction."

I sense it fighting to keep its natural impulses in check, like it's fending off an overwhelming desire to simply rip Kalad's head straight off.

"Of course, of course," Kalad replies, and already, beyond his fear, I can see the cogs of his clever mind whirring into life, calculating. "For you, there is no difference. The worker and the colony are one, always striving for the same goal."

"It is… the natural order."

The Craver stands up to its full height, hauling Kalad off the ground and holding him aloft. Although they're face-to-face, the Cavemaster's feet dangle uselessly above the rutted floor of the hatchery.

"For Cravers, yes," Kalad splutters, both hands pulling tight on the collar of his suit so he can breathe, "but not for others." Terror fills his eyes. "Not for us Pilgrims."

Carefully, I reach behind my back, slip my gun into my hand. I can't let Kalad be slaughtered by this monster. Even he deserves better than that. I'm ready to shoot, but the Craver stays its execution.

"You did not... attack the nest?"

"No!" Kalad cries, his voice a whispery husk. "My people did, but I didn't." He chokes out a last few words. "And I'm here to right that wrong."

Kalad, still the great betrayer.

The Craver releases him, and he crumples to the ground, clutching his neck, his breaths coming in rasping gasps.

"You steal from the nest."

Kalad gets himself onto his knees, body doubled up like an act of supplication. "Only so I might give," he gasps, "the Cravers the vengeance they deserve." He sits up, still resting on his knees, gestures at the pilfered embryos. "I plan to hatch these soldiers in secret back on the Pilgrim fleet. I will help them reach maturity, then release them. If I'm lucky no Pilgrim will escape."

My mouth goes dry.

The real monster here is Kalad.

If *this* is his plan, it seems absurd. A handful of Craver soldiers shouldn't be underestimated, especially launching a surprise assault from the inside, but they'd be snuffed out by Pilgrim security before too long.

Is it a ruse, a grasping at straws—saying something, anything that might sway this Craver monstrosity? Or is the Cavemaster really this desperate? The Horizon's lurch towards religious fanaticism, together with his waning influence, might've provoked him to act while he still had some agency.

What is certain is that he intended to steal Craver eggs.

"Your plan is flawed," the Craver replies. "Without the right signals, the young will tear you apart."

"But you can prevent that, can't you?" A beatific smile lights Kalad's face. "This encounter was fated—for both our sakes. We can work together."

"No!" I shout.

Kalad and the Craver turn.

The gun is in my hand, but I keep it lowered.

"Sewa?" Kalad's eyes go wide. "How...?"

The Craver gazes down at Kalad. "You know them?"

"Yes," he replies. "But we are enemies. And she's come to try and thwart my plans."

An appeal to an alliance.

The gambit seems to work. The Craver takes a menacing step closer, turning its back on Kalad. Power ripples through its hulking frame, eyes sharp, blades sharper. Even if I could get a clean shot away, I wouldn't know where to shoot. Violence isn't the answer. I push my terror away, stay as relaxed as I can.

"I know what happened to you, Craver."

At first I think it doesn't care for my words, but then I notice a slight shift in its stance.

"Her words are poison!"

The Craver moves so fast Kalad doesn't see the blow coming, the monster's whirling fist sending the Cavemaster flying across the chamber. It turns back to me.

"Speak."

Somewhere on the hatchery's edge, Kalad exhales a low moan, but I can't be distracted. Not now. *Focus.*

"There was an accident, wasn't there?" I keep my voice low, out of Kalad's earshot, while pointing at its ravaged side. "You were hurt. Badly hurt. Dust saturated you. Somehow it eked its way into your nervous system, your mind, your very essence. When you came round, you found yourself changed."

"We felt... different."

"For the first time in your life, you felt yourself as a separate thing from the nest." I meet its golden-hued eyes. "And you felt afraid."

"How do you... know this?"

"Same thing happened to me." I glance at Kalad's heaped form, stirring. "I awoke changed. And afraid. With a gulf between me and my people."

The Craver roars. "Our nest was crushed! Our Queen was slaughtered! Afterwards, the Bishops fled."

I raise a hand, placatory.

"Senseless deaths on both sides."

The Craver trembles.

"Please, hear me out," I plead.

It says nothing, so I go on.

"You can walk another path." I take a deep breath, start moving towards the Craver. "One where you're not alone, where you can find others just like you, where you can become whole."

Standing next to the Craver, shadowed by its great, muscular stature, my heart hammers. Over the reek of my own sweat, I can smell its flesh and keratin. Up close, I can see the terrifying engineering that has created this creature, a half-machine, half-natural thing, full of seams and systems. Somewhere in that great mass beats a heart too.

I hear it.

I grip my gun tighter.

"There's a place," I say, looking up at its small head fed by dozens of hydraulic lines. "The Academy. They helped me adapt. And they can help you too."

Beyond the Craver I can hear Kalad shifting, discarded shells splintering as he crawls away.

"We are… curious."

I take a breath. *Maybe I can do this.* I need it to assert its autonomy first, though. I need it to sever its identity to the nest.

"*You* are curious."

"We are curious."

"No, *you* are curious." I meet its eyes. "*You* are not the nest. Say '*I am curious.*'"

Its head twitches.

"I… I… I…" it stutters, the concept triggering some kind of mental distress. "I… I… I…"

It goes still, steadying itself…

A moment later, I know I've lost it.

It moves to grab me, but before it can, I've whipped the gun up to its chest cavity, lodging the barrel through a fold of muscle. The muzzle of the gun quivers against the titanic beat of its heart. I can feel its life in my hands.

It doesn't move, knows it's over.

I'm glad for that small mercy.

"We are Craver," it says, proudly.

Then I pull the trigger.

THIRTY-SEVEN

ㅈƷʃƐʞꟼ ꝊƐ�序ƐƷ

As I stand over the dead Craver I feel not elation but despondency. I wonder if things could've gone differently, that if I'd said other words, it might've been walking by my side, not slain at my feet. I wonder what feats it might've accomplished, what worlds it might've walked, what lives it might've changed for the better.

Or I could've easily been the one killed.

And then Kalad would've been escorting *it* back to the Horizon to help carry out his murderous spree.

By that measure, this is a win.

I should take solace from that.

A worker enters the hatchery, scampering over the dead shells, oblivious to the carnage. Coming to Kalad's spoils, its gaze lingers on the stolen eggs, still cradled in the Cavemaster's abandoned pack.

Of the dead Craver it barely gives a glance.

The nest is truly in its death throes.

Not far off I hear Kalad hustling through the nest, making no effort to silence his tracks. Most likely he thinks I died at the hands of the Craver, and now his only thought is to escape.

Come back and fight another day.

Well, he'll be coming back alright, but in my custody.

With the Dust, his pace is no match for mine.

I record some footage, carefully omitting any evidence of the Dust-enhanced Craver, check my equipment, then move off, determined but controlled. I must seem like a ghost to Kalad. A vengeful spirit from beyond the grave. I don't want him to know my truth.

I don't want anyone on the Horizon to know.

I pass through the Queen's chamber, the hulking matriarch's vast decomposing body, together with her annihilated personal guard of defenders, filling the air with a wicked stench.

The ceaseless lynchpin of the tireless war machine.

What were the Endless thinking?

Ahead, I can hear Kalad's climbing boots scraping against stone, the strain of his breaths, explosive exhalations of air. He's climbing a shaft, still believes he can escape. I go still, seeking the subtle currents that carry the shape of the nest for those who can read their flow. There's another vertical passage a little further on that links up with the original shaft in a crossroads chamber.

I can cut him off.

I hustle, fast but silent.

I get to the chamber as he's climbing over the lip, just in time to draw my gun on him and skewer him in my torchlight.

"It's over, Kalad."

He's blinded, but his eyes still widen in shock.

"What are you?" he spits, hauling himself into a crouched position at the edge of the drop, ready to spring.

"Same as I always was," I say, training my gun on him. "Sewa Eze. The girl you taught to cave."

"No, I killed that girl," he says, shaking his head. "You're something else."

A memory flares, unbidden. I can almost feel his calloused hands around my neck again, the pressure on my windpipe.

I fear him.

I think I always will.

"You left me for dead, but I didn't die."

"Bullshit." His eyes narrow. "Wait... the Dust sump... The Dust did something to you, didn't it?"

"Stand up!" I order. "Now!"

Kalad rises, hands aloft. "That's how you gained the Craver's trust."

The gun shakes in my trembling hand.

"What happened to that freak?"

He knows my secret.

A few words and the whole arcology will know too. I'd be studied, hounded, used. One moment fated as a savior, the next vilified as a monster. The attention would be unbearable. Fleeing from the only home I've known would be the only choice.

A small press of the trigger and all that goes away.

My hand stills. "I killed it."

Come on, rush me.

It's the wrong answer, though.

The wind goes out of his sails, any impulse to charge me ebbing away. He knows I'd shoot.

Damn.

He smiles. "You want me dead, don't you?"

"I want you judged for your crimes."

"Then execute me," he says. "Nobody knows my crimes better than you."

I take a breath. "I'm not your judge."

"Down here, deep in this dying nest? Corpses everywhere, only mindless workers for company?" He gestures with a hand. "No one need know."

He's loving this power over me.

I flick the barrel of the gun, indicating for him to take the passage to the left, a gently rising incline. "Let's go."

We set off, captor and captive.

In the darkness, shuffling forward, only illuminated by slices of my torchlight, he looks weak and pathetic. Strange to think such a man could've committed such evils, threatened such further destruction. We're about halfway back to the surface when he twists his head, speaks over his shoulder.

"I'm right about the Endless, you know."

I shouldn't take the bait, but I can't resist.

"Right or wrong," I reply, "what you did was unforgivable. You tried to kill me, you slaughtered innocent Pilgrims, and you would've seen the rest of us enslaved on Raia. And now, if you weren't joking, you scheme to see Cravers run wild across the Horizon!"

He stops, turns round.

"Still so blind to the Endless threat," he says, patronizingly. "Their remnants will see the galaxy burn, you understand. Just like it did before. We shouldn't be worshipping them, we should be burying them."

My bile rises. "You know what I think?"

He shrugs.

"Twenty years ago, I think a man with an overactive imagination worked himself up into a grotesque, paranoid delusion, got so crazy in the head, that he ended up killing the very people he was supposed to be protecting.

"Then, to stop himself falling apart, to stop the great wave of guilt washing him away, he invested everything in his wild fantasy, somehow convinced himself that only the annihilation of his own people, the Pilgrims, would save the galaxy." I shake my head sadly. "If the consequences hadn't been so lethal, maybe it'd be funny."

In the torchlight, I glimpse something in his eyes.

Remembrance, comprehension, fear.

Then it's gone.

"You're wrong," he says, twisting away, marching on.

I can't leave it.

"Let's say you're right," I say. "Let's say somewhere out there among the remains of the Endless exists a gilded box that once opened will see all life in the galaxy extinguished."

Like a lodestone that can resurrect dead gods.

Kalad steps on a dead Craver, part of its carapace breaking with sharp crack. "Go on."

"The thing is, this situation isn't new."

"What do you mean?"

I remember Oyita's words.

"Civilizations have always faced existential threats." I step over the Craver. "Plagues, nuclear wars, superintelligences. And yet we've come through them. And not through ignorance, but through understanding. Sharing ideas, communicating fears, examining the danger with a cold, clear eye. We wouldn't be standing here otherwise, would we?"

"Survivor's bias."

"What?"

"You're speaking from a survivor's perspective," he says, voice echoing off into the darkness. "Maybe there's countless civilizations who fell to plagues, nuclear wars, whatever. We just don't know about them because they didn't get off planet, and now everything they built is falling into rust and ruin.

"The Endless represent a galactic-wide threat. There's no decontamination zone, no ring-fencing the dangers to one system, never mind one world. Mark my words, digging up the bones of the Endless' civilization will lead to the demise of all."

Could he be right?

I think of Isyander, seeking out the tombs of the Endless, desperate to resurrect the old gods on the very altars where they were slaughtered millennia past.

No less a fanatic than Kalad, really.

"A bit of a leap if you ask me," I reply as we come to a manufacturing chamber, raising my voice to speak over the noise of the machines.

"But what do I know? All I know for sure is that you need to be tried for your crimes. And I'll let wiser heads than mine decide if you should be granted clemency based on your doomsday scenarios."

"You haven't understood anything, have you?" He kicks out at a Craver worker who goes sprawling, before scrabbling back to its feet, confused but passive. "Blessed with Dust but still blind."

"Careful," I warn.

If he riles the nest into violence against us, I'd be well within my rights to kill him on the spot. A nice clean line under everything. No chance of my secret getting out.

The temptation is strong.

He raises a hand, apologetic.

"You know," he says, "long ago, before we became starfarers, before we'd even circled the globe, people would make maps of the world. Rivers and cities, mountains and seas, great continents across the oceans. And the further the eye roamed from the heartlands, the more the landmarks became speculative, the coastlines erratic. Eventually, the eye'd reach *terra incognita*, and the mapmakers would write *Here Be Dragons*." Kalad's eyes light up. "*Dragons!* Fearsome fire-breathing beasts of the skies, wings so vast they could blot out the sun! One attack could see a whole fleet set afire, a whole caravan line torched." He laughs. "Of course, even then they didn't mean *literal* dragons. But they did mean terrible dangers. Unending deserts, storm-wracked seas, icy wastelands. Places anathema to human life. And let me ask you: Do you think for one moment that those warnings discouraged the explorers of the age?"

"Kalad—"

"Of course they didn't!" he shouts. "In fact, those words did the opposite. They drew in the explorers, like moths to the flames." He bends down, fetches up a splintered piece of the mechanical intestines of a dead Craver. "The same is true of the remnants of the Endless' civilization. The most we can hope for is that one day, if we're lucky, they'll be entirely forgotten."

Somewhere far behind us several ear-splitting screeches echo through the nest, punctuating Kalad's forebodings. They're simply the reflexive contortions of a dying colony, but the timing feels prophetic. Not something I want to be in the middle of, though, whatever they herald.

"Keep moving."

Kalad tosses the piece, spins, and sets off.

I follow, gun trained.

"At the time of your judgment," I say, "you won't justify your actions, then?"

"And trample over everything I believe in?" He pauses, looks upwards. "No, I will not."

Kalad, the martyr.

Except no one will know.

Only me. And Liandra.

"They'll paint you a psychopath."

"They would anyway." He presses on. "At least this way I won't have betrayed my beliefs. What you decide to say, of course, is on you, but if you care for the fate of the galaxy you'll stay quiet too."

"And buy into your fantasies?"

"Call it a harmless indulgence."

Not so harmless when you tried to kill me.

"I'll do as my conscience dictates."

We trek on in silence, my senses heightened to every shadow, every musty scent, every scratch and rumble. I keep thinking Kalad will try something, some last ruse to attempt an escape, but he trudges on sedately. Maybe he fears me, this apparition returned from the dead, fears I'll end him like I ended the Craver. Not much farther now. Stay alert.

Soon his fate will be out of my hands.

Soon I won't have control over my secret.

"I'm curious," Kalad says, breaking the silence. "How *did* you get off that moon?"

His voice seems extra loud in the quiet of the nest.

"I was rescued by a friend of yours."

"A friend?"

I let him stew a little. "Well, maybe friend is a bit strong," I say. "I mean, how would you characterize your relationship with your co-conspirator?"

Kalad stops.

He reaches out a hand to the tunnel wall.

"Zarva?" he whispers. "Zarva Rachkov."

"You didn't hear?" I keep my distance, a few paces behind Kalad. "Rachkov abandoned the Empire when they realized Zelevas had no intention of repatriating the Pilgrims."

Kalad slaps the wall. "And I thought the Niris had played me!" He turns, wearing a bittersweet smile. His eyes narrow. "Now it all starts to make sense. Rachkov became your mentor in the ways of

Dust. I wonder, did they sense you on that moon? Is that something the Dust-tainted can do?"

Now it's my turn to be surprised.

That *would* explain how the Niris found me.

"Zarva died on Raia."

Kalad's shoulders slump. His voice is heavy when he speaks. "Rachkov's dead?"

"We were with the resistance when we were ambushed by Empire forces," I say, voice trembling. "They gave their life to help us escape. I'll never forget that."

Kalad shakes his head. "A little light left the galaxy the day that Niris died." He starts to move towards me, then thinks the better of it, stops. "I'm sorry, Sewa."

I nod.

"For what it's worth," I say, "come the end, I think Zarva had found peace."

Kalad fixes me with a long look.

"Maybe that's all any of us can ask for."

He turns away, starts off again.

Strangely, as we get closer to the surface, the mood lightens. Kalad recounts tales from the long rambling exchanges he had with the Niris, and, in turn, I share my memories of Rachkov too. *Funny.* There's likely no one else within fifty light years who could have this conversation. One day, I vow, I'll speak to others who knew the Niris.

We exit the nest, march across the asteroid's scarred ground, the stars bright overhead. Helmets back on, we talk in staccato bursts, our words punctuated by static. In other circumstances, we could be returning from a caving expedition, but at the crest of the first hill we're met by a security team and everything snaps back into focus.

I feel relief, but also anxiety.

I don't feel like we're entirely on the same side.

They seize Kalad, relieve me of my weapon.

I feel vulnerable—more vulnerable than when I stalked through the nest, maybe even more vulnerable than when I confronted the Craver.

I am Pilgrim, but I am also something else.

Something only Kalad knows.

THIRTY-EIGHT

⊅ꝫ↑Σᛕꝫ ⸵↑ꝰꝫᛕ

We cross the asteroid, head for the capital vessel. A trident of soldiers surround Kalad, while I walk behind, side-by-side with the fourth. Everywhere I look, Pilgrims stop and stare.

A pair loading supplies into the *Fortitude*'s hold pause from their work and convene on the ship's landing ramp, while an engineer working on repairs to a shuttle's underbelly emerges from the shadows, gives me the deadeye. I can feel their shock. I wonder what exactly they know. All they can see across the pitted surface is their Cavemaster in restraints, a seeming outsider trailing in his wake.

We reach the capital vessel, decontaminate. Our small group parts company with little fanfare. Kalad is being taken straight to the brig, while I am to be escorted elsewhere. A few steps along a dimly lit corridor, somebody steps out of the shadows.

"I'll take it from here, Nilith."

Liandra.

The soldier's uncertain. I keep my expression neutral, hiding my relief at seeing my ally again.

"I have direct orders."

"I know your orders," Liandra states, staring down the soldier she used to command. "Dismissed, Nilith."

Nilith hesitates, then nods. Soon enough her footfalls on the hard grid-metal floor have fallen to silence.

Liandra gives a sigh of relief.

"That trick isn't going to work much longer."

"What's happening?"

"Walk with me," she replies, setting off.

I comply.

"I'm taking you to the Overseer."

"Artak?"

"Yes, Artak."

"He knows I'm here?"

"After you left for the nest," she says, defensively, "I got worried. I organized for a security team to follow. Word got out."

I guess it was only a matter of time.

"What did you tell them?"

"Just what you told me. That Kalad attempted to kill you on that moon. That he was the one who planted the beacon." Liandra stops. "It's the truth, isn't it?"

"It is," I say. "You read the correspondence, right?"

"I didn't have time," she replies. "And now Artak has taken possession of the data crystal."

He'll get quite the surprise reading those files.

Liandra gives me a long look. "Something else?"

I nod.

Damn. He really did get in my head with his apocalypse talk.

"When you spoke to Artak," I say, "did you mention what I said about Kalad's reasons? That he thought the pursuit of the Endless would see the galaxy fall?"

Liandra shakes her head.

"I didn't get into that."

"Good." I glance around to check nobody's in earshot. "This is going to sound crazy, but… you need to keep that to yourself. The very idea… it's dangerous… it could become a self-fulfilling prophecy." I give her a steely look. "Never, ever, speak of it, Liandra."

"You think he might be right?"

"Maybe."

She shakes her head, incredulous.

"Sometimes I think we Pilgrims would be better off forgetting about the Endless. Not for those reasons. But because they've become an obsession for us."

"You'll stay silent, then?"

She nods.

"I'm glad," I say.

We start walking again.

The exchange has made me feel grubby, tainted, like Kalad's own paranoia has seeped under my skin.

"You should know something," Liandra says, keeping her voice low. "Many Pilgrims will be suspicious of you. After the 'accident' on the moon, Kalad did a good job of insinuating that you might've been up to something."

"Like what?"

"Like you might've been planning to ditch the Horizon, even that you might've been in league with Ito."

"But it was never Ito!"

"I know," Liandra says softly. "And soon all the Horizon will know too. But right now all they see is their Cavemaster in the brig, and the girl they thought dead, resurrected. Some will side with Kalad."

She rubs her temple, while a couple of Novitiates pass, then speaks again. "People will have questions. They'll wonder how you escaped, where you've been, in what circles you've been mixing."

"And I'll tell them."

Everything except the Dust.

That's my truth. Nobody else's.

I can see she wants more.

"I was rescued by Zarva Rachkov."

"The Empire puppet?" Liandra says, eyes wide. "The one who's been hunting us for years?"

I nod. "It's a long story."

"Give me the bare bones, then," she says, moving off again. "We've still got some ways before we reach Artak."

So I do.

I tell her no lies, omit only a few *personal* details. Near the end, with difficulty, I recount how we found my father's grave in the Raian wilds.

"After that we made contact with the Pilgrim resistance," I say, swiftly wrapping things up. "And they got me back to the Horizon."

"Thank the stars." Liandra pulls me into a fierce hug. "Your father might be gone, but you've still got family here."

I hug back, tentatively.

The sense of loss is still raw, overpowering.

Liandra says, "I'm just glad I know now."

Mother and Rina should know too.

And they should learn the truth from me. Nobody else. Soon as Artak's done with me, that's my next stop. Not long after, Liandra hands me over to the pair of sentries standing guard outside the House of Faith.

"We'll talk later," she says, disappearing into the shadows.

With a heavy grunt, the sentries push ajar the obscenely tall, ornately carved doors. We slip through the slender crack, and the door closes again with a reverberating thud. Ecclesiastical refrains echo through the dimly lit chamber, while colorful friezes depicting proclaimed, yet largely speculative, Endless events gaze down from the vast canvas of the walls. As a callow religion born in a fiery blaze less than a century ago, when it came to the trappings, the Pilgrim founders borrowed wholesale from their homeworld's more ancient faiths.

I could be in a backwater church on Raia.

Except Artak has made this place his seat-of-power.

I spy him at the head of a long, semi-circular table, sat ramrod straight in a high-backed chair, surrounded by his closest advisors. Aside from a discreet terminal embedded in the table's obsidian surface, the whole scene could be lifted from medieval times. Liandra's leadership feels a long time ago.

"Sewa Eze," he cries when he sees me. "A phoenix from the flames!"

"Overseer," I offer, deferentially.

I am led to the middle of the half-circle, where Artak and his advisors can each gaze upon me unimpeded, like a prisoner in a panopticon. No seat is offered.

"Child," he says, "it warms my heart to see you alive, but your return has—" he gazes up at a frieze, finding the right words "—disturbed the tranquility across the Horizon."

"I would've thought the proximity of a Craver nest," I reply, exaggerating my perplexed expression, "even one in its death throes, would've shattered any chance of tranquility."

My attempt at levity is not appreciated.

One of the scribes taps out something on their tablet. I realize my every word is going to be recorded and pored over later. Omissions, inconsistencies, lies. Any slips will be rooted out with ruthless efficiency.

I am an unpredictable element.

And I need to be controlled.

I'm just glad I got to rehearse my story with Liandra.

They will not know what I am.

Artak presses the tips of his fingers together.

"The Horizon of Light is not the place you left," he says. "Less beguiled by fanciful ideas, more respectful of our origins, more understanding of our one true mission."

"Tor?"

He fixes me with a hard look. "To live in accordance with scripture.

"Now," Artak says, "I understand you make grave accusations against our Cavemaster. Accusations, so severe, in fact, that I would have been deemed irresponsible had I not placed the accused under immediate arrest."

The faintest hint of a smile crosses the Overseer's lips.

Artak and Kalad's mutual animosity goes back a long way.

"However," he continues, "it is also right that this matter is investigated with the utmost urgency, so the accused's guilt is either established or refuted at the earliest opportunity."

Several figures emerge from the shadows, take seats, while everyone else except the scribe departs. I'm a little taken aback. I expected a thorough interrogation from Artak, but I thought Kalad's case would undergo a civil hearing.

An independent judge, legal counsel, public scrutiny.

This is the trial, though.

A secret trial.

"Justice in session."

The ordeal lasts for hours.

With forensic attention, one of Artak's deputies, a devoted priest I remember for being an authority on scripture, interrogates me on the precise sequence of events on the moon, digging deeper and deeper into every little detail from the mood of the party on the first day to how Kalad gripped my neck as he tried to drown me.

Artak listens with rapt attention, every so often interrupting proceedings to ask innocuous questions that invariably have a sting in the tail. *Trying to catch me out.*

I keep to the truth, only lying about the Dust.

I tricked him into believing he'd drowned me, I tell them. After he'd gone, I managed to climb back out through the cold and dark. When I reached the surface I was alone.

It isn't that far from what happened.

Lies are easier to hide when they're seeded in the truth. And when your life depends on it. Already, less than a day back, I know that should they ever discover they have a super-soldier in their midst, they will make me a tool. A tool with a single purpose.

To be a servant of the faith.

Hunting unbelievers. Acclaiming the Endless. Seeking Tor.

I don't want to live in that cage.

They must not know.

The questions turn naturally to my original investigation into who planted the beacon. *Who knew of the investigation? How did Ito become the prime suspect? When did I realize Kalad might be the traitor?*

This is firmer ground, no reason for me to hide or invent anything, and I answer everything fully, confidently. When I ask if Artak has examined the correspondence between Kalad and Rachkov yet, a hubbub erupts. Artak calls order.

"Not in depth, but I have seen them," he says. "If corroborated, these exchanges constitute the most damning evidence against Cavemaster Kalad." He locks eyes with me. "I am most curious as to how these messages came into your possession."

I hold my tongue.

Artak cricks his neck. "Yet, that tale can wait for another day. We will adjourn this session, while the evidence is assessed. Thank you for your testimony, Sewa Eze."

"We're done?"

"For today."

I try not to let my relief show, but inwardly I am happy. I should have nothing to fear once I get a good night's rest, get some time to make the story of the last few months watertight.

"May I remind you that you are to remain on the Horizon at all times," Artak adds, coldly. "After all, we don't want you to go missing again, do we?"

Like that could even happen.

They'll watch my every move.

Until they're satisfied I pose no threat, I will be considered a security risk. I need to be very careful with my movements, my use of the archives, my words, so as not to give them any hint I am more than what I pretend.

"Of course."

I leave the House of Faith, calves aching, body stiff.

Outside, somebody hobbles out of the shadows, propelled along by a pair of crutches.

"Sewa!"

Their face is hidden in darkness by a hood, but I can recognize that voice anywhere.

"Oba."

We stand a few paces apart, taking each other in, both understanding that neither of us are the same people. Then we come together in a fierce, clumsy hug, one of Oba's crutches lifting horizontal, while he keeps his balance with the other.

Under his cowl his body feels gaunt.

"I didn't think—"

"I didn't think—"

We laugh.

Maybe not so different too.

We stay embraced, neither of us wanting to break off.

"I'm so happy to see you, Oba."

"I can't believe you're really here," he whispers in my ear. "You're a phantom, right?"

"No, I'm 100 percent real."

We pull apart, both grinning ear to ear.

"Let's get out of here," Oba says, then lowers his voice. "This place gives me the creeps."

I'm happy to oblige. We set off, Oba setting a fast pace, despite his crutches. Behind, I sense someone following us, discreet and far away enough that anybody else wouldn't notice.

"Something up?" Oba asks.

I nearly tell him we're being followed, but that would provoke questions I wouldn't be able to answer.

"No, it's nothing," I say, hating the lie.

He gives a brief tilt back of his head.

Whatever you say.

We walk in silence.

I want to tell him there's things I can't tell him, but that would only lead to dangers, so I hold my tongue.

"Last time I saw you," I finally say, "you were in the medical bay, entombed in that glass chamber, hooked up to a dozen machines."

Like he wants to be reminded of that day.

"And I can see you've come a long way since," I add, brightly. "The recovery's going well, then?"

Oba shrugs. "My recovery's over. At least for now."

"What?"

"With all the fighting, medical resources are stretched thin. Life-saving interventions are the priority right now."

Understandable. Limb regrowth or replacement for his frostbitten extremities might have to wait.

"Must be hard," I say, "wanting to cave and everything, and just having to wait. But it'll come in time."

"Maybe."

"Maybe?"

Oba stops, turns to me.

"There's rumors... the maimed might never get full treatment."

"The hell?"

"Some religious doctrine." Oba stares up at the passage ceiling. "Truth is we're useful symbols for the leadership. Walking, talking reminders of the 'sacrifices we've made.'"

"That's insane." My voice rises. "How can you fulfill your duties? How can you be a caver?"

I regret the words immediately.

"I can't." He shakes his head, looks at me with a grimace. "Not like this, anyway. And they've already assigned me to other duties. I spend most of my time working in the archives."

"The archives?"

A Pilgrim passes the other way, gives us a severe look.

"Come on," he says, and we start off again. "I'll tell you about the archives later."

Too depressing, I guess.

"So, how's your Papa, how are your brothers?"

"They're okay."

Oba flicks out his right crutch, mashes a scuttling beetle.

I don't push further.

He'll tell me when he's ready.

"Alright, enough of my crappy life," he says, eyes twinkling. "Let's talk about your adventures." Straight away, I can see he's worried he's been tactless. "You have had adventures, right?"

I smile. "I have."

"Well?" His voice is relieved and excited.

"I'll tell you all about them soon," I say. "I'll tell you everything, I swear." Well, almost everything. "So many places, so many characters. It's been a wild journey, Oba, but right now I just need to see my family."

"Yeah, of course."

"They're alive then?" I ask, hopeful. "Still on the *Reverent*?"

Oba nods. "I visit them."

"You do?"

"We've got some things in common," he says, wistfully. "Well, one thing."

A lump comes to my throat, knowing they're still here, knowing they've had Oba's companionship, knowing my news will bring them both peace and devastation.

"Hey, they're okay," Oba says, stopping and squeezing my arm. "Your Ma's a little more devout these days, and Rina's a little more cheeky, but they're okay."

I wipe a tear from the corner of my eye.

Tell him.

"I found my father's grave, Oba."

The color drains from his cheeks.

"Sewa, I'm…"

"We found it on Raia, in the middle of a snowy wilderness," I say, knowing there are no easy words. "It was beautiful, in its way."

"Damn."

Oba hugs me again.

This time there's no stopping the tears.

Afterwards, he steps back.

"Did you…"

I can see him struggling to find the right words.

"Did I find out why he left?"

Oba nods.

"No, I didn't."

THIRTY-NINE

ㅈㅋ↑Σㅏꓘ ꓘ↑Σㄷ

The *Reverent* is silent, its communal spaces empty.

The inhabitants are either off-vessel or keeping to their chambers. Not like before, when from dawn till dusk Pilgrims spilt out of their homes, lighting up the place with life and color. No sign of Old Mina sitting on her weaved rug muttering Endless scripture. None of the Oko family eating around their usual big wok of spicy rice. No Tall Hands bartering over whatever he'd scavenged from the latest wreck dive.

Different times.

Today, the quiet feels oppressive.

Or maybe that's just my paranoia.

After all, right now, somewhere else on the Horizon, Kalad is being interrogated. If he talks, my secret could be common knowledge across the arcology before the day's end.

Life would never be the same again.

I come to my family chambers, notice the call-screen is broken, grimy with dust. Guess they don't get many visitors these days. It feels weird to stand here when so much has happened, like this isn't really my home any longer. I take a moment to compose myself, then knock.

No answer.

Oba warned me she might feign being out, even if she was likely in, so I knock again, more insistent.

I hear a scrabbling noise.

"Rina!"

Mother's voice is scolding, but still unmistakable.

"Ma, Rina," I manage, my words catching in my throat. "It's me. It's Sewa."

The door shoots open, and my little sister's standing there, mouth agape. She's not as little as I remember, but her eyes haven't changed, still as bright and mischievous as ever. She grins madly as her shock gives way to joy. She's not much shorter than me now, but she leaps up, linking her arms around my neck, and I pull her into me, squeezing her, enveloping her, inhaling her.

I've missed this so much.

Eventually, I gently put her down.

"Rina, Rina, Rina!" I exclaim, my fingers brushing her exquisite braids, our eyes locked together. "I am *so* happy to see you again."

Not leaping this time, she hugs me again.

"I've missed you, big sister," she cries. "What happened to your hair?"

I rub my fuzzy scalp. "New style."

She drags me inside, interleaving her fingers between my own, while closing the door with her other hand. The chamber is dim, the two recessed bunks on either side dark. Flickering candles illuminate the gloom, musty with the smell of old votives. In Mother's usual chair, I spy the silhouette of a trembling figure.

"Mother?" I ask, my eyes adjusting to the light.

She stands up, hand over her mouth, wet eyes wide.

"Is that really you, Sewa?"

"It's really me."

Dressed in loose robes with her hair pulled up into a braided swirl, she carries the air of a devout Pilgrim.

"Praise the Endless!"

I step over, dragging Rina with me, and Mother takes my free hand, strokes it, with love but also an edge of rebuke. The wayward child has returned. I am a source of shame as well as joy. After Father left, I never liked living here. Everything was a reminder of his absence. With Mother's increasing devotion to the faith, home became a more and more oppressive place. Today that suffocating feeling is only magnified, the religious trappings multiplied, father's absence crystallized.

"Are you hungry, child?"

One wall, I remember, that used to be shelves brimming with a bric-a-brac of child's toys, now only contains a stern looking mural. An abstract rendering of an Endless figure, all straight lines and virtue. I imagine Mother prostrating herself beneath it, where once Rina and I played.

"No, Mother, I'm not hungry."

I see the words sting, see the old barriers coming up.

"I'm sorry, Mother," I add. "Long day. I'm just tired."

"They said you'd died."

I did.

Then the Dust made me anew.

"I survived."

I say no more, instead freeing my hand, stepping away. On a shelved recess I spy a real, ink and paper, photograph. A shot of Father, standing on some windswept world, laughing, arm beckoning the photographer closer.

Mother steps close. "I always loved that picture."

I suddenly feel for her, feel for this interstitial life she's been left with since he left, half stuck in the past, half grasping for a future that is more than just waiting and hoping.

"Mother, Rina," I begin. "I found him."

"You found him?"

I can hear both her hope and despair.

If he's alive, why didn't he come back?

Rina looks up at me, confused, and I pull her tight.

"He died on Raia. A few years ago."

Rina buries her head into my midriff, head shuddering, while Mother grips my arm, unsteady.

"May the Endless rest his soul."

They're no saints, I want to say. And in no position to grant anyone peace, least of all Father. But who am I to deny her this salve?

"I'm sorry, Mother," I say as I stroke Rina's hair.

"Oh, Kendro."

She picks up the photo, gazes tenderly at Father, then presses it to her breast, eyes closed.

"How did he…?"

I wrap an arm around her too, wondering whether I should spare her the harsh truth. No, better she knows.

"Executed," I whisper in her ear.

"Oh, Kendro."

"He didn't suffer," I say. "And we should take comfort knowing he lived life, you know, pursuing what he thought was right."

That hits a nerve.

She shrugs my arm off.

"What he thought was *right*?" she cries, slapping the photo back down, wiping her eyes. "He left us, for what? Do we even know?"

No, we don't.

I could mention the Academy, that he wanted to speak with its leader, Isyander, but that would only lead her deeper into the mists surrounding Father's life.

"I'm sure it was for the best reasons," I say, defensively. "Something that would've helped all Pilgrims. He wouldn't have left us otherwise."

Mother scoffs. "You didn't know him like I did."

Now I wonder if I'm the one deceiving myself.

"What do you mean?"

"He was obsessed with the past."

"He was a historian!" I throw up a hand. "Of course he was obsessed with the past. It was his passion, his life!"

"To the exclusion of his family?"

"He was a great father!"

"Tell that to Rina."

"Mother!"

At those words my little sister detaches herself from my side and retreats to her bunk, burying her head in her blankets, her small frame quivering with tears. I try to comfort her, but she shrugs me off.

"I think I should go." I grit my teeth, grasping for some words that offer the hope of later reconciliation. "Let you grieve in peace."

"Wait."

Mother proceeds into the second, smaller room, and I follow her to the threshold, saying nothing. While she potters among the storage units looking for something, I stare, goggle-eyed, at what used to be Mother and Father's quarters, or more truthfully, by the time he left, his study. When he left, Mother moved fully into the main room with us, effectively mothballing this space.

As always, it's still locked in time.

Everything's as I remember it. My childhood drawings, the familiar woven bedspread laid out neatly over the bottom bunk where they slept, Father's antiquarian tomes stacked on an ornate side table between the pair of beautiful, natural wood armchairs that Father snagged from a derelict Raian space yacht and presented to Mother as a name day gift.

She's still living that day.

I suddenly feel guilty arguing with her, challenging her interpretation of events, and my anger dissipates.

"What are you looking for, Mother?"

She mutters something, and I step into the room, seat myself in one of the chairs. As I glance at the bunks from this vantage point I experience a strange sense of déjà vu.

Where have I seen this?

It's not an old memory—
The photograph!

While Mother still has her back to me, I reach inside my suit, pull out the picture. I shiver. The photo's like a window on the past, like I can hold up this little magic rectangle and see back in time. Father and I sit together on the edge of the bunk, Father holding me in his lap, one of his arms wrapped across my chest, the other pressed up against the lower bunk's ceiling. My head's flung back, laughing, but Father's eyes are trained on the camera, full of tender sadness. I take it all in greedily, almost wishing I could slip through that window, be there again.

Then I notice something odd.

Father's hand, the one whose palm is pressed up against the roof of the bunk, isn't flat. Three of his fingers are tucked in, but his index finger and thumb are visible.

Pointing.

I jump up, head over to the beds, carefully scan the underside of the upper bunk. I can't see anything unusual so I sit on the lower bunk and trace my fingers over the smooth surface.

Nothing, not even a hint of any hidden joins.

Now you're imagining things…

Undeterred, I get to my feet, step onto the first rung of the ladder that leads up to the top bunk. Funny how this climb up to what once used to be my bed used to feel like a great undertaking. Now I can see across the whole top bunk from the bottom rung.

I glance over at Mother.

She's on her knees, delving deep into one of the floor-level storage units. I wrest up the mattress, dismayed to see nothing hidden beneath it, and even more dismayed when my grasping hand finds nothing else further down the bed between the mattress and the bunk's floor.

It's as I'm patting the underside of the mattress, more in frustration than hope, when I feel something hard-edged inside. Exploring with my fingers, I trace out its contours.

Rectangular-shaped, no bigger than my hand.

A tablet?

Heart racing, I examine the edge of the mattress. A small rip, just large enough for a pinched hand, gives me access. I thrust my hand in, breathless, thinking of Father doing likewise all those years ago. And then it's between my fingers—not the cold sleekness of a tablet, but something warmer, textured.

It snags on the rip, but I wriggle it out.

A journal. Well-worn with a dark, wrinkled sleeve.

The smell of the leather is rich, unforgettable.

Using my thumb, I rifle-flick through the pages, page after page brimming with elegant writing, sketches, asides. Actual handwriting! A rarity, perhaps even a violation, in our culture where everything is digitized, replicable, transparent. And not just any writings, Father's writings!

Profane writings, no doubt.

I am thrilled.

"There it is!" Mother says.

For an awful moment I think she's been watching me, that she means the journal in my hands, but when I glance down at her, she's still occupied in the guts of the storage unit. As she shuffles out, I squirrel away my prize.

"What are you doing up there?"

I'm still standing on the lowest rung of the ladder, looking across my old bunk. "Nothing," I say, stepping down. "Just looking at my old drawings."

"They always make me smile."

She gets to her feet, clutching a fabric backpack.

"I hoped he'd give this to you himself one day," she says, brushing a layer of dust off the pack, "when he... well... I'm giving it to you now instead."

She holds it out.

It's Father's old caving backpack, a high-quality piece of gear made with smart materials so that it shapes itself to the caver's physique. I remember him wearing it when he took me on my first caving expeditions, a little creeped out by its shifting form that made it seem alive.

I take it, happy.

"I'll take good care of it."

I put it on, sense it shifting.

"It fits you well," Mother says, twirling me around. I'm not sure if she's making a joke, but then I see her sly grin.

"Strange that."

Inside my suit, I feel the journal pressing against my chest, close to my beating heart. I feel ravenous, hungry to devour these words in one voracious sitting.

Father's thoughts.

Maybe some answers too.

He might be gone, but wearing his pack, carrying his words, I feel closer to him than I have for a long time.

I give Mother a long hug. "We'll get through this."

Back in the main room I stop by Rina's bunk, sit next to her stilled form. Her face is still pressed into her blankets, but she no longer shudders with sadness.

"Hey," I say, rubbing her back, "it'll be okay."

She tilts her head a little, listening.

"Hard, but okay."

She gives a small nod, twists around. Her eyes are raw, her cheeks streaked red.

"Promise you'll never leave us again," she whispers.

I squeeze her wrist, but I can't give her those words.

I have seen things. I know things.

I give her a final hug then leave.

FORTY

ᛉᐸᎬᛕᛏ

Living under Mother and Rina's toes after all this time alone feels too much, so I install myself in the chamber's other room. I make a cursory effort to tidy what had become Father's study, happy to feel his presence. Over the next few days, I read his journal whenever I get the chance, whenever I'm confident I'm not being watched.

It isn't often.

I take what I can.

A few pages out on a long trek; deep in one of the asteroid's unexplored cave systems; under the covers at night. He wrote in a tiny cursive, writing in the margins, filling each page with thousands of words, like he knew he couldn't waste a scrap of paper, like he knew he wouldn't run out of things to say.

Never too long, never too much.

These are dangerous ideas.

A part of me is more afraid of getting caught with this than having my own secret exposed. Not because the writings are incendiary which they most certainly are, but because it would feel like a betrayal.

A betrayal of Father's trust.

These words are for my eyes alone.

When I read, I hear his voice. Whispering back, I can almost feel like we're having a conversation. Of course, it's not the same as him being here, but it's something, and it gives me solace.

Forced to read in snippets turns out to be a blessing in disguise. The writing is rich, chaotic, one moment devoted to the history of a dig, the next a frustration with bureaucracy, the next a sketch of Endless technology. Not devouring too much at once allows me to think deeply about what I've just read. It often feels like Father's feeling out his own thoughts on the subjects as he commits the words to the page.

I turn the ideas over in my mind as if I play with toy puzzles, examining them, fiddling with them, if not exactly solving them, then coming to a newfound appreciation for their intricacies.

Father was obsessed with the Endless.

Not the usual theological enquiries that occupied the attentions of the faithful, but the cold, hard anthropological study of their vast culture.

What did their social strata look like?

How did they maintain political control?

When they arrived on inhabited worlds, how did they treat indigenous populations?

Because, in Pilgrim theology, the Endless are considered infallible—a higher form of life that Pilgrims should never doubt, never question—his research was only ever grudgingly tolerated by the religious authorities. Everything went through a secret cabal named the Standing Committee for Scholarly Research into the Endless (SCSRE), and nearly all his work on these subjects was deemed "potentially obscene" and unfit for public consumption. And so, he worked alone, unacknowledged, a major strand of his life's work known only to a handful of disapproving figures, forever struggling against the orthodoxy.

It must've worn him down, this constant suppression.

Of Kalad's trial I hear little, my own daily interrogations in front of the Overseer and his inner circle now focusing on my time away from the Horizon. Again, I keep to the rough truth, only omitting some episodes that would only raise awkward questions.

Like my time at the Academy.

And the search for my father.

Instead I tell them that after Zarva rescued me, we spent many weeks on the run from the United Empire. The Niris, I explain, had decided to abandon Zelevas's side after the attack on the Horizon, when he realized the deal he tried to secretly broker with Kalad—the repatriation of Pilgrims on Raia—was never going to happen.

Of course, I say, Zelevas was incandescent.

So we laid low, kept to backwaters.

I mention the fabled Academy in passing, telling them Zarva had burnt his bridges when he joined up with the Empire, so it wasn't like we had any obvious refuge. A few, I can see, recognize the name, their eyes lighting up when I mention it, but when I give them the impression I don't know much more than its name, their enthusiasm wanes.

Outside the daily interrogations, I carry on reading the journal whenever I can. As I read through Father's early years in the field, unflattering Endless conjectures are the apex of the inflammatory material. All that changes on the fifth day though. The journal hides something much more explosive. I'm sat on a simple bench reading in the *Reverent*'s hydroponics gardens, the journal hidden in the cut-out recess of a book of holy scripture, when the realization dawns.

He thought the Horizon had been infiltrated.

In shock, as if the secret might leap out from the page, I slam the book shut, startling a pair of passing acolytes. They eye me with displeasure, move on without speaking. I lean back, tip my head back, and close my eyes. Keeping the book clutched tight, I breathe deep on the oxygenated air, its sweet, fresh edge refreshing yet heady.

Even in the privacy of his journal, Father kept his deepest suspicions hidden, but knowing him, reading between the lines, I can sense that he strongly believed outside forces had infiltrated. At every Endless dig or site, no matter how slight, somebody had always been there first. Subtle signs, not in the least obvious to an untrained eye, yet over many expeditions, he began to see patterns. Disturbances in the undergrowth, unexplained tracks, most of all, the sense of things missing. At first, I could tell, he'd suspected the Pilgrim military had swept the sites, but any investigations along that line had always come up empty. Nothing in the manifests, no tip-offs from trusted military contacts, no hints from the leadership. After that the trail went cold, no mention of anything unusual, and that's when I knew his suspicions had grown even darker.

He was afraid.

Afraid his own words might fall into the enemy's hands. He must've feared being exposed, maybe even killed. He must've suspected whoever the infiltrator was, they were powerful, well connected, able to get wind of events before they happened.

In hindsight, the Horizon's infiltration isn't a huge revelation. We are wanderers who venerate the Endless, seek out its relics, its homeworld. Many of the galaxy's players would like to know what we learn.

Was this the reason he left?

To hunt the enemy within from *without*?

Of course! He deemed staying on the Horizon too risky. He knew pursuing this course while here would put his life in great jeopardy. And not only his life.

The lives of his family too.

Our lives. Ma, Rina, me.

He was protecting us.

All while trying to protect the Pilgrims.

I open my eyes to the canopy, slices of azure sky visible through the fronds and branches. I feel a sense of weight lifting, his death no longer a meaningless cruelty. He was doing what he thought was *right*. Not only for him. For us. For all Pilgrims. The grief is still there, raw and painful, but it's tempered by the knowledge he was staying loyal to what mattered.

Everything is falling into place.

Isyander revealed Father had visited a Sophon waystation shortly after leaving the Horizon. No wonder. He must've first suspected the infiltrator was a Sophon agent. And that would make perfect sense! They'd been instrumental in the Pilgrim's inception, knew our plight, knew our tech, better than we did ourselves. What better way to uncover the Endless' remnants than infiltrating the wandering tribes who worshipped that very same civilization? Nomads whose very survival depended on always moving, evading their hunters, keeping to the lost, dark backwaters of the galaxy…

But then his suspicions moved onto the Academy.

Suppose the infiltrator *was* an Academy agent.

Suppose Father *never* learned the truth, *never* got word out.

My stomach drops.

The agent could still be here.

I glance up and down the path, chilled, then look across the gardens, past the great, gnarled tree that occupies the heart of hydroponics. Several other Pilgrims are dotted around, some in contemplation while they lean over the upper balustrades, others walking leisurely through the greenery. They all *look* nonchalant, lost in own private worlds…

Wait, wait, wait. Think this through.

I need to move. Still gripping the tome tight, I get up as casually as I can muster, stretch my legs, and head out of the gardens. The book of scripture feels like a ball and chain, marking me as a prisoner, noisy, drawing attention, fooling nobody. At the first opportunity I squirrel the journal away into my suit, throw the hollowed-out book into an incinerator.

Why would Isyander want to infiltrate the Pilgrims?

Same reason the Sophons would, I think.

Keeping tabs. Charting the galaxy. Securing Endless artifacts. And, truth be told, maybe he'd have even more incentive given his special interest in the lodestones.

Motive is clear then.

And means and opportunity?

Tick and tick.

I steady myself on the passage wall. Father's suspicions were right. *They're here.* And they must know I'm here, too. Isyander would've relayed the information as soon as he became aware of my existence. I just pray that they don't know that I know. Overseer Artak's not the only one watching me.

Would Isyander sacrifice my life to protect his agent? I don't know. Maybe. Probably. What is each of us worth to him? I imagine he takes a very utilitarian outlook.

I give a bitter laugh.

I'm stuck with a similar dilemma to the one my father faced all those years ago. Stay on the Horizon, uncover the agent, or head out into the galaxy and make contact with Muldaur.

Who's more vital to find?

The infiltrator or the rebel?

As I'm thinking, a soldier materializes out of the dark of the passage.

"Sewa Eze?"

"Yes?"

"Follow me," he says. "Overseer Artak wishes to resume your testimony. Now."

"Help me understand, child."

Like always, Artak sits at the head of the semi-circular table, the flickering light of the hall accentuating the shadows of his face, while I stand in the position of judgment. He flicks a hand and a hawk-faced advisor a couple of seats to his left recaps some of my previous testimony.

"Once free from the attentions of the Empire you searched long and hard for the remnants of the Horizon, scouring old haunts and virgin systems alike, but the trail went cold. After that you headed for the one place you thought you might have a chance of picking up the Horizon's trail again—Raia.

"Do you really expect us to believe," he continues, "that you, a hated Pilgrim youth, together with a Niris traitor who'd likely be executed on the spot, or worse, voluntarily stepped into Zelevas's own backyard on the slim hope you might get a lead on the Horizon?"

I glance at Artak.

"Answer the question."

I need to give him something, convince him that I can be trusted, that I'm not hiding anything.

"We both had our reasons."

All eyes wait for my next words.

"Some of you might remember that many years ago my father left the Horizon. Where he went, why he went, was a mystery." As I suspected, from the knowing glances between themselves, some of these figures must've sat on the Standing Committee that Father faced. "During my time with the Niris, however, Rachkov told me that my father had come to Raia. More than that, the Niris confessed that they were instrumental in seeing my father incarcerated on the world too. So, as you can see, as well as seeking clues to this arcology's whereabouts, we both had other reasons too. Rachkov wanted redemption. I wanted to find my father."

Artak speaks. "And did you? Find Kendro?"

"My father died in a Raian labor camp."

After a collective intake of breath, the hall falls dead silent.

"My sincere condolences. Stepping out from the protective wing of the Horizon is never to be taken lightly." He pauses, lets his gaze wander across the assembled observers. "And certainly not without the leadership's blessing."

My jaw tightens.

Artak's words are as much a warning for others as a rebuke of my father, but I still want to scream.

He did it for the Horizon! For all of you.

I can't say that though. Isyander's agent is likely still among us, watching, listening, picking the bones.

Artak raises his brows. *Anything to say?*

He suspects my own disappearance wasn't entirely accidental, or maybe, that there's more to my story.

His intuition isn't wrong.

Most of all, he's warning *me*.

Know your place.

I stay silent.

"And Rachkov?" Artak adds. "Did *they* find redemption?"

I close my eyes, still hear the explosion. "They did."

Artak narrows his eyes.

"Why *was* your father on Raia, child?"

I drop my head.

"I don't know."

"Not even an inkling?" Artak asks. "Over the years, you must've asked yourself this question a thousand times. Did you not find answers on Raia?"

I look up, embracing the old feelings of shame and dejection that his departure provoked. I still remember the taunts of the other kids, the pitying words of the adults.

"Only more questions, Overseer."

"Like?"

"Why that place, the Academy, interested him so much? Was there somebody there he wanted to find? Was he out for revenge? To find allies? The Endless fascinated him too, of course. It was his life's work. Maybe he just wanted to learn their secrets, secure a powerful relic?" I take a breath. "I like to think whatever he was doing though, he was doing it for the Horizon, for all of us."

My muddled ramblings look to have done the trick.

The advisor to Artak's immediate right is whispering in the Overseer's ear, probably reminding him of my father's lax faith. Speculations as to the Endless' galactic machinations are not what this audience needs to hear.

"Thank you, child," Artak says. "Hearsay is not the remit of this court, though. Let us proceed with the facts."

After that exchange, they don't go easy on me, but some of the distrust ebbs away. Most of my testimony from this episode can in time be corroborated by the Raian resistance.

That doesn't stop me worrying though.

At the back of my mind, I'm convinced Kalad's already revealed my secret, that they're simply letting me dig my own grave, letting my deceptions get bigger and bigger.

Stupid girl, thinking you can deceive us.

"And I believe that concludes your testimony," Overseer Artak says finally, glancing around his inner circle.

Heads nod.

"That's it?" I ask, keeping the hope from my voice.

"Unless you have something else to confess?" Artak's hands are bridged, his face neutral.

Am I being given a last chance?

I shake my head.

"Then your testimony is over."

I turn away, head for the doors, every step glacial, my footfalls the only sound in the vast hall. I feel all eyes on me. The guard at the door reaches for the handle…

"Sewa."

I stop dead, turn.

I do my best to keep the tremor from my voice. "Yes, Overseer?"

Artak eyes narrow.

He senses my fear.

"Why so tense?"

Any denial would be a mistake, but I need to give him something plausible.

"These sessions," I say, "they bring back a lot of painful memories. I just want them to be over."

Artak considers, nods.

"Still, I'm surprised you haven't enquired as to your former Cavemaster's fate. After all, he tried to kill you, then left you for dead. If I was in your place, I think I'd want to know."

A cold dread assails me.

Did Kalad talk?

"I... I trust justice will be served."

"It will be." Artak gets up, shifts his robes, then unhurriedly crosses the chamber. "Cavemaster Kalad," he says, clasping my hands, "is to be executed as a traitor."

"Executed?"

"At dawn, tomorrow." He squeezes my hands. "I hope that gives you some solace, child."

I feel sick.

The Pilgrims have never executed their criminals.

"I need to see him."

Artak is taken aback. "Why?"

To learn what he divulged.

I can't say that though.

"Deep down, in my bones, I still fear him," I say, feeling out the words. *A half truth.* "If I can see him... see him broken... that's my best chance of healing."

As I speak I bring forth the memory of his hands around my neck. I remember my raw animal fear, and I embrace the terrifying feeling, let it grip me again.

Artak sees it.

He addresses the guard.

"Take her to him."

FORTY-ONE

ᚱ⊲Ɛⵕⵕ ⵕƐⵕ

Kalad's cell is a dim, low-ceilinged, rectangular space, four paces wide and six long, the only furnishings a single-piece bed extruded from the wall. Everything is still and silent, Kalad himself a dark figure sat at the far end of the bed, back straight, hands on knees. The door glides closed.

My stomach tightens. I can smell his sweat, and when he turns his head, I see the glint of perspiration on his brow and shaved head. I picture him doing press-ups, squats. The space is claustrophobic, but nothing as compared to the crawl-shafts cavers navigate. No, what must be eating him alive is the incarceration. And the death sentence.

He gives a wry smile.

"I thought they'd sent another Priest."

Not out of concern for your soul.

They're still fishing…

"What did you tell them?"

I stay near the door, not wanting to take a single step closer. Even in his imprisonment, even though he will be executed tomorrow, I'm still afraid of him.

"Sit down," he instructs, pointing at his ear.

They're listening.

I hesitate, then perch myself at the other end of the bed.

"Closer," he says. "I won't bite."

I shift along, hating this feeling.

I feel myself shaking.

He twists, our knees almost touching. "I see the past still has its grip on you."

I wonder if his choice of words is deliberate.

"That day… that day you tried to take my life…" I stare down at my hands. "I didn't lose my life, but you took something else. Something near as valuable—"

"Your trust in others."

I nod, not looking at him.

Cavemaster Kalad had been like a second father. This man next to me was someone else. That's how my mind reconciled the betrayal.

"You gave me a hard choice," Kalad says. "One I would make again though, without hesitation. Some things are bigger than any one life." He exhales. "But I never wanted to cause you pain."

I harden.

Fuck this guy.

"I think you're wrong," I say, voice trembling.

He shrugs. "Soon, it won't matter what I think," he says. "But let me tell you this. Carrying secrets? That isn't easy. Not trusting anyone? Even harder. But if that's the path you choose, then you need to resolve yourself."

I'll do what I need to do.

We sit for a while, unspeaking.

All I can hear is my heart beating.

"You asked me what I told them," he says, eventually. He leans in close, cups his hand over my ear. "Nothing they didn't already know."

Nothing on his true motives?

Nothing on my real nature?

I feel a sliver of glee—and shame.

Less than a day and my secret will be safe.

"Why?" I whisper back, urgent. "Why didn't you tell them what I've become?"

"Because it would serve no purpose except spite," he replies. "And I didn't want to die full of spite."

Yet you would murder Pilgrims for your beliefs.

Strange, the codes by which others live.

I don't thank him. He doesn't deserve that. He does it for himself, not me. Part of me is grateful, though.

I keep my voice low. "And the Endless?"

"You know what I believe." He gives me a hard look. "They need to be forgotten."

Father thought the opposite, spent half his life seeking to learn their ways, their culture—and their sins. And yet maybe that only helped Isyander's plan get a little closer to fruition.

Maybe they should be buried.

I can't believe that though.

"You're wrong, Kalad."

"Am I?"

I stare down at my hands.

They are rough and calloused, but Dust courses through these hands, through this body. I am still flesh and blood, yet my transformation is profound, the cerebral pathways of my very mind redrawn and strengthened. I shudder as I imagine the power a being of pure Dust would wield.

My burdens feel heavier than ever.

Tell him.

"Isyander's close to resurrecting the Lost."

Kalad's eyes go wide, horrified.

"And," I add, "we might've helped that day arrive."

He shakes his head, confused.

I lean close. "Isyander has an insider on the Horizon," I whisper. "Maybe more than one. For years, they've been passing on intel back to the Academy. Relics too."

Kalad looks crestfallen.

"Everything I feared is coming to pass."

I've never seen him so despondent.

"You know who it is?" he asks, hopeful.

I shake my head, deflating him again. "My father suspected an infiltrator," I say. "But he never learnt who they were. That's why he left—to track them down from *outside*."

"And yet he still failed."

"At least he tried!"

I glance at the cell door, catch the guard peering in.

I give him a nod. *I'm okay.*

I turn back to Kalad, grit my teeth. I can't ask anybody else, and tomorrow it'll be too late.

"What should I do?"

"Pray."

I shake my head. Kalad's defeatism is the last thing I need. I move to get up and leave, but he grabs my forearm.

"Sorry," he says, "I didn't mean that."

"Then what?" I pull away my arm.

"You should fight," he says, locking eyes. "Fight like your father."

The guard raps on the door. "Time's up!"

I turn back to Kalad. "Meaning?"

"I think you know."

"Visitor, step over to the door!"

"You better go," Kalad says.

I stand up. "I will fight."

"Never think you can't make a difference, Sewa."

I get to the door and it slides open.

"I hope you find peace, Cavemaster."

I step past the soldier, and the door hisses closed. I slump against the wall, close my eyes. I *will* fight. I will do *something*. But I won't be like Kalad. No collateral damage.

The guard slaps my shoulder.

"You okay?"

I open my eyes, nod.

"You're brave," he says. "Confronting him like that. I don't know if I could do that."

I catch my breath. "I wasn't sure I could either."

The guard lingers.

"Say it."

"Did it help?"

In his face I see such naked curiosity, that he must have his own demons to confront.

I nod. "I'm not afraid of him now."

The guard's eyes widen with joy, like I've given him a religious epiphany. And it's true. My fear of Kalad, the man, has gone. What I don't tell him though is that a new fear has sprung up in its stead.

The fear of making the wrong choice.

Do I stay or go?

FORTY-TWO

· ⋀⟨Σⱪ⟨ ⱬⱽ⟨ ·

The next morning, to little fanfare, Kalad is executed.

Only a small circle of observers witness the act, and regarding his crimes all the leadership announce on the matter is that Kalad was judged a traitor to all Pilgrims.

I guess they want to suppress any talk of repatriation.

Any return to Raia would mean an existential threat to the arcologies. And any dreams of finding Tor.

Out of sight, out of mind.

Kalad would relate.

Ideas, he'd say, need minds. They're only dangerous once they take root inside people's heads.

Like the apotheosis of the Endless.

His remains are expelled into the gravity well of a rocky inner world. His corpse will likely burn up on entry through the thin atmosphere, but should his charred bones survive the journey, in time they'll be decomposed by the planet's rudimentary life-forms.

I suspect he'd be happy with that.

For me, his death is a double-edged sword.

My secret is safe.

Aside from the infiltrator, nobody within fifty light years knows of the Dust that courses through my veins, and all that do know are sworn to secrecy by the Academy code.

Here, I can be a normal Pilgrim again.

On the other hand, with Kalad gone, I am alone.

I can pretend to be normal, but I cannot deny the truth.

Every day that I keep it to myself, every day that I choose to trust no one with the knowledge—not my mother or sister, not Oba, not

Liandra—is a day I further erode the slender bridge that connects me to the lives of others.

I am becoming an island.

It doesn't help that the Horizon no longer feels like home.

For the first time in years we have escaped the attentions of the Empire, yet there is no celebratory mood. Instead, there is a solemnity, a sense of getting back to our religious duties.

Living in accordance with scripture while we seek Tor.

Piety is the watchword.

Devotions, votives, prayer.

Pilgrims come together often—for work, for meals, for worship—but say nothing. Not as in the absence of conversation, even though the arcology is certainly a quieter realm, but rather the absence of meaningful exchange. Talk is limited to the mission, to scripture, to incidental matters.

Never anything true, never anything intimate.

At least in public.

Everyone fears they are being watched, judged.

I feel it too.

It's hard to resist the groupthink, much easier to simply drift along as a good little believer. To tell a joke is now a small act of rebellion. I'm certain I haven't heard unbridled laughter since my return.

Always, I'm wondering if the infiltrator is nearby, watching, observing, reporting. Sometimes I close my eyes, listen to the whisper of the Dust in my blood, sensing if it feels a nearby kindred spirit, but I always open my eyes none the wiser.

Maybe they're not even here anymore.

I feel paralyzed.

Every day, somewhere out among the stars, Isyander's project to resurrect the Lost gets closer. I want to leave, join the Academy rebellion, but I am torn. Rina needs guidance, stability. My departure might see her spiral, seek sanctuary in piety.

Stay and I can be her pillar.

And who says I can change anything out there anyway?

Isn't that a glimmer of the same megalomania that drives Isyander, Zelevas, and every other despot?

Here, I *know* I can make a difference.

In fifty-six days the Horizon of Light will rendezvous with another Pilgrim arcology, the Crimson Star, on the outskirts of the Regul system, a galactic trade crossroads in a lawless region beyond the reach of the Empire. A perfect place to abandon ship, put out feelers, catch a ride.

Fifty-six days. Long enough to really think it through. Not too long that it'll be too late. I will spend as much time as I can with Rina and Ma, sharing stories, creating memories.

Then, I will make a choice.

Not simply let things happen.

Like Oba I am assigned to archives.

Our manifest purpose is to find clues, no matter how slight, that might help identify traces of the Endless. Vessels, shrines, outposts, and, of course, worlds, most notably Tor. We do this by reading the Pilgrim holy texts forensically, and cross-referencing anything tangible with other sources—stellar geography, anthropological study, even ancient literature.

For example, a parable that mentions two Endless wanderers walking across a windswept desert with twisted trees, beneath a night sky that features three distinct moons, would be a reason to sift the galactic database for such worlds.

The theory is nonsense, of course.

No one dare utter it, but the holy texts, brilliantly and vibrantly written as they are by those who claimed communion with the Endless, are, at best, fictionalized accounts of long forgotten events, or, at worst, complete works of fantasy. The scholars, savants, philosophers, observers, and servants, who wrote or assembled the writings that compose the entirety of the holy texts, though, cannot be doubted.

And so we read.

And so, I surmise, the true purpose of this otherwise pointless endeavor is to make Pilgrims of the Horizon of Light arcology, especially those whose faith is somewhat questionable, intimately familiar with scripture.

Through suffocation, we will believe.

At least that's what they hope.

The silver lining, though, is my time with Oba.

Every morning he comes to my chambers at dawn. We walk together to daybreak devotions, listen to a sermon, say our mantras, then head for the archives.

When we are alone, we speak freely.

Like old times.

Well, almost.

Some things I have to keep to myself.

One day, while finishing midday repast in the main refectory, long after most Pilgrims have eaten, Oba leans closer, lowers his voice. "When you're reading scripture, do you ever get the feeling you're reading something that actually happened?"

I do.

Some of the passages chime with the flotsam I've amassed over the past year. Kalad's confessions, things I learnt at the Academy, conversations with Zarva.

And Father's writings, of course.

I shrug. "I don't know."

"I mean," he whispers, "we both know it's largely Necro crap, but do you ever think any of it's real? Do you even think any of their civilization's still left beyond the ruins?"

"They built the gates," I reply, avoiding eye contact as I mop up the juices on my plate with a crust of bread. "Maybe that's all that's left."

I hate lying to him.

And they're not even the worst lies.

I downplay the Endless because Kalad's still in my head, because some part of me believes that they—or their remnants—really might still be an existential threat to the whole galaxy.

They did disappear, after all.

But lying about who I am?

That's a whole other level.

And one that keeps him at arm's length.

"Yeah, you're probably right," he says. "They vanished tens of thousands of years ago. Nature's a beast. What lasts?"

He starts telling me about how Raia had this phase in their history when they worried about the nuclear waste they had to bury and how they could ensure future generations would always know where it was, would always stay away, no matter what happened. It became a whole scientific discipline. Nuclear semiotics. The nuclear waste had half-lives of thousands, sometimes millions of years, so any warnings needed to work across shifts of language, culture, technology…

My mind drifts.

What lasts indeed?

I think of the Dust in my veins.

Will it lose its potency, will it just die, if its power is not flexed? I haven't caved or climbed for weeks. Last time was in the icy caverns of a frozen planet, while high above, a couple of ships got repaired in the local collective's orbital shipyard.

I'm beginning to suffocate, beginning to go crazy.

The urge to cave is like a hunger.

One I'm struggling to sate.

I snap out of the downward spiral.

"Come on, let's get back."

More weeks pass.

Oba and I are shifted to a dig expedition after our stint with the archives finishes. It's hard, backbreaking work, sifting for the remains of some primitive culture who may or may not have had interactions with the mighty Endless.

At least I'm still with Oba.

He stays on the surface, restricted by his disabilities, while I descend into the caverns and fissures of a vast canyon system where the culture made their home. The canyon is ideal for caving, but it teems with Pilgrims night and day, and I daren't risk fully expressing my skills.

It drives me insane.

I guess it's good the hunger is still there.

It means the Dust is still alive, craving.

But for how much longer?

One day, at dusk, while we wait for one of the transport vessels to return us to the orbiting arcology, I sit with Oba overlooking the canyon. The sky is a blend of bruised reds and purples, and the scent of desert pines mingles with the smell of a charcoal fire. Far off, I hear scripture being recited.

Oba picks up a handful of tiny pebbles, tosses them over the precipice, each one skittering along the ground, then disappearing over the edge.

We're growing apart.

The thin veil that once divided us feels more like a brick wall now, the burden of my lies weighing heavier with every passing day.

He doesn't know who I am.

Not really.

He brushes off his hands, leans back to rest on his elbows, gazing at the sunset. "Discover any new paths today?"

He means caving paths through the canyon.

I know he misses the thrill of a session as much as I miss being able to fully cut loose.

"Actually, yeah," I reply. "We found a small cleft in one of the communal halls. Tricky descent, but it leads places. This site is more extensive than anyone thought."

I go on, describing the technical aspects of the descent, hoping that even if he can't take part himself, he can experience a vicarious pleasure. My words have the opposite effect.

"Sublime," he utters, crestfallen.

Tears are in his eyes, and he sees that I see.

He gets up, levering up on his crutches, then moves closer to the edge, back to me. A slight breeze comes over the chasm, rustling his hair.

I feel awful.

"I'm sorry, I didn't mean…" I trail off. "One day you'll cave again. They'll fix you up. I know it."

"Will they?"

I stay silent.

How can I say they will when I don't know?

Something's breaking between us.

"I need to tell you things."

He turns his head, wiping his eyes. "What things?"

"Lots of things." I take a deep breath. "For one, the fact I died on that moon."

"What?" Oba frowns. "But you survived."

"I died, Oba." I stare down at the stone. "Kalad killed me. I don't know how long I was gone, but… I was reborn in Dust. I'm changed, Oba."

There, the secret's out.

My mouth is dry, my heart beating hard.

Oba blinks, grips his temple.

"Say something," I say.

He shakes his head, grins. "I knew there was something different about you."

In that moment I know everything's going to be okay. I spring up, hug him harder than I've hugged anyone.

"I'm so glad you know," I whisper. "I've felt so alone."

"You're not alone." He hugs back hard with one arm, leaning on one crutch while the other scrapes against the rock. "Now, I want to hear everything."

And I tell him.

I leave nothing out.

My superhuman skills, coming to trust Zarva, my interlude at the Academy where I learnt of the Endless' slaughter of the Lost. Isyander's dangerous project to bring them back. Raia and the gulag and the resistance. I even tell him about Kalad's apocalyptic prophecies.

And the infiltrator.

Only thing I leave out is the choice I will make in thirty-odd days, when we reach Regul.

That's for me alone.

By the time I'm done the blood-red sun has fallen beneath the horizon and the first stars dapple the darkening skies. We're last aboard the transport vessel, but I walk with a skip in my step, feeling free for the first time in a long time. Side-by-side in our drop-seats, ready for the vertical stake-off, Oba turns to me grinning.

"Seriously?" he whispers, over the whirr of the spooling-up engines. "You're a genuine caving ninja now?"

"I am." I feel the sides of my mouth lifting, his smile infectious. "And I can't wait to show you."

"Damn straight. I gotta see this."

The rest of his words are lost in the full roar of the engine, and as the acceleration kicks in, we scream like excited children, no care in the world.

And so I show him.

Not often, opportunities are scarce, but in the cracks of our lives, we head out to isolated places. Sometimes early before our work shift starts, sometimes late when most of the arcology sleeps. The locations might change—a derelict vessel, a natural cavern system, a ruined cityscape—but the thrill never gets old.

Oba watches from afar, sometimes finding a vantage point where he can observe most of a run, other times simply hunkering down somewhere and connecting to my helmet-cam. He's become more proficient in his limitations, but he is still far from the caver he once was. Despite my skills being another step beyond, he watches with a child-like glee that never wavers.

Sometimes he times me, coaxing me to go even faster. Even if I indulge him, push myself even harder, I get no more pleasure than the simple fact of being seen.

He is the totality of my audience.

But I think he is enough.

Our lives settle into a comfortable rhythm.

Things with Rina and Mother are good.

We wander like an ancient nomadic people, moving between systems, foraging, seeking, fulfilling our duties. We see no sign of the United Empire, our enemy far away, focused on other matters—other arcologies, perhaps.

Not that I ask.

Whatever Overseer Artak and the religious leadership strive for, I decide, is not my concern. I have found equilibrium. Maybe I can live like this.

The day we reach Regul draws close.

"That was intense, Sewa!"

Oba offers a hand, and I clasp it, levering up over the lip of the waterfall onto a large rock. I'm soaked to the skin, the climb taking me through the brunt of the tumbling, cold waters as they cascaded down.

Even for me it was little hairy.

Only a handful of days now.

Inside, I feel the Dust pulsing, invigorated.

The twin suns of the world bathe us in a warming light, matching the fire that burns inside, and as I look out over the vast valley below, I see an unbroken rainforest full of life and color.

Somewhere among those trees, Pilgrims are scavenging.

Out of the corner of my eye, I catch Oba gazing at me, like he often does, with a look of wonder.

"Knock it off," I say, my breaths still heavy.

"You're a force of nature," he says, shaking his head. "Every time I think I've seen your limit, you crash right through, take it to another level. That Academy must be some place."

"Dust is a gift."

He picks up a stone, rolls it between his hands. "Sewa, you might not want to hear this, but I'm your best friend, so I'm going to say this straight." He tosses the stone over the falls, watches it plummet into the mist. "You're squandering this gift."

His words sting.

"I use it as much as I can."

"For what? For kicks? For my amusement?"

"No, so I can be myself."

He snorts. "These lives? Working the archives, the digs, the fields, all the rank-and-file stuff. This isn't you. This isn't your life. How can you be yourself if nobody knows who you really are?"

"You know," I say. "And that's enough."

"For you, maybe. But not for me."

"What are you saying?"

"I'm saying you've got a way outta here. I haven't. Tomorrow I'm gonna wake up and ten years'll have passed. And I'll still be working these gigs, fixed legs or not. And that's fine. That's who I am. But you? You can do things. You think I wouldn't give anything to have what you've got? But you're hiding away, letting the days slip through your fingers. And that's not right. Hanging around this arcology is a waste of your time. Most of all, it's an insult to me and every Pilgrim like me."

"This is my home."

"This *was* your home!" he snaps. "Now it's just your comfort blanket—and a thin one at that!"

"You want me to leave?"

"I want you to live."

I am living, I want to say, but I can't bring myself to say the words. I can see the hurt in his eyes, the pain of voicing these thoughts.

I sigh. "And Rina?"

"Your Ma's becoming more like her old self every day. Rina'll be fine. And I'll look out for her too," Oba says. "I used to have a little sister myself."

Oh boy. Leona.

"Oba," I say. "It's not that simple."

"Isn't it? I'll tell you what's simple. Every day I come by, we have good times, right?" he says. "Reminiscing, poking fun, going on these little missions. You know what the best part of my day is?" He lets the question hang. "The short walk between my place and yours, 'cause during that walk I let myself think that when I get there, you'd be gone. I'd knock on your door and nothing would happen. You'd have left."

He gives me a long look. "That simple."

He spins away, hobbles over the rocks towards the river's banks, the only sound the ceaseless roar of the waters tumbling over the edge of the falls.

I turn back to the spectacular vista, thinking.

EPILOGUE

⨤⧎⅃⧎⧄⧄⨤

He wakes, limbs stiff, body heavy.

Sunk into his berth, he remembers they've landed on a hub world, the gravity of the planet a little higher than what he's used to off-world. While he lies in the darkness, slowly coming round, he recalls the descent—passing the orbital station near Regul's system gate, before leaving behind the majority of the arcology in orbit and dropping through magenta-tinged skies.

Sick vistas.

Mama would've enjoyed.

They landed on a vast plateau overlooking the capital, stationed on an interstellar parking lot, joining thousands of other vessels of every size and shape and origin.

Vessels of the Crimson Star are out there.

The world is a trading hub, far from any borders of the galaxy's major players, and overseen by an independent collective. If there's any such thing as a safe haven, this is it. Today, the higher-ups will meet with their counterparts, while the rank-and-file will go out and wander the souks and backstreets.

Trade is the excuse, but really it's for the R&R.

He smiles, his usual excitement of this hour supercharged.

Stretching, he commands his quarter's lights to come on, partial illumination, then swivels to an upright position on the side of his berth. The space is small yet seems smaller from the mess that is a hallmark of his life. He rubs his calves, runs his fingers over the stumps of his toes.

The cold never goes away.

A few minutes later he's washed and dressed.

He drains a hot infusion, leaves.

Maybe today's the day.

He hobbles through the passages of the vessel in his usual fashion, a skip in his step, even despite the extra gravity. Their daily routine takes them to the refectory before most Pilgrims have risen, but even so, he still passes a few of the usual regulars who like to get up early too.

Praying, pruning shrubs, sipping tea.

Smiles greet his own smile.

Some bless him, appealing to the Endless' grace, while others cannot hide the pity in their eyes.

It never sours his mood.

Not at this hour.

He hopes for what he always hopes for, but another part of his mind imagines the adventures they'll have together in the teeming metropolis. Discovering strange games and customs, spotting life-forms—natural or otherwise—that they've never seen before, challenging each other to eat the most disgusting looking so-called delicacies.

Maybe some free running if they can find a quiet space.

He's sure the city won't disappoint.

He comes to the Eze's family door, knocks.

No answer.

Surely they haven't all overslept today?

"Aduka, Rina?" He knocks again, harder, and the door cracks open, unlocked. "Anybody there?"

Still nothing.

"Heads-up, I'm coming in."

The main room is empty, no sign of either Rina or her mother. Their beds are unmade, their blankets crumpled. He glances over at the door to Sewa's room, sees it is open. His heart beats faster.

He enters.

The room is still, dim, except for a small lamp spilling a circle of light on her desk. He turns in circles, scarcely believing that she's not there, expecting that his eyes have deceived him and she's still under her covers.

She always waits for him here. Always.

An envelope stands on the desk in the light, and he glimpses a name.

Oba.

That's when he knows.

He picks it up, sits down on the side of her bed, tears coming. Opening it he finds a picture of the pair of them, arm-in-arm, dirty-faced but grinning, back from years earlier when life was nothing but a pure adventure.

Thick as thieves, he remembers people saying.

He turns it over, sees Sewa's flowing handwriting.

He doesn't read it, not yet, just flips it back and stares at the picture. For a time, he cries, joy and sadness mingling.

Any residual warmth in the bed is gone.

Still clutching the photo, he wipes his eyes, leaves their quarters, and navigates his way up to the *Reverent*'s gallery. Aduka and Rina are there, clutching one another, and when they see him, Aduka beckons him over. She squeezes his hand.

He notices both hold their own envelopes.

Dawn is breaking over the mountains to the east, and fine sunlight grazes the highest minarets and obelisks of the stirring metropolis. In the dark swathe of the city, lights twinkle, and hundreds of thin ribbons of smoke trail upwards.

His gaze tracks the line of a long, wide thoroughfare. At its heart a large edifice towers over a circular plaza which seethes with motion. They could be worshippers heading to dawn prayers, or workers coming and going from a central station, but he imagines it is a vast market teeming with life and color.

He imagines her there, threading her way through the throng, sampling the cuisine, talking with the stallholders, delighted by it all.

He reads her message.

O,

You were right. Girl's gotta save the galaxy — even if she doesn't have the first clue. Simple, right? I know it's gonna land you in a heap of trouble but... please show them who I am. They'll understand in time.

I got your back, S.

P.S. Don't lay a finger on my gear.
P.P.S. I'm kidding. It's all yours. For now.

He grins.

His stomach growls, but he's going to forgo the daybreak repast. He can eat later, in the city. If he's fast, he can be down there before the sun's fully up.

He won't see her, he knows that.

But knowing she's out there?

That'll be enough.

THE END

ACKNOWLEDGEMENTS

ᒪᔦ᙭ᐸᒍᗡᕧᒍᕃᒪᕃ᙭ᑲᐊ

They say it takes a village to raise a child. The same could be said for writing a novel. Except for village read world. Or, more accurately, worlds. First and foremost, this work would not exist without the rich tapestry of the Endless Universe, conceived in the anarchic mind of Amplitude's visionary Narrative Director, Jeff Spock, and embroidered over the decade and a half since by countless Amplitudians as they helped create *Endless Space I & II*, *Endless Legend*, *Dungeon of the Endless*, and much more besides. Of course, Jeff would be the first to admit the Endless Universe draws from a rich well of science fiction and fantasy, and I must also pay a large debt to the corpus of speculative fiction I read, watched, and played through my youth and beyond. So thank-you to Iain M Banks for the Culture, Glen Larson for *Battlestar Galactica*, and Simtex for *Master of Orion* to name a few touchstones.

For improving my craft I am indebted to scores, if not hundreds, of teachers, instructors, fellow writers, editors, and other creatives. Notably the Clarion class of 2006, Writers of the Future 2007, and numerous ongoing workshops including Critters, Codex, Online Writing Workshop, and Villa Diodai Expat Writers Workshop who have given me invaluable feedback. Special thanks to Jeff Carlson, Brad Beaulieu, Aliette de Bodard, and Ruth Nestvold. At this juncture, I would also be remiss not to acknowledge the many privileges of geography, health, and education, that have permitted me to pursue the author's path.

For *Shadow of the Endless* specifically, I am most grateful to my many beta readers, especially to my fellow Amplitude wordsmith, Bridget Behrmann, and Fenton Coulthurst, my editor at Titan.

Beyond the Deep by William Stone and Barbara am Ende provided a terrifying yet grounded insight into the world of caving that underpinned much of the backdrop. Marketing-wise, Max von Knorring, Niels Kooijman and the rest of the Amplitude team have been tireless champions of the work from its earliest days, all the way through launch plans and beyond. Thanks to all at Titan Publishing for pulling everything together. I must give special mention to Aurélien Rantet, not only for the stunning cover art, but also for his vast body of Endless work that inspires anew every day.

Lastly, I am endlessly grateful for the nurturing love of both my immediate and wider family, who have given me their unconditional support from day one. Thank-you to my wife, Eloise Calandre, for your brainstorming, dramatizing insights, cheerleading, and periodic funk-breaking pep talks. Most of all, thank-you to my daughter, Alexia, for your fire and spirit.

ABOUT THE AUTHOR

ꓕƎ⊂Ꝺꓘ ꓘꓱ⊂ ꓕꝺꓘꓱ⊂Ʃ

Stephen Gaskell writes about aliens, apocalypses, and weird science. A graduate of University College, Oxford, his work has been published in numerous venues including *Clarkesworld*, *Interzone*, and *Year's Best Military SF and Space Opera*. An expert on the Endless Universe, he is currently Lead Writer at Amplitude Studios, where he imagines star spanning adventures while fighting with game designers.

For more fantastic fiction, author events,
exclusive excerpts, competitions, limited editions and more

VISIT OUR WEBSITE
titanbooks.com

LIKE US ON FACEBOOK
facebook.com/titanbooks

FOLLOW US ON TWITTER AND INSTAGRAM
@TitanBooks

EMAIL US
readerfeedback@titanemail.com